I stood absolutely motionless, not breathing, for the Peacemaker Colt was pointed directly at my right thigh.

Unconsciously, almost, I braced my leg to meet the impending shock. Defensively, this was a very good move, about as useful as holding up a sheet of newspaper in front of me. I wished to God that Colonel Sam Colt had gone in for inventing something else, something useful, like safety pins.

Very slowly, very steadily, I raised both hands, palms outward, until they were level with my shoulders.

The gleaming eyes stared unwinkingly at me. The smile, the head cocked slightly to one side, the negligent relaxation of the body—the aura in that tiny cabin of a brooding and sardonic menace was so heavy as to be almost palpable. There was something evil, something frighteningly unnatural and wrong and foreboding in the man's stillness and silence and cold-blooded cat-and-mouse indifference. I could smell death in the air.

FACETT CREST BOOKS

by Alistair MacLean

WHEN EIGHT BELLS TOLL

ALISTAIR MacLEAN

FAWCETT CREST • NEW YORK

To Paul and Xenia

A Fawcett Crest Book
Published by Ballantine Books

ISBN 0-449-20636-X

This edition published by arrangement with
Doubleday and Company

Manufactured in the United States of America

First Fawcett Crest Edition: September 1967
First Ballantine Books Edition: June 1983
Second Printing: December 1984

The Peacemaker Colt has now been in production, without change in design, for a century. Buy one today and it would be indistinguishable from the one Wyatt Earp wore when he was the Marshal of Dodge City. It is the oldest hand gun in the world, without question the most famous and, if efficiency in its designated task of maiming and killing be taken as criterion of its worth, then it is also probably the best hand gun ever made. It is no light thing, it is true, to be wounded by some of the Peacemaker's more highly esteemed competitors, such as the Luger or Mauser: but the high-velocity, narrow-calibre, steel-cased shell from either of those just goes straight through you, leaving a small neat hole in its wake and spending the bulk of its energy on the distant landscape whereas the large and unjacketed soft-nosed lead bullet from the Colt mushrooms on impact, tearing and smashing bone and muscle and tissue as it goes and expending all its energy on you.

In short when a Peacemaker's bullet hits you in, say, the leg, you don't curse, step into shelter, roll and light a cigarette one-handed then smartly shoot your assailant between the eyes. When a Peacemaker bullet hits your leg you fall to the ground unconscious, and if it hits the thigh bone and you are lucky enough to survive the torn arteries and shock, then you will never walk again without crutches because a totally disintegrated femur leaves the surgeon with no option but to cut your leg off. And so I stood absolutely motionless, not breathing, for the Peacemaker Colt that had prompted this unpleasant train of thought was pointed directly at my right thigh.

Another thing about the Peacemaker: because of the very heavy and varying trigger pressures required to operate the semiautomatic mechanism, it can be wildly inaccurate unless held in a strong and steady hand. There was no such hope here. The hand that held the Colt, the hand that lay so lightly

5

yet purposefully on the radio operator's table, was the steadiest hand I'd ever seen. It was literally motionless. I could see the hand very clearly. The light in the radio cabin was very dim, the rheostat of the angled table lamp had been turned down until only a faint pool of yellow fell on the scratched metal of the table, cutting the arm off at the cuff, but the hand was very clear. Rock-steady, the gun could have lain no quieter in the marbled hand of a statue. Beyond the pool of light I could half sense, half see the dark outline of a figure leaning back against the bulkhead, head slightly tilted to one side, the white gleam of unwinking eyes under the peak of a hat. My eyes went back to the hand. The angle of the Colt hadn't varied by a fraction of a degree. Unconsciously, almost, I braced my right leg to meet the impending shock. Defensively, this was a very good move, about as useful as holding up a sheet of newspaper in front of me. I wished to God that Colonel Sam Colt had gone in for inventing something else, something useful, like safety pins.

Very slowly, very steadily, I raised both hands, palms outward, until they were level with my shoulders. The careful deliberation was so that the nervously inclined wouldn't be deceived into thinking that I was contemplating anything ridiculous, like resistance. It was probably a pretty superfluous precaution as the man behind that immobile pistol didn't seem to have any nerves and the last thought I had in my head was that of resistance. The sun was long down but the faint red afterglow of sunset still loomed on the northwest horizon and I was perfectly silhouetted against it through the cabin doorway. The lad behind the desk probably had his left hand on the rheostat switch ready to turn it up and blind me at an instant's notice. And there was that gun. I was paid to take chances. I was paid even to step, on occasion, into danger. But I wasn't paid to act the part of a congenital and suicidal idiot. I hoisted my hands a couple of inches higher and tried to look as peaceful and harmless as possible. The way I felt, that was no feat.

The man with the gun said nothing and did nothing. He remained completely still. I could see the white blur of teeth now. The gleaming eyes stared unwinkingly at me. The smile, the head cocked slightly to one side, the negligent relaxation of the body—the aura in that tiny cabin of a brooding and sardonic menace was so heavy as to be almost palpable. There was something evil, something frighteningly unnatural and wrong and foreboding in the man's stillness and silence and cold-blooded cat-and-mouse indifference. Death was waiting to reach out and touch with his icy forefinger in that tiny cabin. In spite of two Scots grandparents I'm in no way psychic or fey or second-sighted, as far as extrasensory perception goes I've about the same degree of receptive sensitivity as a lump of old lead. But I could smell death in the air.

"I think we're both making a mistake," I said. "Well, you are. Maybe we're both on the same side." The words came with difficulty, a suddenly dry throat and tongue being no aid to clarity of elocution, but they sounded all right to me, just as I wanted them to sound, low and calm and soothing. Maybe he was a nut case. Humor him. Anything. Just stay alive. I nodded to the stool at the front corner of his desk. "It's been a hard day. Okay if we sit and talk? I'll keep my hands high, I promise you."

The total reaction I got was nil. The white teeth and eyes, the relaxed contempt, that iron gun in that iron hand. I felt my own hands begin to clench into fists and hastily unclenched them again, but I couldn't do anything about the slow burn of anger that touched me for the first time.

I smiled what I hoped was a friendly and encouraging smile and moved slowly towards the stool. I faced him all the time, the cordial smile making my face ache and the hands even higher than before. A Peacemaker Colt can kill a steer at sixty yards, God only knew what it would do to me. I tried to put it out of my mind, I've only got two legs and I'm attached to them both.

I made it with both still intact. I sat down, hands still high, and started breathing again. I'd stopped breathing but hadn't been aware of it, which was understandable enough as I'd had other things on my mind, such as crutches, bleeding to death, and suchlike matters that tend to grip the imagination.

The Colt was as motionless as ever. The barrel hadn't followed me as I'd moved across the cabin, it was still pointing rigidly at the spot where I'd been standing ten seconds earlier.

I moved fast going for that gun hand, but it was no break-neck dive. I didn't, I was almost certain, even have to move fast, but I haven't reached the advanced age in which my chief thinks he honors me by giving me all the dirtiest jobs going by ever taking a chance when I don't have to.

I eat all the right foods, take plenty of exercise and, even although no insurance company in the world will look at me, their medical men would pass me any time, but even so I couldn't tear that gun away. The hand that had looked like marble felt like marble, only colder. I'd smelled death all right, but the old man hadn't been hanging around with his scythe at the ready, he'd been and gone and left this lifeless shell behind him. I straightened, checked that the windows were curtained, closed the door noiselessly, locked it as quietly and switched on the overhead light.

There's seldom any doubt about the exact time of a murder in an old English country house murder story. After a cursory examination and a lot of pseudo-medical mumbo-jumbo, the good doctor drops the corpse's wrist and says, "The decedent deceased at 11:57 last night" or words to that effect, then, with a thin deprecatory smile magnanimously conceding that he's a member of the fallible human race, adds, "Give or take a minute or two." The good doctor outside the pages of the detective novel finds it rather more difficult. Weight, build, ambient temperature, and cause of death all bear so heavily and often unpredictably on the cooling of the body that the estimated time of death may well lie in a span of several hours.

I'm not a doctor, far less a good one, and all I could tell about the man behind the desk was that he had been dead long enough for rigor mortis to set in but not long enough for it to wear off. He was stiff as a man frozen to death in a Siberian winter. He'd been gone for hours. How many, I'd no idea.

He wore four gold bands on his sleeves, so that would seem to make him the captain. The captain in the radio cabin. Captains are seldom found in the radio cabin and never behind the desk. He was slumped back in his chair, his head to one side, the back of it resting against a jacket hanging from a hook on the bulkhead, the side of it against a wall cabinet. Rigor mortis kept him in that position but he should have slipped to the floor or at least slumped forward on to the table before rigor mortis had set in.

There were no outward signs of violence that I could see but on the assumption that it would be stretching the arm of coincidence a bit far to assume that he had succumbed from natural causes while preparing to defend his life with his Peacemaker I took a closer look. I tried to pull him upright but he wouldn't budge. I tried harder, I heard the sound of cloth ripping, then suddenly he was upright, then fallen over to the left of the table, the right arm pivoting stiffly around and upwards, the Colt an accusing finger pointing at heaven.

I knew now how he had died and why he hadn't fallen forward before. He'd been killed by a weapon that projected from his spinal column, between maybe the sixth and seventh vertebrae, I couldn't be sure, and the handle of this weapon had caught in the pocket of the jacket on the bulkhead and held him there.

My job was one that had brought me into contact with a fair number of people who had died from a fair assortment of unnatural causes, but this was the first time I'd ever seen a man who had been killed by a chisel. A half-inch wood chisel, apparently quite ordinary in every respect except that its wooden handle had been sheathed by a bicycle's rubber hand grip, the kind that doesn't show fingerprints. The blade was embedded to a depth of at least four inches and even allowing for an edge honed to a razor sharpness it had taken a man as powerful as he was violent to strike that blow. I tried to jerk the chisel free, but it wouldn't come. It often happens that way with a knife: bone or cartilage that has been pierced by a sharp instrument locks solid over the steel when an attempt is made to withdraw it. I didn't try again. The chances were that the killer himself had tried to move it and failed. He wouldn't have wanted to abandon a handy little sticker like that if he could help it. Maybe someone had interrupted him. Or maybe he had a large supply of half-inch wooden chisels and could afford to leave the odd one lying around carelessly in someone's back.

Anyway, I didn't really want it. I had my own. Not a chisel but a knife. I eased it out of the plastic sheath that had been sewn into the inner lining of my coat, just behind the neck. It didn't look so much, a four-inch handle and a little double-edged three-inch blade. But that little blade could slice through a two-inch manilla with one gentle stroke and the point was the point of a lancet. I looked at it and looked at the inner door behind the radio table, the one that led to the radio operator's sleeping cabin, then I slid a little fountain pen torch from my breast pocket, crossed to the outer door, switched off the overhead lamp, did the same for the table lamp and stood there waiting.

How long I stood there I couldn't be sure. Maybe two minutes, maybe as long as five. Why I waited, I don't know. I told myself I was waiting until my eyes became adjusted to the almost total darkness inside the cabin, but I knew it wasn't that. Maybe I was waiting for some noise, the slightest imagined whisper of stealthy sound, maybe I was waiting for something, anything, to happen—or maybe I was just scared

9

to go through that inner door. Scared for myself? Perhaps I was. I couldn't be sure. Or perhaps I was scared of what I would find behind that door. I transferred the knife to my left hand—I'm right-handed but ambidextrous in some things—and slowly closed my fingers round the handle of the inner door.

It took me all of twenty seconds to open that door the twelve inches that was necessary for me to squeeze through the opening. In the very last half-inch the damned hinges creaked. It was a tiny sound, a sound you wouldn't normally have heard two yards away. With my steel-taut nerves in the state they were in, a six-inch naval gun going off in my ear would have sounded muffled by contrast. I stood petrified as any graven image, the dead man by my side was no more immobile than I. I could hear the thump of my accelerating heartbeat and savagely wished the damned thing would keep quiet.

If there was anyone inside waiting to flash a torch in my face and shoot me, knife me or do a little fancy carving up with a chisel, he was taking his time about it. I treated my lungs to a little oxygen, stepped soundlessly and sideways through the opening. I held the flash at the full outstretched extent of my right arm. If the ungodly are going to shoot at a person who is shining a torch at them they generally aim in the very close vicinity of the torch as the unwary habitually hold a torch in front of them. This, as I had learnt many years previously from a colleague who'd just had a bullet extracted from the lobe of his left lung because of this unwariness, was a very unwise thing to do. So I held the torch as far from my body as possible, drew my left arm back with the knife ready to go, hoped fervently that the reactions of any person who might be in that cabin were slower than mine and slid forward the switch of the torch.

There was someone there all right, but I didn't have to worry about his reactions. Not any more. He'd none left. He was lying face down on the bunk with that huddled shapeless look that belongs only to the dead. I made a quick traverse of the cabin with the pencil beam. The dead man was alone. As in the radio cabin, there was no sign of a struggle.

I didn't even have to touch him to ascertain the cause of death. The amount of blood that had seeped from that half-inch incision in his spine wouldn't have filled a teaspoon. I wouldn't have expected to find more; when the spinal column has been neatly severed the heart doesn't go on pumping long enough to matter a damn. There would have been a little more internal bleeding, but not much.

The curtains were drawn. I quartered every foot of the deck, bulkheads, and furniture with my flash. I don't know what I expected to find: what I found was nothing. I went out, closed the door behind me and searched the radio cabin with the same results. There was nothing more for me here, I had found all I wanted to find, all I had never wanted to find. And I never once looked at the faces of the two dead men. I didn't have to, they were faces I knew as well as the face that looked back at me every morning out of my shaving mirror. Seven days previously they had dined with me and our chief in our favorite pub in London and they had been as cheerful and relaxed as men in their profession can ever be, their normal still watchfulness overlaid by the momentary savoring of the lighter side of life they knew could never really be for them. And I had no doubt they had gone on being as still and watchful as ever, but they hadn't been watchful enough and now they were only still. What had happened to them was what inevitably happened to people in our trade, which would inevitably happen to myself when the time came. No matter how clever and strong and ruthless you were, sooner or later you would meet up with someone who was cleverer and stronger and more ruthless than yourself. And that someone would have a half-inch wood chisel in his hand and all your hardly won years of experience and knowledge and cunning counted for nothing for you never saw him coming and you never saw him coming because you had met your match at last and then you were dead.

And I had sent them to their deaths. Not willingly, not knowingly, but the ultimate responsibility had been mine. This had all been my idea, my brain-child and mine alone, and I'd overridden all objections and fast-talked our very doubtful and highly skeptical chief into giving if not his enthusiastic approval at least his grudging consent. I'd told the two men, Baker and Delmont, that if they played it my way no harm would come to them so they'd trusted me blindly and played it my way and now they lay dead beside me. No hesitation, gentlemen, put your faith in me, only see to it that you make your wills first of all.

There was nothing more to be done here now. I'd sent two men to their deaths and that couldn't be undone. It was time to be gone.

I opened the outer door the way you'd open the door to a

cellar you knew to be full of cobras and black widow spiders. The way *you* would open the door, that is: were cobras and black widow spiders all I had to contend with aboard that ship, I'd have gone through that door without a second thought, they were harmless and almost lovable little creatures compared to some specimens of Homo sapiens that were loose on the decks of the freighter *Nantesville* that night.

With the door opened at its fullest extent I just stood there. I stood there for a long time without moving a muscle of body or limbs, breathing shallowly and evenly, and when you stand like that even a minute seems half a lifetime. All my being was in my ears. I just stood there and listened. I could hear the slap of waves against the hull, the occasional low metallic rumble as the *Nantesville* worked against wind and tide on its moorings, the low moan of the strengthening night wind in the rigging, and, once, the far-off lonely call of a curlew. Lonesome sounds, safe sounds, sounds of the night and nature. Not the sounds I was listening for. Gradually, these sounds too became part of the silence. Foreign sounds, sounds of stealth and menace and danger, there were none. No sound of breathing, no slightest scrape of feet on steel decks, no rustle of clothing, nothing. If there was anyone waiting out there he was possessed of a patience and immobility that was superhuman and I wasn't worried about superhumans that night, just about humans, humans with knives and guns and chisels in their hands. Silently I stepped out over the storm sill.

I've never paddled along the nighttime Orinoco in a dugout canoe and had a thirty-foot anaconda drop from a tree, wrap a coil around my neck and start constricting me to death and what's more I don't have to go there now to describe the experience for I know exactly what it feels like. The sheer animal power, the feral ferocity of the pair of huge hands that closed round my neck from behind was terrifying, something I'd never known of, never dreamed of. After the first moment of blind panic and shocked paralysis, there was only one thought in my mind: it comes to us all and now it has come to me, someone who is cleverer and stronger and more ruthless than I am.

I lashed back with all the power of my right foot but the man behind me knew every rule in the book. His own right foot, travelling with even more speed and power than mine, smashed into the back of my swinging leg. It wasn't a man behind me, it was a centaur and he was shod with the biggest set of horseshoes I'd ever come across. My leg didn't feel as if it had been broken, it felt as if it had been cut in half. I felt his left toe behind my left foot and stamped on it with every vicious ounce of power left in me but when my foot came down his toe wasn't there any more. All I had on my feet was a pair of thin rubber swimming moccasins and the agonizing jar from the steel deck plates shot clear to the top of my head. I reached up my hands to break his little fingers but he knew all about that too for his fingers were clenched into iron-hard balls with the second knuckle grinding into the carotid artery. I wasn't the first man he'd strangled and unless I did something pretty quickly I wasn't going to be the last either. In my ears I could hear the hiss of compressed air escaping under high pressure and behind my eyes the shooting lines and flashes of color were deepening and brightening by the moment.

What saved me in those first few seconds were the folded hood and the thick rubberized canvas neck ruff of the scuba suit I was wearing under my coat. But it wasn't going to save me many seconds longer; the life's ambition of the character behind me seemed to be to make his knuckles meet in the middle of my neck. With the progress he was making that wouldn't take him too long, he was halfway there already.

I bent forward in a convulsive jerk. Half of his weight came on my back, that throttling grip not easing a fraction, and at the same time he moved his feet as far backward as possible—the instinctive reaction to my move, he would have thought that I was making a grab for one of his legs. When I had him momentarily off-balance I swung round in a short arc till both our backs were towards the sea. I thrust backwards with all my strength, one, two, three steps, accelerating all the way. The *Nantesville* didn't boast of any fancy teak guard-rails, just small-section chain, and the small of the strangler's back took our combined charging weights on the top chain.

If I'd taken that impact I'd have broken my back or slipped enough discs to keep an orthopaedic surgeon in steady employment for months. But no shouts of agony from this lad. No gasps, even. Not a whisper or sound. Maybe he was a deaf mute—I'd heard of several deaf mutes possessed of this phenomenal strength, part of nature's compensatory process, I suppose.

But he'd been forced to break his grip, to grab swiftly at the upper chain to save us both from toppling over the side

13

into the cold dark waters of Loch Houron. I thrust myself away and spun round to face him, my back against the radio office bulkhead. I needed that bulkhead, too—any support while my swimming head cleared and a semblance of life came back into my numbed right leg.

I could see him now as he straightened up from the guard-rail. Not clearly—it was too dark for that—but I could see the white blur of face and hands and the general outline of his body.

I'd expected some towering giant of a man, but he was no giant—unless my eyes weren't focussing properly, which was likely enough. From what I could see in the gloom he seemed a compact and well enough made figure, but that was all. He wasn't even as big as I was. Not that that meant a thing—George Hackenschmidt was a mere five foot nine and a paltry fourteen stone when he used to throw the Terrible Turk through the air like a football and prance around the training ring with eight hundred pounds of cement strapped to his back just to keep him in trim. I had no compunction of false pride about running from a smaller man and as far as this character was concerned the farther and faster the better. But not yet: My right leg wasn't up to it. I reached my hand behind my neck and brought the knife down, holding it in front of me, the blade in the palm of my hand so that he couldn't see the sheen of steel in the faint starlight.

He came at me calmly and purposefully, like a man who knew exactly what he intended to do and was in no doubt at all as to the outcome of his intended action. God knows I didn't doubt he had reason enough for his confidence. He came at me sideways so that my foot couldn't damage him, with his right hand extended at the full stretch of his arm. A one track mind. He was going for my throat again. I waited till his hand was inches from my face then jerked my own right hand violently upwards. Our hands smacked solidly together as the blade sliced cleanly through the center of his palm.

He wasn't a deaf mute after all. Three short unprintable words, an unjustified slur on my ancestry, and he stepped quickly backwards, rubbed the back and front of his hand against his clothes then licked it in a queer animal-like gesture. He peered closely at the blood, black as ink in the starlight, welling from both sides of his hand.

"So the little man has a little knife, has he?" he said softly. The voice was a shock. With this caveman-like strength I'd

14

have expected a caveman-like intelligence and voice to match, but the words came in the calm, pleasant, cultured almost accentless speech of the well-educated southern Englishman. "We shall have to take the little knife from him, shan't we?" He raised his voice. "Captain Imrie?" At least, that's what the name sounded like.

"Be quiet, you fool!" The urgent irate voice came from the direction of the crew accommodation aft. "Do you want to—"

"Don't worry, Captain." The eyes didn't leave me. "I have him. Here by the wireless office. He's armed. A knife. I'm just going to take it away from him."

"You have him? You have him? Good, good, good!" It was the kind of a voice a man uses when he's smacking his lips and rubbing his hands together: it was also the kind of voice that a German or Austrian uses when he speaks English. The short guttural "gut" was unmistakable. "Be careful. This one I want alive. Jacques! Henry! Kramer! All of you. Quickly! The bridge. Wireless office."

"Alive," the man opposite me said pleasantly, "can also mean not quite dead." He sucked some more blood from the palm of his hand. "Or will you hand over the knife quietly and peaceably? I would suggest—"

I didn't wait for more. This was an old technique. You talked to an opponent who courteously waited to hear you out, not appreciating that halfway through some well-turned phrase you were going to shoot him through the middle when, lulled into a sense of temporary false security, he least expected it. Not quite cricket, but effective, and I wasn't going to wait until it took effect on me. I didn't know how he would come at me but I guessed it would be a dive, either head or feet first and that if he got me down on the deck I wouldn't be getting up again. Not without assistance. I took a quick step forward, flashed my torch a foot from his face, saw the dazzled eyes screw shut for the only fraction of time I'd ever have and kicked him. It wasn't as hard as it might have been, owing to the fact that my right leg still felt as if it were broken, nor as accurate, because of the darkness, but it was a pretty creditable effort in the circumstances and it should have left him rolling and writhing about the deck, whooping in agony. Instead he just stood there, unable to move, bent forward and clutching himself with his hands. He was more than human, all right. I could see the sheen of his eyes, but I couldn't see the expression in them, which was

15

just as well as I don't think I would have cared for it very much.

I left. I remembered a gorilla I'd once seen in Basle Zoo, a big black monster who used to twist heavy truck tires into figures of eight for light exercise. I'd as soon have stepped inside that cage as stay around that deck when this lad became more like his old self again. I hobbled forward round the corner of the radio office, climbed up a liferaft and stretched myself flat on the deckhead.

The nearest running figures, some with torches, were already at the foot of the companionway leading up to the bridge. I had to get right aft to the rope with the rubber-covered hook I'd swung up to swarm aboard. But I couldn't do it until the midships decks were clear. And then, suddenly, I couldn't do it at all: now that the need for secrecy and stealth was over, someone had switched on the cargo loading lights and the midships and foredecks were bathed in a brilliant dazzle of white. One of the foredeck arc lamps was on a jumbo mast, just for'ard of and well above where I was lying. I felt as exposed as a fly pinned to a white ceiling. I flattened myself on that deckhead as if I were trying to push myself through it.

They were up the companionway and by the radio office now. I heard the sudden exclamations and curses and knew they'd found the hurt man: I didn't hear his voice so I assumed he wasn't able to speak yet.

The curt, authoritative German-accented voice took command.

"You cackle like a flock of hens. Be silent. Jacques, you have your machine pistol?"

"I have my pistol, Captain." Jacques had the quiet competent sort of voice that I would have found reassuring in certain circumstances but didn't very much care for in the present ones.

"Go aft. Stand at the entrance to the saloon and face for-'ard. Cover the midships decks. We will go to the forepeak and then come aft in line abreast and drive him to you. If he doesn't surrender to you, shoot him through the legs. I want him alive."

God, this was worse than the Peacemaker Colt. At least that fired only one shot at a time. I'd no idea what kind of machine pistol Jacques had, probably it fired bursts of a dozen or more. I could feel my right thigh muscle begin to stiffen again, it was becoming almost a reflex action now.

16

"And if he jumps over the side, sir?"

"Do I have to tell you, Jacques?"

"No, sir."

I was just as clever as Jacques was. He didn't have to tell me either. That nasty dry taste was back in my throat and mouth again. I'd a minute left, no more, and then it would be too late. I slid silently to the side of the radio office roof, the starboard side, the side remote from the spot where Captain Imrie was issuing curt instructions to his men, lowered myself soundlessly to the deck and made my way to the wheelhouse.

I didn't need my torch in there, the backwash of light from the big arc lamps gave me all the illumination I wanted. Crouching down, to keep below window level, I looked around and saw what I wanted right away—a metal box of distress flares.

Two quick flicks of the knife severed the lashings that secured the flare box to the deck. One piece of rope, perhaps ten feet in all, I left secured to a handle of the box. I pulled a plastic bag from the pocket of my coat, tore off the coat and the yachtsman's rubber trousers that I was wearing over my scuba suit, stuffed them inside and secured the bag to my waist. The coat and trousers had been essential. A figure in a dripping rubber diving suit walking across the decks of the *Nantesville* would hardly have been likely to escape comment whereas in the dusk and with the outer clothing I had on I could have passed for a crewman and, indeed, had done so twice at a distance: equally important, when I'd left the port of Torbay in my rubber dinghy it had been broad daylight and the sight of a scuba-clad figure putting to sea towards evening wouldn't have escaped comment either as the curiosity factor of the inhabitants of the smaller ports of the Western Highlands and Islands did not, I had discovered, lag noticeably behind that of their mainland brethren. Some would put it even more strongly than that.

Still crouching low, I moved out through the wheelhouse door on to the starboard wing of the bridge. I reached the outer end and stood up straight. I had to, I had to take the risk, it was now or never at all, I could hear the crew already beginning to move forward to start their search. I lifted the flare box over the side, eased it down the full length of the rope and started to swing it slowly, gently, from side to side, like a leadsman preparing to cast his lead.

The box weighed at least forty pounds, but I barely noticed the weight. The pendulum arc increased with every swing I made. It had reached an angle of about forty-five degrees on each swing now, pretty close to the maximum I could get and both time and my luck must be running out, I felt about as conspicuous as a trapeze artist under a dozen spotlights and just about as vulnerable too. As the box swung aft on its last arc I gave the rope a final thrust to achieve all the distance and momentum I could, opened my hands at the extremity of the arc and dropped down behind the canvas wind dodger. It was as I dropped that I remembered I hadn't holed the damned box, I had no idea whether it would float or sink but I did have a very clear idea of what would happen to me if it didn't sink. One thing for sure, it was too late to worry about it now.

I heard a shout come from the main deck, some twenty or thirty feet aft of the bridge. I was certain I had been seen but I hadn't. A second after the shout came a loud and very satisfactory splash and a voice I recognized as Jacques' shouting: "He's gone over the side. Starboard abaft the bridge. A torch, quick!" He must have been walking aft as ordered, seen this dark blur falling, heard the splash and come to the inevitable conclusion. A dangerous customer who thought fast, was Jacques. In three seconds he'd told his mates all they required to know: what had happened, where and what he wanted done as the necessary preliminary to shooting me full of holes.

The men who had been moving forward to start the sweep for me now came running aft, pounding along the deck directly beneath where I was crouching on the wing of the bridge.

"Can you see him, Jacques?" Captain Imrie's voice, very quick, very calm.

"Not yet, sir."

"He'll be up soon." I wished he wouldn't sound so damned confident. "A dive like that must have knocked most of the breath out of him. Kramer, two men and into the boat. Take lamps and circle around. Henry, the box of grenades. Carlo, the bridge, quick. Starboard searchlight."

I'd never thought of the boat, that was bad enough, but the grenades! I felt chilled. I knew what an underwater explosion, even a small explosion, can do to the human body, it was twenty times as deadly as the same explosion on land. And I had to, I just had to, be in that water in minutes. But at least I could do something about that searchlight, it was only two feet above my head. I had the power cable in my

18

left hand, the knife in my right and had just brought the two into contact when my mind stopped thinking about those damned grenades and started working again. Cutting that cable would be about as clever as leaning over the wind dodger and yelling "Here I am, come and catch me"—a dead giveaway that I was still on board. Clobbering Carlo from behind as he came up the ladder would have the same effect. And I couldn't fool them twice. Not people like these. Hobbling as fast as I could I passed through the wheelhouse on to the port wing, slid down the ladder and ran towards the forepeak. The foredeck was deserted.

I heard a shout and the harsh chatter of some automatic weapon—Jacques and his machine pistol, for a certainty. Had he imagined he'd seen something, had the box come to the surface, had he actually seen the box and mistaken it for me in the dark waters? It must have been the last of these—he wouldn't have wasted ammunition on anything he'd definitely recognised as a box. Whatever the reason, it had all my blessing. If they thought I was floundering about down there, riddled like a Gruyère cheese, then they wouldn't be looking for me up here.

They had the port anchor down. I swung over the side, got my feet in the hawse pipe, reached down and grabbed the chain. The international athletics board should have had their stopwatches on me that night, I must have set a new world record for shinning down anchor chains.

The water was cold but my exposure suit took care of that. It was choppy, with a heavy tide running, both of which suited me well. I swam down the port side of the *Nantesville*, underwater for ninety percent of the time, and I saw no one and no one saw me: all the activity was on the starboard side of the vessel.

My aqualung unit and weights and flippers were where I had left them, tied to the top of the rudder post—the *Nantesville* was not much more than halfway down to her marks and the top of the post not far underwater. Fitting on an aqualung in choppy seas with a heavy tide running isn't the easiest of tasks but the thought of Kramer and his grenades was a considerable help. Besides, I was in a hurry to be gone for I had a long way to go and many things to do when I arrived at my destination.

I could hear the engine note of the lifeboat rising and falling as it circled off the ship's starboard side but at no time did it come within a hundred feet of me. No more shots were fired and Captain Imrie had obviously decided against using the grenades. I adjusted the weights around my waist, dropped down into the dark safety of the waters, checked my direction on my luminous wrist compass and started to swim. After five minutes I came to the surface and after another five felt my feet ground on the shores of the rocky islet where I'd cached my rubber dinghy.

I clambered up on the rocks and looked back. The *Nantesville* was ablaze with light. A searchlight was shining down into the sea and the lifeboat still circling around. I could hear the steady clanking of the anchor being weighed. I hauled the dinghy into the water, climbed in, unshipped the two stubby oars and paddled off to the southwest. I was still within effective range of the searchlight but its chances of picking up a black-clad figure in a low-silhouette black dinghy on those black waters were remote indeed.

After a mile I shipped the oars and started up the outboard. Or tried to start it up. Outboards always work perfectly for me, except when I'm cold, wet, and exhausted. Whenever I really need them, they never work. So I took to the stubby oars again and rowed and rowed and rowed, but not for what seemed any longer than a month. I arrived back at the *Firecrest* at ten to three in the morning.

2 • TUESDAY: 3 A.M.—DAWN

"Calvert?" Hunslett's voice was a barely audible murmur in the darkness.

"Yes." Standing there above me on the *Firecrest*'s deck, he was more imagined than seen against the blackness of the night sky. Heavy clouds had rolled in from the southwest and the last of the stars were gone. Big heavy drops of cold rain were beginning to spatter off the surface of the sea. "Give me a hand to get the dinghy aboard."

"How did it go?"

"Later. This first." I climbed up the accommodation ladder, painter in hand. I had to lift my right leg over the gunwale. Stiff and numb and just beginning to ache again, it could barely take my weight. "And hurry. We can expect company soon."

"So that's the way of it," Hunslett said thoughtfully. "Uncle Arthur *will* be pleased about this."

I said nothing to that. Our employer, Rear-Admiral Sir Arthur Arnford-Jason, K.C.B. and most of the rest of the alphabet, wasn't going to be pleased at all. We heaved the dripping dinghy inboard, unclamped the outboard and took them both on to the foredeck.

"Get me a couple of waterproof bags," I said. "Then start getting the anchor chain in. Keep it quiet—leave the brake pawl off and use a tarpaulin."

"We're leaving?"

"We would if we had any sense. We're staying. Just get the anchor up and down."

By the time he'd returned with the bags I'd the dinghy deflated and in its canvas cover. I stripped off my aqualung and scuba suit and stuffed them into one of the bags along with the weights, my big-dialled waterproof watch and the combined wrist compass and depth gauge. I put the outboard in the other bag, restraining the impulse just to throw the damn thing overboard: an outboard motor was a harmless

21

enough object to have aboard any boat, but we already had one attached to the wooden dinghy hanging from the davits over the stern.

Hunslett had the electric windlass going and the chain coming in steadily. An electric windlass is in itself a pretty noiseless machine: when weighing anchor all the racket comes from four sources—the chain passing through the hawse pipe, the clacking of the brake pawl over the successive stops, the links passing over the drum itself and the clattering of the chain as it falls into the chain locker. About the first of these we could do nothing: but with the brake pawl off and a heavy tarpaulin smothering the sound from the drum and chain locker, the noise level was surprisingly low. Sound travels far over the surface of the sea, but the nearest anchored boats were almost two hundred yards away—we had no craving for the company of other boats in the harbor. At two hundred yards, in Torbay, we felt ourselves uncomfortably close: but the sea bed shelved fairly steeply away from the little town and our present depth of twenty fathoms was the safe maximum for the sixty fathoms of chain we carried.

I heard the click as Hunslett's foot stepped on the deck switch. "She's up and down."

"Put the pawl in for a moment. If that drum slips, I'll have no hands left." I pulled the bags right for'ard, leaned out under the pulpit rail and used lengths of heaving line to secure them to the anchor chain. When the lines were secure I lifted the bags over the side and let them dangle from the chain.

"I'll take the weight," I said. "Lift the chain off the drum—we'll lower it by hand."

Forty fathoms is 240 feet of chain and letting that lot down to the bottom didn't do my back or arms much good at all, and the rest of me was a long way below par before we started. I was pretty close to exhaustion from the night's work, my neck ached fiercely, my leg only badly and I was shivering violently. I know of various ways of achieving a warm rosy glow but wearing only a set of underclothes in the middle of a cold, wet and windy autumn night in the Western Isles is not one of them. But at last the job was done and we were able to go below. If anyone wanted to investigate what lay at the foot of our anchor chain he'd need a steel articulated diving suit.

Hunslett pulled the saloon door to behind us, moved

around in the darkness adjusting the heavy velvet curtains, then switched on a small table lamp. It didn't give much light but we knew from experience that it didn't show up through the velvet, and advertising the fact that we were up and around in the middle of the night was the last thing I wanted to do.

Hunslett had a dark narrow saturnine face, with a strong jaw, black bushy eyebrows and thick black hair—the kind of face which is so essentially an expression in itself that it rarely shows much else. It was expressionless now and very still.

"You'll have to buy another shirt," he said. "Your collar's too tight. Leaves marks."

I stopped towelling myself and looked in a mirror. Even in that dim light my neck looked a mess. It was badly swollen and discolored, with four wicked looking bruises where the thumbs and forefinger joints had sunk deep into the flesh. Blue and green and purple they were, and they looked as if they would be there for a long time to come.

"He got me from behind. He's wasting his time being a criminal, he'd sweep the board at the Olympic weightlifting. I was lucky. He also wears heavy boots." I twisted around and looked down at my right calf. The bruise was bigger than my fist and if it missed out any of the colors of the rainbow I couldn't offhand think which one. There was a deep red gash across the middle of it and blood was ebbing slowly along its entire length. Hunslett gazed at it with interest.

"If you hadn't been wearing that tight scuba suit, you'd have most like bled to death. I better fix that for you."

"I don't need bandages. What I need is a Scotch. Stop wasting your time. Oh, hell, sorry, yes, you'd better fix it, we can't have our guests sloshing about ankle deep in blood."

"You're very sure we're going to have guests?"

"I half expected to have them waiting on the doorstep when I got back to the *Firecrest*. We're going to have guests, all right. Whatever our pals aboard the *Nantesville* may be, they're no fools. They'll have figured out by this time that I could have approached only by dinghy. They'll know damn well that it was no nosey-parker local prowling about the ship—local lads in search of a bit of fun don't go aboard anchored ships in the first place. In the second place the locals wouldn't go near Beul nan Uamh—the mouth of the grave—in daylight, far less at nighttime. Even the Pilot says the place has an evil reputation. And in the third place no

23

local lad would get aboard as I did, behave aboard as I did or leave as I did. The local lad would be dead."

"I shouldn't wonder. And?"

"So we're not locals. We're visitors. We wouldn't be staying at any hotel or boarding house—too restricted, couldn't move. Almost certainly we'll have a boat. Now, where would our boat be? Not to the north of Loch Houron for with a forecast promising a southwest Force six strengthening to Force seven, no boat is going to be daft enough to hang about a lee shore in that lot. The only holding ground and shallow enough sheltered anchorage in the other direction, down the Sound for forty miles, is in Torbay—and that's only four or five miles from where the *Nantesville* was lying at the mouth at Loch Houron. Where would you look for us?"

"I'd look for a boat anchored at Torbay. Which gun do you want?"

"I don't want any gun. You don't want any gun. People like us don't carry guns."

"Marine biologists don't carry guns," he nodded. "Employees of the Ministry of Agriculture and Fisheries don't carry guns. Civil Servants are above reproach. So we play it clever. You're the boss."

"I don't feel clever any more. And I'll take long odds that I'm not your boss any more. Not after Uncle Arthur hears what I have to tell him."

"You haven't told *me* anything yet." He finished tying the bandage round my leg and straightened. "How's that feel?"

I tried it. "Better. Thanks. Better still when you've taken the cork from that bottle. Get into pyjamas or something. People found fully dressed in the middle of the night cause eyebrows to go up." I towelled my head as vigorously as my tired arms would let me. One wet hair on my head and eyebrows wouldn't just be lifting, they'd be disappearing into hairlines. "There isn't much to tell and all of it is bad."

He poured me a large drink, a smaller one for himself, and added water to both. It tasted the way Scotch always does after you've swum and rowed for hours and damn near got yourself killed in the process.

"I got there without trouble. I hid behind Carrara Point till it was dusk and then paddled out to the Bogha Nuadh. I left the dinghy there and swam underwater as far as the stern of the ship. It was the *Nantesville* all right. Name and flag were different, a mast was gone and the white superstructure was now black—but it was her all right. Near as dammit didn't make it—it was close to the turn of the tide but it took me thirty minutes against that current. Must be wicked at the full flood or ebb."

"They say it's the worst on the West Coast—worse even than Coirebhreachan."

"I'd rather not be the one to find out. I had to hang on to the stern post for ten minutes before I'd got enough strength back to shin up that rope."

"You took a chance."

"It was near enough dark. Besides," I added bitterly, "there are some precautions intelligent people don't think to take about crazy ones. There were only two or three people in the after accommodation. Just a skeleton crew aboard, seven or eight, no more. All the original crew have vanished completely."

"No sign of them anywhere?"

"No sign. Dead or alive, no sign at all. I had a bit of bad luck. I was leaving the after accommodation to go to the bridge when I passed someone a few feet away. I gave a half wave and grunted something and he answered back, I don't know what. I followed him back to the quarters. He picked up a phone in the galley and I heard him talking to someone, quick and urgent. Said that one of the original crew must have been hiding and was trying to get away. I couldn't stop him—he faced the door as he was talking and he had a gun in his hand. I had to move quickly. I walked to the bridge structure—"

"You what? When you knew they were on to you? Mr. Calvert, you want your bloody head examined."

"Uncle Arthur will put it less kindly. It was the only chance I'd ever have. Besides, if they thought it was only a terrified member of the original crew they wouldn't have been so worried: if this guy had seen me walking around dripping wet in a scuba suit he'd have turned me into a colander. He wasn't sure. On the way for'ard I passed another bloke without incident—he'd left the bridge superstructure before the alarm had been given, I suppose. I didn't stop at the bridge. I went right for'ard and hid behind the winchman's shelter. For about ten minutes there was a fair bit of commotion and a lot of flashlight work around the bridge island, then I saw and heard them moving aft—must have thought I was still in the after accommodation.

"I went through all the officers' cabins in the bridge island.

No one. One cabin, an engineer's, I think, had smashed furniture and a carpet heavily stained with dry blood. Next door, the captain's bunk had been saturated with blood."

"They'd been warned to offer no resistance."

"I know. Then I found Baker and Delmont."

"So you found them. Baker and Delmont." Hunslett's eyes were hooded, gazing down at the glass in his hand. I wished to God he'd show some expression on that dark face of his.

"Delmont must have made a last second attempt to send a call for help. They'd been warned not to, except in emergency, so they must have been discovered. He'd been stabbed in the back with a half-inch wood chisel and then dragged into the radio officer's cabin which adjoined the radio office. Some time later Baker had come in. He was wearing an officer's clothes—some desperate attempt to disguise himself, I suppose. He'd a gun in his hand, but he was looking the wrong way and the gun was pointing the wrong way. The same chisel in the back."

Hunslett poured himself another drink. A much larger one. Hunslett hardly ever drank. He swallowed half of it in one gulp. He said: "And they hadn't all gone aft. They'd left a reception committee."

"They're very clever. They're very dangerous. Maybe we've moved out of our class. Or I have. A one-man reception committee, but when that one man was this man, two would have been superfluous. I know he killed Baker and Delmont. I'll never be so lucky again."

"You got away. Your luck hadn't run out."

And Baker's and Delmont's had. I knew he was blaming me. I knew London would blame me. I blamed myself. I hadn't much option. There was no one else to blame.

"Uncle Arthur," Hunslett said. "Don't you think—"

"The hell with Uncle Arthur. Who cares about Uncle Arthur? How in God's name do you think I feel?" I felt savage and I know I sounded it. For the first time a flicker of expression showed on Hunslett's face. I wasn't supposed to have any feelings.

"Not that," he said. "About the *Nantesville*—now that she's been identified *as* the *Nantesville,* now we know her new name and flag—what were they, by the way?"

"*Alta Fjord*. Norwegian. It doesn't matter."

"It does matter. We radio Uncle Arthur—"

"And have our guests find us in the engine room with earphones round our heads. Are you mad?"

"You seem damned sure they'll come."

"I *am* sure. You too. You said so."

"I agree this is where they would come. *If* they came."

"If they come. *If* they come. Good God, man, for all that they know I was aboard that ship for hours. I may have the names and full descriptions of all of them. As it happens I couldn't identify any of them and their names may or may not mean anything. But they're not to know that. For all they know I'm on the blower right now bawling out descriptions to Interpol. The chances are at least even that some of them are on file. They're too good to be little men. Some must be known."

"In that case they'd be too late anyway. The damage would be done."

"Not without the sole witness who could testify against them."

"I think we'd better have those guns out."

"No."

"Then for God's sake let's get out of here."

"No."

"You don't blame me for trying?"

"No."

"Baker and Delmont. Think of them."

"I'm thinking of nothing else but them. You don't have to stay."

He set his glass down very carefully. He was really letting himself go tonight, he'd allowed that dark craggy face its second expression in ten minutes and it wasn't a very encouraging one. Then he picked up his glass and grinned.

"You don't know what you're saying," he said kindly. "Your neck—that's what comes from the blood supply to the brain being interrupted. You're not fit to fight off a teddy bear. Who's going to look after you if they start playing games?"

"I'm sorry," I said. I meant it. I'd worked with Hunslett maybe ten times in the ten years I'd known him and it had been a stupid thing for me to say. About the only thing Hunslett was incapable of was leaving your side in time of trouble. "You were speaking of Uncle?"

"Yes. We know where the *Nantesville* is. Uncle could get a Navy boat to shadow her, by radar if—"

"I know where she was. She upped anchor as I left. By dawn she'll be a hundred miles away—in any direction."

"She's gone? We've scared them off? They're going to love

this." He sat down heavily, then looked at me. "But we have her new description—"

"I said that didn't matter. By tomorrow she'll have another description. The *Hoko Maru* from Yokohama, with green topsides, Japanese flag, different masts—"

"An air search. We could—"

"By the time an air search could be organised they'd have twenty thousand square miles of sea to cover. You've heard the forecast. It's bad. Low cloud—and they'd have to fly under the low cloud. Cuts their effectiveness by ninety percent. And poor visibility and rain. Not a chance in a hundred, not one in a thousand of positive identification. And if they do locate them—if—what then? A friendly wave from the pilot? Not much else he can do."

"The Navy. They could call up the Navy—"

"Call up what Navy? From the Med? Or the Far East? The Navy has very few ships left and practically none in those parts. By the time any naval vessel could get to the scene it would be night again and the *Nantesville* to hell and gone. Even if a naval ship did catch up with it, what then? Sink it with gunfire—with maybe the twenty-five missing crew members of the *Nantesville* locked up in the hold?"

"A boarding party?"

"With the same twenty-five ex-crew members lined up on deck with pistols at their backs and Captain Imrie and his thugs politely asking the Navy boys what their next move was going to be?"

"I'll get into my pyjamas," Hunslett said tiredly. At the doorway he paused and turned. "If the *Nantesville* has gone, her crew—the new crew—have gone too and we'll be having no visitors after all. Had you thought of that?"

"No."

"I don't really believe it either."

They came at twenty past four in the morning. They came in a very calm and orderly and law-abiding and official fashion, they stayed for forty minutes and by the time they had left I still wasn't sure whether they were our men or not.

Hunslett came into my small cabin, starboard side forward, switched on the light and shook me. "Wake up," he said loudly. "Come on. Wake up."

I was wide awake. I hadn't closed an eye since I'd lain down. I groaned and yawned a bit without overdoing it, then opened a bleary eye. There was no one behind him.

"What is it? What do you want?" A pause. "What the hell's up? It's just after four in the morning."

"Don't ask me what's up," Hunslett said irritably. "Police. Just come aboard. They say it's urgent."

"Police? Did you say, 'police'?"

"Yes. Come on, now. They're waiting."

"Police? Aboard our boat? What—"

"Oh, for God's sake! How many more nightcaps did you have last night after I went to bed? Police. Two of them and two Customs. It's urgent, they say."

"It better bloody well be urgent. In the middle of the bloody night. Who do they think we are—escaped train robbers? Haven't you told them who we are? Oh, all right, all right, all *right!* I'm coming."

Hunslett left, and thirty seconds afterwards I joined him in the saloon. Four men sat there, two police officers and two Customs officials. They didn't look a very villainous bunch to me. The older, bigger policeman got to his feet. A tall, burly, brown-faced sergeant in his late forties, he looked me over with a cold eye, looked at the near-empty whisky bottle with the two unwashed glasses on the table, then looked back at me. He didn't like wealthy yachtsmen. He didn't like wealthy yachtsmen who drank too much at nighttime and were bleary-eyed, bloodshot and tousle-haired at the following crack of dawn. He didn't like wealthy effete yachtsmen who wore red silk dragon Chinese dressing gowns with a Paisley scarf to match tied negligently round the neck. I didn't like them very much myself, especially the Paisley scarf, much in favor though it was with the yachting fraternity: but I had to have something to conceal those bruises on my neck.

"Are you the owner of this boat, sir?" the sergeant inquired. An unmistakable West Highland voice and a courteous one, but it took him all his time to get his tongue round the "sir."

"If you would tell me what makes it any of your damn business," I said unpleasantly, "maybe I'll answer that and maybe I won't. A private boat is the same as a private house, Sergeant. You have to have a warrant before you shove your way in. Or don't you know the law?"

"He knows the law," one of the Customs men put in. A small dark character, smooth-shaven at four in the morning, with a persuasive voice, not West Highland. "Be reasonable. This is not the sergeant's job. We got him out of bed almost three hours ago. He's just obliging us."

I ignored him. I said to the sergeant: "This is the middle of the night in a lonely Scottish bay. How would you feel if four unidentified men came aboard in the middle of the night?" I was taking a chance on that one, but a fair chance. If they were who I thought they might be and if I were who they thought I might be, then I'd never talk like that. But an innocent man would. "Any means of identifying yourselves?"

"Identifying myself?" The sergeant stared coldly at me. "I don't have to identify myself. Sergeant MacDonald. I've been in charge of the Torbay police station for eight years. Ask any man in Torbay. They all know me." If he was who he claimed to be this was probably the first time in his life that anyone had asked him for identification. He nodded to the seated policeman. "Police Constable MacDonald."

"Your son?" The resemblance was unmistakable. "Nothing like keeping it in the family, eh, Sergeant?" I didn't know whether to believe him or not, but I felt I'd been an irate householder long enough. A degree less truculence was in order. "And Customs, eh? I know the law about you, too. No search warrants for you boys. I believe the police would like your powers. Go anywhere you like and ask no one's permission beforehand. That's it, isn't it?"

"Yes, sir." It was the younger Customs man who answered. Medium height, fair hair, running a little to fat, Belfast accent, dressed like the other in blue overcoat, peaked hat, brown gloves, smartly creased trousers. "We hardly ever do, though. We prefer cooperation. We like to ask."

"And you'd like to ask to search this boat, is that it?" Hunslett said.

"Yes, sir."

"Why?" I asked. Puzzlement now in my voice. And in my mind. I just didn't know what I had on my hands. "If we're all going to be so courteous and cooperative, could we have any explanation?"

"No reason in the world why not, sir." The older Customs man was almost apologetic. "A truck with contents valued at £12,000 was hi-jacked on the Ayrshire coast last night—night before last, that is, now. In the news this evening. From information received, we know it was transferred to a small boat. We think it came north."

"Why?"

"Sorry, sir. Confidential. This is the third port we've visited and the thirteenth boat—the fourth in Torbay—that we've been on in the past fifteen hours. We've been kept on the run,

30

I can tell you." An easy friendly voice, a voice that said: "You don't really think we suspect you. We've a job to do, that's all."

"And you're searching all boats that have come up from the south. Or you think have come from there. Fresh arrivals, anyway. Has it occurred to you that any boat with hijacked goods on board wouldn't dare pass through the Crinan Canal? Once you're in there, you're trapped. For four hours. So he'd have to come round the Mull of Kintyre. We've been here since this afternoon. It would take a pretty fast boat to get up here in that time."

"You've got a pretty fast boat here, sir," Sergeant MacDonald said. I wondered how the hell they managed it, from the Western Isles to the East London docks every sergeant in the country had the same wooden voice, the same wooden face, the same cold eye. Must be something to do with the uniform. I ignored him.

"What are we—um—supposed to have stolen?"

"Chemicals. It was an ICI truck."

"Chemicals?" I looked at Hunslett, grinned, then turned back to the Customs officer. "Chemicals, eh? We're loaded with them. But no £12,000 worth, I'm afraid."

There was a brief silence. MacDonald said: "Would you mind explaining, sir?"

"Not at all." I lit a cigarette, the little mind enjoying its big moment, and smiled. "This is a government boat, Sergeant MacDonald. I thought you would have seen the flag. Ministry of Agriculture and Fisheries. We're marine biologists. Our after cabin is a floating laboratory. Look at our library here." Two shelves loaded with technical tomes. "And if you've still any doubt left I can give you two numbers, one in Glasgow, one in London, that will establish our bona-fides. Or phone the lock-master in the Crinan sea basin. We spent last night there."

"Yes, sir." The lack of impression I had made on the sergeant was total. "Where did you go in your dinghy this evening?"

"I beg your pardon, Sergeant?"

"You were seen to leave this boat in a black rubber dinghy about five o'clock this evening." I'd heard of icy fingers playing up and down one's spine but it wasn't fingers I felt then, it was a centipede with a hundred icy boots on. "You went out into the Sound. Mr. McIlroy, the postmaster, saw you."

"I hate to impugn the character of a fellow Civil Servant but he must have been drunk." Funny how an icy feeling could make you sweat. "I haven't got a black rubber dinghy. I've never owned a black rubber dinghy. You just get out your little magnifying glass, Sergeant, and if you find a black rubber dinghy I'll make you a present of the brown wooden dinghy, which is the only one we have on the *Firecrest*."

The wooden expression cracked a little. He wasn't so certain now. "So you weren't out?"

"I *was* out. In our own dinghy. I was just round the corner of Garbh Island there, collecting some marine samples from the Sound. I can show them to you in the after cabin. We're not here on a holiday, you know."

"No offence, no offence." I was a member of the working classes now, not a plutocrat, and he could afford to thaw a little. "Mr. McIlroy's eyesight isn't what it was and everything looks black against the setting sun. You don't *look* the type, I must say, who'd land on the shores of the Sound and bring down the telephone wires to the mainland."

The centipede started on again and broke into a fast gallop. Cut off from the mainland. How very convenient for somebody. I didn't spend any time wondering who had brought the wires down—it had been no act of God, I was sure of that.

"Did you mean what I thought you to mean, Sergeant?" I said slowly. "That you suspected me—"

"We can't take chances, sir." He was almost apologetic now. Not only was I a working man, I was a man working for the Government. All men working for the Government are ipso facto respectable and trustworthy citizens.

"But you won't mind if we take a little look round?" The dark-haired Customs officer was even more apologetic. "The lines are down and, well, you know . . ." His voice trailed off and he smiled. "If you were the hi-jackers—I appreciate now that it's a chance in a million, but still—and if we didn't search—well, we'd be out of a job tomorrow. Just a formality."

"I wouldn't want to see that happen, Mr.—ah—"

"Thomas. Thank you. Your ship's papers? Ah, thank you." He handed them to the younger man. "Let's see now. Ah, the wheelhouse. Could Mr. Durran here use the wheelhouse to make copies? Won't take five minutes."

"Certainly. Wouldn't he be more comfortable here?"

"We're modernized now, sir. Portable photo copier. Standard on the job. Has to be dark. Won't take five minutes. Can we begin in this laboratory of yours?"

A formality, he'd said. Well, he was right there, as a search it was the least informal thing I'd ever come across. Five minutes after he'd gone to the wheelhouse Durran came aft to join us and he and Thomas went through the *Firecrest* as if they were looking for the Koh-i-nor. To begin with, at least. Every piece of mechanical and electrical equipment in the after cabin had to be explained to them. They looked in every locker and cupboard. They rummaged through the ropes and fenders in the large stern locker aft of the laboratory and I thanked God I hadn't followed my original idea of stowing the dinghy, motor, and scuba gear in there. They even examined the after toilet. As if I'd be careless enough to drop the Koh-i-nor in there.

They spent most time of all in the engine room. It was worth examining. Everything looked brand new, and gleamed. Two big 100 hp diesels, diesel generator, radio generator, hot and cold water pumps, central heating plant, big oil and water tanks and the two long rows of lead-acid batteries. Thomas seemed especially interested in the batteries.

"You carry a lot of reserve there, Mr. Petersen," he said. He'd learnt my name by now, even though it wasn't the one I'd been christened with. "Why all the power?"

"We haven't even got enough. Care to start those two engines by hand? We have eight electric motors in the lab—and the only time they're used, in harbor, we can't run either the engines or generators to supply juice. Too much interference. A constant drain." I was ticking off my fingers. "Then there's the central heating, hot and cold water pumps, radar, radio, automatic steering, windlass, power winch for the dinghy, echo-sounder, navigation lights, cooker—"

"You win, you win." He'd become quite friendly by this time. "Boats aren't really in my line. Let's move forward, shall we?"

The remainder of the inspection, curiously, didn't take long. In the saloon I found that Hunslett had persuaded the Torbay police force to accept the hospitality of the *Firecrest*. Sergeant MacDonald hadn't exactly become jovial, but he was much more human than when he'd come on board. Constable MacDonald, I noticed, didn't seem so relaxed. He looked positively glum. Maybe he didn't approve of his old man consorting with potential criminals.

If the examination of the saloon was cursory, that of the

two forward cabins was positively perfunctory. Back in the saloon, I said:

"Sorry I was a bit short, gentlemen. I like my sleep. A drink before you go?"

"Well." Thomas smiled. "We don't want to be rude either. Thank you."

Five minutes and they were gone. Thomas didn't even glance at the wheelhouse—Durran had been there, of course. He had a quick look at one of the deck lockers but didn't bother about the others. We were in the clear. A civil good-bye on both sides and they were gone. Their boat, a big indeterminate shape in the darkness, seemed to have plenty of power.

"Odd," I said.

"What's odd?"

"That boat. Any idea what it was like?"

"How could I?" Hunslett was testy. He was as short of sleep as I was. "It was pitch dark."

"That's just the point. A gentle glow in their wheelhouse—you couldn't even see what that was like—and no more. No deck lights, no interior lights, no navigation lights even."

"Sergeant MacDonald has been looking out over this harbor for eight years. Do you need lights to find your way about your own living room after dark?"

"I haven't got twenty yachts and cruisers in my living room swinging all over the place with wind and tide. And wind and tide doesn't alter my own course when I'm crossing my living room. There are only three boats in the harbor carrying anchor lights. He'll have to use something to see where he's going."

And he did. From the direction of the receding sound of engines a light stabbed out into the darkness. A five-inch searchlight, I would have guessed. It picked up a small yacht riding at anchor less than a hundred yards ahead of it, altered to starboard, picked up another, altered to port, then swung back on course again.

"'Odd' was the word you used," Hunslett murmured. "Quite a good word, too, in the circumstances. And what are we to think of the alleged Torbay police force?"

"You talked to the sergeant longer than I did. When I was aft with Thomas and Durran."

"I'd like to think otherwise," Hunslett said inconsequentially. "It would make things easier, in a way. But I can't.

34

He's a genuine old-fashioned cop and a good one, too. I've met too many. So have you."

"A good cop and an honest one," I agreed. "This is not his line of country and he was fooled. It is our line of country and we were fooled. Until now, that is."

"Speak for yourself."

"Thomas made one careless remark. An off-beat remark. You didn't hear it—we were in the engine room." I shivered, maybe it was the cold night wind. "It meant nothing—not until I saw that they didn't want their boat recognised again. He said: 'Boats aren't really in my line.' Probably thought he'd been asking too many questions and wanted to reassure me. Boats not in his line—a Customs officer and boats not in his line. They only spend their lives aboard boats, examining boats, that's all. They spend their lives looking and poking in so many odd corners and quarters that they know more about boats than the designers themselves. Another thing, did you notice how sharply dressed they were? A credit to Carnaby Street."

"Customs officers don't usually go around in oil-stained overalls."

"They've been living in those clothes for twenty-four hours. This is the what—the thirteenth boat they've searched in that time. Would you still have knife-edged creases to your pants after that lot? Or would you say they'd only just taken them from the hangers and put them on?"

"What else did they say? What else did they do?" Hunslett spoke so quietly that I could hear the note of the engines of the Customs' boat fall away sharply as their searchlight lit up the low-water stone pier, half a mile away. "Take an undue interest in anything?"

"They took an undue interest in everything. Wait a minute, though, wait a minute. Thomas seemed particularly intrigued by the batteries, by the large amount of reserve electrical power we had."

"Did he now? Did he indeed? And did you notice how lightly our two Customs friends swung aboard their launch when leaving?"

"They'll have done it a thousand times."

"Both of them had their hands free. They weren't carrying anything. They should have been carrying something."

"The photo copier. I'm getting old."

"The photo copier. Standard equipment my ruddy foot. So

if our fair-haired pal wasn't busy photo-copying he was busy doing something else."

We moved inside the wheelhouse. Hunslett selected the larger screwdriver from the tool rack beside the echo-sounder and had the face-plate off our R.T./D.F. set inside sixty seconds. He looked at the interior for five seconds, looked at me for the same length of time, then started screwing the face-plate back into position. One thing was certain, we wouldn't be using that transmitter for a long time to come.

I turned away and stared out through the wheelhouse windows into the darkness. The wind was still rising, the black sea gleamed palely as the whitecaps came marching in from the southwest, the *Firecrest* snubbed sharply on her anchor chain and, with the wind and the tide at variance, she was beginning to corkscrew quite noticeably now. I felt desperately tired. But my eyes were still working. Hunslett offered me a cigarette. I didn't want one, but I took one. Who knew, it might even help me to think. And then I had caught his wrist and was staring down at his palm.

"Well, well," I said. "The cobbler should stick to his last."

"He what?"

"Wrong proverb. Can't think of the right one. A good workman uses only his own tools. Our pal with the penchant for smashing valves and condensers should have remembered that. No wonder my neck was twitching when Durran was around. How did you cut yourself?"

"I didn't cut myself."

"I know. But there's a smear of blood on your palm. He's been taking lessons from Peter Sellers, I shouldn't wonder. Standard southern English on the *Nantesville*, northern Irish on the *Firecrest*. I wonder how many other accents he has up his sleeve—behind his larynx, I should say. And I thought he was running to a little fat. He's running to a great deal of muscle. You noticed he never took his gloves off, even when he had that drink?"

"I'm the best noticer you ever saw. Beat me over the head with a club and I'll notice anything." He sounded bitter. "Why didn't they clobber us? You, anyway? The star witness?"

"Maybe we *have* moved out of our class. Two reasons. They couldn't do anything with the cops there, genuine cops as we've both agreed, not unless they attended to the cops too. Only a madman would deliberately kill a cop and whatever those boys may lack it isn't sanity."

"But why cops in the first place?"

"Aura of respectability. Cops are above suspicion. When a uniformed policeman shoves his uniformed cap above your gunwale in the dark watches of the night, you don't whack him over the head with a marlin-spike. You invite him aboard. All others you might whack, especially if we had the bad consciences we might have been supposed to have."

"Maybe. It's arguable. And the second point?"

"They took a big chance, a desperate chance, almost, with Durran. He was thrown to the wolves to see what the reaction would be, whether either of us recognised him."

"Why Durran?"

"I didn't tell you. I shone a torch in his face. The face didn't register, just a white blur with screwed-up eyes half-hidden behind an upflung hand. I was really looking lower down, picking the right spot to kick him. But they weren't to know that. They wanted to find out if we would recognise him. We didn't. If we had done so we'd either have started throwing the crockery at him or yelped for the cops to arrest them—if we're against them then we're with the cops. But we didn't. Not a flicker of recognition. Nobody's as good as that. I defy any man in the world to meet up again in the same night with a man who has murdered two other people and nearly murdered himself without at least twitching an eyebrow. So the immediate heat is off, the urgent necessity to do us in has become less urgent. It's a safe bet that if we didn't recognise Durran, then we recognised nobody on the *Nantesville* and so we won't be burning up the lines to Interpol."

"We're in the clear?"

"I wish to God we were. They're on to us."

"But you said—"

"I don't know how I know," I said irritably. "I know. They went through the after end of the *Firecrest* like a Treble Chance winner hunting for the coupon he's afraid he's forgotten to post. Then halfway through the engine-room search—click!—just like that and they weren't interested any more. At least Thomas wasn't. He'd found out something. You saw him afterwards in the saloon, the fore cabins and the upper deck. He couldn't have cared less."

"The batteries?"

"No. He was satisfied with my explanation. I could tell. I don't know why, I only know I'm sure."

"So they'll be back."

"They'll be back."

"I get the guns out now?"

"There's no hurry. Our friends will be sure we can't communicate with anyone. The mainland boat calls here only twice a week. It came today and won't be back for four days. The lines to the mainland are down and if I thought for a moment they wouldn't stay down I should be back in kindergarten. Our transmitter is out. Assuming there are no carrier pigeons in Torbay, what's the only remaining means of communication with the mainland?"

"There's the *Shangri-la*." The *Shangri-la*, the nearest craft to ours, was white, gleaming, a hundred and twenty feet long and wouldn't have left her owner a handful of change from a quarter of a million pounds when he'd bought it. "She'll have a couple of thousand quids' worth of radio equipment aboard. Then there are two, maybe three yachts big enough to carry transmitters. The rest will carry only receivers, if that."

"And how many transmitters in Torbay harbor will still be in operating condition tomorrow?"

"One."

"One. Our friends will attend to the rest. They'll have to. We can't warn anyone. We can't give ourselves away."

"The insurance companies can stand it." He glanced at his watch. "This would be a nice time to wake up Uncle Arthur."

"I can't put it off any longer." I wasn't looking forward to talking to Uncle Arthur.

Hunslett reached for a heavy coat, pulled it on, made for the door and stopped. "I thought I'd take a walk on the upper deck. While you're talking. Just in case. A second thought—I'd better have that gun now. Thomas said they'd already checked three boats in the harbor. MacDonald didn't contradict him, so it was probably true. Maybe there *are* no serviceable transmitters left in Torbay now. Maybe our friends just dumped the cops ashore and are coming straight back for us."

"Maybe. But those yachts are smaller than the *Firecrest*. Apart from us, there's only one with a separate wheelhouse. The others will carry transmitters in the saloon cabin. Lots of them sleep in their saloon cabins. The owners would have to be banged on the head first before the radios could be attended to. They couldn't do that with MacDonald around."

"You'd bet your pension on that? Maybe MacDonald didn't always go aboard."

"I'll never live to collect my pension. But maybe you'd better have that gun."

The *Firecrest* was just over three years old. The Southampton boatyard and marine-radio firm that had combined to build her had done so under conditions of sworn secrecy to a design provided by Uncle Arthur. Uncle Arthur had not designed her himself although he had never said so to the few people who knew of the existence of the boat. He'd pinched the idea from a Japanese-designed Indonesian-owned fishing craft that had been picked up with engine failure off the Malaysian coast. Only one engine had failed though two were installed, but still she had been not under command, an odd circumstance that had led the alert Engineer Lieutenant on the frigate that had picked her up to look pretty closely at her: the net result of his investigations, apart from giving this splendid inspiration to Uncle Arthur, was that the crew still languished in a Singapore prisoner of war camp.

The *Firecrest*'s career had been chequered and inglorious. She had cruised around the Eastern Baltic for some time, without achieving anything, until the authorities in Memel and Leningrad, getting tired of the sight of her, had declared the *Firecrest* persona non grata and sent it back to England. Uncle Arthur had been furious, especially as he had to account to a parsimonious Under-Secretary for the considerable expenses involved. The Waterguard had tried their hand with it at catching smugglers and returned it without thanks. No smugglers. Now for the first time ever it was going to justify its existence and in other circumstances Uncle Arthur would have been delighted. When he heard what I had to tell him he would have no difficulty in restraining his joy.

What made the *Firecrest* unique was that while she had two screws and two propeller shafts, she had only one engine. Two engine casings, but only one engine, even though that one engine was a special job fitted with an underwater bypass exhaust valve. A simple matter of disengaging the fuel pump coupling and unscrewing four bolts on top—the rest were dummies—enabled the entire head of the starboard diesel engine to be lifted clear away, together with the fuel lines and injectors. With the assistance of the seventy foot telescopic radio mast housed inside our aluminum foremast, the huge gleaming transmitter that took up eighty percent of the space inside the starboard engine casing could have sent a signal to the moon, if need be: as Thomas had observed, we had power and to spare. As it happened I didn't want to send a signal to the moon, just to Uncle Arthur's combined office and home in Knightsbridge.

The other twenty percent of space was taken up with a motley collection of material that even the Assistant Commissioner in New Scotland Yard wouldn't have regarded without a thoughtful expression on his face. There were some packages of pre-fabricated explosives with amatol, primer, and chemical detonator combined in one neat unit with a miniature timing device that ranged from five seconds to five minutes, complete with sucker clamps. There was a fine range of burglar's house-breaking tools, bunches of skeleton keys, several highly sophisticated listening devices, including one that could be shot from a Very-type pistol, several tubes of various harmless looking tablets which were alleged, when dropped in some unsuspecting character's drink, to induce unconsciousness for varying periods, four pistols and a box of ammunition. Anyone who was going to use that lot in one operation was in for a busy time indeed. Two of the pistols were Lugers, two were 4.25 German Lilliputs, the smallest really effective automatic pistol on the market. The Lilliput had the great advantage that it could be concealed practically anywhere on your person, even upside down in a spring-loaded clip in your lower left sleeve—if, that was, you didn't get your suits cut in Carnaby Street.

Hunslett lifted one of the Lugers from its clamp, checked the loading indicator and left at once. It wasn't that he was imagining that he could already hear stealthy footsteps on the upper deck, he just didn't want to be around when Uncle Arthur came on the air. I didn't blame him, I didn't really want to be around then either.

I pulled out the two insulated rubber cables, fitted the powerfully spring-loaded saw-toothed metal clamps on to the battery terminals, hung on a pair of earphones, turned on the set, pulled another switch that actuated the call-up and waited. I didn't have to tune in, the transmitter was permanently pre-set, and pre-set on a VHF frequency that would have cost the license of any ham operator who dared wander anywhere near it for transmission purposes.

The red receiver warning light came on. I reached down and adjusted the magic eye control until the green fans met in the middle.

"This is station SPFX," a voice came. "Station SPFX."

"Good morning. This is Caroline. May I speak to the manager, please?"

"Will you wait, please?" This meant that Uncle Arthur was in bed. Uncle Arthur was never at his best on rising. Three minutes passed and the earphones came to life again.

"Good morning, Caroline. This is Annabelle."

"Good morning. Location 481, 281." You wouldn't find those references in any Ordnance Survey Map, there weren't a dozen maps in existence with them. But Uncle Arthur had one. And so had I.

There was a pause, then: "I have you, Caroline. Proceed."

"I located the missing vessel this afternoon. Four or five miles northwest of here. I went on board tonight."

"You did what, Caroline?"

"Went on board. The old crew has gone home. There's a new crew aboard. A smaller crew."

"You located Betty and Dorothy?" Despite the fact that we both had scramblers fitted to our radio phones, making intelligible eavesdropping impossible, Uncle Arthur always insisted that we speak in a roundabout riddle fashion and used code names for his employees and himself. Girls' names for our surnames, initials to match. An irritating foible, but one that we had to observe. He was Annabelle, I was Caroline, Baker was Betty, Delmont Dorothy, and Hunslett Harriet. It sounded like a series of Caribbean hurricane warnings.

"I found them." I took a deep breath. "They won't be coming home again, Annabelle."

"They won't be coming home again," he repeated mechanically. He was silent for so long that I began to think that he had gone off the air. Then he came again, his voice empty, remote. "I warned you of this."

"Yes, Annabelle, you warned me of this."

"And the vessel?"

"Gone."

"Gone where?"

"I don't know. Just gone. North, I suppose."

"North, you suppose." Uncle Arthur never raised his voice, when he went on it was as calm and impersonal as ever, but the sudden disregard of his own rules about circumlocution betrayed the savage anger in his mind. "North where? Iceland? A Norwegian fjord? To effect a trans-shipment of cargo anywhere in a million square miles between the mid-Atlantic and the Barents Sea? And you lost her. After all the time, the trouble, the planning, the expense, you've lost her!" He

41

might have spared me that bit about the planning, it had been mine all the way. "And Betty and Dorothy." The last words showed he'd taken control of himself again.

"Yes, Annabelle, I've lost her." I could feel the slow anger in myself. "And there's worse than that, if you want to listen to it."

"I'm listening."

I told him the rest and at the end of it he said: "I see. You've lost the vessel. You've lost Betty and Dorothy. And now our friends know about you, the one vital element of secrecy is gone forever and every usefulness and effectiveness you might ever have had is completely negated." A pause. "I shall expect you in my office at nine P.M. tonight. Instruct Harriet to take the boat back to base."

"Yes, sir." The hell with his Annabelle. "I had expected that. I've failed. I've let you down. I'm being pulled off."

"Nine o'clock tonight, Caroline. I'll be waiting."

"You'll have a long wait, Annabelle."

"And what might you mean by that?" If Uncle Arthur had had a low silky menacing voice then he'd have spoken those words in a low silky menacing voice. But he hadn't, he'd only this flat level monotone and it carried infinitely more weight and authority than any carefully modulated theatrical voice that had ever graced a stage.

"There are no planes to this place, Annabelle. The mail boat doesn't call for another four days. The weather's breaking down and I wouldn't risk our boat to try to get to the mainland. I'm stuck here for the time being, I'm afraid."

"Do you take me for a nincompoop, sir?" Now he was at it. "Go ashore this morning. An air-sea rescue helicopter will pick you up at noon. Nine P.M. at my office. Don't keep me waiting."

This, then, was it. But one last try. "Couldn't you give me another twenty-four hours, Annabelle?"

"Now you're being ridiculous. And wasting my time. Goodbye."

"I beg of you, sir."

"I'd thought better of you than that. Goodbye."

"Goodbye. We may meet again sometime. It's not likely. Goodbye."

I switched the radio off, lit a cigarette and waited. The call-up came through in half a minute. I waited another half-minute and switched on. I was very calm. The die was cast and I didn't gave a damn.

42

"Caroline? Is that you, Caroline?" I could have sworn to a note of agitation in his voice. This was something for the record books.

"Yes."

"What did you say? At the end there?"

"Goodbye. You said goodbye. I said goodbye."

"Don't quibble with me, sir! You said—"

"If you want me aboard that helicopter," I said, "you'll have to send a guard with the pilot. An armed guard. I hope they're good. I've got a Luger, and you know I'm good. And if I have to kill anyone and go into court, then you'll have to stand there beside me because there's no single civil action or criminal charge that even you, with all your connections, can bring against me that would justify the sending of armed men to apprehend me, an innocent man. Further I am no longer in your employ. The terms of my civil service contract state clearly that I can resign at any moment, provided that I am not actively engaged on an operation at that moment. You've pulled me off, you've recalled me to London. My resignation will be on your desk as soon as the mail can get through. Baker and Delmont weren't your friends. They were my friends. They were my friends ever since I joined the service. You have the temerity to sit there and lay all the blame for their deaths on my shoulders when you know damn well that every operation must have your final approval, and now you have the final temerity to deny me a one last chance to square accounts. I'm sick of your damned soulless service. Goodbye."

"Now wait a moment, Caroline." There was a cautious, almost placatory note to his voice. "No need to go off half-cocked." I was sure that no one had ever talked to Rear-Admiral Sir Arthur Arnford-Jason like that before but he didn't seem particularly upset about it. He had the cunning of a fox, that infinitely agile and shrewd mind would be examining and discarding possibilities with the speed of a computer, he'd be wondering whether I was playing a game and if so how far he could play it with me without making it impossible for me to retreat from the edge of the precipice. Finally he said quietly: "You wouldn't want to hang around there just to shed tears. You're on to something."

"Yes, sir, I'm on to something." I wondered what in the name of God I was on to.

"I'll give you twenty-four hours, Caroline."

"Forty-eight."

"Forty-eight. And then you return to London. I have your word?"

"I promise."

"And Caroline?"

"Sir?"

"I didn't care for your way of talking there. I trust we never have a repetition of it."

"No, sir. I'm sorry, sir."

"Forty-eight hours. Report to me at noon and midnight." A click. Uncle Arthur was gone.

The false dawn was in the sky when I went on deck. Cold heavy slanting driving rain was churning up the foam-flecked sea. The *Firecrest*, pulling heavily on her anchor chain, was swinging slowly through an arc of forty degrees, corkscrewing quite heavily now on the outer arc of the swing, pitching in the center of them. She was snubbing very heavily on the anchor and I wondered uneasily how long the lengths of heaving line securing the dinghy, outboard and scuba gear to the chain could stand up to this sort of treatment.

Hunslett was abaft the saloon, huddling in what little shelter it afforded. He looked up at my approach and said: "What do you make of that?" He pointed to the palely gleaming shape of the *Shangri-la*, one moment on our quarter, the next dead astern as we swung on our anchor. Lights were burning brightly in the forepart of her superstructure, where the wheelhouse would be.

"Someone with insomnia," I said. "Or checking to see if the anchor is dragging. What do you think it is—our recent guests laying about the *Shangri-la*'s radio installation with crowbars? Maybe they leave lights on all night."

"Came on just ten minutes ago. And look, now—they're out. Funny. How did you get on with Uncle?"

"Badly. Fired me, then changed his mind. We have forty-eight hours."

"Forty-eight hours? What are you going to do in forty-eight hours?"

"God knows. Have some sleep first. You too. Too much light in the sky for callers now."

Passing through the saloon, Hunslett said, apropos of nothing: "I've been wondering. What did you make of P. C. MacDonald? The young one."

"What do you mean?"

"Well, glum, downcast. Heavy weight on his shoulders."

"Maybe he's like me. Maybe he doesn't like getting up in

44

the middle of the night. Maybe he has girl trouble and if he has I can tell you that P. C. MacDonald's love life is the least of my concerns. Goodnight."

I should have listened to Hunslett more. For Hunslett's sake.

3 • TUESDAY: 10 A.M.—10 P.M.

I need my sleep, just like anyone else. Ten hours, perhaps only eight, and I would have been my own man again. Maybe not exuding brightness, optimism, and cheerfulness, the circumstances weren't right for that, but at least a going concern, alert, perceptive, my mind operating on what Uncle Arthur would be by now regarding as its customary abysmal level but still the best it could achieve. But I wasn't given that ten hours. Nor even the eight. Exactly three hours after dropping off I was wide awake again. Well, anyway, awake. I would have had to be stone deaf, drugged, or dead to go on sleeping through the bawling and thumping that was currently assailing my left ear from what appeared to be a distance of not more than twelve inches.

"Ahoy, there, *Firecrest!* Ahoy there!" Thump, thump, thump on the boat's side. "Can I come aboard? Ahoy, there! Ahoy, ahoy, ahoy!"

I cursed this nautical idiot from the depths of my sleep-ridden being, swung a pair of unsteady legs to the deck and levered myself out of the bunk. I almost fell down, I seemed to have only one leg left, and my neck ached fiercely. A glance at the mirror gave quick external confirmation of my internal decrepitude. A haggard unshaven face, unnaturally pale, and bleary bloodshot eyes with dark circles under them. I looked away hurriedly, there were lots of things I could put up with first thing in the morning, but not sights like that.

I opened the door across the passage. Hunslett was sound asleep and snoring. I returned to my own cabin and got busy with the dressing gown and Paisley scarf again. The iron-lunged thumping character outside was still at it, if I didn't hurry he would be roaring out avast there any moment. I combed my hair into some sort of order and made my way to the upper deck.

It was a cold, wet, and windy world. A grey, dreary, unpleasant world, why the hell couldn't they have let me sleep

46

on. The rain was coming down in slanting sheets, bouncing inches high off the decks, doubling the milkiness of the spume-flecked sea. The lonely wind mourned through the rigging and the lower registers of sound and the steep-sided wind-truncated waves, maybe three feet from tip to trough, were high enough to make passage difficult if not dangerous for the average yacht tender.

They didn't make things in the slightest difficult or dangerous for the yacht tender that now lay alongside us. It maybe wasn't as big—it looked it at first sight—as the *Firecrest*, but it was big enough to have a glassed-in cabin for'ard, a wheelhouse that bristled and gleamed with controls and instrumentations that would have been no disgrace to a VC 10, and, abaft that, a sunken cockpit that could have sunbathed a football team without overcrowding. There were three crewmen dressed in black oilskins and fancy French navy hats with black ribbons down the back, two of them each with a boathook round one of the *Firecrest*'s guard-rail stanchions. Half a dozen big inflated spherical rubber fenders kept the *Firecrest* from rubbing its plebeian paintwork against the whitely varnished spotlessness of the tender alongside and it didn't require the name on the bows or the crew's hats to let me know that this was the tender that normally took up most of the after-deck on the *Shangri-la*.

Amidships a stocky figure, clad in a white vaguely naval brass-buttoned uniform and holding above his head a golf umbrella that would have had Joseph green with envy, stopped banging his gloved fist against the *Firecrest*'s planking and glared up at me.

"Ha!" I've never actually heard anyone snort out a word but this came pretty close to it. "There you are at last. Took your time about it, didn't you? I'm soaked, man, soaked!" A few spots of rain did show up quite clearly on the white seersucker. "May I come aboard?" He didn't wait for any permission, just leapt aboard with surprising nimbleness for a man of his build and years and nipped into the *Firecrest*'s wheelhouse ahead of me, which was pretty selfish of him as he still had his umbrella and all I had was my dressing gown. I followed and closed the door behind me.

He was a short, powerfully built character, fifty-five I would have guessed, with a heavily tanned jowled face, close-cropped iron-grey hair with tufted eyebrows to match, long straight nose and a mouth that looked as if it had been closed with a zip fastener. A good-looking cove, if you liked that type of looks. The dark darting eyes looked me up and down and if he was impressed by what he saw he made a heroic effort to keep his admiration in check.

"Sorry for the delay," I apologised. "Short of sleep. We had the Customs aboard in the middle of the night and I couldn't get off after that." Always tell everyone the truth if there's an even chance of that truth coming out anyway, which in this case there was: gives one a reputation for forthright honesty.

"The Customs?" He looked as if he intended to say "pshaw" or "fiddlesticks" or something of that order, then changed his mind and looked up sharply. "An intolerable bunch of busybodies. And in the middle of the night. Shouldn't have let them aboard. Sent them packing. Intolerable. What the deuce did they want?" He gave the distinct impression of having himself had some trouble with the Customs in the past.

"They were looking for stolen chemicals. Stolen from some place in Ayrshire. Wrong boat."

"Idiots!" He thrust out a stubby hand, he'd passed his final judgment on the unfortunate Customs and the subject was now closed. "Skouras. Sir Anthony Skouras."

"Petersen." His grip made me wince, less from the sheer power of it than from the gouging effect of the large number of thickly encrusted rings that adorned his fingers. I wouldn't have been surprised to see some on his thumbs but he'd missed out on that. I looked at him with new interest. "Sir Anthony Skouras. I've heard of you of course."

"Nothing good. Columnists don't like me because they know I despise them. A Cypriot who made his shipping millions through sheer ruthlessness, they say. True. Asked by the Greek government to leave Athens. True. Became a naturalized British citizen and bought a knighthood. Absolutely true. Charitable works and public services. Money can buy anything. A baronetcy next but the market's not right at the moment. Price is bound to fall. Can I use your radio transmitter? I see you have one."

"What's that?" The abrupt switch had me off-balance, no great achievement the way I was feeling.

"Your radio transmitter, man! Don't you listen to the news? All those major defense projects cancelled by the Pentagon. Price of steel tumbling. Must get through to my New York broker at once!"

48

"Sorry. Certainly you may—but, but your own radio-telephone? Surely—"

"It's out of action." His mouth became more tight-lipped then ever and the inevitable happened: it disappeared. "It's urgent, Mr. Petersen."

"Immediately. You know how to operate this model?"

He smiled thinly, which was probably the only way he was capable of smiling. Compared to the cinema-organ job he'd have aboard the *Shangri-la,* asking him if he could operate this was like asking the captain of a transatlantic jet if he could fly a Tiger Moth. "I think I can manage, Mr. Petersen."

"Call me when you're finished. I'll be in the saloon." He'd be calling me before he'd finished, he'd be calling me before he'd even started. But I couldn't tell him. Word gets around. I went down to the saloon, contemplated a shave and decided against it. It wouldn't take that long.

It didn't. He appeared at the saloon door inside a minute, his face grim.

"Your radio is out of order, Mr. Petersen."

"They're tricky to operate, some of those older jobs," I said tactfully. "Maybe if I—"

"I say it's out of order. I mean it's out of order."

"Damned odd. It was working—"

"Would you care to try it, please?"

I tried it. Nothing. I twiddled everything I could lay hands on. Nothing.

"A power failure, perhaps," I suggested. "I'll check—"

"Would you be so good as to remove the face-plate, please?"

I stared at him in perplexity, switching the expression, after a suitable interval, to shrewd thoughtfulness. "What do you know, Sir Anthony, that I don't?"

"You'll find out."

So I found out and went through all the proper motions of consternation, incredulity and tight-lipped indignation. Finally I said: "You knew. How did you know?"

"Obvious, isn't it?"

"Your transmitter," I said slowly. "It's just more than out of order. You had the same midnight caller."

"And the *Orion.*" The mouth vanished again. "The big blue ketch lying close in. Only other craft in the harbor apart from us with a radio transmitter. Smashed. Just come from there."

"Smashed? Theirs as well? But who in God's name—it must be the work of a madman."

"Is it? Is it the work of a madman? I know something of those matters. My first wife—" He broke off abruptly and gave an odd shake of the head, then went on slowly: "The mentally disturbed are irrational, haphazard, purposeless, aimless in their behavior patterns. This seems an entirely irrational act, but an act with a method and a purpose to it. Not haphazard. It's planned. There's a reason. At first I thought the reason was to cut off my connection with the mainland. But it can't be that. By rendering me temporarily incommunicado nobody stands to gain. I don't stand to lose."

"But you said the New York Stock—"

"A bagatelle," he said contemptuously. "Nobody likes to lose money." Not more than a few million anyway. "No, Mr. Petersen, I am not the target. We have here an A and a B. A regards it as vital that he remains in constant communication with the mainland. B regards it as vital that A doesn't. So B takes steps. There's something damned funny going on in Torbay. And something big. I have a nose for such things."

He was no fool but then not many morons have ended up as multimillionaires. I couldn't have put it better myself. I said: "Reported this to the police yet?"

"Going there now. After I've made a phone call or two." The eyes suddenly became bleak and cold. "Unless our friend has smashed up the two public call boxes in the main street."

"He's done better than that. He's brought down the lines to the mainland. Somewhere down the Sound. No one knows where."

He stared at me, wheeled to leave, then turned, his face empty of expression. "How did you know that?" The tone matched the face.

"Police told me. They were aboard with the Customs last night."

"The police? That's damned odd. What were the police doing here?" He paused and looked at me with his cold measuring eyes. "A personal question, Mr. Petersen. No impertinence intended. A question of elimination. What are *you* doing here? No offence."

"No offence. My friend and I are marine biologists. A working trip. Not our boat—the Ministry of Agriculture and Fisheries." I smiled. "We have impeccable references, Sir Anthony."

"Marine biology, eh? Hobby of mine, you might say. Lay-

50

man, of course. Must have a talk sometime." He was speaking absent-mindedly, his thoughts elsewhere. "Could you describe the policeman, Mr. Petersen?"

I did and he nodded. "That's him all right. Odd, very odd. Must have a word with Archie about this."

"Archie?"

"Sergeant MacDonald. This is my fifth consecutive season's cruising based on Torbay. The South of France and the Aegean can't hold a candle to these waters. Know quite a few of the locals pretty well by this time. He was alone?"

"No. A young constable. His son, he said. Melancholy sort of lad."

"Peter MacDonald. He has reason for his melancholy, Mr. Petersen. His two young brothers, sixteen years old, twins, died a few months back. At an Inverness school, lost in a late snowstorm in the Cairngorms. The father is tougher, doesn't show it so much. A great tragedy. I knew them both. Fine boys."

I made some appropriate comment but he wasn't listening.

"I must be on my way, Mr. Petersen. Put this damned strange affair in MacDonald's hands. Don't see that he can do much. Then off for a short cruise."

I looked through the wheelhouse windows at the dark skies, the whitecapped seas, the driving rain. "You picked a day for it."

"The rougher the better. No bravado. I like a millpond as well as any man. Just had new stabilisers fitted in the Clyde—we got back up here only two days ago—and it seems like a good day to try them out." He smiled suddenly and put out his hand. "Sorry to have barged in. Taken up far too much of your time. Seemed rude, I suppose. Some say I am. You and your colleague care to come aboard for a drink tonight? We eat early at sea. Eight o'clock, say? I'll send the tender." That meant we didn't rate an invitation to dinner, which would have made a change from Hunslett and his damned baked beans, but even an invitation like this would have given rise to envious tooth-gnashing in some of the stateliest homes in the land: it was no secret that the bluest blood in England, from Royalty downwards, regarded a holiday invitation to the island Skouras owned off the Albanian coast as the conferment of the social cachet of the year or any year. Skouras didn't wait for an answer and didn't seem to expect one. I didn't blame him. It would have been many years since Skouras had discovered that it was an immutable law of human nature, human nature being what it is, that no one ever turned down one of his invitations.

"You'll be coming to tell me about your smashed transmitter and asking me what the devil I intend to do about it," Sergeant MacDonald said tiredly. "Well, Mr. Petersen, I know all about it already. Sir Anthony Skouras was here half an hour ago. Sir Anthony had a lot to say. And Mr. Campbell, the owner of the *Orion*, has just left. He'd a lot to say, too."

"Not me, Sergeant. I'm a man of few words." I gave him what I hoped looked like a self-deprecatory smile. "Except, of course, when the police and Customs drag me out of bed in the middle of the night. I take it our friends have left?"

"Just as soon as they'd put us ashore. Customs are just a damn nuisance." Like myself, he looked as if he could do with some hours' sleep. "Frankly, Mr. Petersen, I don't know what to do about the broken radio transmitters. Why on earth—who on earth would want to do a daft vicious thing like that?"

"That's what I came to ask you."

"I can go aboard your boat," MacDonald said slowly. "I can take out my notebook, look around and see if I can't find any clues. I wouldn't know what to look for. Maybe if I knew something about fingerprinting and analysis and microscopy I might just find out something. But I don't. I'm an island policeman, not a one-man Flying Squad. This is CID work and we'd have to call in Glasgow. I doubt if they'd send a couple of detectives to investigate a few smashed radio valves."

"Old man Skouras draws a lot of water."

"Sir?"

"He's powerful. He has influence. If Skouras wanted action I'm damned sure he could get it. If the need arose and the mood struck him I'm sure he could be a very unpleasant character indeed."

"There's not a better man or a kinder man ever sailed into Torbay," MacDonald said warmly. That hard brown face could conceal practically anything that MacDonald wanted it to conceal but this time he was hiding nothing. "Maybe his ways aren't my ways. Maybe he's a hard, aye, a ruthless businessman. Maybe, as the papers hint, his private life wouldn't bear investigation. That's none of my business. But if you were to look for a man in Torbay to say a word against him, you'll have a busy time on your hands, Mr. Petersen."

"You've taken me up wrongly, Sergeant," I said mildly. "I don't even know the man."

"No. But we do. See that?" He pointed through the side window of the police station to a large Swedish-style timber building beyond the pier. "Our new village hall. Town hall, they call it. Sir Anthony gave us that. Those six wee chalets up the hill there? For old folks. Sir Anthony again—every penny from his own pocket. Who takes all the school children to the Oban Games—Sir Anthony on the *Shangri-la*. Contributes to every charity going and now he has plans to build a boatyard to give employment to the young men of Torbay—there's not much else going since the fishing boats left."

"Well, good for old Skouras," I said. "He seems to have adopted the place. Lucky Torbay. I wish he'd buy me a new radio transmitter."

"I'll keep my eyes and ears open, Mr. Petersen. I can't do more. If anything turns up I'll let you know at once."

I told him thanks, and left. I hadn't particularly wanted to go there, but it would have looked damned odd if I hadn't turned up to add my pennyworth to the chorus of bitter complaint.

I was very glad that I had turned up.

The midday reception from London was poor. This was due less to the fact that reception is always better after dark than to the fact that I couldn't use our telescopic radio mast: but it was fair enough and Uncle's voice was brisk and businesslike and clear.

"Well, Caroline, we've found our missing friends," he said.

"How many?" I asked cautiously. Uncle Arthur's ambiguous references weren't always as clear as Uncle Arthur imagined them to be.

"All twenty-five." That made it the former crew of the *Nantesville*. "Two of them are pretty badly hurt but they'll be all right." That accounted for the blood I had found in the captain's and one of the engineers' cabins.

"Where?" I asked.

He gave me a map reference. Just north of Wexford. The *Nantesville* had sailed from Bristol, she couldn't have been more than a few hours on her way before she'd run into trouble.

"Exactly the same procedure as on the previous occasions," Uncle Arthur was saying. "Held in a lonely farmhouse for a couple of nights. Plenty to eat and drink and blankets to keep the cold out. Then they woke up one morning and found their guards had gone."

"But a different procedure in stopping the—our friend?" I'd almost said *Nantesville* and Uncle Arthur wouldn't have liked that at all.

"As always. We must concede them a certain ingenuity, Caroline. After having smuggled men aboard in port, then using the sinking fishing-boat routine, the police launch routine and the yacht with the appendicitis case aboard, I thought they would be starting to repeat themselves. But this time they came up with a new one—possibly because it's the first time they've hi-jacked a ship during the hours of darkness. Carley rafts, this time, with about ten survivors aboard dead ahead of the vessel. Oil all over the sea. A weak distress flare that couldn't have been seen a mile away and probably was designed that way. You know the rest."

"Yes, Annabelle." I knew the rest. After that the routine was always the same. The rescued survivors, displaying a marked lack of gratitude, would whip out pistols, round up the crew, tie black muslin bags over their heads so that they couldn't identify the vessel that would appear within the hour to take them off, march them on board the unknown vessel, land them on some lonely beach during the dark, then march them again, often a very long way indeed, till they arrived at their prison. A deserted farmhouse. Always a deserted farmhouse. And always in Ireland, three times in the north and now twice in the south. Meantime the prize crew sailed the hi-jacked vessel to God alone knew where and the first the world knew of the disappearance of the pirated vessel was when the original crew, released after two or three days' painless captivity, would turn up at some remote dwelling and start hollering for the nearest telephone.

"Betty and Dorothy," I said. "Were they still in safe concealment when the crew were taken off?"

"I imagine so. I don't know. Details are still coming in and I understand the doctors won't let anyone see the captain yet." Only the captain had known of the presence aboard of Baker and Delmont. "Forty-one hours now, Caroline. What have you done?"

For a moment I wondered irritably what the devil he was

talking about. Then I remembered. He'd given me forty-eight hours. Seven were gone.

"I've had three hours' sleep." He'd consider that an utter waste of time, his employees weren't considered to need sleep. "I've talked to the constabulary ashore. And I've talked to a wealthy yachtsman, next boat to us here. We're paying him a social call tonight."

There was a pause. "You're doing *what* tonight, Caroline?"

"Visiting. We've been invited. Harriet and I. For drinks."

This time the pause was markedly longer. Then he said: "You have forty-one hours, Caroline."

"Yes, Annabelle."

"We assume you haven't taken leave of your senses."

"I don't know how the unanimous informed opinion might be about that. I don't think I have."

"And you haven't given up? No, not that. You're too damn stiff necked and—and—"

"Stupid?"

"Who's the yachtsman?"

I told him. It took me some time, partly because I had to spell out names with the aid of his damned code book, partly because I gave him a very full account of everything Skouras had said to me and everything Sergeant MacDonald had said about Skouras. When his voice came again it was cagey and wary. As Uncle Arthur couldn't see me I permitted myself a cynical grin. Even Cabinet Ministers found it difficult to make the grade as far as Skouras' dinner table, but the permanent Under-Secretaries, the men with whom the real power of government lies, practically had their own initialled napkin rings. Under-Secretaries were the bane of Uncle Arthur's life.

"You'll have to watch your step very carefully here, Caroline."

"Betty and Dorothy aren't coming home any more, Annabelle. Someone has to pay. I want someone to pay. You want someone to pay. We all do."

"But it's inconceivable that a man in his position, a man of his wealth—"

"I'm sorry, Annabelle. I don't understand."

"A man like that. Dammit all, I know him well, Caroline. We dine together. First name terms. Know his present wife even better. Ex-actress. A philanthropist like that. A man who's spent five consecutive seasons there. Would a man like

55

that, a millionaire like that, spend all that time, all that money, just to build up a front—"

"Skouras?" The code name. Interrogatory, incredulous, as if it had just dawned upon me what Uncle Arthur was talking about. "I never said I suspected him, Annabelle. I have no reason to suspect him."

"Ah!" It's difficult to convey a sense of heartfelt gladness, profound satisfaction and brow-mopping relief in a single syllable, but Uncle Arthur managed it without any trouble. "Then why go?" A casual eavesdropper might have thought he detected a note of pained jealousy in Uncle Arthur's voice, and the casual eavesdropper would have been right. Uncle Arthur had only one weakness in his makeup—he was a social snob of monumental proportions.

"I want aboard. I want to see this smashed transmitter of his."

"Why?"

"A hunch, let me call it, Annabelle. No more."

Uncle Arthur was going in for the long silences in a big way today. Then he said: "A hunch? A *hunch?* You told me this morning you were onto something."

"There's something else. I want you to contact the Post Office Savings Bank, Head Office, in Scotland. After that, the Records files of some Scottish newspapers. I suggest the *Glasgow Herald*, the *Scottish Daily Express* and, most particularly, the West Highland weekly, the *Oban Times.*"

"Ah!" No relief this time, just satisfaction. "This is more like it, Caroline. What do you want and why?"

So I told him what I wanted and why, lots more of the fancy code work, and when I'd finished he said: "I'll have my staff onto this straightaway. I'll have all the information you want by midnight."

"Then I don't want it, Annabelle. Midnight's too late for me. Midnight's no use to me."

"Don't ask the impossible, Caroline." He muttered something to himself, something I couldn't catch, then: "I'll pull every string, Caroline. Nine o'clock."

"Four o'clock, Annabelle."

"Four o'clock this afternoon?" When it came to incredulity he had me whacked on the side. "Four hours' time? You *have* taken leave of your senses."

"You can have ten men on it in ten minutes. Twenty in twenty minutes. Where's the door that isn't open to you? Especially the door of the Assistant Commissioner. Profes-

56

sionals don't kill for the hell of it. They kill because they must. They kill to gain time. Every additional hour is vital to them. And if it's vital to them, how much more so it is to us. Or do you think we're dealing with amateurs, Annabelle?"

"Call me at four," he said heavily. "I'll see what I have for you. What's your next move, Caroline?"

"Bed," I said. "I'm going to get some sleep."

"Of course. Time, as you said, is of the essence. You mustn't waste it, must you, Caroline?" He signed off. He sounded bitter. No doubt he was bitter. But then, insomnia apart, Uncle Arthur could rely on a full quota of sleep during the coming night. Which was more than I could. No certain foreknowledge, no second sight, just a hunch, but not a small one, the kind of hunch you couldn't have hidden behind the Empire State Building. Just like the one I had about the *Shangri-la*.

I only managed to catch the last fading notes of the alarm as it went off at ten minutes to four. I felt worse than I had done when we'd lain down after a miserable lunch of corned beef and reconstituted powdered potatoes—if old Skouras had had a spark of human decency, he'd have made that invitation for dinner. I wasn't only growing old I felt old. I'd been working too long for Uncle Arthur. The pay was good but the hours and working conditions—I'd have wagered that Uncle Arthur hadn't even set eyes on a tin of corned beef since World War II—were shocking. And all this constant worrying, chiefly about life expectancy, helped wear a man down.

Hunslett came out of his cabin as I came out of mine. He looked just as old as I did. If they had to rely on a couple of aging crocks like us, I thought morosely, the rising generation must be a pretty sorry lot.

Passing through the saloon, I wondered bitterly about the identity of all those characters who wrote so glibly about the Western Isles in general and the Torbay area in particular as being a yachtsman's paradise without equal in Europe. Obviously, they'd never been there. Fleet Street was their home and home was a place they never left, not if they could help it. An ignorant bunch of travel and advertising copy writers who regarded King's Cross as the northern limits of civilization. Well, maybe not all that ignorant, at least they were smart enough to stay south of King's Cross.

Four o'clock on an autumn afternoon, but already it was

more night than day. The sun wasn't down yet, not by a very long way, but it might as well have been for all the chance it had of penetrating the rolling masses of heavy dark cloud hurrying away to the eastwards to the inky blackness of the horizon beyond Torbay. The slanting sheeting rain that foamed whitely across the bay further reduced what little visibility there was to a limit of no more than four hundred yards. The village itself, half a mile distant and nestling in the dark shadow of the steeply rising pine-covered hills behind, might never have existed. Off to the northwest I could see the navigation lights of a craft rounding the headland, Skouras returning from his stabiliser test run. Down in the *Shangri-la*'s gleaming galley a master chef would be preparing the sumptuous evening meal, the one to which we hadn't been invited. I tried to put the thought of that meal out of my mind, but I couldn't, so I just put it as far away as possible and followed Hunslett into the engine room.

Hunslett took the spare earphones and squatted beside me on the deck, notebook on his knee. Hunslett was as competent in shorthand as he was in everything else. I hoped that Uncle Arthur would have something to tell us, that Hunslett's presence there would be necessary. It was.

"Congratulations, Caroline," Uncle Arthur said without preamble. "You really are onto something." As far as it is possible for a dead flat monotone voice to assume an overtone of warmth, then Uncle Arthur's did just that. He sounded positively friendly. More likely it was some freak of transmission or reception but at least he hadn't started off by bawling me out.

"We've traced those Post Office Savings books," he went on. He rattled off book numbers and details of times and amounts of deposits, things of no interest to me, then said: "Last deposits were on December 27th. Ten pounds in each case. Present balance is £78,14.6d. Exactly the same in both. And those accounts have not been closed."

He paused for a moment to let me congratulate him, which I did, then he continued.

"That's nothing, Caroline. Listen. Your queries about any mysterious accidents, deaths, disappearances off the west coasts of Inverness-shire or Argyll, or anything happening to people from that area. We've struck oil, Caroline, we've really struck oil. My God, why did we never think of this before. Have your pencil ready?"

"Harriet has."

"Here we go. This seems to have been the most disastrous sailing season for years in the west of Scotland. But first, one from last year. The *Pinto,* a well-found sea-worthy forty-five foot motor cruiser left Kyle of Lochalsh for Oban at eight A.M. September 4th. She should have arrived that afternoon. She never did. No trace of her has ever been found."

"What was the weather at that time, Annabelle?"

"I thought you'd ask me that, Caroline." Uncle Arthur's combination of modesty and quiet satisfaction could be very trying at times. "I checked with the Met. office. Force one, variable. Flat calm, cloudless sky. Then we come to this year. April 6th and April 26th. The *Evening Star* and the *Jeannie Rose.* Two East Coast fishing boats—one from Buckie, the other from Fraserburgh."

"But both based on the West Coast?"

"I wish you wouldn't try to steal my thunder," Uncle Arthur complained. "Both were based on Oban. Both were lobster boats. The *Evening Star,* the first one to go, was found stranded on the rocks off Islay. The *Jeannie Rose* vanished without a trace. No member of either crew was ever found. Then again on the seventeenth of May. This time a well-known racing yacht, the *Cap Gris Nez,* an English built and owned craft, despite her name, highly experienced skipper, navigator, and crew, all of them longtime and often successful competitors on RORC races. That class. Left Londonderry for the north of Scotland in fine weather. Disappeared. She was found almost a month later—or what was left of her—washed up on the Isle of Skye."

"And the crew?"

"Need you ask? Never found. Then the last case, a few weeks ago—August 8th. Husband, wife, two teenage children, son and daughter. Converted lifeboat, the *Kingfisher.* By all accounts a pretty competent sailor, been at it for years. But he'd never done any night navigation, so he set out one calm evening to do a night cruise. Vanished. Boat and crew."

"Where did he set out from."

"Torbay."

That one word made his afternoon. It made mine, too. I said: "And do you still think the *Nantesville* is hell and gone to Iceland or some remote fjord in northern Norway?"

"I never thought anything of the kind." Uncle's human relationship barometer had suddenly swung back from friendly to normal, normal lying somewhere between cool and glacial. "The significance of the dates will not have escaped you?"

"No, Annabelle, the significance has not escaped me." The Buckie fishing boat, the *Evening Star,* had been found washed up on Islay three days after the SS *Holmwood* had vanished off the south coast of Ireland. The *Jeannie Rose* had vanished exactly three days after the MV *Antara* had as mysteriously disappeared in the St. George's Channel. The *Cap Gris Nez,* the RORC racer that had finally landed up on the rocks of the Island of Skye had vanished the same day as the MV *Headley Pioneer* had disappeared somewhere, it was thought, off Northern Ireland. And the converted lifeboat, *Kingfisher,* had disappeared, never to be seen again, just two days after the SS *Hurricane Spray* had left the Clyde, also never to be seen again. Coincidence was coincidence and I classed those who denied its existence with intellectual giants like the twentieth-century South African president who stoutly maintained that the world was flat and that an incautious step would take you over the edge with results as permanent as they would be disastrous: but this was plain ridiculous. The odds against such a perfect matching of dates could be calculated only in astronomical terms: while the complete disappearance of the crews of four small boats that had come to grief in so very limited an area was the final nail in the coffin of coincidence. I said as much to Uncle.

"Let us not waste time by dwelling upon the obvious, Caroline," Uncle said coldly, which was pretty ungracious of him as the idea had never even entered his head until I had put it there four hours previously. "The point is—what is to be done? Islay to Skye is a pretty big area. Where does this get us?"

"How much weight can you bring to bear to secure the cooperation of the television and radio networks?"

There was a pause, then: "What do you have in mind, Caroline?" Uncle at his most forbidding.

"An insertion of an item in their news bulletins."

"Well." An even longer pause. "It was done daily during the war, of course. I believe it's been done once or twice since. Can't compel them, of course—they're a pretty stuffy lot, both the BBC and the ITA." His tone left little doubt as to his opinion of those diehard reactionaries who brooked no interference, an odd reaction from one who was himself a pastmaster of brookmanship of this nature. "If they can be persuaded that it's completely apolitical and in the national interests there's a chance. What do you want?"

"An item that a distress signal has been received from a

sinking yacht somewhere south of Skye. Exact position unknown. Signals ceased, the worst feared, an air-sea search to be mounted at first light tomorrow. That's all."

"I may manage it. Your reason, Caroline?"

"I want to look around. I want an excuse to move around without raising eyebrows."

"You're going to volunteer the *Firecrest* for this search and then poke around where you shouldn't?"

"We have our faults, Annabelle, Harriet and I, but we're not crazy. I wouldn't take this tub across the Serpentine without a favorable weather forecast. It's blowing a Force seven outside. And a boat search would take a lifetime too long in those parts. What I had in mind was this. At the very eastern tip of Torbay Island, about five miles from the village, there's a small deserted sandy cove, semicircular and well protected by steep bluffs and pine trees. Will you please arrange to have a long range helicopter there exactly at dawn?"

"And now it's your turn to think I am crazy," Uncle Arthur said coldly. That remark about the sea-keeping qualities of his own brainchild, the *Firecrest,* would have rankled badly. "I'm supposed to snap my fingers and hey presto! A helicopter will be there at dawn."

"That's fourteen hours from now, Annabelle. At five o'clock this morning you were prepared to snap your fingers and have a helicopter here by noon. Seven hours. Exactly half the time. But that was for something important, like getting me down to London to give me the bawling out of a lifetime before firing me."

"Call me at midnight, Caroline. I hope to God you know what you are doing."

I said: "Yes, sir," and hung up. I didn't mean, Yes, sir, I knew what I was doing, I meant, Yes, sir, I hoped to God I knew what I was doing.

If the carpet in the *Shangri-la*'s saloon had cost a penny under five thousand pounds, then old Skouras must have picked it up secondhand somewhere. Twenty by thirty, bronze and russet and gold, but mainly gold, it flowed across the deck like a field of ripe corn, an illusion heightened both by its depth and the impediment it offered to progress. You had to wade through the damn thing. I'd never seen an item of furnishing like it in my life except for the curtains that covered two-thirds of the bulkhead space. The curtains made the carpet look rather shoddy. Persian or Afghanistan, with a heavy gleaming weave that gave a shimmering shot-silk effect with every little movement of the *Shangri-la*, they stretched all the way from deckhead to deck. What little of the bulkheads that could be seen were sheathed in a satiny tropical hardwood, the same wood as was used for the magnificent bar that took up most of the after bulkhead of the saloon. The opulently upholstered settees and armchairs and bar stools, dark green leather with gold piping, would have cost another fortune, even the trade-in value of the beaten copper tables scattered carelessly about the carpet would have fed a family of five for a year. At the Savoy Grill.

On the port bulkhead hung two Cézannes, on the starboard two Renoirs. The pictures were a mistake. In that room they didn't have a chance. They'd have felt more at home in the galley.

So would I. So, I was pretty sure, would Hunslett. It wasn't merely that our sports coats and Paisley scarves clashed violently with the decor in general and the black ties and dinner jackets of our host and his other guests in particular. It wasn't even that the general run of conversation might have been specifically designed to reduce Hunslett and myself to our proper status of artisans and pretty inferior artisans at that. All this talk about debentures and mergers and cross-options and takeovers and millions and millions of dollars has a pretty demoralising effect on the lower classes, but you didn't need to have the IQ of a genius to realise that this line of talk wasn't being aimed specifically at us; to the lads with the black ties debentures and takeovers were the stuff and staff of life and so a principal staple of conversation. Besides, this wish to be somewhere else obviously didn't apply only to us: at least two others, a bald-headed goatee-bearded merchant banker by the name of Henry Biscarte and a big bluff Scots lawyer by the name of MacCallum were just as uncomfortable as I felt, but showed it a great deal more.

A silent movie picture of the scene would have given no clue as to what was wrong. Everything was so very comfortable, so very civilised. The deep armchairs invited complete relaxation. A blazing if superfluous log fire burned in the hearth. Skouras was the smiling and genial host to the life. The glasses were never empty—the press of an unheard bell brought a white-jacketed steward who silently refilled glasses and as silently departed again. All so urbane, so wealthy, so pleasantly peaceful. Until you put in the movie sound track, that was. That was when you wished you were in the galley.

Skouras had his glass refilled for the fourth time in the forty-five minutes we had been there, smiled at his wife sitting in the armchair across the fire from him, lifted his glass in a toast. "To you, my dear. To your patience with putting up with us all so well. A most boring trip for you, most boring. I congratulate you."

I looked at Charlotte Skouras. Everybody looked at Charlotte Skouras. There was nothing unusual in that, millions of people had looked at Charlotte Skouras when she had been the most sought-after actress in Europe. Even in those days she'd been neither particularly young nor beautiful, she didn't have to be because she'd been a great actress and not a beautiful but bone-headed movie star. Now she was even older and less good-looking and her figure was beginning to go. But men still looked at her. She was somewhere in her late thirties, but they would still be looking at her when she was in her bath chair. She had that kind of face. A worn face, a used face, a face that had been used for living and laughing and thinking and feeling and suffering, a face with brown tired wise knowing eyes a thousand years old, a face that had more quality and character in every little line and wrinkle—and heaven only knew there was no shortage of these—than in a whole battalion of the fringe-haired darlings of contemporary society, the ones in the glossy magazines, the ones who week after week stared out at you with their smooth and beautiful faces, with their beautiful and empty eyes. Put them in the same room as Charlotte Skouras and no one would ever have seen them. Mass-produced carbon copies of chocolate boxes are no kind of competition at all for a great painter's original in oils.

"You are very kind, Anthony." Charlotte Skouras had a deep slow slightly foreign accented voice and, just then, a tired strained smile that accorded well with the darkness under the brown eyes. "But I am never bored. Truly. You know that."

"With this lot as guests?" Skouras' smile was as broad as ever. "A Skouras board meeting in the Western Isles instead of your blue-blooded favorites on a cruise in the Levant? Take Dollmann here." He nodded to the man by his side, a tall thin bespectacled character with receding thin dark hair who looked as if he needed a shave but didn't. John Dollmann, the managing director of the Skouras' shipping lines. "Eh, John? How do you rate yourself as a substitute for

63

young Viscount Horley? The one with sawdust in his head and fifteen million in the bank?"

"Poorly, I'm afraid, Sir Anthony." Dollman was as urbane as Skouras himself, as apparently unconscious of anything untowards in the atmosphere. "Very poorly. I've a great deal more brains, a great deal less money and I've no pretensions to being a gay and witty conversationalist."

"Young Horley *was* rather the life and soul of the party, wasn't he? Especially when I wasn't around," Skouras added thoughtfully. He looked at me. "You know him, Mr. Petersen?"

"I've heard of him. I don't move in those circles, Sir Anthony." Urbane as all hell, that was me.

"Um." Skouras looked quizzically at the two men sitting close by myself. One, rejoicing in the good Anglo-Saxon name of Hermann Lavorski, a big jovial twinkling-eyed man with a great booming laugh and an inexhaustible supply of risqué stories, was, I'd been told, his accountant and financial adviser. I'd never seen anyone less like an accountant and finance wizard, so that probably made him the best in the business . . . The other, a middle-aged, balding, Sphinx-faced character with a drooping handlebar moustache of the type once sported by Wild Bill Hickok and a head that cried out for a bowler hat, was Lord Charnley, who, in spite of his title, found it necessary to work as a broker in the City to make ends meet. "And how would you rate our two good friends here, Charlotte?" This with another wide and friendly smile at his wife.

"I'm afraid I don't understand." Charlotte Skouras looked at her husband steadily, not smiling.

"Come now, come now, of course you understand. I'm still talking about the poor company I provide for so young and attractive a woman as you." He looked at Hunslett. "She *is* a young and attractive woman, don't you think, Mr. Hunslett?"

"Well, now." Hunslett leaned back in his armchair, fingers judiciously steepled, an urbanely sophisticated man entering into the spirit of things. "What is youth, Sir Anthony? I don't know." He smiled across at Charlotte Skouras. "Mrs. Skouras will never be old. As for attractive—well, it's a bit superfluous to ask that. For ten million European men—and for myself—Mrs. Skouras was the most attractive actress of her time."

"*Was*, Mr. Hunslett? *Was?*" Old Skouras was leaning forward in his chair now, the smile a shadow of his former self. "But now, Mr. Hunslett?"

"Mrs. Skouras' producers must have employed the worst cameramen in Europe." Hunslett's dark, saturnine face gave nothing away. He smiled at Charlotte Skouras. "If I may be pardoned for so personal a remark."

If I'd had a sword in my hand and the authority to use it, I'd have knighted Hunslett on the spot. After, of course, having first had a swipe at Skouras.

"The days of chivalry are not yet over," Skouras smiled. I saw MacCallum and Biscarte, the bearded banker, stir uncomfortably in their seats. It was damnably awkward. Skouras went on: "I only meant, my dear, that Charnley and Lavorski here are poor substitutes for sparkling young company like Welshblood, the young American oil man, or Domenico, that Spanish count with the passion for amateur astronomy. The one who used to take you on the afterdeck to point out the stars in the Aegean." He looked again at Charnley and Lavorski. "I'm sorry, gentlemen, you just wouldn't do at all."

"I don't know if I'm all that insulted," Lavorski said comfortably. "Charnley and I have our points. Um—I haven't seen young Domenico around for quite some time." He'd have made an excellent straight man, would Lavorski, trained to say his lines at exactly the right time.

"You won't see him around for a very much longer time," Skouras said grimly. "At least not in my yacht or in any of my houses." A pause. "Or near anything I own. I promised him I'd see the color of his noble Castilian blood if I ever clapped eyes on him again." He laughed suddenly. "I must apologise for even bringing that nonentity's name into the conversation. Mr. Hunslett. Mr. Petersen. Your glasses are empty."

"You've been very kind, Sir Anthony. We've enjoyed ourselves immensely." Bluff old, stupid old Calvert, too obtuse to notice what was going on. "But we'd like to get back. It's blowing up badly tonight and Hunslett and I would like to move the *Firecrest* into the shelter of Garve Island." I rose to a window, pulling one of his Afghanistan or whatever curtains to one side. It felt as heavy as a stage fire curtain, no wonder he needed stabilisers with all that topweight on. "That's why we left our navigation and cabin lights on. To see if we'd moved. She dragged a fair bit earlier this evening."

"So soon? So soon?" He sounded genuinely disappointed. "But of course, if you're worried—" He pressed a button, not the one for the steward, and the saloon door opened. The man who entered was a small weather-beaten character with two gold stripes on his sleeves. Captain Black, the *Shangri-la*'s skipper. He'd accompanied Skouras when we'd been briefly shown around the *Shangri-la* after arriving aboard, a tour that had included an inspection of the smashed radio transmitter. No question about it, their radio was well and truly out of action.

"Ah, Captain Black. Have the tender brought alongside at once, will you. Mr. Petersen and Mr. Hunslett are anxious to get back to the *Firecrest* as soon as possible."

"Yes, sir. I'm afraid there'll be a certain delay, Sir Anthony."

"Delay?" Old Skouras could put a frown in his voice without putting one on his face.

"The old trouble, I'm afraid," Captain Black said apologetically.

"Those bloody carburetors," Skouras swore. "You were right, Captain Black, you were right. Last tender I'll ever have with petrol engines fitted. Let me know as soon as she's all right. And detail one of the hands to keep an eye on the *Firecrest* to see that she doesn't lose position. Mr. Petersen's afraid she'll drag."

"Don't worry, sir." I didn't know whether Black was speaking to Skouras or myself. "She'll be all right."

He left. Skouras spent some time in extolling diesel engines and cursing petrol ones, pressed some more whisky on Hunslett and myself and ignored my protests, which were based less on any dislike of whisky in general or Skouras in particular than on the fact that I didn't consider it very good preparation for the night that lay ahead of me. Just before nine o'clock he pressed a button by his arm rest and the doors of a cabinet automatically opened to reveal a 23-inch TV set.

Uncle Arthur hadn't let me down. The newscaster gave quite a dramatic account of the last message received from the TSDY *Moray Rose,* reported not under command and making water fast somewhere to the south of the Island of Skye. A full-scale air and sea search, starting at dawn the next day, was promised.

Skouras switched the set off. "The sea's crowded with damn fools who should never be allowed outside a canal basin. What's the latest on the weather? Anyone know?"

"There was a Hebrides Force Eight warning on the 1758 shipping forecast," Charlotte Skouras said quietly. "Southwest, they said."

"Since when did you start listening to forecasts?" Skouras demanded. "Or to the radio at all? But of course, my dear, I'd forgotten. Not so much to occupy your time these days, have you? Force eight and southwest, eh? And the yacht would be coming down from the Kyle of Lochalsh, straight into it. They must be mad. And they have a radio—they sent a message. That makes them stark staring lunatics. Whether they didn't listen to the forecast or whether they listened and still set out, they must have been lunatics. Get them everywhere."

"Some of those lunatics may be dying, drowning now. Or already drowned," Charlotte Skouras said. The shadows under the brown eyes seemed bigger and darker than ever, but there was still life in those brown eyes.

For perhaps five seconds Skouras, face set, stared at her and I felt that if I snapped my fingers there would be a loud tinkling or crashing sound, the atmosphere was as brittle as that. Then he turned away with a laugh and said to me: "The little woman, eh, Petersen. The little mother—only she has no children. Tell me, Petersen, are you married?"

I smiled at him while debating the wisdom of throwing my whisky glass in his face or clobbering him with something heavy, then decided against it. Apart from the fact that it would only make matters worse, I didn't fancy the swim back to the *Firecrest*. So I smiled and smiled, feeling the knife under the cloak, and said: "Afraid not, Sir Anthony."

"Afraid not? Afraid not?" He laughed his hearty goodfellowship laugh, the kind I can't stand, and went on cryptically: "You're not so young to be sufficiently naïve to talk that way, come now, are you, Mr. Petersen?"

"Thirty-eight and never had a chance," I said cheerfully. "The old story, Sir Anthony. The ones I'd have wouldn't have me. And vice-versa." Which wasn't quite true. The driver of a Bentley with, the doctors have estimated, certainly not less than a bottle of whisky inside him, had ended my marriage before it was two months old—and also accounted for the savagely scarred left side of my face. It was then that Uncle Arthur had prised me from my marine salvage business and since then no girl with any sense would ever have contemplated marrying me if she'd known what my job was. What made it even more difficult was the fact that I couldn't tell her in the first place. And the scars didn't help.

"You don't look a fool to me," Skouras smiled. "If I may say so without offence." That was rich, old Skouras worrying about giving offence. The zip fastener of a mouth softened into what, in view of his next words, I correctly interpreted in advance as being a nostalgic smile. "I'm joking, of course. It's not all that bad. A man must have his fun. Charlotte?"

"Yes?" The brown eyes wary, watchful.

"There's something I want from our stateroom. Would you— "

"The stewardess. Couldn't she—?"

"This is personal, my dear. And as Mr. Hunslett has pointed out, at least by inference, you're a good deal younger than I am." He smiled at Hunslett to show that no offence was intended. "The picture on my dressing table."

"What!" She suddenly sat forward in her armchair, hands reaching for the fronts of the arm rests as if about to pull herself to her feet. Something touched a switch inside Skouras and the smiling eyes went bleak and hard and cold, changing their direction of gaze fractionally. It lasted only a moment because his wife had caught it even before I did, because she sat forward abruptly, smoothing down the short sleeves of her dress over suntanned arms. Quick and smooth, but not quite quick enough. For a period not more than two seconds the sleeves had ridden nearly all the way up to her shoulders—and nearly four inches below those shoulders each arm had been encircled by a ring of bluish-red bruises. A continuous ring. Not the kind of bruises that are made by blows or finger pressure. The kind that is made by a rope.

Skouras was smiling again, pressing the bell to summon the steward. Charlotte Skouras rose without a further word and hurried quickly from the room. I could have wondered if I'd only imagined this momentary tableau I'd seen, but I knew damned well I hadn't. I was paid not to have an imagination of that kind.

She was back inside a moment, a picture frame maybe six by eight in her hand. She handed it to Skouras and sat down quickly in her own chair. This time she was very careful with the sleeves, without seeming to be.

"My wife, gentlemen," Skouras said. He rose from his armchair and handed round a photograph of a dark-eyed, dark-haired woman with a smiling face that emphasised the high Slavonic cheekbones. "My first wife. Anna. We were married for thirty years. Marriage isn't all that bad. That's Anna, gentlemen."

If I'd a gram of human decency left in me I should have knocked him down and trampled all over him. For a man to state openly in company that he kept the picture of his former wife by his bedside and then impose upon his present wife the final and utter humiliation and degradation of fetching it was beyond belief. That and the rope burns on his present wife's arms made him almost too good for shooting. But I couldn't do it, I couldn't do anything about it. The old coot's heart was in his voice and his eyes. If this was acting, it was the most superb acting I had ever seen, the tear that trickled down from his right eye would have rated an Oscar any year since cinema had begun. And if it wasn't acting then it was just the picture of a sad and lonely man, no longer young, momentarily oblivious of this world, gazing desolately at the only thing in this world that he loved, that he ever had loved or ever would love, something gone beyond recall. And that was what it was.

If it hadn't been for the other picture, the picture of the still, proud, humiliated Charlotte Skouras staring sightlessly into the fire, I might have felt a lump in my own throat. As it happened, I'd no difficulty in restraining my emotion. One man couldn't, however, but it wasn't sympathy for Skouras that got the better of him. MacCallum, the Scots lawyer, pale-faced with outrage, rose to his feet, said something in a thick voice about not feeling well, wished us goodnight and left. The bearded banker left on his heels. Skouras didn't see them go, he'd fumbled his way back to his seat and was staring before him, his eyes as sightless as those of his wife. Like his wife, he was seeing something in the depths of the flames. The picture lay face down on his knee. He didn't even look up when Captain Black came in and told us the tender was ready to take us back to the *Firecrest*.

When the tender had left us aboard our own boat we waited till it was halfway back to the *Shangri-la*, closed the saloon door, unbuttoned the studded carpet and pulled it back. Carefully I lifted a sheet of newspaper and there, on the thin film of flour spread out on the paper below it, were four perfect sets of footprints. We tried out two for'ard cabins, the engine room and the after cabin, and the silk threads we'd so laboriously fitted before our departure to the *Shangri-la* were all snapped.

69

Somebody, two at least to judge from the footprints, had been through the entire length of the *Firecrest*. They could have had at least a clear hour for the job, so Hunslett and I spent a clear hour trying to find out why they had been there. We found nothing, no reason at all.

"Well," I said, "at least we know now why they were so anxious to have us aboard the *Shangri-la.*"

"To give them a clear field here? That's why the tender wasn't ready—it was here."

"What else?"

"There's something else. I can't put my finger on it. But there's something else."

"Let me know in the morning. When you call Uncle at midnight, ask him to dig up what information he can on those characters on the *Shangri-la* and about the physician who attended the late Lady Skouras. There's a lot I want to know about the late Lady Skouras." I told him what I wanted to know. "Meantime, let's shift this boat over to Garve Island. I've got to be up at three-thirty—you've all the time for sleep in the world."

I should have listened to Hunslett. Again I should have listened to Hunslett. And again for Hunslett's sake. But I didn't know then that Hunslett was to have time for all the sleep in the world.

4 • WEDNESDAY: 5 A.M.—DUSK

As the saying went in those parts, it was as black as the earl of hell's waistcoat. The sky was black, the woods were black, and the icy heavy driving rain reduced what little visibility there was to just nothing at all. The only way to locate a tree was to walk straight into it, the only way to locate a dip in the ground was to fall into it. When Hunslett had woken me at three-thirty with a cup of tea he told me that when he'd been speaking to Uncle Arthur at midnight—I'd been asleep—he was left in no doubt that although the helicopter had been laid on Uncle had been most unenthusiastic and considered the whole thing a waste of time. It was a rare occasion indeed when I ever felt myself in total agreement with Uncle Arthur but this was one of those rare occasions.

It was beginning to look as if I'd never even find that damned helicopter anyway. I wouldn't have believed that it could have been so difficult to find one's way across five miles of wooded island at nighttime. It wasn't even as if I had to contend with rivers or rushing torrents or cliffs or precipitous clefts in the ground or any kind of dense or tangled vegetation. Torbay was just a moderately wooded gently sloping island and crossing from one side to the other of it would have been only an easy Sunday afternoon stroll for a fairly active octogenarian. I was no octogenarian, though I felt like one, but then this wasn't a Sunday afternoon.

The trouble had started from the moment I'd landed on the Torbay shore opposite Garve Island. From the moment I'd tried to land. Wearing rubber-soled shoes and trying to haul a rubber dinghy over slippery seaweed-covered rocks, some as much as six feet in diameter, to a shoreline twenty interminable yards away is, even in broad daylight, a bone-breaking job: in pitch darkness it's almost as good a way as any for a potential suicide to finish off the job with efficiency and dispatch. The third time I fell I smashed my torch. Several bone-jarring bruises later my wrist compass went the same way. The attached depth gauge, almost inevitably, remained intact. A depth gauge is a great help in finding your way through a trackless wood at night.

After deflating and caching the dinghy and pump I'd set off along the shoreline remote from the village of Torbay. It was logical that if I followed this long enough I'd be bound to come to the sandy cove at the far end of the island where I was to rendezvous with the helicopter. It was also logical that, if the tree line came right down to the shore, if that shore was heavily indented with little coves and if I couldn't see where I was going, I'd fall into the sea with a fair degree of regularity. After I'd hauled myself out for the third time I gave up and struck inland. It wasn't because I was afraid of getting wet—as I hadn't seen much point in wearing a scuba suit for walking through a wood and sitting in a helicopter I'd left it aboard and was already soaked to the skin. Nor was it because of the possibility that the hand distress flares I'd brought along for signalling the helicopter pilot, wrapped though they were in oilskin, might not stand up to this treatment indefinitely. The reason why I was now blundering my blind and painful way through the wood was that if I'd stuck to the shoreline my rate of progress there wouldn't have brought me to the rendezvous before midday.

My only guides were the wind-lashed rain and the lie of the land. The cove I was heading for lay to the east, the near-gale force wind was almost due west so as long as I kept that cold stinging rain on the back of my neck I'd be heading in approximately the right direction: as a check on that, the island of Torbay has a spinal hog's back, covered in pines to the top, running its east-west length and when I felt the land falling away to one side or the other it meant I was wandering. But the rain-laded wind swirled unpredictably as the wood alternately thinned and became dense again, the hog's back had offshoots and irregularities and as a result of the combination of the two I lost a great deal of time. Half an hour before dawn—by my watch, that was, it was still as black as the midnight hour—I was beginning to wonder if I could possibly make it in time.

And I was beginning to wonder if the helicopter could make it either. There was no doubt in my mind that it could land—that eastern cove was perfectly sheltered—but whether it could get there at all was another question. I had a vague idea that helicopters were unmanageable above certain windspeeds but had no idea what the windspeeds were. And if the helicopter didn't turn up, then I was faced with the long cold wet trudge back to where I had hidden the dinghy and then an even longer, colder and hungry wait until darkness fell at night and I could get out to the *Firecrest* unseen. Even now, I had only twenty-four hours left. By nightfall I would have only twelve. I began to run.

Fifteen minutes and God knows how many iron-hard tree trunks later I heard it, faint and intermittent at first, then gradually swelling in strength—the clattering roar of a helicopter engine. He was early, damn him, he was far too early, he'd land there, find the place deserted and take off for base again. It says much for my suddenly desperate state of mind that it never occurred to me how he could even begin to locate, far less land in, that sandy cove in a condition of darkness that was still only a degree less than total. For a moment I even contemplated lighting a flare to let the pilot know that I was at least there or thereabouts and had the flare halfway out of my pocket before I shoved it back again. The arrangement had been that the flare would be lit only to show the landing strip in the sand: if I lit one there and then he might head for it, strike the tops of the palm trees and that would be the end of that.

I ran even faster. It had been years since I'd run more than a couple of hundred yards and my lungs were already wheezing and gasping like a fractured bellows in a blacksmith's shop. But I ran as hard as I could. I cannoned into trees, I tripped over roots, fell into gullies, had my face whipped time and again by low-spreading branches, but above all I cannoned into those damned trees. I stretched my arms before me but it did no good, I ran into them all the same. I picked up a broken branch I'd tripped over and held it in front of me but no matter how I pointed it the trees always seemed to come at me from another direction. I hit every tree in the island of Torbay. I felt the way a bowling ball must feel after a hard season in a bowling alley, the only difference, and a notable one, being that whereas the ball knocked the skittles down, the trees knocked me down. Once, twice, three times I heard the sound of the helicopter engine disappearing away to the east, and the third time I was sure he was gone for good. But each time it came back. The sky was lightening to the east now, but still I couldn't see the helicopter: for the pilot, everything below would still be as black as night.

The ground gave way beneath my feet and I fell. I braced

myself, arms outstretched, for the impact as I struck the other side of the gully. But my reaching hands found nothing. No impact. I kept on falling, rolling and twisting on a heathery slope, and for the first time that night I would have welcomed the appearance of a pine tree, any kind of tree, to stop my progress. I don't know how many trees there were on that slope, I missed the lot. If it was a gully, it was the biggest gully on the Island of Torbay. But it wasn't a gully at all, it was the end of Torbay. I rolled and bumped over a suddenly horizontal grassy bank and landed on my back in soft wet sand. Even while I was whooping and gasping and trying to get my knocked-out breath back into my lungs I still had time to appreciate the fortunate fact that kindly providence and a few million years had changed the jagged rocks that must have once fringed that shore into a nice soft yielding sandy beach.

I got to my feet. This was the place, all right. There was only one such sandy bay, I'd been told, in the east of the Isle of Torbay and there was now enough light for me to see that this was indeed just that, though a lot smaller than it appeared on the chart. The helicopter was coming in again from the east, not, as far as I could judge, more than three or four hundred feet up. I ran halfway down to the water's edge, pulled a hand flare from my pocket, slid away the waterproof covering and tore off the ignition strip. It flared into life at once, a dazzling blue-white magnesium light so blinding that I had to clap my free hand over my eyes. It lasted for only thirty seconds, but that was enough. Even as it fizzled and sputtered its acrid and nostril-wrinkling way to extinction the helicopter was almost directly overhead. Two vertically downward pointing searchlights, mounted fore and aft on the helicopter, switched on simultaneously, interlocking pools of brilliance on the pale white sand. Twenty seconds later the skids sank into the soft sand, the rackety clangour of the motor died away and the blades idled slowly to a stop. I'd never been in a helicopter in my life but I'd seen plenty: in the half-darkness this looked like the biggest one I'd ever seen.

The right-hand door opened and a torch shone in my face as I approached. A voice, Welsh as the Rhondda Valley, said: "Morning. You Calvert?"

"Me. Can I come aboard?"

"How do I know you're Calvert?"

"I'm telling you. Don't come the hard man, laddie. You've no authority to make an identification check."

"Have you no proof? No papers?"

"Have you no sense? Haven't you enough sense to know that there are some people who *never* carry any means of identification? Do you think I just happened to be standing here, five miles from nowhere, and that I just happened to be carrying flares in my pocket? You want to join the ranks of the unemployed before sunset?" A very auspicious beginning to our association.

"I was told to be careful." He was as worried and upset as a cat snoozing on a sun-warmed wall. Still a marked lack of cordiality. "Lieutenant Scott Williams, Fleet Air Arm. Takes an admiral to sack me. Step up."

I stepped up, closed the door and sat. He didn't offer to shake hands. He flicked on an overhead light and said: "What the hell's happened to your face?"

"What's the matter with my face?"

"Blood. Hundreds of little scratches."

"Pine needles." I told him what had happened. "Why a machine this size? You could ferry a battalion in this one."

"Fourteen men, to be precise. I do lots of crazy things, Calvert, but I don't fly itsy-bitsy two-bit choppers in this kind of weather. Be blown out of the sky. With only two of us, the long-range tanks are full."

"You can fly all day?"

"More or less. Depends how fast we go. What do you want from me?"

"Civility, for a start. Or don't you like early morning rising?"

"I'm an Air-Sea Rescue pilot, Calvert. This is the only machine on the base big enough to go out looking in this kind of weather. I should be out looking, not out on some cloak-and-dagger joy ride. I don't care how important it is, there's people maybe clinging to a life raft fifty miles out in the Atlantic. That's my job. But I've got my orders. What do you want?"

"The *Moray Rose?*"

"You heard? Yes, that's her."

"She doesn't exist. She never has existed."

"What are you talking about? The news broadcasts—"

"I'll tell you as much as you need to know, Lieutenant. It's essential that I be able to search this area without arousing suspicion. The only way that can be done is by inventing an iron-clad reason. The foundering *Moray Rose* is that reason. So we tell the tale."

"Phony?"

"Phony."

"You can fix it?" he said slowly. "You can fix a news broadcast?"

"Yes."

"Maybe you could get me fired at that." He smiled for the first time. "Sorry, sir. Lieutenant Williams—Scotty to you—is now his normal cheerful willing self. What's on?"

"Know the coastlines and islands of this area well?"

"From the air?"

"Yes."

"I've been here twenty months now. Air-Sea Rescue and in between Army and Navy exercises and hunting for lost climbers. Most of my work is with the Marine Commandos. I know this area at least as well as any man alive."

"I'm looking for a place where a man could hide a boat. A fairly big boat. Forty feet—maybe fifty. Might be in a big boathouse, might be under overhanging trees up some creek, might even be in some tiny secluded harbor normally invisible from the sea. Between Islay and Skye."

"Well, now, is that all. Have you any idea how many hundreds of miles of coastline there is in that lot, taking in all the islands? Maybe thousands. How long do I have for this job? A month?"

"By sunset today. Now, wait. We can cut out all the centers of population, and by that I mean anything with more than two or three houses together. We can cut out known fishing grounds. We can cut out regular steamship routes. Does that help?"

"A lot. What are we really looking for?"

"I've told you."

"Okay, okay, so mine is not to reason why. Any idea where you'd like to start, any ideas for limiting the search?"

"Let's go due east to the mainland. Twenty miles up the coast, then twenty south. Then we'll try Torbay Sound and the Isle of Torbay. Then the islands farther west and north."

"Torbay Sound has a steamer service."

"Sorry, I should have said a daily service. Torbay has a bi-weekly service."

"Fasten your seat belt and get on those earphones. We're going to get thrown around quite a bit today. I hope you're a good sailor."

"And the earphones?" They were the biggest I'd ever seen, four inches wide with inch-thick linings of what looked like sorbo rubber. A spring loaded swing microphone was attached to the headband.

"For the ears," the lieutenant said kindly. "So that you don't get perforated drums. And so you won't be deaf for a week afterwards. If you can imagine yourself inside a steel drum in the middle of a boiler factory with a dozen pneumatic chisels hammering outside you'll have some idea of what the racket is like once we start up."

Even with the earphone muffs on, it sounded exactly like being in a steel drum in a boiler factory with a dozen pneumatic chisels hammering on the outside. The earphones didn't seem to have the slightest effect at all, the noise came hammering and beating at you through every facial and cranial bone, but on the one and very brief occasion when I cautiously lifted one phone to find out what the noise was like without them and if they were really doing any good at all, I found out exactly what Lieutenant Williams meant about perforated drums. He hadn't been joking. But even with them on, after a couple of hours my head felt as if it were coming apart. I looked occasionally at the dark lean face of the young Welshman beside me, a man who had to stand this racket day in, day out, the year round. He looked quite sane to me. I'd have been in a padded cell in a week.

I didn't have to be in that helicopter a week. Altogether, I spent eight hours' flying time in it and it felt like a leap year.

Our first run northwards up the mainland coast produced what was to be the first of many false alarms that day. Twenty minutes after leaving Torbay we spotted a river, a small one but still a river, flowing into the sea. We followed it upstream for a mile, then suddenly the trees, crowding down close to the banks on both sides, met in the middle where the river seemed to run through some rocky gorge.

I shouted into the microphone. "I want to see what's there."

Williams nodded. "We passed a place a quarter of a mile back. I'll set you down."

"You've got a winch. Couldn't you lower me?"

"When you know as much as I do about the effect of forty to fifty mile an hour winds in steep-sided valleys," he said, "you'll never even talk about such things. Not even in a joke. I want to take this kite back home again."

So he turned back and set me down without much difficulty in the shelter of a bluff. Five minutes later I'd reached the beginning of the overhanging stretch. Another five minutes and I was back in the helicopter.

"What luck?" the lieutenant asked.

"No luck. An ancient oak tree right across the river, just at the entrance to the overhang."

"Could be shifted."

"It weighs two or three tons, it's imbedded feet deep in the mud and it's been there for years."

"Well, well, we can't be right first time, every time."

A few more minutes and another river mouth. It hardly looked big enough to take a boat of any size, but we turned up anyway. Less than half a mile from its mouth the river foamed whitely as it passed through rapids. We turned back.

By the time it was fully daylight we had reached the northern limit of possibility in this area. Steep-sided mountains gave way to precipitous cliffs that plunged almost vertically into the sea.

"How far does this go north?" I asked.

"Ten, twelve miles to the head of Loch Lairg."

"Know it?"

"Flown up there a score of times."

"Caves?"

"Nary a cave."

I hadn't really thought that there would be. "What about the other side?" I pointed to the west where the mountainous shoreline, not five miles away yet barely visible through the driving rain and low scudding cloud, ran in an almost sheer drop from the head of Loch Lairg to the entrance to Torbay Sound.

"Even the gulls can't find a foothold there. Believe me."

I believed him. We flew back the way we had come as far as our starting point on the coast, then continued southwards. From the Isle of Torbay to the mainland the sea was an almost unbroken mass of foaming white, big white-capped rollers marching eastwards across the darkened Firth, long creamy lines of spume torn from the wave tops veining the troughs between. There wasn't a single craft in sight, even the big drifters had stayed home, it was as bad as that. In that buffeting gale force wind our big helicopter was having a bad time of it now, violently shaking and swaying like an out-of-control express train in the last moments before it leaves the track: one hour's flying in those conditions had turned me against helicopters for life. But when I thought of what it would be like down there in a boat in that seething maelstrom of a firth I could feel a positive bond of attachment growing between me and that damned helicopter.

We flew twenty miles south—if the way we were being jarred and flung through the air could be called flying—but covered sixty miles in that southing. Every little sound between the islands and the mainland, every natural harbor, every sea-loch and inlet had to be investigated. We flew very low most of the time, not much above two hundred feet: sometimes we were forced down to a hundred feet—so heavy was the rain and so powerful the wind now battering against the streaming windscreen that the wipers were almost useless and we had to get as low as possible to see anything at all. As it was, I don't think we missed a yard of the coastline of the mainland or the close inshore islands. We saw everything. And we saw nothing.

I looked at my watch. Nine-thirty. The day wearing on and nothing achieved. I said: "How much more of this can the helicopter stand?"

"I've been 150 miles out over the Atlantic in weather a damn sight worse than this." Lieutenant Williams showed no signs of strain or anxiety or fatigue, if anything he seemed to be enjoying himself. "The point is how much more can *you* stand?"

"Very little. But we'll have to. Back to where you picked me up and we'll make a circuit of the coast of Torbay. South coast first, then north up the west coast, then east past Torbay and down the southern shore of the Sound."

"Yours to command." Williams brought the helicopter round to the northwest in a swinging slide-slipping movement that didn't do my stomach any good. "You'll find coffee and sandwiches in that box there." I left the sandwiches and coffee where they were.

It took us almost forty minutes to cover the twenty-five miles to the eastern tip of the Isle of Torbay, that wind took us two steps back for every three forward. Visibility was so bad that Williams flew on instruments the whole way and with that violent cross-wind blowing he should have missed our target by miles. Instead he hit that sandy cove right on the nose as if he'd been flying in on a radio beacon. I was beginning to have a very great deal of confidence in Williams, a man who knew exactly what he was doing: I was beginning to have no confidence at all in myself and to wonder if I had any idea in the world what I was doing. I thought about Uncle

79

Arthur and quickly decided I'd rather think about something else.

"There." Williams pointed. We were about halfway along the south coast of Torbay. "A likely setup, wouldn't you say?"

And a likely setup it was. A large white three-story stone-built Georgian house, set in a clearing about a hundred yards back from and thirty yards above the shore. There are dozens of such houses scattered in the most unlikely positions in some of the most barren and desolate islands in the Hebrides. Heaven only knew who built them, why or how. But it wasn't the house that was the focal point of interest in this case, it was the big boathouse on the edge of a tiny land-locked harbor. Without a further word from me Williams brought the big machine down neatly in the shelter of the trees behind the house.

I unwrapped the polythene bag I'd been carrying under my shirt. Two guns. The Luger I stuck in my pocket, the little German Lilliput I fixed to the spring clip in my left sleeve. Williams stared unconcernedly ahead and began to whistle to himself.

Nobody had lived in that house for years. Part of the roof had fallen in, years of salt air erosion had removed all paint-work and the rooms, when I looked in through the cracked and broken windows, were bare and crumbling with long strips of wallpaper lying on the floor. The path down to the little harbor was completely overgrown with moss. Every time my heel sunk into the path a deep muddy mark was left behind, the first made there for a long, long time. The boat-shed was big enough, at least sixty by twenty, but that was all that could be said for it. The two big doors had three hinges apiece and two huge padlocks where they met in the middle. Padlocks and hinges alike were almost eaten through by rust. I could feel the heavy tug of the Luger in my pocket and the weight made me feel faintly ridiculous. I went back to the helicopter.

Twice more in the next twenty minutes we came across al-most identical situations. Big white Georgian houses with big boathouses at their feet. I knew they would be false alarms but I had to check them both. False alarms they were. The last occupants of those houses had been dead before I'd been born. People had lived in those houses once, people with families, big families, people with money and ambition and confidence and no fear at all of the future. Not if they had built houses as big as those. And now the people were gone and all that was left were those crumbling, mouldering monuments to a misplaced faith in the future. Some years previously I'd seen houses in plantations in South Carolina and Georgia, houses widely dissimilar but exactly the same, white-porticoed ante-bellum houses hemmed in by evergreen live oaks and overgrown with long grey festoons of Spanish moss. Sadness and desolation and a world that was gone forever.

The west coast of the Isle of Torbay yielded nothing. We gave the town of Torbay and Garve Island a wide berth and flew eastwards down the southern shore of the Sound with the gale behind us. Two small hamlets, each with its disintegrating pier. Beyond that, nothing.

We reached the sandy cove again, flew north till we reached the northern shore of the Sound, then westwards along this shore. We stopped twice, once to investigate a tree-overhung land-locked harbor less than forty yards in diameter, and again to investigate a small complex of industrial buildings which had once, so Williams said, produced a fine-quality sand that had been one of the ingredients in a famous brand of toothpaste. Again, nothing.

At the last place we stopped for five minutes. Lieutenant Williams said he was hungry. I wasn't. I'd become used to the helicopter by now but I wasn't hungry. It was midday. Half our time gone and nothing accomplished. And it was beginning to look very much as if nothing was going to be accomplished. Uncle Arthur would be pleased. I took the chart from Williams.

"We have to pick and choose," I said. "We'll have to take a chance. We'll go up the Sound to Dolman Head, opposite Garve Island, then go up Loch Hynart." Loch Hynart was a seven mile long loch, winding and many-islanded, that ran more or less due east, nowhere more than half a mile wide, deep into the heart of the mountain massif. "Back to Dolman Point again, then along the southern shore of the mainland peninsula again as far as Carrara Point. Then east along the southern shore of Loch Houron."

"Loch Houron." Williams nodded. "The wildest waters and the worst place for boats in the west of Scotland. Last place I'd go looking, Mr. Calvert, that's for sure. From all accounts you'll find nothing there but wrecks and skeletons. There are more reefs and skerries and underwater rocks and overfalls and whirlpools and tidal races in twenty miles there than in the whole of the rest of Scotland. Local fishermen won't go near the place." He pointed at the chart. "See this passage between Dubh Sgeir and Ballara Island, the two islands at the mouth of Loch Houron? That's the most feared spot of all. You should see the grip fishermen get on their whisky glasses when they talk about it. Beul nan Uamh, it's called. The mouth of the grave."

"They're a cheery lot, hereabouts. It's time we were gone."

The wind blew as strongly as ever, the sea below looked as wicked as ever, but the rain had stopped and that made our search all that much easier. The stretch of the Sound from the sand quarry to Dolman Point yielded nothing. Neither did Loch Hynart. Between Loch Hynart and Carrara Point, eight miles to the west, there were only two tiny hamlets crouched against the water's edge, their backs to the barren hills behind, their inhabitants—if there were any inhabitants—subsisting on God alone knew what. Carrara Point was storm-torn desolation itself. Great jagged broken fissured cliffs, huge fanged rocks rising from the sea, massive Atlantic breakers smashing in hundred-foot-high spray against the cliffs, the rocks, and the tiny-seeming lighthouse at the foot of the cliffs. If I were Sir Billy Butlin looking for the site for my latest holiday camp, I wouldn't have spent too much time on Carrara Point.

We turned north now, then northeast, then east, along the southern shore of Loch Houron.

Many places have evil reputations. Few at first seeing live up to those reputations. But there are a few. In Scotland, the Pass of Glencoe, the scene of the infamous massacre, is one of them. The Pass of Brander is another. And Loch Houron was beyond all doubt another.

It required no imagination at all to see this as a dark and deadly and dangerous place. It looked dark and deadly and dangerous. The shores were black and rocky and precipitous and devoid of any form of vegetation at all. The four islands strung out in a line to the east were a splendid match for the hospitable appearance of the shores. In the far distance the northern and the southern shores of the loch came close together and vanished in a towering vertical cleft in the sinister brooding mountains. In the lee of the islands the waters were black as midnight but elsewhere it was a seething boiling white, the waters wickedly swirling, churning, spinning in evil-looking whirlpools as it passed across overfalls or forced its way through the narrow channels between the islands or between the islands and the shore. Water in torment. In the Beul nan Uamh—the mouth of the grave—between the first two islands the rushing leaping milk-white waters looked like floodwater in the Mackenzie River rapids in springtime, when the snows melt. A yachtsman's paradise. Only a madman would take his boat into these waters.

Apparently there were still a few madmen around. We'd just left the first of the islands, Dubh Sgeir, to port, when I caught sight of a narrow break in the cliffs on the southern mainland. A small rock-girt bay, if bay it could be called, about the size of a couple of tennis courts, almost completely enclosed from the sea, the entrance couldn't have been more than ten yards wide. I glanced at the chart—Little Horseshoe Bay, it was called. Not original, but very apt. There was a boat in there, a fairly big one, a converted MFV by the looks of her, anchored fore and aft in the middle of the bay. Behind the bay was a little plateau, mossy or grass-covered, I couldn't tell which, and, behind that, what looked like a dried-up river bed rising steeply into the hills behind. On the little plateau were four khaki-colored tents, with men working at them.

"This could be it?" Williams said.

"This could be it."

This wasn't it. A glance at the thin, wispy-bearded, pebble-bespectacled lad who came hurrying forward to greet me when I stepped on to the ground was all the proof I required that this was indeed not it. Another glance at the seven or eight bearded, scarved and duffel-coated characters behind him who had not, as I'd thought, been working but were struggling to prevent their tents from being blown away by the wind, was almost superfluous proof. That lot couldn't have hi-jacked a rowing boat. The MFV, I could see now, was down by the stern and listing heavily to starboard.

"Hallo, hallo, hallo," said the character with the wispy beard. "Good afternoon, good afternoon. By Jove, are we glad to see you!"

I looked at him, shook the outstretched hand, glanced at the listing boat and said mildly: "You may be shipwrecked, but those are hardly what I'd call desperate straits. You're not on a deserted island. You're on the mainland. Help is at hand!"

"Oh, we know where we are all right." He waved a deprecating hand. "We put in here three days ago but I'm afraid our boat was holed in a storm during the night. Most unfortunate, most inconvenient."

"Holed as she lay there? Just as she's moored now?"

"Yes, indeed."

"Bad luck. Oxford or Cambridge?"

"Oxford, of course." He seemed a bit huffed at my ignorance. "Combined geological and marine biological party."

"No shortage of rocks and sea water hereabouts," I agreed. "How bad is the damage?"

"A holed plank. Sprung. Too much for us, I'm afraid."

"All right for food?"

"Of course."

"No transmitter?"

"Receiver only."

"The helicopter pilot will radio for a shipwright and engineer to be sent out as soon as the weather moderates. Goodbye."

His jaw fell about a couple of inches. "You're off? Just like that?"

"Air-Sea Rescue. Vessel reported sinking last night."

"Ah, that. We heard."

"Thought you might be it. Glad for your sakes you're not. We've a lot of ground to cover yet."

We continued eastwards towards the head of Loch Houron. Halfway there I said: "Far enough. Let's have a look at those four islands out in the loch. We'll start with the most easterly one first of all—what's it called, yes, Eilean Oran—then make our way back towards the mouth of Loch Houron again."

"You said you wanted to go all the way to the top."

"I've changed my mind."

"You're the man who pays the piper," he said equably. He was a singularly incurious character, was young Lieutenant Williams. "Northward ho for Eilean Oran."

We were over Eilean Oran in three minutes. Compared to Eilean Oran, Alcatraz was a green and lovely holiday resort. Half a square mile of solid rock and never a blade of grass in sight. But there was a house. A house with smoke coming from its chimney. And beside it a boat-shed, but no boat. The smoke meant an inhabitant, at least one inhabitant, and however he earned his living he certainly didn't do it from tilling the good earth. So he would have a boat, a boat for fishing for his livelihood, a boat for transportation to the mainland, for one certain thing among the manifold uncertainties of

84

this world was that no passenger vessel had called at Eilean Oran since Robert Fulton had invented the steamboat. Williams set me down not twenty yards from the shed.

I rounded the corner of the boathouse and stopped abruptly. I always stop abruptly when I'm struck in the stomach by a battering ram. After a few minutes I managed to whoop enough air into my lungs to let me straighten up again.

He was tall, gaunt, grey, in his middle sixties. He hadn't shaved for a week or changed his collarless shirt in a month. It wasn't a battering ram he'd used after all, it was a gun, none of your fancy pistols, just a good old-fashioned double-barrelled twelve-bore shotgun, the kind of gun that at close range—six inches in this case—can give points even to the Peacemaker Colt when it comes to blowing your head off. He had it aimed at my right eye. It was like staring down the Mersey tunnel. When he spoke I could see he'd missed out on all those books that laud the unfailing courtesy of the Highlander.

"And who the hell are you?" he snarled.

"My name's Johnson. Put that gun away. I—"

"And what the hell do you want here?"

"How about trying the 'Ceud Mile Failte' approach?" I said. "You see it everywhere in these parts. A hundred thousand welcomes—"

"I won't ask again, mister."

"Air-Sea Rescue. There's a missing boat—"

"I haven't seen any boat. You can just get to hell off my island." He lowered his gun till it pointed at my stomach, maybe because he thought it would be more effective there or make for a less messy job when it came to burying me. "Now!"

I nodded to the gun. "You could get prison for this."

"Maybe I could and maybe I couldn't. All I know is that I don't like strangers on my island and that Donald MacEachern protects his own."

"And a very good job you make of it, too, Donald," I said approvingly. The gun moved and I said quickly: "I'm off. And don't bother saying 'haste ye back' for I won't be."

As we rose from the island Williams said: "I just caught a glimpse. That was a gun he had there?"

"It wasn't the outstretched hand of friendship they're always talking about in those parts," I said bitterly.

"Who is he? What is he?"

"He's an undercover agent for the Scottish Tourist Board in secret training to be their goodwill ambassador abroad. He's not any of those I'm looking for, that I know. He's not a nut case, either—he's as sane as you are. He's a worried man and a desperate one."

"You didn't look in the shed. You wanted to find out about a boat. Maybe there was someone pointing a gun at him."

"That was one of the thoughts that accounted for my rapid departure. I could have taken the gun from him."

"You could have got your head blown off."

"Guns are my business. The safety catch was in the 'On' position."

"Sorry." Williams' face showed how out of his depth he was, he wasn't as good at concealing his expressions as I was. "What now?"

"Island number two to the west here." I glanced at the chart. "Craigmore."

"You'll be wasting your time going there." He sounded very positive. "I've been there. Flew out a badly injured man to a Glasgow hospital."

"Injured how?"

"He'd cut himself to the thigh bone with a flensing knife. Infection had set in."

"A flensing knife? For whales? I'd never heard—"

"For sharks. Basking sharks. They're as common as mackerel hereabouts. Catch them for their livers—you can get a ton of liver oil from a good-sized one." He pointed to the chart, to a tiny mark on the North Coast. "Craigmore village. Been abandoned, they say, from before the First World War. We're coming up to it now. Some of those old boys built their homes in the damnedest places."

Some of those old boys had indeed built their homes in the damnedest places. If I'd been compelled to build a home either there or at the North Pole I'd have been hard put to it to make a choice. A huddle of four small grey houses built out near the tip of a foreland, several wicked reefs that made a natural breakwater, an even more wicked-looking entrance through the reefs and two fishing boats swinging and rolling wildly at anchor inside the reefs. One of the houses, the one nearest the shore, had had its entire seaward wall cut away. On the twenty or thirty feet of sloping ground that separated the house from the sea I could see three unmistakable sharks.

A handful of men appeared at the open end of the house and waved at us.

"That's their flensing shed," Williams said. "Haul them from the water straight up inside."

"It's one way of making a living. Can you put me down?"

"What do you think, Mr. Calvert?"

"I don't think you can." Not unless he set his helicopter down on top of one of the little houses, that was. "You winched this sick man up?"

"Yes. And I'd rather not winch you down, if you don't mind. Not in this weather and not without a crewman to help me. Unless you're desperate."

"Not all that desperate. Would you vouch for them?"

"I'd vouch for them. They're a good bunch. I've met the boss, Tim Hutchinson, an Aussie about the size of a house, several times. Most of the fishermen on the West Coast would vouch for them."

"Fair enough. The next island is Ballara."

We circled Ballara once. Once was enough. Not even a barnacle would have made his home in Ballara.

We were over the channel between Ballara and Dubh Sgeir now and the Beul nan Uamh was a sight to daunt even the stoutest-hearted fish. It certainly daunted me, five minutes in that lot whether in a boat or scuba suit and that would have been that. The ebb-tide and the wind were in head-on collision and the result was the most spectacular witches' cauldron I'd ever seen. There were no waves as such, just a bubbling swirling seething maelstrom of whirlpools, overfalls, and races, running no way and every way, gleaming boiling white in the overfalls and races, dark and smooth and evil in the hearts of the whirlpools. Not a place to take Aunty Gladys out in a rowboat for a gentle paddle in the quiet evenfall.

Oddly enough, close in to the east and south coast of Dubh Sgeir, one *could* have taken Aunty Gladys out. In those tidal races between islands a common but not yet clearly understood phenomenon frequently leaves an undisturbed stretch of water close in to one or other of the shores, calm and smooth and flat, a millpond with a sharply outlined boundary between it and the foaming races beyond. So it was here. For almost a mile between the most southerly and easterly headlands of Dubh Sgeir, for a distance of two or three hundred yards out from the shore, the waters were black and still. It was uncanny.

"Sure you really want to land here?" Williams asked.

"Is it tricky?"

"Easy. Helicopters often land on Dubh Sgeir. Not mine—others. It's just that you're likely to get the same reception here as you got on Eilean Oran. There are dozens of privately owned islands off the West Coast and none of them likes uninvited visitors. The owner of Dubh Sgeir hates them."

"This world-famous Highland hospitality becomes positively embarrassing at times. The Scotsman's home is his castle, eh?"

"There *is* a castle here. The ancestral home of the Clan Dalwhinnie. I think."

"Dalwhinnie's a town, not a clan."

"Well, something unpronounceable." That was good, considering that he like as not hailed from Rhosllanerchrugog or Pontrhydfendgaid. "He's the clan chief. Lord Kirkside. Ex-Lord Lieutenant of the shire. Very important citizen but a bit of a recluse now. Seldom leaves the place except to attend Highland Games or go south about once a month to flay the Archbishop of Canterbury in the Lords."

"Must be difficult for him to tell which place he's at, at times. I've heard of him. Used to have a very low opinion of the Commons and made a long speech to that effect every other day."

"That's him. But not any more. Lost his older son—and his future son-in-law—in an air accident some time ago. Took the heart from the old boy, so they say. People in those parts think the world of him."

We were round to the south of Dubh Sgeir now and suddenly the castle was in sight. Despite its crenellated battlements, round towers and embrasures, it didn't begin to rank with the Windsors and Balmorals of this world. A pocket castle. But the site had the Windsors and Balmorals whacked to the wide. It grew straight out of the top of a hundred and fifty foot cliff and if you leaned too far out of your bedroom window the first thing to stop your fall would be the rocks a long, long way down. You wouldn't even bounce once.

Below the castle and a fair way to the right of it a cliff fall belonging to some bygone age had created an artificial foreshore some thirty yards wide. From this, obviously at the cost of immense labor, an artificial harbor had been scooped out, the boulders and rubble having been used for the construction of a horseshoe breakwater with an entrance of not more than six or seven yards in width. At the inner end of this harbor a boathouse, no wider than the harbor entrance and less than twenty feet in length, had been constructed against the cliff face. A boathouse to berth a good-sized rowboat, no more.

Williams took his machine up until we were two hundred feet above the castle. It was built in the form of a hollow square with the landward side missing. The seaward side was dominated by two crenellated towers, one topped by a twenty foot flagpole and flag, the other by an even taller TV mast. Aesthetically, the flagpole had it every time. Surprisingly the island was not as barren as it had appeared from the sea. Beginning some distance from the castle and expending clear to the cliff-bound northern shore of the island ran a two hundred yard wide stretch of what seemed to be flat smooth turf, not the bowling green standard but undoubtedly grass of the genuine variety as testified to by the heads-down position of a handful of goats that browsed close to the castle. Williams tried to land on the grass but the wind was too strong to allow him to hold position: he finally put down in the eastern lee of the castle close but not too close to the cliff edge.

I got out, keeping a wary eye on the goats, and was rounding the landward corner of the castle when I almost literally bumped into the girl.

I've always known what to look for in a suddenly encountered girl in a remote Hebridean island. A kilt, of course, a Hebridean girl without a kilt was unthinkable, a Shetland two-piece and brown brogues: and that she would be a raven-haired beauty with wild, green, fey eyes went without saying. Her name would be Deirdre. This one wasn't like that at all, except for the eyes, which were neither green nor fey but certainly looked wild enough. What little I could see of them, that was. Her blonde hair was cut in the uniform peekaboo scalloped style of the day, the one where the long side hair meets under the chin and the central fringe is hacked off at eyebrow level, a coiffure which in any wind above Force one allows no more than ten percent of the face to be seen at any one time. Below hair level she wore a horizontally striped blue and white sailor's jersey and faded blue denim pants that must have been fixed on with a portable sewing machine as I didn't see how else she could have got into them. Her tanned feet were bare. It was comforting to see that the civilising influence of television reached even the remoter outposts of empire.

I said: "Good afternoon, Miss—um—"

"Engine failure?" she asked coldly.

"Well, no—"

"Mechanical failure? Of any kind? No? Then this is private property. I must ask you to leave. At once, please."

There seemed to be little for me here. An outstretched hand and a warm smile of welcome and she'd have been on my lists of suspects at once. But this was true to established form, the weary stranger at the gates receiving not the palm of the hand but the back of it. Apart from the fact that she lacked a blunderbuss and had a much better figure she had a great deal in common with Mr. MacEachern. I bent forward to peer through the wind-blown camouflage of blonde hair. She looked as if she had spent most of the night and half the morning down in the castle wine cellars. Pale face, pale lips, dark smudges under the blue-grey eyes. But clear blue-grey eyes.

"What the hell's the matter with you?" she demanded.

"Nothing. The end of a dream. Deirdre would never have talked like that. Where's your old man?"

"My old man?" The one eye I could see had the power turned up to its maximum shrivelling voltage. "You mean my father?"

"Sorry. Lord Kirkside." It was no feat to guess that she was Lord Kirkside's daughter, hired help are too ignorant to have the execrable manners of their aristocratic betters.

"I'm Lord Kirkside." I turned round to see the owner of the deep voice behind me, a tall rugged-looking character in his fifties, hawk nose, jutting grey eyebrows and moustache, grey tweeds, grey deer stalker, hawthorne stick in hand. "What's the trouble, Sue?"

Sue. I might have known. Exit the last vestige of the Hebridean dream. I said: "My name is Johnson. Air-Sea Rescue. There was a boat, the *Moray Rose,* in bad trouble somewhere south of Skye. If she'd been not under command but still afloat she might have come drifting this way. We wondered—"

"And Sue was going to fling you over the cliff before you had a chance to open your mouth?" He smiled down affectionately at his daughter. "That's my Sue. I'm afraid she doesn't like newspapermen."

"Some do and some don't. But why pick on me?"

"When you were twenty-one could you, as the saying goes, tell a newspaperman from a human being? I couldn't. But I

90

can now, a mile away. I can also tell a genuine Air-Sea Rescue helicopter when I see one. And so should you too, young lady. I'm sorry, Mr. Johnson, we can't help you. My men and I spent several hours last night patrolling the clifftops to see if we could see anything. Lights, flares, anything. Nothing, I'm afraid."

"Thank you, sir. I wish we had more voluntary cooperation of this kind." From where I stood I could see, due south, the gently rocking masts of the Oxford's field expedition's boat in Little Horseshoe Bay. The boat itself and the tents beyond were hidden behind the rocky eastern arm of the bay. I said to Lord Kirkside: "But why newspapermen, sir? Dubh Sgeir isn't quite as accessible as Westminster."

"Indeed, Mr. Johnson." He smiled, not with his eyes. "You may have heard of—well, of our family tragedy. My elder boy, Jonathon, and John Rollinson—Sue's fiancé."

I knew what was coming. And after all those months she had those smudges under her eyes. She must have loved him a lot. I could hardly believe it.

"I'm no newspaperman, sir. Prying isn't my business." It wasn't my business, it was my life, the *raison d'etre* for my existence. But now wasn't the time to tell him.

"The air accident. Jonathon had his own private Beechcraft." He waved towards the stretch of green turf running to the northern cliffs. "He took off from here that morning. They—the reporters—wanted on-the-spot reporting. They came by helicopter and boat—there's a landing stage to the west." Again the mirthless smile. "They weren't well received. Care for a drink? You and your pilot?" Lord Kirkside, for all the reputation Williams had given him, seemed to be cast in a different mould from his daughter and Mr. Donald MacEachern: on the other hand, as the Archbishop of Canterbury knew to his cost, Lord Kirkside was a very much tougher citizen than either his daughter or Mr. MacEachern.

"Thank you, sir. I appreciate that. But we haven't many hours of daylight left."

"Of course, of course. How thoughtless of me. But you can't have much hope left by this time."

"Frankly, none. But, well, you know how it is, sir."

"We'll cross our fingers for that one chance in a million. Good luck, Mr. Johnson." He shook my hand and turned away. His daughter hesitated then held out her hand and smiled. A fluke of the wind had blown the hair off her face, and when she smiled like that, sooty eyes or not, the end of

Deirdre and the Hebridean dream didn't seem to be of so much account after all. I went back to the helicopter.

"We're getting low on both fuel and time," Williams said. "Another hour or so and we'll have the dark with us. Where now, Mr. Calvert?"

"North. Follow this patch of grass—seems it used to be used as a light aircraft runway—out over the edge of the cliff. Take your time."

So he did, taking his time as I'd asked him, then continued on a northward course for another ten minutes. After we were out of sight of watchers on any of the islands we came round in a great half-circle to west and south and east and headed back for home.

The sun was down and the world below was more night than day as we came in to land on the sandy cove on the eastern side of the Isle of Torbay. I could just vaguely distinguish the blackness of the tree-clad island, the faint silvery gleam of the sand and the semicircular whiteness where the jagged reef of rocks fringed the seaward approach to the cove. It looked a very dicey approach indeed to me but Williams was as unworried as a baby's show mother who has already slipped the judge a five-pound note. Well, if he wasn't going to worry, neither was I: I knew nothing about helicopters but I knew enough about men to recognise a superb pilot when I sat beside one. All I had to worry about was that damned walk back through those Stygian woods. One thing, I didn't have to run this time.

Williams reached up his hand to flick on the landing lights, but the light came on a fraction of a second before his fingers touched the switch. Not from the helicopter but from the ground. A bright light, a dazzling light, at least a five-inch searchlight located between the high-water line of the cove and the tree-line beyond. For a moment the light wavered, then steadied on the cockpit of the helicopter, making the interior bright as the light from the noon-day sun. I twisted my head to one side to avoid the glare. I saw Williams throw up a hand to protect his eyes, then slump forward wearily, dead in his seat, as the white linen of his shirt turned red and the center of his chest disintegrated. I flung myself forwards and downwards to try to gain what illusory shelter I could from the cannonading submachine shells shattering the windscreen. The helicopter was out of control, dipping sharply forwards and spinning slowly on its axis. I reached out to grab the controls from the dead man's hands but even as I did the trajectory of the bullets changed, either because the man with the machine gun had altered his aim or because he'd been caught off balance by the sudden dipping of the helicopter. An abruptly mad cacophony of sound, the iron clangour of steel-nosed bullets smashing into the engine casing mingled with the banshee ricochet of spent and mangled shells. The engine stopped, stopped as suddenly as if the ignition had been switched off. The helicopter was completely out of control, lifeless in the sky. It wasn't going to be in the sky much longer but there was nothing I could do about it. I braced myself for the jarring moment of impact when we struck the water, and when the impact came it was not just jarring, it was shattering to a degree I could never have anticipated. We'd landed not in the water but on the encircling reef of rocks.

I tried to get at the door but couldn't make it; we'd landed nose down and facing seawards on the outside of the reefs and from the position where I'd been hurled under the instrument panel the door was above and beyond my reach. I was too dazed, too weak, to make any real effort to get at it. Icy water poured in through the smashed windscreen and the fractured floor of the fuselage. For a moment everything was as silent as the grave, the hiss of the flooding waters seemed only to emphasise the silence, then the machine gun started again. The shells smashed through the top of the windscreen above me. Twice I felt angry tugs on the right shoulder of my coat and I tried to bury my head even more deeply into the freezing waters. Then, due probably to a combination of an accumulation of water in the nose and the effect of the fusillade of bullets aft, the helicopter lurched forwards, stopped momentarily, then slid off the face of the reef and fell like a stone, nose first, to the bottom of the sea.

Among the more ridiculous and wholly unsubstantiated fic-
tions perpetuated by people who don't know what they are
talking about is the particularly half-witted one that death by
drowning is peaceful, easy and, in fact, downright pleasant.
It's not. It's a terrible way to die. I know, because I was
drowning and I didn't like it one little bit. My ballooning
head felt as if it were being pumped full of compressed air,
my ears and eyes ached savagely, my nostrils, mouth and
stomach were full of sea water and my bursting lungs felt as
if someone had filled them with petrol and struck a match.
Maybe if I opened my mouth, maybe if to relieve that
flaming agony that was my lungs I took that one great gasping breath that would be the last I would ever take, maybe
then it would be quiet and pleasant and peaceful. On the
form to date, I couldn't believe it.

The damned door was jammed. After the beating the fuselage had taken, first of all in smashing into the reef and then
into the seabed, it would be a miracle if it hadn't jammed. I
pushed the door, I pulled at it, I beat at it with clenched fists.
It stayed jammed. The blood roared and hissed in my ears,
the flaming vise around my chest was crushing my ribs and
lungs, crushing the life out of me. I braced both feet on the
instrument panel, laid both hands on the door handle. I thrust
with my legs and twisted with my hands, using the power and
the leverage a man can use only when he knows he is dying.
The door handle sheared, the thrust of my legs carried me
backwards and upwards towards the after end of the fuselage
and suddenly my lungs could take no more. Death couldn't
be worse than this agony. The air rushed out through my wa-
ter-filled mouth and nostrils and I sucked in this one great
gasping breath, this lungful of sea water, this last I would
ever take.

It wasn't a lungful of water, it was a lungful of air. Noxious compressed air laden with the fumes of petrol and oil,

but air for all that. Not the tangy salt-laden air of the Western Isles, not the wine-laden air of the Aegean, the pine-laden air of Norway or the sparkling champagne air of the high Alps. All those I'd tasted and all of them put together were a thin and anaemic substitute for this marvellous mixture of nitrogen and oxygen and petrol and oil that had been trapped in an air pocket under the undamaged upper rear part of the helicopter's fuselage, the only part of the plane that hadn't been riddled by machine-gun bullets. This was air as it ought to be.

The water level was around my neck. I took half-a-dozen deep whooping breaths, enough to ease the fire in my lungs and the roaring and hissing and dizziness in my head to tolerable levels, then pushed myself backwards and upwards to the extreme limit of the fuselage. The water was at chest level now. I moved a hand around in the blind darkness to try to estimate the amount of air available to me. Impossible to judge accurately, but enough, I guessed, compressed as it was, to last for ten to fifteen minutes.

I moved across to the left of the fuselage, took a deep breath and pushed myself forwards and downwards. Eight feet behind the pilot's seat was the passenger door, maybe I could force that. I found it right away, not the door but the opening where the door had been. The impact that had jammed the door on the right-hand side where I'd been had burst this door open. I pushed myself back to the upper part of the fuselage again and helped myself to a few more deep breaths of that compressed air. It didn't taste quite so good as it had the first time.

Now that I knew I could go at any time I was in no hurry to leave. Up above, guns in hand, those men would be waiting and if there was one outstanding attribute that characterized their attitude to work on hand, it was a single-minded thoroughness. Where those lads were concerned, a job half-done was no job at all. They could only have come there by boat and that boat would have been very nearby. By this time it would be even nearer by, it would be sitting directly over the spot where the helicopter had gone down and the crew wouldn't be sitting around with drinks in their hands congratulating themselves on their success, they'd be lining the side with searchlights or flashes and waiting to see if anyone would break surface. With their guns in their hands.

If I ever got back to the *Firecrest* again, if I ever got in touch with Uncle Arthur again, I wondered dully what I would say to him. Already I'd lost the *Nantesville*, already I'd been responsible for the deaths of Baker and Delmont, already I'd given away to the unknown enemy the secret of my identity—if that hadn't been obvious after the fake Customs officers had smashed our transmitter it was bitterly obvious now—and now I'd lost Lieutenant Scott Williams his life and the Navy a valuable helicopter. Of Uncle Arthur's forty-eight hours only twelve were left now, and nothing could be more certain than when Uncle Arthur had finished with me, I wouldn't be allowed even those twelve hours. After Uncle Arthur had finished with me my days as an investigator would be finished, and finished forever; with the kind of references he'd give me I wouldn't even qualify as a store detective in a street barrow. Not that it would make any difference what Uncle Arthur thought now. Baker and Delmont and Williams were gone. There was a heavy debt that had to be paid and the matter was out of Uncle Arthur's hands now. On the form to date, I thought bleakly, there wasn't one bookmaker in the land who would have given odds of one in a thousand of that debt ever being repaid. Only a fool bets against a certainty.

I wondered vaguely how long the men up top would wait—my conviction that they would be waiting was absolute. And then I felt a dry salty taste in my mouth that had nothing to do with the steadily deteriorating quality of air. It was pretty foul by this time, but a man can survive a surprisingly long time in foul air and there was enough oxygen left in that heavily tainted atmosphere to last me for a good few minutes yet.

The question was not how long they would wait but how long I could wait. Or had I already waited too long? I could feel the panic in my throat like some solid lump in my windpipe completely obstructing my breathing and had to make a conscious physical effort to force it down.

I tried to recall all I could from my marine salvage days. How long had I been under water and how deep down was I? How long had that dive down from the surface of the sea to the bottom taken? Under those conditions time loses all meaning. Say forty seconds. Just over halfway down I'd taken my last gulp of air before the water in the fuselage had flooded over my head. And then a minute, probably a minute and a half, fighting with that jammed door. Since then a minute to recover, half a minute to locate that open door, and then how long since? Six minutes, seven? Not less than seven.

I couldn't reckon on a total of less than ten minutes. The lump was back in my throat again.

How deep was I? That was the life-or-death question. I could tell from the pressure that I was pretty deep. But how deep? Ten fathoms? Fifteen? Twenty? I tried to recall the chart of Torbay Sound. There were eighty fathoms in the deepest channel and the channel was pretty close to the southern shore at this point, so that the water was steep-to. God above, I might even be in twenty-five fathoms. If I was, well, that was it. Finish. How did the decompression tables go again? At thirty fathoms a man who has been under water for ten minutes requires to spend eighteen minutes for decompression stops on the way up. When you breathe air under pressure, the excess nitrogen is stored in the tissues: when you begin to surface this nitrogen is carried by the blood stream to the lungs and is eliminated in respiration; and if you rise too rapidly respiration can't cope with it and nitrogen bubbles form in the blood, causing the agonising and crippling diver's bends. Even at twenty fathoms I'd require a six-minute halt for decompression on the way up and if there was one certain fact in life it was that decompression stops were out for me. I'd be a broken man. What I did know for certain was that every additional second I remained there would make the bends all the more agonising and crippling when they finally struck. All at once the prospect of surfacing beneath the steady guns and the pitiless eyes of the men above seemed positively attractive compared to the alternative. I took several deep breaths to get as much oxygen as possible into my blood stream, exhaled to the fullest extent, took a long final breath to fill every last cubic millimetre in every last nook and cranny in my lungs, dived under the water, pushed my way out through the doorway and made for the surface.

I'd lost count of time on the way down and I now lost all count of time on the way up. I swam slowly and steadily using enough power to assist my progress through the water, but not so much as prematurely to use up all the stored oxygen. Every few seconds I let a little air escape from my mouth, not much, just enough to ease the pressure in my lungs. I looked up but the waters above me were as black as ink, there could have been fifty fathoms above my head for any trace of light I could see. And then suddenly, quite some time before the air supply was exhausted and before my lungs had begun to hurt again, the water was a shade less than pitch black and my head struck something hard and un-yielding. I grabbed it, held on, surfaced, sucked in some lung-fuls of that cold salt wonderful air and waited for the de-compression pains to start, those sharply agonising twinges in the joints of the limbs. But none came. I couldn't have been more than fifteen fathoms down and even then I should have felt something. It had probably been something nearer ten.

During the past ten minutes my mind had taken as much a beating as any other part of me but it would have to have been in very much poorer shape than it was for me not to recognise what I was clinging to. A boat's rudder, and if any confirmation had been required the milkily phosphorescent water being turned up by the two slowly turning screws a couple of feet ahead of me would have been all that was re-quired. I'd surfaced right under their boat. I was lucky. I might have surfaced right under one of their propellers and had my head cut in half. Even now, if the man at the wheel suddenly decided to go astern I'd be sucked into the vortex of one or another of the screws and end up like something that had passed through a turnip-cutting machine. But I'd been through too much to cross any bridges before I came to them.

Off the port I could see, sharply illuminated by a couple of powerful lights from the boat's deck, the reef where we'd crashed. We were about forty yards away and, relative to the reefs, stationary in the water, the engines turning just enough to maintain the boat's position against the effect of wind and tide. Now and again a searchlight patrolled the dark waters all around. I couldn't see anything of the men on deck, but I didn't have to be told what they were doing, they were wait-ing and watching and the safety catches would be off. Nor could I see anything of the boat itself but I made up my mind that, even though I couldn't recognise it, I'd know it if I ever came across it again. I took out the knife from the sheath behind my neck and cut a deep vee notch in the trail-ing edge of the rudder.

For the first time, I heard voices. I heard four voices and I had no difficulty in the world in identifying any of them. If I lived to make Methuselah look a teenager I'd never forget any one of them.

"Nothing on your side, Quinn?" Captain Imrie, the man who had organised the manhunt for me aboard the *Nantes-ville*.

"Nothing on my side, Captain." I could feel the hairs rise

98

on the nape of my neck. Quinn. Durran. The bogus Customs officer. The man who had almost, but not quite, strangled me to death.

"Your side, Jacques?" Captain Imrie again.

"Nothing, sir." The machine pistol specialist. "Eight minutes since we've been here, fifteen since they went under. A man would require pretty good lungs to stay down that long, Captain."

"Enough," Imrie said. "There'll be a bonus for all of us for this night's work. Kramer?"

"Captain Imrie?" A voice as guttural as Imrie's own.

"Full ahead. Up the Sound."

I thrust myself backwards and dived deep. The waters above my head boiled into turbulent, phosphorescent life. I stayed deep, maybe ten feet down, heading for the reef. How long I swam like that, I don't know. Certainly less than a minute, my lungs weren't what they used to be, not even what they had been fifteen minutes ago; but when I was forced to the surface I'd my dark oilskin over my head.

I needn't have bothered. I could see the faintly shimmering outline of the disappearing wake, no more. The searchlights were extinguished; when Captain Imrie decided a job was finished, then that job was finished. Predictably, the boat was in complete darkness with neither interior nor navigation lights showing.

I turned and swam slowly towards the reef. I reached a rock and clung to it until a measure of strength returned to my aching muscles, to my exhausted body. I would not have believed that fifteen minutes could have taken so much out of a man. I stayed there for five minutes. I could have stayed there for an hour. But time was not on my side. I slipped into deep water again and made for the shore.

Three times I tried and three times I failed to pull myself up from the rubber dinghy over the gunwales of the *Firecrest*. Four feet, no more. Just four feet. A Matterhorn. A ten-year-old could have done it. But not Calvert. Calvert was an old, old man.

I called out for Hunslett, but Hunslett did not come. Three times I called, but he did not come. The *Firecrest* was dark and still and lifeless. Where the hell was he? Asleep? Ashore? No, not ashore, he'd promised to stay aboard in case word came through at any time from Uncle Arthur. Asleep, then, asleep in his cabin. I felt the blind unreasoning anger rise.

This was too much, after what I had been through this was too much. Asleep. I shouted at the top of my voice and hammered feebly on the steel hull with the butt of my Luger. But he didn't come.

The fourth time I made it. It was touch and go, but I made it. For a few seconds, dinghy painter in hand, I teetered on my stomach on the edge of the gunwale, then managed to drag myself aboard. I secured the painter and went in search of Hunslett. There were words I wished to have with Hunslett.

I never used them. He wasn't aboard. I searched the *Firecrest* from forepeak to the after stowage locker, but no Hunslett. No signs of a hasty depature, no remnants of a meal on the saloon table or unwashed dishes in the galley, no signs of any struggle, everything neat and in good order. Everything as it ought to have been. Except that there was no Hunslett.

For a minute or two I sat slumped in the saloon settee trying to figure out a reason for his absence, but only for a minute or two. I was in no condition to figure out anything. Wearily I made my way out to the upper deck and brought dinghy and outboard over the side. No fancy tricks about securing them to the anchor chain this time: apart from the fact that it was, the way I felt, physically impossible, the time for that was past. I deflated the dinghy and stowed it, along with the outboard, in the after locker. And if someone came aboard and started looking? If someone came aboard and started looking he'd get a bullet through him. I didn't care if he claimed to be a police superintendent or an assistant commissioner or the top Customs official in the country, he'd get a bullet through him, in the arm or leg, say, and I'd listen to his explanations afterwards. If it was one of my friends, one of my friends from *Nantesville* or the reef back there, he got it through the head.

I went below. I felt sick. The helicopter was at the bottom of the sea. The pilot was down there with it, half his chest shot away by machine-gun bullets. I'd every right to feel sick. I stripped off my clothes and towelled myself dry and the very action of towelling seemed to drain away what little strength was left to me. Sure I'd had a hard time in the last hour, all this running and slipping and stumbling through the dark woods, locating and blowing up the dinghy and dragging it over those damned seaweed covered boulders had taken it out of me, but I was supposed to be fit, it shouldn't

100

have left me like this. I was sick, but the sickness was in the heart and mind, not in the body.

I went into my cabin and laboriously dressed myself in fresh clothes, not forgetting the Paisley scarf. The rainbow colored bruises that Quinn had left on my neck had now swollen and spread to such an extent that I had to bring the scarf right up to the lobes of my ears to miss them. I looked in the mirror. It might have been my grandfather staring back at me. My grandfather on his deathbed. My face had that drawn and waxy look that one normally associates with approaching dissolution. Not an all-over waxiness though, there was no blood on my face now but the pine needles had left their mark. I looked like someone with galloping impetigo. I felt like someone with galloping bubonic plague.

I checked that the Luger and the little Lilliput—I'd put them both back in their waterproof covering after leaving Dubh Sgeir—were still in working order. They were. In the saloon I poured myself a stiff three fingers of whisky. It went down my throat like a ferret down a burrow after a rabbit, one moment there, the next vanished in the depths. The weary old red corpuscles hoisted themselves to their feet and started trudging around again. It seemed a reasonable assumption that if I encouraged them with some more of the same treatment they might even break into a slow gallop and I had just closed my hand around the bottle when I heard the sound of an approaching engine. I put the bottle back in the rack, switched out the saloon lights although they would have been invisible from outside through the velvet curtains—and took up position behind the open saloon door.

I was pretty sure the precautions were unnecessary, ten to one this was Hunslett coming back from shore, but why hadn't he taken the dinghy, still slung on the davits aft? Probably someone, for what Hunslett had regarded as an excellent reason, had persuaded him to go ashore and was now bringing him back.

The motorboat's engine slowed, went into neutral, astern, then neutral again. A slight bump, the murmur of voices, the sound of someone clambering aboard and then the engine opening up again.

The footfalls passed over my head as the visitor—there was only one set of footfalls—made his way towards the wheelhouse door. The springy confident step of a man who knew what he was about. There was only one thing wrong with that springy confident step. It didn't belong to Hunslett.

I flattened myself against the bulkhead, took out the Luger, slid off the safety catch and prepared to receive my visitor in what I had now come to regard as the best traditions of the Highlands.

I heard the click as the wheelhouse door opened, the louder click as it was shut by a firm hand. A pool of light from a flashlight preceded the visitor down the four steps from the wheelhouse to the saloon. He paused at the door of the steps and the light moved away as he made to locate the light switch. I stepped round the door and did three things at once—I hooked an arm around his neck, brought up a far from gentle knee into the small of his back and ground the muzzle of the Luger into his right ear. Violent stuff, but not unnecessarily violent stuff, it might have been my old friend Quinn. The gasp of pain was enough to show that it wasn't.

"This isn't a hearing aid you feel, friend. It's a Luger pistol. You're one pound pressure from a better world. Don't make me nervous."

The better world seemed to have no appeal for him. He didn't make me nervous. He made an odd gurgling noise in his throat, he was trying either to speak or breathe, but he stood motionless, head and back arched. I eased the pressure a little.

"Put that light switch on with your left hand. Slowly. Carefully."

He was very slow, very careful. The saloon flooded with light.

"Raise your hands above your head. As high as you can reach."

He was a model prisoner, this one, he did exactly as he was told. I turned him round, propelled him into the center of the room and told him to face me.

He was of medium height, nattily dressed in an Astrakhan coat and a fur Cossack hat. He had a beautifully trimmed white beard and moustache, with a perfectly symmetrical black streak in the center of the beard, the only one of its kind I had ever seen. The tanned face was red, either from anger or near-suffocation. From both, I decided. He lowered his hands without permission, sat on the settee, pulled out a monocle, screwed it into his right eye and stared at me with cold fury. I gave him look for look, stare for stare, pocketed the Luger, poured a whisky and handed it to Uncle Arthur. Rear-Admiral Sir Arthur Arnford-Jason, K.C.B., and all the rest of the alphabet.

102

"You should have knocked, sir," I said reproachfully.

"I should have knocked." His voice sounded half-strangled, maybe I had exerted more pressure than had been necessary. "Do you always greet your guests this way?"

"I don't have guests, sir. I don't have friends, either. Not in these Western Isles. All I have is enemies. Anyone who comes through that door is an enemy. I didn't expect to see you here, sir."

"I hope not. In view of that performance, I hope not." He rubbed his throat, drank some whisky and coughed. "Didn't expect to be here myself. Do you know how much bullion was aboard the *Nantesville?*"

"Close on a million, I understood."

"That's what I understood. Eight millions! Think of it, eight million pounds' worth. All this gold that's being shovelled back from Europe into the vaults at Fort Knox usually goes in small lots, eight 28-lb. ingots at a time. For safety. For security. In case anything goes wrong. But the Bank knew that nothing could go wrong this time, they knew our agents were aboard, they were behind with their payments, so they cleverly loaded six hundred and forty ingots without telling anyone. Eight million. The Bank is hopping mad. The Government is hopping mad. And everyone is taking it out on me."

And he's come up here to take it out on me. I said, "You should have let me know. That you were coming."

"I tried to. You failed to keep your noon-day schedule. The most elementary of crimes, Calvert, and the most serious. You failed to keep a schedule. You or Hunslett. Then I knew things were going from bad to worse. I knew I had to take over myself. So I came by plane and RAF rescue launch." That would have been the high-speed launch I'd seen taking a bad battering in the Sound as we had headed down towards the cove. "Where's Hunslett?"

"I don't know, sir."

"You don't know?" He was using his quiet unemphatic tone, the one I didn't care for very much. "You're out of your depth in this one, Calvert, aren't you?"

"Yes, sir. I'm afraid he's been removed by force. I'm not sure how. What have you been doing in the past two hours, sir?"

"Explain yourself." I wished he'd stop screwing that damned monocle into his eye. It was no affectation, that monocle, he was nearly blind on that side, but it was an irritating mannerism. At that moment, anything would have irritated me.

"That RAF launch that dropped you off here just now. It should have been here at least two hours ago. Why didn't you come aboard then?"

"I did. We almost ran the *Firecrest* down in the darkness as we came round the headland. No one here. So I went and had some dinner. Nothing but baked beans aboard this damned boat as far as I could see."

"The Columba Hotel wouldn't offer you much more. Toast below the beans, if you were lucky." The Columba was Torbay's only hotel.

"I had smoked trout, filet mignon and an excellent bottle of hock. I dined aboard the *Shangri-la*." This with the slight hint of a smile. Uncle Arthur's Achilles' heel was showing again: Uncle Arthur loved a lord like nobody's business, and a knight with a seven-figure income was as good as a lord any day.

"The *Shangri-la?*" I stared at him, then remembered. "Of course. You told me. You know Lady Skouras well. No, you said you knew her very well and her husband well. How is my old pal Sir Anthony?"

"Very well," he said coldly. Uncle Arthur had as much humor as the next man, but discussing titled millionaires in tones of levity was not humorous.

"And Lady Skouras?"

He hesitated. "Well—"

"Not so well. Pale, drawn, unhappy, with dark smudges under her eyes. Not unlike myself. Her husband mistreats her and mistreats her badly. Mentally and physically. He humiliated her in front of a group of men last night. And she had rope burns on her arms. Why would she have rope burns on her arms, Sir Arthur?"

"Impossible. Quite fantastic. I knew the former Lady Skouras, the one who died this year in hospital. She—"

"She was undergoing treatment in a mental hospital. Skouras as good as told me."

"No matter. She adored him. He adored her. A man can't change like that. Sir Anthony—Sir Anthony's a gentleman."

"Is he? Tell me how he made his first millions. You saw Lady Skouras, didn't you?"

"I saw her," he said slowly. "She was late. She arrived with the filet mignon." He didn't seem to find anything funny in that. "She didn't look very well and she's a bruise on her

104

right temple. She'd fallen climbing aboard from the tender and hit her head against a guard-rail."

"Hit her head against her husband's fist, more like. To get back to the first time you boarded the *Firecrest* this evening. Did you search it?"

"I searched it. All except the after cabin. It was locked. I assumed there was something in there you didn't want chance callers to see."

"There was something in there that callers, not chance, didn't want *you* to see," I said slowly. "Hunslett. Hunslett under guard. They were waiting for word of my death, then they'd have killed Hunslett or kept him prisoner. If word came through that I hadn't been killed, then they'd have waited until my return and taken me prisoner too. Or killed us both. For by then they would have known that I knew too much to be allowed to live. It takes time, a long time, to open up a strong room and get all those tons of gold out and they know their time is running out. They're desperate now. But they still think of everything."

"They were waiting for word of your death," Uncle Arthur said mechanically. "I don't understand."

"That helicopter you laid on for me, sir. We were shot down tonight after sunset. The pilot's dead and the machine is at the bottom of the sea. They believe me to be dead also."

"I see. You go from strength to strength, Calvert." The absence of reaction was almost total, maybe he was getting punch drunk by this time, more likely he was considering the precise phraseology that would return me to the ranks of the unemployed with economy and dispatch. He lit a long, thin and very black cheroot and puffed meditatively. "When we get back to London remind me to show you my confidential report on you."

"Yes, sir." So this was how it was coming.

"I was having dinner with the Under-Secretary just forty-eight hours ago. One of the things he asked me was which country had the best agents in Europe. Told him I'd no idea. But I told him who I thought, on the balance of probabilities, was the best in Europe. Philip Calvert."

"That was very kind of you, sir." If I could remove that beard, whisky, cheroot and monocle, at least three of which were obscuring his face at any given moment, his expression might have given me some faint clue as to what was going on in that devious mind. "You were going to fire me thirty-six hours ago."

"If you believe that," Uncle Arthur said calmly, "you'll believe anything." He puffed out a cloud of foul smoke and went on: "One of the comments in your reports states: 'Unsuitable for routine investigation. Loses interest and becomes easily bored. Operates at his best only under extreme pressure. At this level he is unique.' It's on the files, Calvert. I don't cut off my right hand."

"No, sir. Do you know what you are, sir?"

"A Machiavellian old devil," Uncle Arthur said with some satisfaction. "You know what's going on?"

"Yes, sir."

"Pour me another whisky, my boy, a large one, and tell me what's happened, what you know and what you think you know."

So I poured him another whisky, a large one, and told him what had happened, what I knew and as much of what I thought I knew as seemed advisable to tell him.

He heard me out, then said: "Loch Houron, you think?"

"Loch Houron it must be. I spoke to no one else, anywhere else, and to the best of my knowledge no one else saw me. Someone recognised me. Or someone transmitted my description. By radio. It must have been by radio. The boat that was waiting for Williams and myself came from Torbay or somewhere near Torbay, a boat from Loch Houron could never have made it to the eastern end of the Sound of Torbay in five times the time we took. Somewhere near here, on land or sea, is a transceiver set. Somewhere out on Loch Houron, there's another."

"This University expedition boat you saw on the south shore of Loch Houron. This alleged University expedition. It would have a radio transmitter aboard."

"No, sir. Boys with beards." I rose, pulled back the saloon curtains on both sides, then sat down again. "I told you their boat was damaged and listing. She'd been riding moored fore and aft in plenty of water. They didn't hole it themselves and it wasn't holed by any act of nature. Somebody kindly obliged. Another of those odd little boating incidents that occur with such profusion up and down the West Coast."

"Why did you pull those curtains back?"

"Another of those odd little boating incidents, sir. One that's about to happen. Some time tonight people will be coming aboard. Hunslett and I, those people think, are dead. At least, I'm dead and Hunslett is dead or a prisoner. But

106

they can't leave an abandoned *Firecrest* at anchor to excite suspicion and invite investigation. So they come in a boat, up anchor, and take the *Firecrest* out into the Sound, followed by their own boat. Once there, they'll slice through the flexible salt water cooling intake, open the salt water cock, take to their own boat and lift their hats as the *Firecrest* goes down to join the helicopter. As far as the big wide innocent world is concerned, Hunslett and I will just have sailed off into the sunset."

"And the gulfs will have washed you down," Uncle Arthur nodded. "You are very sure of this, Calvert?"

"You might say I'm absolutely certain."

"Then why open those blasted curtains?"

"The scuttling party may be coming from anywhere and they may not come for hours. The best time to scuttle a boat in close waters is at slack tide, when you can be sure that it will settle exactly where you want it to settle, and slack tide is not until one o'clock this morning. But if someone comes panting hotfoot aboard soon after those curtains are opened, then that will be proof enough that the radio transmitter we're after, and our friends who are working the transmitter, are somewhere in this bay, ashore or afloat."

"How will it be proof?" Uncle Arthur said irritably. "Why should they come, as you say, panting hotfoot?"

"They know they have Hunslett. At least, I assume they have, I can't think of any other reason for his absence. They think they know I'm dead, but they can't be sure. Then they see the beckoning oil lamp in the window. What is this, they say to themselves, Calvert back from the dead? Or a third, or maybe even a third and a fourth colleague of Calvert and Hunslett that we don't know of. Whether it's me or my friends, they must be silenced. And silenced at once. Wouldn't you come panting hotfoot?"

"There's no need to treat the matter with levity," Uncle Arthur complained.

"In your own words, sir, if you can believe that, you can believe anything."

"You should have consulted me first, Calvert." Uncle Arthur shifted in his seat, an almost imperceptible motion, though his expression didn't change. He was a brilliant administrator, but the more executive side of the business, the sand-baggings and pushing of people off high cliffs, wasn't exactly in his line. "I've told you that I came to take charge."

"Sorry, Sir Arthur. You'd better change that report, hadn't you? The bit about the best in Europe, I mean."

"*Touché, touché, touché,*" he grumbled. "And they're coming at us out of the dark, is that it? On their way now. Armed men. Killers. Shouldn't we—shouldn't we be preparing to defend ourselves? Dammit, man, I haven't even got a gun."

"You won't need one. You may not agree with me." I handed him the Luger. He took it, checked the indicator and that the safety catch moved easily, then sat there holding it awkwardly in his hand.

"Shouldn't we move, Calvert? We're sitting targets here."

"They won't be here for some time. The nearest house or boat is a mile away to the east. They'll be pushing wind and tide and they daren't use a motor. Whether they're towing a boat or paddling a rubber dinghy they have a long haul ahead of them. Time's short, sir. We have a lot to do tonight. To get back to Loch Houron. The expedition's out, they couldn't pirate a dinghy, far less five oceangoing freighters. Our friend Donald MacEachern acts in a highly suspicious fashion, he's got the facilities there, he's dead worried and he might have had half-a-dozen guns at his back while he had his in my front. But it was all too good to be true, professionals wouldn't lay it on the line like that."

"Maybe that's how professionals would expect a fellow-professional to react. And you said he's worried."

"Maybe the fish aren't biting. Maybe he's involved, but not directly. Then there's the shark fishers. They have the boats, the facilities and, heavens knows, they're tough enough. Against that, they've been based there for years, the place is littered with sharks—it should be easy enough to check if regular consignments of liver oil are sent to the mainland—and they're well known and well thought of along the coast. They'll bear investigating. Then there's Dubh Sgeir. Lord Kirkside and his lovely daughter Sue."

"Lady Susan," Uncle Arthur said. It's difficult to invest an impersonal, inflectionless voice with cool reproach, but he managed it without any trouble. "I know Lord Kirkside, of course"—his tone implied that it would be remarkable if he didn't—"and while I may or may not be right about Sir Anthony, and I will lay you a hundred to one, in pounds, that I am, I'm convinced that Lord Kirkside is wholly incapable of any dishonest or illegal action."

"Me, too. He's a very tough citizen, I'd say, but on the side of the angels."

"And his daughter? I haven't met her."

"Very much a girl of today. Dressed in the modern idiom, speaks in the modern idiom, I'm tough and I'm competent and I can take care of myself, thank you. She's not tough at all, just a nice old-fashioned girl in new-fashioned clothes."

"So that clears them." Uncle Arthur sounded relieved. "That leaves us the expedition, in spite of your sneers, or MacEachern's place, or the shark fishers. I go for the shark fishers myself."

I let him go for wherever he wanted to. I thought it was time I went to the upper deck and told him so.

"It won't be long now?"

"I shouldn't think so, sir. We'll put out the lights in the saloon here—it would look very odd if they peered in the windows and saw no one here. We'll put on the two sleeping cabin lights and the stern light. That will destroy their night-sight. The after deck will be bathed in light. For'ard of that, as far as they are concerned, it will be pitch dark. We hide in the dark."

"Where in the dark?" Uncle Arthur didn't sound very confident.

"You stand inside the wheelhouse. All wheelhouse doors are hinged for'ard and open outwards. Keep your hand on the inside handle. Lightly. When you feel it begin to turn, a very slow and stealthy turn, you can bet your boots, wait till the door gives a fraction, then kick the rear edge, just below the handle, with the sole of your right foot and with all the weight you have. If you don't break his nose or knock him overboard you'll at least set him in line for a set of false teeth. I'll take care of the other or others."

"How?"

"I'll be on the saloon roof. It's three feet lower than the wheelhouse roof so they can't see me silhouetted against the loom of the stern light even if they approach from the bows."

"But what are you going to do?"

"Clobber him or them. A nice big Stilson from the engine room with a rag round it will do nicely."

"Why don't we just dazzle them with torches and tell them to put their hands up?" Uncle Arthur clearly didn't care for my proposed modus operandi.

"Three reasons. These are dangerous and deadly men and you never give them warning. Not the true sporting spirit, but it helps you survive. Then there will almost certainly be night glasses trained on the *Firecrest* at this very moment. Finally, sound carries very clearly over water and the wind is blowing towards Torbay. Shots, I mean."

He said no more. We took up position and waited. It was still raining heavily with the wind still from the west. For once the rain didn't bother me, I'd a full set of oilskins on. I just lay there, spread-eagled on the saloon coach roof, occasionally easing the fingers of my hands, the right round the Stilson, the left round the little knife. After fifteen minutes they came. I heard the gentle scuff of rubber on our starboard side—the side of the wheelhouse door. I pulled on the cord which passed through the rear window of the wheelhouse. The cord was attached to Uncle Arthur's hand.

There were only two of them. My eyes were perfectly tuned to the dark by this time and I could easily distinguish the shape of the first man coming aboard just below where I lay. He secured a painter and waited for his mate. They moved forward together.

The leading man gave a cough of agony as the door smashed, fair and square, as we later established, into his face. I wasn't so successful. The second man had catlike reactions and had started to drop to the deck as the Stilson came down. I caught him on back or shoulder, I didn't know which, and dropped on top of him. In one of his hands he'd have either a gun or knife and if I'd wasted a fraction of a second trying to find out which hand and what he had in it, I'd have been a dead man. I brought down my left hand and he lay still.

I passed the other man lying moaning in agony in the scuppers, brushed by Uncle Arthur, pulled the saloon curtains to and switched on the lights. I then went out, half-pulled, half-lifted the moaning man through the wheelhouse door, down the saloon steps and dropped him on the carpet. I didn't recognise him. That wasn't surprising, his own mother or wife wouldn't have recognised him. Uncle Arthur was certainly a man who believed in working with a will and he'd left the plastic surgeon a very tricky job.

"Keep your gun on him, sir," I said. Uncle Arthur was looking down at his handiwork with a slightly dazed expression. What one could see of his face behind the beard seemed slightly paler than normal. "If he breathes, kill him."

"But—but look at his face, man. We can't leave—"

"You look at this, sir." I stooped and picked up the

weapon that had fallen from the man's hand as I'd dropped him to the floor. "This is what is technically known to the United States' police departments as a whippet. A shotgun with two-thirds of the barrel and two-thirds of the stock sawn off. If he'd got you first, you wouldn't have any face left at all. I mean that literally. Do you still feel like playing Florence Nightingale to the fallen hero?" That wasn't at all the way one should talk to Uncle Arthur, there would be a few more entries in the confidential report when we got back. If we got back. But I couldn't help myself, not then. I passed by Uncle Arthur and went out.

In the wheelhouee I picked up a small torch, went outside and shone it down into the water, hooding it with my hand so that the beam couldn't have been seen fifty yards away. They had a rubber dinghy, all right—and an outboard motor attached. The conquering heroes, bathed in that warm and noble glow of satisfaction that comes from the comforting realisation of a worth-while job well done, had intended to make it home the easy way.

Looping a heaving line round the outboard's cylinder head and hauling alternately on the heaving line and painter, I had both dinghy and outboard up and over in two minutes. I unclamped the outboard, lugged the dinghy round to the other side of the superstructure, the side remote from the inner harbor, and examined it carefully in the light of the torch. Apart from the manufacturer's name there was no mark on it, nothing to indicate to which craft it belonged. I sliced it to ribbons and threw it over the side.

Back in the wheelhouse, I cut a twenty foot length from a roll of PVC electric wiring cable, went outside again and lashed the outboard to the dead man's ankles. I searched his pockets. Nothing, I'd known there would be nothing, I was dealing with professionals. I hooded the torch and looked at his face. I'd never seen him before. I took from him the pistol still clutched in his right hand, undid the spring clips holding the guard chains in place above the gunwale slots for our companionway ladder, then eased first the outboard and then the man over the side. They vanished into the dark waters of Torbay harbor without the whisper of a splash. I went inside, closing wheelhouse and saloon doors behind me.

Uncle Arthur and the injured man had reversed positions by this time. The man was on his feet now, leaning drunkenly against the bulkhead, dabbing his face with a blood-stained towel Uncle Arthur must have found, and moaning from time to time. I didn't blame him, if I'd a broken nose, most of my front teeth displaced and a jaw that might or might not have been fractured, I'd have been moaning too. Uncle Arthur, gun in one hand and some more of my Scotch in the other, was sitting on the settee and contemplating his bloody handiwork with an odd mixture of satisfaction and distaste. He looked at me as I came in, nodded towards the prisoner.

"Making a fearful mess of the carpet," he complained. "What do we do with him?"

"Hand him over to the police."

"The police? You had your reservations about the police, I thought."

"Reservations is hardly the word. We have to make the break some time."

"Our friend outside, as well?"

"Who?"

"This fellow's—ah—accomplice."

"I threw him over the side."

Uncle Arthur made the mess on the carpet even worse. He spilt whisky all over it. He said: "You what?"

"There's no worry." I pointed downwards. "Twenty fathoms and thirty pounds of metal attached to his ankles."

"At—at the bottom of the sea?"

"What did you expect me to do with him? Give him a state funeral? I'm sorry, I didn't tell you, he was dead. I had to kill him."

"Had to? Had to?" He seemed upset. "Why, Calvert?"

"There's no 'why.' There's no justification needed. I killed him or he killed me, and then you, and now we'd both be where he is. Do you have to justify killing men who have murdered at least three times, probably oftener? And if that particular character wasn't a murderer, he came tonight to murder. I killed him with as little thought and compunction and remorse as I'd have tramped on a black widow spider."

"But you can't go around acting like a public executioner."

"I can and I will. As long as it's a choice between them and me."

"You're right, you're right." He sighed. "I must confess that reading your reports of an operation is quite different from being with you on one. But I must also confess that it's rather comforting having you around at times like this. Well, let's put this man in cells."

"I'd like to go to the *Shangri-la* first, sir. To look for Hunslett."

"I see. To look for Hunslett. Has it occurred to you, Calvert, that if they are hostile to us, as you admit is possible, that they may not let you look for Hunslett?"

"Yes, sir. It's not my intention to go through the *Shangri-la,* a gun in each hand, searching for him. I wouldn't get five feet. I'm just going to ask for him, if anyone has seen him. Assuming they really are the bandits, don't you think it might be most instructive, sir, to observe their reactions when they see a dead man walking aboard, especially a dead man coming alongside from a boat to which they'd shortly beforehand dispatched a couple of killers? And don't you think it will become more and more instructive to watch them as time passes by with no sign of First and Second Murderers entering left?"

"Assuming they are the bandits, of course."

"I'll know before we say goodbye to them."

"And how do we account for our knowing one another?"

"If they're white as the driven snow, we don't have to account to them. If they're not, they won't believe a damned word either of us say anyway."

I collected the roll of flex from the wheelhouse and led our prisoner to the after cabin. I told him to sit down with his back to one of the bulkhead generators and he did. Resistance was the last thought in his mind. I passed a few turns of flex around his waist and secured him to the generator: his feet I secured to one of the stanchions. His hands I left free. He could move, he could use the towel and the bucket of cold fresh water I left to administer first aid to himself whenever he felt like it. But he was beyond the reach of any glass or sharp instrument with which he could either free himself or do himself in. On the latter score I wasn't really worried one way or another.

I started the engines, weighed anchor, switched on the navigation lights and headed for the *Shangri-la.* Quite suddenly, I wasn't tired any more.

6 • WEDNESDAY: 8:40 P.M.—10:40 P.M.

Less than two hundred yards from the *Shangri-la* the anchor clattered down into fifteen fathoms of water. I switched off the navigation lights, switched on all the wheelhouse lights, passed into the saloon and closed the door behind me.

"How long do we sit here?" Uncle Arthur asked.

"Not long. Better get into your oilskins now, sir. Next really heavy shower of rain and we'll go."

"They'll have had their night glasses on us all the way across the bay, you think?"

"No question of that. They'll still have the glasses on us. They'll be worried stiff, wondering what the hell has gone wrong, what's happened to the two little playmates they sent to interview us. *If* they are the bandits."

"They're bound to investigate again."

"Not yet. Not for an hour or two. They'll wait for their two friends to turn up. They may think that it took them longer than expected to reach the *Firecrest* and that we'd upped anchor and left before they got there. Or they may think they'd trouble with their dinghy." I heard the sudden drumming of heavy rain on the coach roof. "It's time to go."

We left by the galley door, felt our way aft, quietly lowered the dinghy into the water and climbed down the transom ladder into it. I cast off. Wind and tide carried us in towards the harbor. Through the driving rain we could dimly see the *Shangri-la's* riding light as we drifted by about a hundred yards from her port side. Halfway between the *Shangri-la* and the shore I started up the outboard motor and made back towards the *Shangri-la*.

The big tender was riding at the outer end of a boom which stretched out from the *Shangri-la's* starboard side about ten feet for'ard of the bridge. The stern of the tender was about fifteen out from the illuminated gangway. I approached from astern, upwind, and closed in on the gangway. An oilskinned figure wearing one of the *Shangri-la's* crew's

114

fancy French sailor hats came running down the gangway and took the painter.

"Ah, good evening, my man," Uncle Arthur said. He wasn't putting on the style, it was the way he talked to most people. "Sir Anthony is aboard?"

"Yes, sir."

"I wonder if I could see him for a moment?"

"If you could wait a—" The sailor broke off and peered at Sir Arthur. "Oh, it's—it's the Admiral, sir."

"Admiral Arnford-Jason. Of course—you're the fellow who ran me ashore to the Columba after dinner."

"Yes, sir. I'll show you to the saloon, sir."

"My boat will be all right here for a few moments." The unspoken implication was that I was his chauffeur.

"Perfectly, sir."

They climbed the gangway and went aft. I spent ten seconds examining the portable lead that served the gangway light, decided that it wouldn't offer much resistance to a good hefty tug, then followed the two men aft. I passed by the passage leading to the saloon and hid behind a ventilator. Almost at once the sailor emerged from the passage and made his way for'ard again. Another twenty seconds and he'd be yelling his head off about the mysteriously vanished chauffeur. I didn't care what he did in twenty seconds.

When I reached the partly open saloon door I heard Sir Arthur's voice.

"No, no, I really am most sorry to break in upon you like this. Well, yes, thank you, a small one if you will. Yes, soda, please." Uncle Arthur really was having a go at the whisky tonight. "Thank you, thank you. Your health, Lady Skouras. Your health, gentlemen. Mustn't delay you. Fact is, I wonder if you can help us. My friend and I are most anxious, really most anxious. I wonder where he is, by the way? I thought he was right behind—"

Cue for Calvert. I turned down the oilskin collar that had been obscuring the lower part of my face, removed the sou'-wester that had been obscuring most of the upper part of my face, knocked politely and entered. I said: "Good-evening, Lady Skouras. Good-evening, gentlemen. Please forgive the interruption, Sir Anthony."

Apart from Uncle Arthur there were six of them gathered round the fire at the end of the saloon. Sir Anthony standing, the others seated. Charlotte Skouras, Dollmann, Skouras' managing director, Lavorski, his accountant, Lord Charnley, his broker and a fifth man I didn't recognise. All had glasses in their hands.

Their reaction to my sudden appearance, as expressed by their faces, was interesting. Old Skouras showed a half-frowning, half-speculative surprise. Charlotte Skouras gave me a strained smile of welcome: Uncle Arthur hadn't been exaggerating when he spoke of that bruise, it was a beauty. The stranger's face was non-committal, Lavorski's inscrutable, Dollmann's rigid as if carved from marble and Lord Charnley's for a fleeting moment that of a man walking through a country churchyard at midnight when someone taps him on the shoulder. Or so I thought. I could have imagined it. But there was no imagination about the sudden tiny snapping sound as the stem of the glass fell soundlessly on to the carpet. A scene straight from Victorian melodrama. Our aristocratic broker friend had something on his mind. Whether the others had or not it was difficult to say. Dollmann, Lavorski, and, I was pretty sure, Sir Arthur could make their faces say whatever they wanted them to say.

"Good lord, Petersen!" Skouras' tone held surprise but not the surprise of a person welcoming someone back from the grave. "I didn't know you two knew each other."

"My goodness, yes. Petersen and I have been colleagues for years, Tony. UNESCO, you know." Uncle Arthur always gave out that he was a British delegate to UNESCO, a cover that gave him an excellent reason for his frequent trips abroad. "Marine biology may not be very cultural, but it's scientific and educational enough. Petersen's one of my star performers. Lecturing, I mean. Done missions for me in Europe, Asia, Africa, and South America." Which was true enough, only they weren't lecture missions. "Didn't even know he was here until they told me at the hotel. But dear me, dear me, musn't talk about ourselves. It's Hunslett. Petersen's colleague. And mine in a way. Can't find him anywhere. Hasn't been in the village. Yours is the nearest boat. Have you seen anything of him, anything at all?"

"Afraid I haven't," Skouras said. "Anybody here? No? Nobody?" He pressed a bell and a steward appeared. Skouras asked him to make enquiries aboard and the steward left. "When did he disappear, Mr. Petersen?"

"I've no idea. I left him carrying out experiments. I've been away all day collecting specimens. Jellyfish." I laughed deprecatingly and rubbed my inflamed face. "The poisonous type, I'm afraid. No sign of him when I returned."

"Could your friend swim, Mr. Petersen?" the stranger asked. I looked at him, a dark thickset character in his middle forties, with black snapping eyes deepset in a tanned face. Expressionlsss faces seemed to be the order of the day there, so I kept mine expressionless. It wasn't easy.

"I'm afraid not," I said quietly. "I'm afraid you're thinking along the same lines as myself. We've no guard-rails aft. A careless step—" I broke off as the steward re-entered and reported that no one had seen a sign of Hunslett, then went on: "I think I should report this to Sergeant MacDonald at once."

Everybody else seemed to think so, too, so we left. The cold slanting rain was heavier than ever. At the head of the gangway I pretended to slip, taking the gangway wandering lead with me. What with the rain, the wind, and the sudden darkness there was quite a bit of confusion and it was the better part of a minute before I was finally hauled on to the landing stage of the companionway. Old Skouras was commiseration itself and offered me a change of clothes at once but I declined politely and went back to the *Firecrest* with Uncle Arthur. Neither of us spoke on the way back.

As we secured the dinghy I said: "When you were at dinner on the *Shangri-la* you must have given some story to account for your presence here, for your dramatic appearance in the RAF rescue launch."

"Yes. It was a good one. I told them a vital UNESCO conference in Geneva was being dead-locked because of the absence of a certain Dr. Spenser Freeman. It happens to be true. In all the papers today. Dr. Freeman is not there because it suits us not to have him there. No one knows that, of course. I told them that it was of vital national importance that he should be there, that we'd received information that he was doing field research in Torbay and that the government had sent me here to get him back."

"Why send the launch away? That would seem odd."

"No. If he's somewhere in the wilds of Torbay I couldn't locate him before daylight. There's a helicopter, I said, standing by to fly him out. I've only to lift the phone to have it here in fifty minutes."

"And, of course, you weren't to know that the telephone lines were out of order. It might have worked—if you hadn't called at the *Firecrest* in the rescue launch *before* you went to the *Shangri-la*. You weren't to know that our friends who were locked in the after cabin when you went aboard would report back that they'd heard an RAF rescue launch here at such and such a time. They might have seen it through a porthole, but even that would be unnecessary, the engines are unmistakable. So now our friends know you're lying like a trooper. The chances are that they've now a very shrewd idea as to who exactly you are. Congratulations, sir. You've now joined the category I've been in for years—no insurance company in the world would issue you a life policy even on a 99 percent premium."

"Our trip to the *Shangri-la* has removed your last doubts about our friends out there?"

"Yes, sir. You saw the reaction of our belted broker, Lord Charnley. And him an aristocrat to boot!"

"A small thing to base a big decision on, Calvert," Uncle Arthur said coldly.

"Yes, sir." I fished my scuba suit from the after locker and led the way below. "I didn't fall into the water by accident. By accident on purpose. I didn't mention that when I was hanging on to the boat's rudder off the reef this evening I cut a notch in it. A deep vee notch. The *Shangri-la's* tender has a deep vee notch in it. Same notch, in fact. Same boat."

"I see. I see indeed." Uncle Arthur sat on the settee and gave me the combination of the cold blue eye and the monocle. "You forgot to give me advance notification of your intentions."

"I didn't forget." I started to change out of my soaking clothes. "I'd no means of knowing how good an actor you are, sir."

"I'll accept that. So that removed your last doubts."

"No, sir. Superfluous confirmation, really. I knew before then. Remember that swarthy character sitting beside Lavorski who asked me if Hunslett could swim. I'll bet a fortune to a penny that he wasn't at the *Shangri-la's* dinner table earlier on."

"You would win. How do you know?"

"Because he was in command of the crew of the boat who shot down the helicopter and killed Williams and hung around afterwards waiting to have a go at me. His name is Captain Imrie. He was the captain of the prize crew of the *Nantesville*."

Uncle Arthur nodded, but his mind was on something else. It was on the scuba suit I was pulling on.

"What the hell do you think you're going to do with that thing?" he demanded.

"Advance notification of intentions, sir. Won't be long. I'm taking a little trip to the *Shangri-la*. The *Shangri-la's* tender, rather. With a little homing device and a bag of sugar. With your permission, sir."

"Something else you forget to tell me, hey, Calvert? Like that breaking off the *Shangri-la's* gangway light was no accident?"

"I'd like to get there before they replace it, sir."

"I can't believe it, I can't believe." Uncle Arthur shook his head. For a moment I thought he was referring to the dispatch with which I had made the uneventful return trip to the *Shangri-la's* tender, but his next words showed that his mind was on higher and more important things. "That Tony Skouras should be up to his neck in this. There's something far wrong. I just *can't* believe it. Good God, do you know he was up for a peerage in the next List?"

"So soon? He told me he was waiting for the price to come down."

Uncle Arthur said nothing. Normally, he would have regarded such a statement as a mortal insult, as he himself automatically collected a life peerage on retirement. But nothing. He was as shaken as that.

"I'd like nothing better than to arrest the lot of them," I said. "But our hands are tied. We're helpless. But now that I know what we do know I wonder if you would do me a favor before we go ashore, sir. There are two things I want to know. One is whether Sir Anthony really was down at some Clyde shipyard a few days ago having stabilisers fitted—a big job that few yards would tackle in a yacht that size. Should find out in a couple of hours. People tell silly and unnecessary lies. Also I'd like to find out if Lord Kirkside has taken the necessary steps to have his dead son's title—he was Viscount somebody or other—transferred to his younger son."

"You get the set ready and I'll ask them anything you like," Uncle Arthur said wearily. He wasn't really listening to me, he was still contemplating with stunned disbelief the possibility that his future fellow peer was up to the neck in skulduggery on a vast scale. "And pass me that bottle before you go below."

At the rate Uncle Arthur was going, I reflected, it was providential that the home of one of the most famous distilleries in the Highlands was less than half a mile from where we were anchored.

I lowered the false head of the starboard diesel to the engine-room deck as if it weighed a ton. I straightened and stood there for a full minute, without moving. Then I went to the engine-room door.

"Sir Arthur?"

"Coming, coming." A few seconds and he was at the doorway, the glass of whisky in his hand. "All connected up?"

"I've found Hunslett, sir."

Uncle Arthur moved slowly forward like a man in a dream.

The transmitter was gone. All our explosives and listening devices and little portable transmitters were gone. That had left plenty of room. They'd had to double him up to get him in, his head was resting on his forearms and his arms on his knees, but there was plenty of room. I couldn't see his face. I could see no marks of violence. Half-sitting, half-lying there he seemed curiously peaceful, a man drowsing away a summer afternoon by a sun-warmed wall. A long summer afternoon because forever was a long time. That's what I'd told him last night, he'd all the time in the world for sleep.

I touched his face. It wasn't cold yet. He'd been dead two to three hours, no more. I turned his face to see if I could find how he had died. His head lolled to one side like that of a broken rag doll. I turned and looked at Sir Arthur. The dreamlike expression had gone, his eyes were cold and bitter and cruel. I thought vaguely of the tales I'd heard, and largely discounted, of Uncle Arthur's total ruthlessness. I wasn't so ready to discount them now. Uncle Arthur wasn't where he was now because he'd answered an advertisement in the *Daily Telegraph*, he'd have been hand-picked by two or three very clever men who would have scoured the country to find the one man with the extraordinary qualifications they required. And they had picked Uncle Arthur, the man with the extraordinary qualifications, and total ruthlessness must have been one of the prime requisites. I'd never really thought of it before.

He said: "Murdered, of course."

"Yes, sir."

"How?"

"His neck is broken, sir."

"His neck? A powerful man like Hunslett?"

"I know a man who could do it with one twist of his hands. Quinn. The man who killed Baker and Delmont. The man who almost killed me."

120

"I see." He paused, then went on, almost absently: "You will, of course, seek out and destroy this man. By whatever means you choose. You can reconstruct this, Calvert?"

"Yes, sir." When it came to reconstruction when it was too damn late, I stood alone. "Our friend or friends boarded the *Firecrest* very shortly after I had left this morning. That is, before daylight. They wouldn't have dared try it after it was light. They overpowered Hunslett and kept him prisoner. Confirmation that he was held prisoner all day comes from the fact that he failed to meet the noon-day schedule. They still held him prisoner when you came aboard. There was no reason why you should suspect that there was anyone aboard—the boat that put them aboard before dawn would have gone away at once. They couldn't leave one of the *Shangri-la's* boats lying alongside the *Firecrest* all day."

"There's no necessity to dot i's and cross t's."

"No, sir. Maybe an hour or so after you departed the *Shangri-la's* tender with Captain Imrie, Quinn, and company aboard turns up: they report that I'm dead. That was Hunslett's death warrant. With me dead they couldn't let him live. So Quinn killed him. Why he was killed this way I don't know. They may have thought shots could be heard, they may not have wanted to use knives or blunt instruments in case they left blood all over the deck. They were intending to abandon the boat till they came back at night, at midnight, to take it out to the Sound and scuttle it and someone might have come aboard in the interim. My own belief is that he was killed this way because Quinn is a psychopath and compulsive killer and liked doing it this way."

"I see. And then they said to themselves: 'Where can we hide Hunslett till we come back at midnight? Just in case someone does come aboard.' And then they said: 'Ha! We know. We'll hide him in the dummy diesel.' So they threw away the transmitter and all the rest of the stuff—or took it with them. It doesn't matter. And they put Hunslett inside." Uncle Arthur had been speaking very quietly throughout and then suddenly, for the first time I'd ever known it, his voice became a shout. "How in the name of God did they know this was a dummy diesel, Calvert? How *could* they have known?" His voice dropped to what was a comparative whisper. "Someone talked, Calvert. Or someone was criminally careless."

"No one talked, sir. Someone was criminally careless. I was. If I'd used my eyes Hunslett wouldn't be lying there now. The night the two bogus Customs officers were aboard I knew that they had got on to something when we were in the engine room here. Up to the time that they'd inspected the batteries they'd gone through the place with a fine-tooth comb. After that they didn't give a damn. Hunslett even suggested that it was something to do with the batteries but I was too clever to believe him." I walked to the workbench, picked up a torch and handed it to Uncle Arthur. "Do you see anything about those batteries that would excite suspicion?"

He looked at me, that monocled eye still ice-cold and bitter, took the torch and examined the batteries carefully. He spent all of two minutes searching, then straightened.

"I see nothing," he said curtly.

"Thomas—the Customs man who called himself Thomas—did. He was on to us from the start. He knew what he was looking for. He was looking for a powerful radio transmitter. Not the tuppence ha' penny job we have up in the wheelhouse. He was looking for signs of a power take-off from those batteries. He was looking for the marks left by screw clamps or by a pair of saw-toothed, powerfully spring-loaded crocodile clips."

Uncle Arthur swore, very quietly, and bent over the batteries again. This time his examination took only ten seconds.

"You make your point well, Calvert." The eyes were still bitter, but no longer glacial.

"No wonder they knew exactly what I was doing today," I said savagely. "No wonder they knew that Hunslett would be alone before dawn, that I'd be landing at that cove this evening. All they required was radio confirmation from someone out in Loch Houron that Calvert had been snooping around there and the destruction of the helicopter was a foregone conclusion. All this damned fol-de-rol about smashing up radio transmitters and making us think that we were the only craft left with a transmitter. God, how blind can you be?"

"I assume that there's some logical thought behind this outburst," Uncle Arthur said coldly.

"That night Hunslett and I were aboard the *Shangri-la* for drinks. I told you that when we returned we knew that we'd had visitors. We didn't know why, then. My God!"

"You've already been at pains to demonstrate the fact that I was no brighter than yourself about the battery. It's not necessary to repeat the process—"

"Let me finish," I interrupted. Uncle Arthur didn't like being interrupted. "They came down to the engine room here. They knew there was a transmitter. They looked at that starboard cylinder head. Four bolts—the rest are dummies—with the paint well and truly scraped off. The port cylinder head bolts without a flake of paint missing. They take off this head, wire into the transceiver lines on the output side of the scrambler and lead out to a small radio transmitter hidden, like as not, behind the battery bank there. They'd have all the equipment with them for they knew exactly what they wanted to do. From then on they could listen in to our every word. They knew all our plans, everything we intended to do, and made their own plans accordingly. They figured—and how right they were—that it would be a damn sight less advantageous for them to let Hunslett and I have our direct communication with you and so know exactly what was going on than to wreck this set and force us to find some other means of communication that they couldn't check on."

"But why—but why destroy the advantage they held by—by—" He gestured at the empty engine casing.

"It wasn't an advantage any longer," I said tiredly. "When they ripped out that set Hunslett was dead and they thought Calvert was dead. They didn't need the advantage any more."

"Of course, of course. My God, what a fiendish brew this is." He took out his monocle and rubbed his eye with the knuckles of his hand. "They're bound to know that we will find Hunslett the first time we attempt to use this radio. I am beginning to appreciate the weight of your remark in the saloon that we might find it difficult to insure ourselves. They cannot know how much we know, but they cannot afford to take chances. Not with, what is it now, a total of seventeen million pounds at stake. They will have to silence us."

"Up and off is the only answer," I agreed. "We've been down here too long already, they might even be on their way across now. Don't let that Luger ever leave your hand, sir. We'll be safe enough under way. But first we must put Hunslett and our friend in the after cabin ashore."

"Yes. Yes, we must put them ashore first."

At the best of times, weighing anchor by electric windlass is not job for a moron, even an alert moron. Even our small windlass had a pull of over 1400 pounds. A carelessly placed hand or foot, a flapping trouser leg or the trailing skirts of an oilskin, any of those being caught up between chain and drum and you can be minus a hand or foot before you can cry out, far less reach the deck switch which is invariably placed abaft the windlass. Doing this on a wet slippery deck is twice as dangerous. Doing it on a wet slippery deck, in total darkness, heavy rain and with a very unstable boat beneath your feet, not to mention having the brake pawl off and the winch covered by a tarpaulin, is a highly dangerous practice indeed. But it wasn't as dangerous as attracting the attention of our friends on the *Shangri-la*.

Perhaps it was because of my total absorption in the job at hand, perhaps because of the muffled clank of the anchor coming inboard, that I didn't locate and identify the sound as quickly as I might. Twice I'd thought I'd heard the far-off sound of a woman's voice, twice I'd vaguely put it down to late-night revelry on one of the smaller yachts in the bay—it would require an IBM computer to work out the gallonage of gin consumed in British yacht harbors after the sun goes down. Then I heard the voice again, much nearer this time, and I put all thought of revelry afloat out of my mind. The only cry of desperation ever heard at a yacht party is when the gin runs out: this soft cry had a different quality of desperation altogether. I stamped on the deck switch, and all sound on the fo'c'sle ceased. The Lilliput was in my hand without my knowing how it had got there.

"Help me!" The voice was low and urgent and desperate. "For God's sake, help me."

The voice came from the water, amidships on the port side. I moved back silently to where I thought the voice had come from and stood motionless. I thought of Hunslett and I didn't move a muscle. I'd no intention of helping anyone until I'd made sure the voice didn't come from some dinghy—a dinghy with two other passengers, both carrying machine guns. One word, one incautious flash of light, a seven pound pull on a trigger and Calvert would be among his ancestors if, that was, they would have anything to do with such a bloody fool of a descendant.

"Please! Please help me! Please!"

I helped her. Not so much because the desperation in the voice was unquestionably genuine as because of the fact that it as unquestionably belonged to Charlotte Skouras.

I pushed through between the scuppers and the lowest guard-rail a rubber tyre fender that was permanently attached to one of the guard-rail stanchions and lowered it to water level. I said: "Lady Skouras?"

"Yes, yes, it's me. Thank God, thank God!" Her voice

didn't come just as easily as that, she was gasping for breath and she had water in her mouth.

"There's a fender at the boat's side. Catch it."

A moment or two, then: "I have it."

"Can you pull yourself up?"

More splashing and gasping, then: "No. No, I can't do it."

"No matter. Wait." I turned round to go for Uncle Arthur but he was already by my side. I said softly in his ear: "Lady Skouras is down there in the water. It may be a trap. I don't think so. But if you see a light, shoot at it."

He said nothing but I felt his arm move as he took the Luger from his pocket. I stepped over the guard-rail and lowered myself till my foot came to rest on the lower part of the tyre. I reached down and caught her arm. Charlotte Skouras was no slender sylph-like figure, she had some bulky package tied to her waist, and I wasn't as fit as I'd been a long, long time ago, say about forty-eight hours, but with a helping hand from Uncle Arthur I managed to get her up on deck. Between us, we half-carried her to the curtained saloon and set her down on the settee. I propped a cushion behind her head and took a good look at her.

She'd never have made the front cover of *Vogue*. She looked terrible. Her dark slacks and shirt looked as if they had spent a month in the sea instead of probably only a few minutes. The long tangled auburn hair was plastered to her head and cheeks, her face was dead-white, the big brown eyes, with the dark half-circles, were wide open and frightened and both mascara and lipstick had begun to run. And she hadn't been beautiful to start with. I thought she was the most desirable woman I'd ever seen. I must be nuts.

"My dear Lady Skouras, my dear Lady Skouras!" Uncle Arthur was back among the aristocracy and showed it. He knelt by her side, ineffectually dabbing at her face with a handkerchief. "What in God's name has happened? Brandy, Calvert, brandy! Don't just stand there, man. Brandy!"

Uncle Arthur seemed to think he was in a pub but, as it happened, I did have some brandy left. I handed him the glass and said: "If you'll attend to Lady Skouras, sir, I'll finish getting the anchor up."

"No, no!" She took a gulp of the brandy, choked on it and I had to wait until she had finished coughing before she went on. "They're not coming for at least two hours yet. I know. I heard. There's something terrible going on, Sir Arthur. I had to come, I had to come."

"Now, don't distress yourself, Lady Skouras, don't distress yourself," Uncle Arthur said, as if she weren't distressed enough already. "Just drink this down, Lady Skouras."

"No, not that!" I got all set to take a poor view of this, it was damned good brandy, then I realised she was talking of something else. "Not Lady Skouras. Never again! Charlotte. Charlotte Meiner. Charlotte."

One thing about women, they always get their sense of priorities right. There they were on the *Shangri-la*, rigging up a home-made atom bomb to throw through our saloon windows and all she could think was to ask us to call her Charlotte. I said: "Why did you have to come?"

"Calvert!" Uncle Arthur's voice was sharp. "Do you mind? Lady—I mean, Charlotte—has just suffered a severe shock. Let her take her time to—"

"No." She struggled to an upright sitting position and forced a wan smile, half-scared, half-mocking. "No, Mr. Peterson, Mr. Calvert, whatever your name, you're quite right. Actresses tend to overindulge their emotions. I'm not an actress any longer." She took another sip of the brandy and a little color came back to her face. "I've known for some time that something was very far wrong aboard the *Shangri-la*. Strange men have been aboard. Some of the old crew were changed for no reason. Several times I've been put ashore with the stewardess in hotels while the *Shangri-la* went off on mysterious journeys. My husband—Sir Anthony—would tell me nothing. He has changed terribly since our marriage—I think he takes drugs. I've seen guns. Whenever those strange men came aboard I was sent to my stateroom after dinner." She smiled mirthlessly. "It wasn't because of any jealousy on my husband's part, you may believe me. The last day or two I sensed that everything was coming to a climax. Tonight, just after you were gone, I was sent to my stateroom. I left, but stayed out in the passage. Lavorski was talking. I heard him saying: 'If your admiral pal is a UNESCO delegate, Skouras, then I'm King Neptune. I know who he is. We all know who he is. It's too late in the day now and they know too much. It's them or us.' And then Captain Imrie—how I hate that man!—said: 'I'll send Quinn and Jacques and Kramer at midnight. At one o'clock they'll open the sea-cocks in the Sound'."

"Charming friends your husband has," I murmured.

She looked at me, half-uncertainly, half-speculatively and

said: "Mr. Petersen or Mr. Calvert—and I heard Lavorski call you Johnson—"

"It *is* confusing," I admitted. "Calvert. Philip Calvert."

"Well, Philip"—she pronounced it the French way and very nice it sounded too—"you are one great bloody fool if you talk like that. You are in deadly danger."

"Mr. Calvert," Uncle Arthur said sourly—it wasn't her language he disapproved of, it was this Christian name familiarity between the aristocracy and the peasants—"is quite aware of the danger. He has unfortunate mannerisms of speech, that's all. You are a very brave woman, Charlotte." Blue-bloods first-naming each other was a different thing altogether. "You took a great risk in eavesdropping. You might have been caught."

"I was caught, Sir Arthur." The smile showed up the lines on either side of her mouth but didn't touch her eyes. "That is another reason why I am here. Even without the knowledge of your danger, yes, I would have come. My husband caught me. He took me into my stateroom." She stood up shakily, turned her back to us and pulled up the sodden dark shirt. Right across her back ran three great blue-red weals. Uncle Arthur stood stock-still, a man incapable of movement. I crossed the saloon and peered at her back. The weals were almost an inch wide and running halfway round her body. Here and there were tiny blood-spotted punctures. Lightly I tried a finger on one of the weals. The flesh was raised and puffy, a fresh weal, as lividly genuine a weal as ever I'd clapped eyes on. She didn't move. I stepped back and she turned to face us.

"It is not nice, is it? It does not feel very nice." She smiled and again that smile. "I could show you worse than that."

"No, no, no," Uncle Arthur said hastily. "That will not be necessary." He was silent for a moment, then burst out: "My dear Charlotte, what you must have suffered. It's fiendish, absolutely fiendish. He must be—he must be inhuman. A monster. A monster, perhaps under the influence of drugs. I would never have believed it!" His face was brick-red with outrage and his voice sounded as if Quinn had him by the throat. Strangled. "No one would ever have believed it!"

"Except the late Lady Skouras," she said quietly. "I understand now why she was in and out of mental homes several times before she died." She shrugged. "I have no wish to go the same way. I am made of tougher stuff than Anna Skouras. So I pick up my bag and run away." She nodded at the small polythene bag of clothes that had been tied to her waist. "Like Dick Whittington, is it not?"

"They'll be here long before midnight when they discover you're gone," I observed.

"It may be morning before they find out. Most nights I lock my cabin door. Tonight I locked it from the outside."

"That helps," I said. "Standing about in those sodden clothes doesn't. There's no point in running away only to die of pneumonia. You'll find towels in my cabin. Then we can get you a room in the Columba hotel."

"I had hoped for better than that." The fractional slump of the shoulders was more imagined than seen, but the dull defeat in the eyes left nothing to the imagination. "You would put me in the first place they would look for me. There is no safe place for me in Torbay. They will catch me and bring me back and my husband will take me into that stateroom again. My only hope is to run away. Your only hope is to run away. Please. Can we not run away together?"

"No."

"A man not given to evasive answers, is that it?" There was a lonely dejection, a proud humiliation about her that did very little for my self-respect. She turned towards Uncle Arthur, took both his hands in hers and said in a low voice: "Sir Arthur. I appeal to you as an English gentleman." Thumbs down on Calvert, that foreign-born peasant. "May I stay? Please?"

Uncle Arthur looked at me, hesitated, looked at Charlotte Skouras, looked into those big brown eyes and was a lost man.

"Of course you may stay, my dear Charlotte." He gave a stiff old-fashioned bow which, I had to admit, went very well with the beard and the monocle. "Yours to command, my dear lady."

"Thank you, Sir Arthur." She smiled at me, not with triumph or satisfaction, just an anxious-to-be-friendly smile. "It would be nice, Philip, to have the consent—what do you say?—unanimous."

"If Sir Arthur wishes to expose you to a vastly greater degree of risk aboard this boat than you would experience in Torbay, that is Sir Arthur's business. As for the rest, my consent is not required. I'm a well-trained civil servant and I obey orders."

"You are gracious to a fault," Uncle Arthur said acidly.

"Sorry, sir." I'd suddenly seen the light and a pretty dazzling beam it was too. "I should not have called your judgment in question. The lady is very welcome. But I think she should remain below while we are alongside the pier, sir."

"A reasonable request and a wise precaution," Sir Arthur said mildly. He seemed pleased at my change of heart, at my proper deference to the wishes of the aristocracy.

"It won't be for long." I smiled at Charlotte Skouras. "We leave Torbay within the hour."

"What do I care what you charge him with?" I looked from Sergeant MacDonald to the broken-faced man with the wet blood-stained towel, then back to MacDonald again. "Breaking and entering. Assault and battery. Illegal possession of a dangerous weapon with intent to create a felony—murder. Anything you like."

"Well, now. It's just not quite as easy as that." Sergeant MacDonald spread his big brown hands across the counter of the tiny police station and looked at the prisoner and myself in turn. "He didn't break and enter, you know, Mr. Petersen. He boarded. No law against that. Assault and Battery? It looks as if he has been the victim and not the perpetrator. And what kind of weapon was he carrying, Mr. Petersen?"

"I don't know. It must have been knocked overboard."

"I see. Knocked overboard, was it. So we have no real proof of any felonious intent."

I was becoming a little tired of Sergeant MacDonald. He was fast enough to cooperate with bogus Customs officers but with me he was just being deliberately obstructive. I said, "You'll be telling me next that it's all a product of my fevered imagination. You'll be telling me next that I just stepped ashore, grabbed the first passerby I saw, hit him in the face with a four-by-two then dragged him up here inventing this tale as I went. Even you can't be so stupid as to believe that."

The brown face turned red and, on the counter, the brown knuckles turned ivory. He said softly: "You'll kindly not talk to me like that."

"If you insist on behaving like a fool I'll treat you as such. Are you going to lock him up?"

"It's only your word against his."

"No. I had a witness. He's down at the old pier now, if you want to see him. Admiral Sir Arthur Arnford-Jason. A very senior civil servant."

"You had a Mr. Hunslett with you last time I was aboard your boat."

"He's down there, too." I nodded at the prisoner. "Why don't you ask a few questions of our friend here?"

"I've sent for the doctor. He'll have to fix his face first. I can't understand a word he says."

"The state of his face doesn't help," I admitted. "But the main trouble is that he speaks in Italian."

"Italian, is it? I'll soon fix that. The owner of the Western Isles cafe is an Italian."

"That helps. There are four little questions he might put to our pal here. Where is his passport, how he arrived in this country, who is his employer, and where does he live."

The sergeant looked at me for a long moment then said slowly: "It's a mighty queer marine biologist that you are, Mr. Petersen."

"And it's a mighty queer police sergeant that you are, Mr. MacDonald. Goodnight."

I crossed the dimly lit street to the sea wall and waited in the shadow of a phone booth. After two minutes a man with a small bag came hurrying up the street and turned into the police station. He was out again in five minutes, which wasn't surprising: there was little a GP could do for what was plainly a hospital job.

The station door opened again and Sergeant MacDonald came hurrying out, long black mackintosh buttoned to the neck. He walked quickly along the sea wall, looking neither to left nor right, which made it very easy for me to follow him, and turned down the old stone pier. At the end of the pier he flashed a torch, went down a flight of steps and began to haul in a small boat. I leaned over the pier wall and switched on my own torch.

"Why don't they provide you with a telephone or radio for conveying urgent messages?" I asked. "You could catch your death of cold rowing out to the *Shangri-la* on a night like this."

He straightened slowly and let the rope fall from his hands. The boat drifted out into the darkness. He came up the steps with the slow heavy tread of an old man and said quietly: "What did you say about the *Shangri-la*?" .   .

"Don't let me keep you, Sergeant," I said affably. "Duty before the idle social chitchat. Your first duty is to your masters. Off you go, now, tell them that one of their hirelings has

130

been severely clobbered and that Petersen has very grave suspicions about Sergeant MacDonald."

"I don't know what you are talking about," he said emptily. "The *Shangri-la*—I'm not going anywhere near the *Shangri-la*."

"Where are you going, then? Do tell. Fishing? Kind of forgotten your tackle, haven't you?"

"And how would you like to mind your own damn business?" MacDonald said heavily.

"That's what I'm doing. Come off it, Sergeant. Think I give a damn about our Italian pal. You can charge him with playing tiddlywinks in the High Street for all I care. I just threw him at you, together with a hint that you yourself were up to no good, to see what the reaction would be, to remove the last doubts in my mind. You reacted beautifully."

"I'm maybe not the cleverest, Mr. Petersen," he said with dignity. "Neither am I a complete idiot. I thought you were one of them or after the same thing as them." He paused. "You're not. You're a Government agent."

"I'm a civil servant." I nodded to where the *Firecrest* lay not twenty yards away. "You'd better come to meet my boss."

"I don't take orders from civil servants."

"Suit yourself," I said indifferently, turned away and looked out over the sea wall. "About your two sons, Sergeant MacDonald. The sixteen-year-old twins who, I'm told, died in the Cairngorms some time back."

"What about my sons?" he said tonelessly.

"Just that I'm not looking forward to telling them that their own father wouldn't lift a finger to bring them back to life again."

He just stood there in the darkness, quite still, saying nothing. He offered no resistance when I took his arm and led him towards the *Firecrest*.

Uncle Arthur was at his most intimidating and Uncle Arthur in full intimidating cry was a sight to behold. He'd made no move to rise when I'd brought MacDonald into the saloon and he hadn't asked him to sit. The blue basilisk stare, channelled and magnified by the glittering monocle, transfixed the unfortunate sergeant like a laser beam.

"So your foot slipped, Sergeant," Uncle Arthur said without preamble. He was using his cold, flat, quite uninflected voice, the one that curled your hair. "The fact that you stand here now indicates that. Mr. Calvert went ashore with a prisoner and enough rope for you to hang yourself and you seized it with both hands. Not very clever of you, Sergeant. You should not have tried to contact your friends."

"They are no friends of mine, sir," MacDonald said bitterly.

"I'm going to tell you as much as you need to know about Calvert—Petersen was a pseudonym—and myself and what we are doing." Uncle Arthur hadn't heard him. "If you ever repeat any part of what I say to anyone, it will cost you your job, your pension, any hope that you will ever again, in whatever capacity, get another job in Britain and several years in prison for contravention of the Official Secrets Act. I myself will personally formulate the charges." He paused, then added in a masterpiece of superfluity: "Do I make myself clear?"

"You make yourself very clear," MacDonald said grimly.

So Uncle Arthur told him all he thought MacDonald needed to know, which wasn't much, and finished by saying: "I am sure we can now count on your hundred percent cooperation, Sergeant."

"Calvert is just guessing at my part in this," he said dully.

"For God's sake!" I said. "You *knew* those Customs officers were bogus. You *knew* they had no photo copier with them. You *knew* their only object in coming aboard was to locate and smash that set and locate any other we might have. You *knew* they couldn't have gone back to the mainland in that launch—it was too rough. The launch, was, in fact, the *Shangri-la's* tender—which is why you left without lights—and no launch left the harbor after your departure. We'd have heard it. The only life we saw after that was when they switched on their lights in the *Shangri-la's* wheelhouse to smash up their own radio—*one* of their own radios, I should have said. And how did you *know* the telephone lines were down in the Sound? You knew they were down, but why did you say Sound? Because you *knew* they had been cut there. Then, yesterday morning, when I asked you if there was any hope of the lines being repaired you said no. Odd. One would have thought that you would have told the Customs boys going back to the mainland to contact the GPO at once. But you *knew* they weren't going back there. And your two sons, Sergeant, the boys supposed to be dead, you forgot to close their accounts. Because you *knew* they weren't dead."

"I forgot about the accounts," MacDonald said slowly.

132

"And all the other points—I'm afraid I'm not good at this sort of thing." He looked at Uncle Arthur. "I know this is the end of the road for me. They said they would kill my boys, sir."

"If you will extend us your full cooperation," Uncle Arthur said precisely, "I will personally see to it that you remain the Torbay police sergeant until you're falling over your beard. Who are 'they'?"

"The only men I've seen is a fellow called Captain Imrie and the two Customs men—Durran and Thomas. Durran's real name is Quinn. I don't know the others' names. I usually meet them in my house, after dark. I've been out to the *Shangri-la* only twice. To see Imrie."

"And Sir Anthony Skouras?"

"I don't know." MacDonald shrugged helplessly. "He's a good man, sir, he really is. Or I thought so. Maybe he is mixed up in this. Anyone can fall into bad company. It's very strange, sir."

"Isn't it? And what's been your part in this?"

"There's been funny things happening in this area in the past months. Boats have vanished. People have vanished. Fishermen have had their nets torn, in harbor, and yacht engines have been mysteriously damaged, also in harbor. This is when Captain Imrie wants to prevent certain boats from going certain places at the wrong time."

"And your part is to investigate with great diligence and a total lack of success," Uncle Arthur nodded. "You must be invaluable to them, Sergeant. A man with your record and character is above suspicion. Tell me, Sergeant, what are they up to?"

"Before God, sir, I have no idea."

"You're totally in the dark?"

"Yes, sir."

"I don't doubt it. This is the way the very top men operate. And you will have no ideas where your boys are being held?"

"No, sir."

"How do you know they're alive?"

"I was taken out to the *Shangri-la* three weeks ago. My sons had been brought there from God only knows where. They were well."

"And are you really so naïve as to believe that your sons will be well and will be returned alive when all this is over? Even although your boys will be bound to know who their

133

captors are and would be available for testimony and identification if the time came for that?"

"Captain Imrie said they would come to no harm. If I cooperated. He said that only fools ever used unnecessary violence."

"You are convinced, then, they wouldn't go the length of murder?"

"Murder! What are you talking about, sir?"

"Calvert?"

"Sir?"

"A large whisky for the sergeant."

"Yes, sir." When it came to lashing out with my private supplies Uncle Arthur was generous to a fault. Uncle Arthur paid no entertainment allowance. So I poured the sergeant a large whisky and, seeing that bankruptcy was inevitable anyway, did the same for myself. Ten seconds later the sergeant's glass was empty. I took his arm and led him to the engine room. When we came back to the saloon in a minute's time the sergeant needed no persuading to accept another glass. His face was pale.

"I told you that Calvert carried out a helicopter reconnaissance today," Uncle Arthur said conversationally. "What I didn't tell you was that his pilot was murdered this evening. I didn't tell you that two other of my best agents have been killed in the last sixty hours. And now, as you've just seen, Hunslett. Do you still believe, Sergeant, that we are dealing with a bunch of gentlemanly law-breakers to whom human life is sacrosanct?"

"What do you want me to do, sir?" Color was back in the brown cheeks again and the eyes were cold and hard and a little desperate.

"You and Calvert will take Hunslett ashore to your office. You will call in the doctor and ask for an official postmortem—we must have an official cause of death. For the trial. The other dead men are probably beyond recovery. You will then row out to the *Shangri-la* and tell Imrie that we brought Hunslett and the other man—the Italian—to your office. You will tell them that you heard us say that we must go to the mainland for new depth-sounding equipment and for armed help and that we can't be back for two days at least. Do you know where the telephone lines are cut in the Sound?"

"Yes, sir. I cut them myself."

"When you get back from the *Shangri-la* get out there and

fix them. Before dawn. Before dawn tomorrow you, your wife and son must disappear. For thirty-six hours. If you want to live. That is understood?"

"I understand what you want done. Not why you want it done."

"Just do it. One last thing. Hunslett has no relations—few of my men have—so he may as well be buried in Torbay. Knock up your local undertaker during the night and make arrangements for the funeral on Friday. Calvert and I would like to be there."

"But—but Friday? That's just the day after tomorrow."

"The day after tomorrow. It will be all over then. You'll have your boys back home."

MacDonald looked at him in long silence, then said slowly: "How can you be sure?"

"I'm not sure at all." Uncle Arthur passed a weary hand across his face and looked at me. "Calvert is. It's a pity, Sergeant, that the Secrets Act will never permit you to tell your friends that you once knew Philip Calvert. If it can be done, Calvert can do it. I think he can. I certainly hope so."

"I certainly hope so, too," MacDonald said sombrely.

Me too, more than either of them, but there was already so much despondency around that it didn't seem right to deepen it, so I just put on my confident face and led MacDonald back down to the engine room.

Three of them came to kill us, not at midnight as promised, but at 10:40 P.M. that night. Had they come five minutes earlier then they would have got us because five minutes earlier we were still tied up to the old stone pier. And had they come and got us that five minutes earlier, then the fault would have been mine for, after leaving Hunslett in the police station I had insisted that Sergeant MacDonald accompany me to use his authority in knocking up and obtaining service from the proprietor of the only chemist's shop in Torbay. Neither of them had been too keen on giving me the illegal help I wanted and it had taken me a full five minutes and the best part of my extensive repertoire of threats to extract from the very elderly chemist the minimum of reluctant service and a small green-ribbed bottle informatively labelled THE TABLETS. But I was lucky and I was back aboard the *Firecrest* just after 10:30 P.M.

The west coast of Scotland doesn't go in much for golden Indian summers and that night was no exception. Apart from being cold and windy, which was standard, it was also black as sin and bucketing heavily, which if not quite standard was at least not so unusual as to excite comment. A minute after leaving the pier I had to switch on the searchlight mounted on the wheelhouse roof. The western entrance to the Sound from Torbay harbor between Torbay and Garve Island, is a quarter of a mile wide and I could have found it easily on a compass course; but there were small yachts, I knew, between the pier and entrance and if any of them was carrying a riding light it was invisible in that driving rain.

The searchlight control was on the wheelhouse deckhead. I moved it to point the beam down and ahead, then traversed it through a forty-degree arc on either side of the bows.

I picked up the first boat inside five seconds, not a yacht riding at its moorings, but a rowing dinghy moving slowly through the water. It was fine on the port bow, maybe fifty yards away. I couldn't identify the man at the oars, the oars wrapped at their middle with some white cloth to muffle the sound of the rowlocks, because his back was towards me. A very broad back. Quinn. The man in the bows was sitting facing me. He wore oilskins and a dark beret and in his hand he held a gun. At fifty yards it's almost impossible to identify any weapon, but this looked like a German Schmeisser machine pistol. Without a doubt Jacques, the machinegun specialist. The man crouched low in the sternsheets was quite unidentifiable, but I could see the gleam of a short gun in his hand. Messrs. Quinn, Jacques, and Kramer coming to pay their respects as Charlotte Skouras had said they would. But much ahead of schedule.

Charlotte Skouras was on my right in the darkened wheelhouse. She'd been there only three minutes, having spent all our time alongside in her darkened cabin with the door closed. Uncle Arthur was on my left, desecrating the clean night air with one of his cheroots. I reached up for a clipped torch and patted my right-hand pocket to see if the Lilliput was still there. It was.

I said to Charlotte Skouras: "Open the wheelhouse door. Put it back on the catch and stand clear." Then I said to Uncle Arthur: "Take the wheel, sir. Hard a port when I call. Then back north on course again."

He took the wheel without a word. I heard the starboard wheelhouse door click on its latch. We were doing no more than three knots through the water. The dinghy was twenty-five yards away, the men in the bows and stern holding up arms to shield their eyes from our searchlight. Quinn had stopped rowing. On our present course we'd leave them at least ten feet on our port beam. I kept the searchlight steady on the boat.

Twenty yards separated us and I could see Jacques lining up his machine pistol on our light when I thrust the throttle lever right open. The note of the big diesel exhaust deepened and the *Firecrest* began to surge forward.

"Hard over now," I said.

Uncle Arthur spun the wheel. The sudden thrust of our single port screw boiled back against the port-angled rudder, pushing the stern sharply to starboard. Flame lanced from Jacques' machine pistol, a silent flame, he'd a silencer on. Bullets ricochetted off our aluminium foremast but missed both light and wheelhouse. Quinn saw what was coming and dug his oars deep but he was too late. I shouted "Midships, now!" pulled the throttle lever back to neutral and jumped out through the starboard doorway on to deck.

We hit them just where Jacques was sitting, breaking off the dinghy's bows, capsizing it and throwing the three men into the water. The overturned remains of the boat and a couple of struggling figures came slowly down the starboard side of the *Firecrest*. My torch picked up the man closer in to our side. Jacques, with the machine pistol held high above his head, instinctively trying to keep it dry though it must have been soaked when he had been catapulted into the water. I held gun hand and torch hand together, aiming down the bright narrow beam. I squeezed the Lilliput's trigger twice and a bright crimson flower bloomed where his face had been. He went down as if a shark had got him, the gun still in the stiffly upstretched arms. It was a Schmeisser machine pistol all right. I shifted the torch. There was only one other to be seen in the water and it wasn't Quinn, he'd either dived under the *Firecrest* or was sheltering under the upturned wreck of the dinghy. I fired twice more at the second figure and he started to scream. The screaming went on for two or three seconds, then stopped in a shuddering gurgle. I heard the sound of someone beside me on the deck being violently sick over the side. Charlotte Skouras. But I'd no time to stay and comfort Charlotte Skouras, she'd no damned right to be out on deck anyway. I had urgent matters to attend to, such as preventing Uncle Arthur from cleaving Torbay's old stone pier in half. The townspeople would not have liked it. Uncle Arthur's idea of midships differed sharply from mine, he'd brought the *Firecrest* round in a three-quarter circle. He would have been the ideal man at the helm of one of those ram-headed Phoenician galleys that specialized in cutting the opposition in two, but as a helmsman in Torbay harbor he lacked something. I jumped into the wheelhouse, pulled the throttle all the way to astern and spun the wheel to port. I jumped out again and pulled Charlotte Skouras away before she got her head knocked off by one of the barnacle-encrusted piles that fronted the pier. Whether or not we grazed the pier was impossible to say but we sure as hell gave the barnacles a nasty turn.

I moved back into the wheelhouse, taking Charlotte Skouras with me. I was breathing heavily. All this jumping in and out through wheelhouse doors took it out of a man. I said: "With all respects, sir, what the hell were you trying to do?"

"Me?" He was as perturbed as a hibernating bear in January. "Is something up, then?"

I moved the throttle to slow ahead, took the wheel from him and brought the *Firecrest* round till we were due north on a compass bearing. I said, "Keep it there, please," and did some more traversing with the searchlight. The waters around were black and empty, there was no sign even of the dinghy. I'd expected to see every light in Torbay lit up like a naval review, those four shots, even in the Lilliput's sharp, light-weight cracks, should have had them all on their feet. But nothing, no sign, no movement at all. The gin bottle levels would be lower than ever. I looked at the compass: north twenty west. Like the honeybee for the flower, the iron filing for the magnet, Uncle Arthur was determinedly heading straight for the shore again. I took the wheel from him, gently but firmly, and said: "You came a bit close to the pier back there, sir."

"I believe I did." He took out a handkerchief and wiped his monocle. "Damn' glass misted up just at the wrong moment. I trust, Calvert, that you weren't just firing at random out there." Uncle Arthur had become a good deal more bellicose in the past hour or so: he'd had a high regard for Hunslett.

"I got Jacques and Kramer. Jacques was the handy one with the automatic arms. He's dead. I think Kramer is too. Quinn got away." What a setup, I thought bleakly, what a setup. Alone with Uncle Arthur on the high seas in the darkness of the night. I'd always known that his eyesight, even in optimum conditions, was pretty poor: but I'd never suspected that, when the sun was down, he was virtually blind as a bat. But unfortunately, unlike the bat, Uncle Arthur wasn't equipped with a built-in radar which would enable him to shy clear of rocks, headlands, islands and suchlike obstructions of a similarly permanent and final nature with which we might go bump in the dark. To all intents and purposes I was single-handed. This called for a radical revision in plans, only I didn't see how I could radically revise anything.

"Not too bad," Uncle Arthur said approvingly. "Pity about Quinn, but otherwise not too bad at all. The ranks of the ungodly are being satisfactorily depleted. Do you think they'll come after us?"

"No. For four reasons. One, they won't know yet what has happened. Two, both their sorties this evening have gone badly and they won't be in a hurry to try any more boarding expeditions for some time. Three, they'd use the tender for this job, not the *Shangri-la* and if they get that tender a hundred yards I've lost all faith in Demerara sugar. Four, there's a mist of fog coming up. The lights of Torbay are obscured already. They can't follow us because they can't find us."

Till that moment the only source of illumination we'd had in the wheelhouse had come from the reflected light of the compass lamp. Suddenly the overhead light came on. Charlotte Skouras' hand was on the switch. Her face was haggard and she was staring at me as if I were the thing from outer space. Not one of those admiring affectionate looks.

"What kind of man are you, Mr. Calvert?" No "Philip" this time. Her voice was lower and huskier than ever and it had a shake in it. "You—you're not human. You kill two men and go on speaking calmly and reasonably as if nothing had happened. What in God's name are you, a hired killer? It's—it's unnatural. Have you no feelings, no emotions, no regrets?"

"Yes, I have. I'm sorry I didn't kill Quinn too."

She stared at me with something like horror in her face, then switched her gaze to Uncle Arthur. She said to him and her voice was almost a whisper: "I saw that man, Sir Arthur. I saw his face being blown apart by the bullets. Mr. Calvert could have—could have arrested him, held him up and handed him over to the police. But he didn't. He killed him. And the other. It was slow and deliberate. Why, why, why?"

"There's no 'why' about it, my dear Charlotte." Sir Arthur sounded almost irritable. "There's no justification needed. Calvert killed them or they killed us. They came to kill us. You told us that yourself. Would you feel any compunction at killing a poisonous snake? Those men were no better than that. As for arresting them!" Uncle Arthur paused, maybe for the short laugh he gave, maybe because he was trying to recall the rest of the homily I'd delivered to him earlier that evening. "There's no intermediate stage in this game. It's kill or be killed. These are dangerous and deadly men and you never give them warning." Good old Uncle Arthur, he'd remembered the whole lecture, practically word for word.

She looked at him for a long moment, her face uncomprehending, looked at me then slowly turned and left the wheelhouse.

I said to Uncle Arthur: "You're just as bad as I am."

She reappeared again exactly at midnight, switching on the

140

light as she entered. Her hair was combed and neat, her face was less puffy and she was dressed in one of those synthetic fibre dresses, white, ribbed and totally failing to give the impression that she stood in need of a good meal. From the way she eased her shoulders I could see that her back hurt. She gave me a faint tentative smile. She got none in return.

I said: "Half-an-hour ago, rounding Carrara Point, I near as dammit carried away the lighthouse. Now I hope I'm heading north of Dubh Sgeir but I may be heading straight into the middle of it. It couldn't be any blacker if you were a mile down in an abandoned coal mine, the fog is thickening, I'm a not very experienced sailor trying to navigate my way through the most dangerous waters in Britain and whatever hope we have of survival depends on the preservation of what night-sight I've slowly and painfully built up over the past hour or so. *Put out that damned light!*"

"I'm sorry." The light went out. "I didn't think."

"And don't switch on any other lights either. Not even in your cabin. Rocks are the least of my worries in Loch Houron."

"I'm sorry," she repeated. "And I'm sorry about earlier on. That's why I came up. To tell you that. About the way I spoke and leaving so abruptly, I mean. I've no right to sit in judgment on others and I think my judgment was wrong. I was just—well, literally shocked. To see two men killed like that, no, not killed, there's always heat and anger about killing, to see two men executed like that, because it was kill or be killed as Sir Arthur said, and then see the person who did it not care . . ." Her voice faded away uncertainly.

"You might as well get your facts and figures right, my dear," Uncle Arthur said. "Three men, not two. He killed one just before you came on board tonight. He had no option. But Philip Calvert is not what any reasonable man would call a killer. He doesn't care in the way you say, because if he did he would go mad. In another way, he cares very much. He doesn't do this job for the money. He's miserably paid for a man of his unique talents." I made a mental note to bring this up next time we were alone. "He doesn't do it for excitement, for—what is the modern expression?—kicks: a man who devotes his spare time to music, astronomy, and philosophy does not live for kicks. But he cares. He cares for the difference between right and wrong, between good and evil, and when that difference is great enough and the evil threatens to destroy the good, then he does not hesitate to take steps to redress the balance. And maybe that makes him better than either you or me, my dear Charlotte."

"And that's not all of it either," I said. "I'm also renowned for my kindness to little children."

"I'm sorry, Calvert," Uncle Arthur said. "No offence and no embarrassment, I hope. But if Charlotte thought it important enough to come up here and apologise, I thought it important enough to set the record straight."

"That's not all Charlotte came up for," I said nastily. "If that's what she came up for in the first place. She came up here because she's consumed with feminine curiosity. She wants to know where we are going."

"Do you mind if I smoke?" she asked.

"Don't strike the match in front of my eyes."

She lit the cigarette and said: "Consumed with curiosity is right. What do you think? Not about where we're going, I know where we're going. You told me. Up Loch Houron. What I want to know is what is going on, what all this dreadful mystery is about, why all the comings and goings of strange men aboard the *Shangri-la*, what is so fantastically important to justify the deaths of three men in one evening, what you are doing here, what you are, who you are. I never really thought you were a UNESCO delegate, Sir Arthur. I know now you're not. Please. I have the right to know, I think."

"Don't tell her," I advised.

"Why ever not?" Uncle Arthur said huffily. "As she says, she is deeply involved, whether she wants it or not. She does have the right to know. Besides, the whole thing will be public knowledge in a day or two."

"You didn't think of that when you threatened Sergeant MacDonald with dismissal and imprisonment if he contravened the Official Secrets Act."

"Merely because he could ruin things by talking out of turn," he said stiffly. "Lady—I mean, Charlotte—is in no position to do so. Not, of course," he went on quickly, "that she would ever dream of doing so. Preposterous. Charlotte is an old and dear friend, a *trusted* friend, Calvert. She shall know."

Charlotte said quietly: "I have the feeling that our friend Mr. Calvert does not care for me overmuch. Or maybe he just does not care for women."

"I care like anything," I said. "I was merely reminding the Admiral of his own dictum: 'Never, never, never'—I forget

142

how many nevers, I think there were four or five—'tell any-one anything unless it's necessary, essential and vital.' In this case it's none of the three."

Uncle Arthur lit another vile cheroot and ignored me. His dictum was not meant to refer to confidential exchanges be-tween members of the aristocracy. He said: "This is the case of the missing ships, my dear Charlotte. Five missing ships, to be precise. Not to mention a fair scattering of very much smaller vessels, also missing or destroyed."

"Five ships," I said. "On April 5th of this year the SS *Holm-wood* disappeared off the south coast of Ireland. It was an act of piracy. The crew was imprisoned ashore, kept under guard for two or three days, then released unharmed. The *Holm-wood* was never heard of again. On April 24th the MV *Antara* vanished in St. George's Channel. On May 17th the MV *Headley Pioneer* disappeared off Northern Ireland, on August 6th the SS *Hurricane Spray* disappeared after leaving the Clyde and, finally, last Saturday, a vessel called the *Nantesville* vanished soon after leaving Bristol. In all cases the crews turned up unharmed.

"Apart from their disappearance and the safe reappear-ances of their crews, those five vessels all had one thing in common—they were carrying extremely valuable and virtual-ly untraceable cargoes. The *Holmwood* had two and a half millions of pounds of South African gold aboard, the *Antara* had a million and a half pounds' worth of uncut Brazilian diamonds for industrial use, the *Headley Pioneer* had close on two million pounds' worth of mixed cut and uncut Andean emeralds from the Muzo mines in Colombia, the *Hurricane Spray*, which had called in at Glasgow en route from Rotter-dam to New York, had just over three million pounds' worth of diamonds, nearly all cut, and the last one, the *Nantesville*"—Uncle Arthur almost choked over this one—"had eight million pounds in gold ingots, reserves being called in by the U.S. Treasury.

"We had no idea where the people responsible for these disappearances were getting their information. Such arrange-ments as to the decision to ship, when, how and how much, are made in conditions of intense secrecy. They, whoever 'they' are, had impeccable sources of information. Calvert says he knows those sources now. After the disappearance of the first three ships and about six million pounds' worth of specie it was obvious that a meticulously organised gang was at work."

"Do you mean to say—do you mean to say that Captain Imrie is mixed up in this?" Charlotte asked.

"Mixed up is hardly the word," Uncle Arthur said drily. "He may well be the directing mind behind it all."

"And don't forget old man Skouras," I advised. "He's pretty deep in the mire, too—about up to his ears, I should say."

"You've no right to say that," Charlotte said quickly.

"No right? Why ever not? What's he to you and what's all this quick defense of the maestro of the bullwhip? How's your back now?"

She said nothing. Uncle Arthur said nothing, in a different kind of way, then went on:

"It was Calvert's idea to hide two of our men and a radio signal transmitter on most of the ships that sailed with cargoes of bullion or specie after the *Headley Pioneer* had vanished. We had no difficulty, as you can imagine, in securing the cooperation of the various exporting and shipping companies and governments concerned. Our agents—we had three pairs working—usually hid among the cargo or in some empty cabin or machinery space with a food supply. Only the masters of the vessels concerned knew they were aboard. They delivered a fifteen second homing signal at fixed—very precisely fixed—but highly irregular intervals. Those signals were picked up at selected receiving stations round the West Coast—we limited our stations to that area for that was where the released crews had been picked up—and by a receiver aboard this very boat here. The *Firecrest*, my dear Charlotte, is a highly unusual craft in many respects." I thought he was going to boast, quietly of course, of his own brilliance in designing the *Firecrest* but he remembered in time that I knew the truth.

"Between May 17th and August 6th, nothing happened. No piracy. We believe they were deterred by the short, light nights. On August 6th, the *Hurricane Spray* disappeared. We had no one aboard that vessel—we couldn't cover them all. But we had two men aboard the *Nantesville*, the ship that sailed last Saturday. Delmont and Baker. Two of our best men. The *Nantesville* was forcibly taken just off the Bristol Channel. Baker and Delmont immediately began the scheduled transmissions. Cross-bearings gave us a completely accurate position at least every half hour.

"Calvert and Hunslett were in Dublin, waiting. As soon—"

"That's right," she interrupted. "Mr. Hunslett. Where is he? I haven't seen—"

"In a moment. The *Firecrest* moved out, not following the *Nantesville* but moving ahead of its predicted course. They reached the Mull of Kintyre and had intended waiting till the *Nantesville* approached there but a southwesterly gale blew up out of nowhere and the *Firecrest* had to run for shelter. When the *Nantesville* reached the Mull of Kintyre area our radio beacon fixes indicated that she was still on a mainly northerly course and that it looked as if she might pass up the Mull of Kintyre on the outside—the western side. Calvert took a chance, ran up Loch Fyne and through the Crinan Canal. He spent the night in the Crinan sea basin. The sea loch is closed at night. Calvert could have obtained the authority to have it opened but he didn't want to: the wind had veered to westerly late that evening and small boats don't move out of Crinan through the Dorus Mor in a westerly gusting up to Force nine. Not if they have wives and families to support—and even if they haven't.

"During the night the *Nantesville* turned out west into the Atlantic. We thought we had lost her. We think we know now why she turned out: she wanted to arrive at a certain place at a certain state of the tide in the hours of darkness, and she had time to kill. She went west, we believe, firstly because it was the easiest way to ride out the westerly gale and, secondly, because she didn't want to be seen hanging around the coast all of the next day and preferred to make a direct approach from the sea as darkness was falling.

"The weather moderated a fair way overnight. Calvert left Crinan at dawn, almost at the very minute the *Nantesville* turned back east again. Radio transmissions were still coming in from Baker and Delmont exactly on schedule. The last transmission came at 1022 hours that morning: after that, nothing."

Uncle Arthur stopped and the cheroot glowed fiercely in the darkness. He could have made a fortune contracting out to the cargo shipping companies as a one-man fumigating service. Then he went on very quickly as if he didn't like what he had to say next, and I'm sure he didn't.

"We don't know what happened. They may have betrayed themselves by some careless action. I don't think so, they were too good for that. Some member of the prize crew may just have stumbled over their hiding place. Again it's unlikely, any man who stumbled over Baker and Delmont wouldn't be doing any more stumbling for some time to come. Calvert thinks, and I agree with him, that by the one unpredictable chance in ten thousand, the prize crew's radio operator happened to be traversing Baker and Delmont's wave band at the very moment they were sending their fifteen second transmission. At that range he'd about have his head blasted off and the rest was inevitable.

"A plot of the *Nantesville's* fixes between dawn and the last transmission showed her course as 082° true. Predicted destination—Loch Houron. Estimated time of arrival—sunset. Calvert had less than a third of the *Nantesville's* distance to cover. But he didn't take the *Firecrest* into Loch Houron because he was pretty sure that Captain Imrie would recognise a radio beacon transmitter when he saw one and would assume that we had his course. Calvert was also pretty sure that if the *Nantesville* elected to continue on that course—and he had a hunch that it would—that any craft found in the entrance to Loch Houron would receive pretty short shrift, either by being run down or sunk by gunfire. So he parked the *Firecrest* in Torbay and was skulking around the entrance to Loch Houron in a frogman's suit and with a motorized rubber dinghy when the *Nantesville* turned up. He went aboard in darkness. The name was changed, the flag was changed, one mast was missing and the superstructure had been repainted. But it was the *Nantesville*.

"Next day Calvert and Hunslett were storm-bound in Torbay but on Wednesday Calvert organised an air search for the *Nantesville* or some place where she might have been hidden. He made a mistake. He considered it extremely unlikely that the *Nantesville* would still be in Loch Houron because Imrie knew that we knew that he had been headed there and therefore would not stay there indefinitely, because the chart showed Loch Houron as being the last place in Scotland where anyone in their sane minds would consider hiding a vessel and because, after Calvert had left the *Nantesville* that evening, she'd got under way and started to move out to Carrara Point. Calvert thought she'd just stayed in Loch Houron till it was dark enough to pass undetected down the Sound of Torbay or round the south of Torbay Island to the mainland. So he concentrated most of his search on the mainland and on the Sound of Torbay and Torbay itself. He thinks now the *Nantesville* is in Loch Houron. We're going there to find out." His cheroot glowed again. "And that's it, my dear. Now, with your permission, I'd like to spend an

146

hour on the saloon settee. Those nocturnal escapades . . ." He sighed, and finished: "I'm not a boy any longer. I need my sleep."

I liked that. I wasn't a boy any longer either and I didn't seem to have slept for months. Uncle Arthur, I knew, always went to bed on the stroke of midnight and the poor man had already lost fifteen minutes. But I didn't see what I could do about it. One of my few remaining ambitions in life was to reach pensionable age and I couldn't make a better start than by ensuring that Uncle Arthur never never laid hands on the wheel of the *Firecrest*.

"But surely that's not it," Charlotte protested. "That's not all of it. Mr. Hunslett, where's Mr. Hunslett? And you said Mr. Calvert was aboard the *Nantesville*. How on earth did he—?"

"There are some things you are better not knowing, my dear. Why distress yourself unnecessarily? Just leave this to us."

"You haven't had a good look at me recently, have you, Sir Arthur?" she asked quietly.

"I don't understand."

"It may have escaped your attention but I'm not a child any more. I'm not even young any more. Please don't treat me as a juvenile. And if you want to get to that settee tonight—"

"Very well. If you insist. The violence, I'm afraid, has not all been one-sided. Calvert, as I said, was aboard the *Nantesville*. He found my two operatives, Baker and Delmont." Uncle Arthur had the impersonal emotionless voice of a man checking his laundry list. "Both men had been stabbed to death. This evening the pilot of Calvert's helicopter was killed when the machine was shot down in the Sound of Torbay. An hour after that Hunslett was murdered. Calvert found him in the *Firecrest's* engine room with a broken neck."

Uncle Arthur's cheroot glowed and faded at least half-a-dozen times before Charlotte spoke. The shake was back in her voice. "They are fiends. Fiends." A long pause, then: "How can you cope with people like that?"

Uncle Arthur puffed a bit more then said candidly: "I don't intend to try. You don't find generals slugging it out hand-to-hand in the trenches. Calvert will cope with them. Goodnight, my dear."

He pushed off. I didn't contradict him. But I knew that

Calvert couldn't cope with them. Not any more, he couldn't. Calvert had to have help. With a crew consisting of a myopic boss and a girl who, every time I looked at her, listened to her or thought of her, started the warning bells clanging away furiously in the back of my head, Calvert had to have a great deal of help. And he had to have it, fast.

After Uncle Arthur had retired, Charlotte and I stood in silence in the darkened wheelhouse. But a companionable silence. You can always tell. The rain drummed on the wheelhouse roof. It was as dark as it ever becomes at sea and the patches of white fog were increasing in density and number. Because of them I had cut down to half speed and with the loss of steerage way and that heavy westerly sea coming up dead astern I'd normally have been hard put to it to control the direction of the *Firecrest:* but I had the auto-pilot on and switched to "Fine" and we were doing famously. The auto-pilot was a much better helmsman than I was. And streets ahead of Uncle Arthur.

Charlotte said suddenly: "What is it you intend to do tonight?"

"You *are* a gourmand for information. Don't you know that Uncle Arthur—sorry, Sir Arthur—and I are engaged upon a highly secret mission. Security is all."

"And now you're laughing at me—and forgetting I'm along on this secret mission too."

"I'm glad you're along and I'm not laughing at you, because I'll be leaving this boat once or twice tonight and I have to have somebody I can trust to look after it when I'm away."

"You have Sir Arthur."

"I have, as you say, Sir Arthur. There's no one alive for whose judgment and intelligence I have greater respect. But at the present moment I'd trade in all the judgment and intelligence in the world for a pair of sharp young eyes. Going by tonight's performance, Sir Arthur shouldn't be allowed out without a white stick. How are yours?"

"Well, they're not so young any more, but I think they're sharp enough."

"So I can rely on you?"

"On me? I—well, I don't know anything about handling boats."

"You and Sir Arthur should make a great team. I saw you star once in a French film about—"

148

"We never left the studio. Even in the studio pool I had a stand-in."

"Well, there'll be no stand-in tonight." I glanced out through the streaming windows. "And no studio pool. This is the real stuff, the genuine Atlantic. A pair of eyes, Charlotte, that's all I require. A pair of eyes. Just cruising up and down till I come back and seeing that you don't go on the rocks. Can you do that?"

"Will I have any option?"

"Nary an option."

"Then I'll try. Where are you going ashore?"

"Eilean Oran and Craigmore. The two innermost islands in Loch Houron. If," I said thoughtfully, "I can find them."

"Eilean Oran and Craigmore." I could have been wrong but I thought the faint French accent a vast improvement on the original Gaelic pronunciation. "It seems so wrong. So very wrong. In the middle of all this hate and avarice and killing. These names—they breathe the very spirit of romance."

"A highly deceptive form of respiration, my dear." I'd have to watch myself, I was getting as bad as Uncle Arthur. "Those islands breathe the very spirit of bare, bleak and rocky desolation. But Eilean Oran and Craigmore hold the key to everything. Of that I'm very sure."

She said nothing. I stared out through the high-speed Kent clear-view screen and wondered if I'd see Dubh Sgeir before it saw me. After a couple of minutes I felt a hand on my upper arm and she was very close to me. The hand was trembling. Wherever she'd come by her perfume it hadn't been bought in a supermarket or fallen out of a Christmas cracker. Momentarily and vaguely I wondered about the grievous impossibility of ever understanding the feminine mind: before fleeing for what she had thought to be her life and embarking upon a hazardous swim in the waters of Torbay harbor, she hadn't forgotten to pack a sachet of perfume in her polythene kit-bag. For nothing was ever surer than that any perfume she'd been wearing had been well and truly removed before I'd fished her out of Torbay harbor.

"Philip?"

Well, this was better than the Mr. Calvert stuff. I was glad Uncle Arthur wasn't there to have his aristocratic feelings scandalized. I said: "Uh-huh?"

"I'm sorry." She said it as if she meant it and I supposed I should have tried to forget that she was once the best actress

149

in Europe. "I'm truly sorry. About what I said—about what I thought—earlier on. For thinking you were a monster. The men you killed, I mean. I—well, I didn't know about Hunslett and Baker and Delmont and the helicopter pilot. All your friends. I'm truly sorry, Philip. Truly."

She was overdoing it. She was also too damn close. Too damn warm. You'd have required a pile-driver in top condition to get a cigarette card between us. And that perfume that hadn't fallen out of a cracker—intoxicating, the ad-boys in the glossies would have called it. And all the time the warning bells were clanging away like a burglar alarm with the St. Vitus' dance. I made a manful effort to do something about it. I put my mind to higher things.

She said nothing. She just squeezed my arm a bit more and even the pile-driver would have gone on strike for piece-work rates. I could hear the big diesel exhaust thudding away behind us, a sound of desolate reassurance. The *Firecrest* swooped down the long overtaking combers, then gently soared again. I was conscious for the first time of a curious meteorological freak in the Western Isles. A marked rise in temperature after midnight. And I'd have to speak to the Kent boys about their guarantee that their clear-view screen wouldn't mist up under any conditions, but maybe that wasn't fair, maybe they'd never visualized conditions like this. I was just thinking of switching off the auto-pilot to give me something to do when she said: "I think I'll go below soon. Would you like a cup of coffee first?"

"As long as you don't have to put on a light to do it. And as long as you don't trip over Uncle Arthur—I mean it, Sir—"

"Uncle Arthur will do just fine," she said. "It suits him." Another squeeze of the arm and she was gone.

The meteorological freak was of short duration. By and by the temperature dropped back to normal and the Kent guarantee became operative again. I took a chance, left the *Firecrest* to its own devices and nipped aft to the stern locker. I took out my scuba diving equipment, together with air cylinders and mask, and brought them forward to the wheelhouse.

It took her twenty-five minutes to make the coffee. Calor Gas has many times the calorific efficiency of standard domestic coal gas and, even allowing for the difficulties of operating in darkness, this was surely a world record for slowness in making coffee at sea. I heard the clatter of crockery as the coffee was brought through the saloon and smiled cynically to myself in the darkness. Then I thought of Hunslett and Baker and Delmont and Williams, and I wasn't smiling any more.

I still wasn't smiling when I dragged myself on to the rocks of Eilean Oran, removed the scuba equipment and set the big, rectangular-based, swivel-headed torch between a couple of stones with its beam staring out to sea. I wasn't smiling, but it wasn't for the same reason that I hadn't been smiling when Charlotte had brought the coffee to the wheelhouse just over half an hour ago. I wasn't smiling because I was in a state of high apprehension and I was in a state of high apprehension because for ten minutes before leaving the *Firecrest* I'd tried to instruct Sir Arthur and Charlotte in the technique of keeping a boat in a constant position relative to a fixed mark on the shore.

"Keep her on a due west compass heading," I'd said. "Keep her bows on to the sea and wind. With the engine at 'Slow' that will give you enough steerage way to keep her head up. If you find yourselves creeping too far forwards, come round to the *south*"—if they'd come round to the north they'd have found themselves high and dry on the rocky shores of Eilean Oran—"Head due east at half speed, because if you go any slower you'll broach to, come sharply round to the north then head west again at slow speed. You can see those breakers on the south shore there. Whatever you do, keep them at least two hundred yards away on the starboard hand when you're going west and a bit more when you're going east."

They had solemnly assured me that they would do just that and seemed a bit chuffed because of what must have been my patent lack of faith in them both, but I'd reason for my lack of faith for neither had shown any marked ability to make a clear distinction between shore breakers and the north-south line of the foaming tops of the waves rolling eastwards toward the mainland. In desperation I'd said I'd place a fixed light on the shore and that that would serve as a permanent guide. I just trusted to God that Uncle Arthur wouldn't emulate the part of an eighteenth-century French sloop's skipper vis-à-vis the smugglers' lamp on a rock-girt Cornish shore and run the damned boat aground under the impression that he was heading for a beacon of hope. He was a very clever man, was Uncle Arthur, but the sea was not his home.

151

The boat-shed wasn't quite empty, but it wasn't far off it. I flashed my small torch around its interior and realised that MacEachern's boat-shed wasn't the place I was after. There was nothing there but a weather-beaten, gunwale-splintered launch, with, amidships, an unboxed petrol engine that seemed to be a solid block of rust.

I came to a house. On its northern side, the side remote from the sea, a light shone through a small window. A light at half past one in the morning. I crawled up to this and hitched a wary eye over the windowsill. A neat, clean, well-cared for small room, with lime washed walls, mat-covered stone floor and the embers of a driftwood fire smouldering in an ingle-nook in the corner. Donald MacEachern was sitting in a cane-bottomed chair, still unshaven, still in his month-old-shirt, his head bent, staring into the dull red heart of the fire. He had the look of a man who was staring into a dying fire because that was all that was left in the world for him to do. I moved round to the door, turned the handle and went inside.

He heard me and turned around, not quickly, just the way a man would turn who knows there is nothing left on earth that can hurt him. He looked at me, looked at the gun in my hand, looked at his own 12-bore hanging on a couple of nails on the wall, then sank back into his chair again.

He said tonelessly: "Who in the name of God are you?"

"Calvert's my name. I was here yesterday." I pulled off my rubber hood and he remembered all right. I nodded to the 12-bore. "You won't be needing that gun tonight, Mr. MacEachern. Anyway, you had the safety catch on."

"You don't miss much," he said slowly. "There were no cartridges in the gun."

"And no one standing behind you, was there?"

"I don't know what you mean," he said tiredly. "Who are you, man? What do you want?"

"I want to know why you gave me the welcome you did yesterday." I put the gun away. "It was hardly friendly, Mr. MacEachern."

"Who are you, sir?" He looked even older than he had yesterday, old and broken and done.

"Calvert. They told you to discourage visitors, didn't they, Mr. MacEachern?" No answer. "I asked some questions tonight of a friend of yours. Archie MacDonald. The Torbay police sergeant. He told me you were married. I don't see Mrs. MacEachern."

He half-rose from his cane chair. The old blood-shot eyes had a gleam to them. He sank back again and the eyes dimmed.

"You were out in your boat one night, weren't you, Mr. MacEachern? You were out in your boat and you saw too much. They caught you and they took you back here and they took Mrs. MacEachern away and they told you that if you ever breathed a word to anyone alive you would never see your wife that way again. Alive, I mean. They told you to stay here in case any chance acquaintances or strangers should call by and wonder why you weren't here and raise the alarm, and just to make sure that you wouldn't be tempted to go to the mainland for help—although heaven knows I would have thought there would be no chance in the world of you being as mad as that—they immobilised your engine. Salt-water impregnated sacks, I shouldn't wonder, so that any chance caller would think it was due to neglect and disuse, not sabotage."

"Aye, they did that." He stared sightlessly into the fire, his voice the sunken whisper of a man who is just thinking aloud and hardly aware that he is speaking. "They took her away and they ruined my boat. And I had my life savings in the back room there and they took that too. I wish I'd had a million pounds to give them. If only they had left my Mairi. She's five years older than myself." He had no defenses left.

"What in the name of God have you been living on?"

"Every other week they bring me tinned food, not much, and condensed milk. Tea I have, and I catch a fish now and then off the rocks." He gazed in the fire, his forehead wrinkling as if he were suddenly realising that I brought a new dimension into his life. "Who are you, sir? Who are you? You're not one of them. And you're not a policeman, I know you're not a policeman. I've seen them. I've seen policemen. But you are a very different kettle of fish." There were the stirrings of life in him now, life in his face and in his eyes. He stared at me for a full minute, and I was beginning to feel uncomfortable under the gaze of those faded eyes, when he said: "I know who you are. I know who you must be. You are a Government man. You are an agent of the British Secret Service."

Well, by God, I took my hat off to the old boy. There I was, looking nondescript as anything and buttoned to the chin in a scuba suit, and he had me nailed right away. So much for the inscrutable faces of the guardians of our country's secrets. I thought of what Uncle Arthur would have said to him, the automatic threats of dismissal and imprisonment if the old man breathed a word. But Donald MacEachern didn't have any job to be dismissed from and after a lifetime on Eilean Oran even a maximum security prison would have looked like a hostelry to which Egon Ronay would have lashed out six stars without a second thought, so as there didn't seem to be much point in threatening him I said instead, for the first time in my life: "I am an agent of the Secret Service, Mr. MacEachern. I am going to bring your wife back to you."

He nodded very slowly, then said: "You will be a very brave man, Mr. Calvert, but you do not know the terrible men who will wait for you."

"If I ever earn a medal, Mr. MacEachern, it will be a case of mistaken identification, but, for the rest, I know very well what I am up against. Just try to believe me, Mr. MacEachern. It will be all right. You were in the war, Mr. MacEachern."

"You know. You were told?"

I shook my head. "Nobody had to tell me."

"Thank you, sir." The back was suddenly very straight. "I was a soldier for twenty-two years. I was a sergeant in the 51st Highland Division."

"You were a sergeant in the 51st Highland Division," I repeated. "There are many people, Mr. MacEachern, and not all of them Scots, who maintain that there was no better in the world."

"And it is not Donald MacEachern who would be disagreeing with you, sir." For the first time the shadow of a smile touched the faded eyes. "There were maybe one or two worse. You make your point, Mr. Calvert. We were not namely for running away, for losing hope, for giving up too easily." He rose abruptly to his feet. "In the name of God, what am I talking about. I am coming with you, Mr. Calvert."

I rose to my feet and touched my hands to his shoulders. "Thank you, Mr. MacEachern, but no. You've done enough. Your fighting days are over. Leave this to me."

He looked at me in silence, then nodded. Again the suggestion of a smile. "Aye, maybe you're right. I would be getting in the way of a man like yourself. I can see that." He sat down wearily in his chair.

I moved to the door. "Goodnight, Mr. MacEachern. She will soon be safe."

"She will soon be safe," he repeated. He looked up at me, his eyes moist, and when he spoke his voice held the same faint surprise as his face. "You know, I believe she will."

"She will. I'm going to bring her back here personally and that will give me more pleasure than anything I've ever done in my life. Friday morning, Mr. MacEachern."

"Friday morning? So soon? So soon!" He was looking at a spot about a billion light years away and seemed unaware that I was standing by the open door. He smiled, a genuine smile of delight, and the old eyes shone. "I'll not sleep a wink tonight, Mr. Calvert. Nor a wink tomorrow night either."

"You'll sleep on Friday," I promised. He couldn't see me any longer, the tears were running down his grey unshaven cheeks, so I closed the door with a quiet hand and left him alone with his dreams.

8 • THURSDAY: 2 A.M.—4:30 A.M.

I had exchanged Eilean Oran for the island of Craigmore and I still wasn't smiling. I wasn't smiling for all sorts of reasons. I wasn't smiling because Uncle Arthur and Charlotte Skouras together made a nautical combination that terrified the life out of me, because the northern tip of Craigmore was much more exposed and reef-haunted than the south shore of Eilean Oran had been, because the fog was thickening, because I was breathless and bruised from big combers hurling me on to unseen reefs on my swim ashore, because I was wondering whether I had any chance in the world of carrying out my rash promise to Donald MacEachern. If I thought a bit more I'd no doubt I could come up with all sorts of other and equally valid reasons why I wasn't smiling, but I hadn't the time to think any more about it, the night was wearing on and I'd much to do before the dawn.

The nearest of the two fishing boats in the little natural harbor was rolling quite heavily in the waves that curled round the reef forming the natural breakwater to the west so I didn't have to worry too much about any splashing sound I might make as I hauled myself up on deck. What I did have to worry about was that damned bright light in its sealed inverted glass by the flensing shed, it was powerful enough to enable me to be seen from the other houses on shore. But my worry about it was a little thing compared to my gratitude for its existence. Out in the wild blue yonder Uncle Arthur could do with every beacon of hope he could find.

It was a typical MFV, about forty-five feet long and with the general look of a boat that could laugh at a hurricane. I went through it in two minutes. All in immaculate condition, not a thing aboard that shouldn't have been there. Just a genuine fishing boat. My hopes began to rise. There was no other direction they could go.

The second MFV was the mirror image of the first, down to the last innocuous inch. It wouldn't be true to say that my

156

hopes were now soaring, but at least they were getting up off the ground where they'd been for a long time.

I swam ashore, parked my scuba equipment above the highwater mark and made my way to the flensing shed, keeping its bulk between the light and myself as I went. The shed contained winches, steel tubs and barrels, a variety of ferocious weapons doubtless used for flensing, rolling cranes, some unidentifiable but obviously harmless machinery, the remains of some sharks and the most fearful smell I'd ever come across in my life. I left, hurriedly.

The first of the cottages yielded nothing. I flashed a torch through a broken window. The room was bare, it looked as if no one had set foot there for half a century, it was only too easy to believe Williams' statement that this tiny hamlet had been abandoned before the First World War. Curiously, the wallpaper looked as if it had been applied the previous day—a curious and largely unexplained phenomenon in the Western Isles. Your grandmother—in those days grandpa would have signed the pledge sooner than lift a finger inside the house—slapped up some wallpaper at ninepence a yard and fifty years later it was still there, as fresh as the day it had been put up.

The second cottage was as deserted as the first.

The third cottage, the one most remote from the flensing shed, was where the shark fishers lived. A logical and very understandable choice, one would have thought, the further away from that olfactory horror the better. Had I the option, I'd have been living in a tent on the other side of the island. But that was a purely personal reaction. The stench of that flensing shed was probably to the shark fishers as is the ammonia-laden, nostril-wrinkling, wholly awful *mist*—liquid manure—to the Swiss farmers: the very breath of being. The symbol of success. One can pay too high a price for success.

I eased open the well-oiled—shark liver oil, no doubt—door and passed inside. The torch came on again. Grandma wouldn't have gone very much on this front parlor but grandpa would cheerfully have sat there watching his beard turn white through the changing seasons without ever wanting to go down to the sea again. One entire wall was given up to food supplies, a miserable couple of dozen crates of whisky and scores upon scores of crates of beer. Australians, Williams had said. I could well believe it. The other three walls—there was hardly a scrap of wallpaper to be seen—was devoted to a form of art, in uninhibited detail and glorious

157

technicolor, of a type not usually to be found in the better-class museums and art galleries. Not grandma's cup of tea at all.

I skirted the furniture which hadn't come out of Harrods and opened the interior door. A short corridor lay beyond. Two doors to the right, three to the left. Working on the theory that the boss of the outfit probably had the largest room to himself, I carefully opened the first door to the right. The flashlight showed it to be a surprisingly comfortable room. A good carpet, heavy curtains, a couple of good armchairs, bedroom furniture in oak, a double bed, and a bookcase. A shaded electric light hung above the bed. Those rugged Australians believed in their home comforts. There was a switch beside the door. I touched it and the overhead lamp came on.

There was only one person in the double bed but even at that he was cramped in it. It's hard to gauge a man's height when he's lying down but if this lad tried to stand up in a room with a ceiling height of less than six feet four inches he'd finish up with concussion. His face was towards me but I couldn't see much of it, it was hidden by a head of thick black hair that had fallen over his brows and the most magnificently bushy black beard I'd ever clapped eyes on. He was sound asleep.

I crossed to the bed, prodded his ribs with the gun barrel and a pressure sufficient to wake a lad of his size and said: "Wake up."

He woke up. I moved a respectable distance away. He rubbed his eyes with one hairy forearm, got his hands under him and heaved himself to a sitting position. I wouldn't have been surprised to see him wearing a bearskin, but no, he was wearing a pair of pyjamas in excellent taste, I might have chosen the color myself.

Law-abiding citizens woken in the dark watches of the night by a gun-pointing stranger react in all sorts of ways, varying from terror to apoplectically purple outrage. The man in the beard didn't react in any of the standard ways at all. He just stared at me from under dark overhanging cliffs of eyebrows and the expression in the eyes was that of a Bengal tiger mentally tucking in his napkin before launching himself on the thirty foot leap that is going to culminate in lunch. I stepped back another couple of paces and said: "Don't try it."

"Put that gun away, sonny boy," he said. The deep rumbling voice seemed to come from the innermost recesses of the Carlsbad cavern. "Put it away or I'll have to get up and clobber you and take it from you."

"Don't be like that," I complained, then added politely: "If I put it away, will you clobber me?"

He considered this for a moment, then said: "No." He reached out for a big black cigar and lit it, his eyes on me all the time. The acrid fumes reached across the room and as it isn't polite for a guest in another's house to rush to open the nearest window without permission I didn't but it was a near thing. No wonder he'd never notice the stench from the flensing shed: compared to this, Uncle Arthur's cheroots came into the same category as Charlotte's perfume.

"My apologies for the intrusion. Are you Tim Hutchinson?"

"Yeah. And you, sonny boy?"

"Philip Calvert. I want to use one of your boats' transmitters to contact London. I also need your help. How urgently you can't imagine. A good many lives and millions of pounds can be lost in the next twenty-four hours."

He watched a particularly noxious cloud of this Vesuvian poison gas drift up to the cringing ceiling, then bent his eyes on me again. "Ain't you the little kidder, now, sonny boy."

"I'm not kidding, you big black ape. And, while we're at it, we'll dispense with the 'sonny boy.' Timothy."

He bent forward, the deep-set coal-black eyes not at all as friendly as I would have liked, then relaxed with a laugh. "Touché, as my French governess used to say. Maybe you ain't kidding at that. What are you, Calvert?"

In for a penny, in for a pound. This man would grant his cooperation for nothing less than the truth. And he looked like a man whose cooperation would be very well worth having. So, for the second time that night and the second time in my life, I said: "I'm an agent of the British Secret Service." I was glad that Uncle Arthur was out there fighting for his life on the rolling deep, his blood pressure wasn't what it ought to have been and a thing like this, twice in one night, could have been enough to see him off.

He considered my reply for some time, then said: "The Secret Service. I guess you have to be at that. Or a nut case. But you blokes never tell."

"I had to. It would have been obvious anyway when I tell you what I have to tell you."

"I'll get dressed. Join you in the front room in two minutes.

159

Help yourself to a Scotch there." The beard twitched and I deduced from this that he was grinning. "You should find some, somewhere."

I went out, found some somewhere and was conducting myself on the grand tour of the Craigmore art gallery when Tim Hutchinson came in. He was dressed all in black, trousers, sailor's jersey, mackinaw, and seaboots. Beds were deceptive, he'd probably passed the six foot four mark when he was about twelve and had just stopped growing. He glanced at the collection and grinned.

"Who would have thought it?" he said. "The Guggenheim and Craigmore. Hotbeds of culture, both of them. Don't you think the one with the earrings looks indecently overdressed?"

"You must have scoured the great galleries of the world," I said reverently.

"I'm no connoisseur. Renoir and Matisse are my cup of tea." It was so unlikely that it had to be true. "You look like a man in a hurry. Just leave out all the inessentials."

I left out the inessentials, but not one of the essentials. Unlike MacDonald and Charlotte, Hutchinson got not only the truth but the whole truth.

"Well, if that isn't the most goddamned story any man ever heard. And right under our bloody noses." It was hard to tell at times whether Hutchinson was Australian or American—I learnt later that he'd spent many years tuna-fishing in California. "So it was you in that chopper this afternoon. Brother, you've had a day and then some. I retract that 'sonny boy' crack. One of my more ill-advised comments. What do you want, Calvert?"

So I told him what I wanted, his own personal assistance that night, the loan of his boats and crews for the next twenty-four hours and the use of a radio transmitter immediately. He nodded.

"Count on us. I'll tell the boys. You can start using that transmitter right away."

"I'd rather go out with you to our boat right away," I said, "leave you there and come back in myself to transmit."

"You lack a mite confidence in your crew, hey?"

"I'm expecting to see the bows of the *Firecrest* coming through that front door any minute."

"I can do better than that. I'll roust out a couple of the boys, we'll take the *Charmaine*—that's the MFV nearest the flensing shed—out to the *Firecrest*, I'll go aboard, we'll cruise

160

around till you get your message off, then you come aboard the *Firecrest* while the boys take the *Charmaine* back again."

I thought of the maelstrom of white breakers outside the mouth of the alleged harbor. I said: "It won't be too dangerous to take an MFV out on a night like this?"

"What's wrong with a night like this? It's a fine fresh night. You couldn't ask for better. This is nothing, I've seen the boys take a boat out there, six o'clock in a black December evening, into a full gale."

"What kind of emergency was that?"

"A serious one, admittedly." He grinned. "We'd run out of supplies and the boys wanted to get to Torbay before the pubs shut. Straight up, Calvert."

I said no more. It was obviously going to be a great comfort to have Hutchinson around with me for the rest of the night. He turned towards the corridor and hesitated: "Two of the boys are married. I wonder——"

"There'll be no danger for them. Besides, they'll be well rewarded for their work."

"Don't spoil it, Calvert." For a man with such a deep rumbling voice he could make it very soft at times. "We don't take money for this kind of work."

"I'm not hiring you," I said tiredly. I'd quite enough people fighting me already without Tim Hutchinson joining their ranks. "There's an insurance reward. I have been instructed to offer you half."

"Ah, now, that's very different indeed. I'll be delighted to relieve the insurance companies of their excess cash at any time. But not half, Calvert, not half. Not for a day's work, not after all you've done. Twenty-five percent to us, seventy-five percent to you and your friends."

"Half is what you get. The other half will be used to pay compensation for those who have suffered hardship. There's an old couple on Eilean Oran, for instance, who are going to be wealthy beyond their dreams for the rest of their days."

"You get nothing?"

"I get my salary, the size of which I'd rather not discuss, as it's a sore point. Civil servants are not permitted to accept gratuities."

"You mean to say you get beaten up, shot down, half-drowned and suffer another couple of murder attempts just for a lousy pay check? What makes you tick, Calvert? Why the hell do you do it?"

"That's not an original question. I ask myself the same

question about twenty times a day, rather more often recently. It's time we were gone."

"I'll get the boys up. They'll be tickled pink by those gold watches or whatever the insurance boys will be handing over. Engraved, of course. We insist on that."

"The reward will be in cash, not kind. Depends how much of the stolen goods are recovered. We're pretty sure to recover all the *Nantesville*'s cargo. Chances are that we'll recover the lot. The award is ten percent. Yours will be five. The minimum you and your boys will pick up will be four hundred thousand pounds: the maximum will be eight hundred and fifty. Thousands pounds, I mean."

"Say that in English." He looked as if the London Post Office tower had fallen on top of him. So I said it again, and after a time he only looked as if a telegraph pole had fallen on him and said carefully: "At rates like that, a man might expect a fair bit of cooperation. Say no more. Put right out of your head any thoughts you had of advertising in the *Telegraph*. Tim Hutchinson is your man."

And Tim Hutchinson was undoubtedly my man. On a night like that, dark as doomsday, rain sluicing down and a thickening mist making it impossible—for me, at least—to tell the difference between a naturally breaking sea and a wave foaming over a reef, Tim Hutchinson was my man. Cheap at half a million.

He was one of that rare breed, that very rare breed, of naturals to whom the sea is truly home. Twenty years daily polishing and refining in every conceivable condition a rarely bestowed gift with which you must be born in the first place and anyone can be like this. Just as the great Grand Prix drivers, the Carraciolas and Nuvolaris and Clarks operate on a level incomprehensible to highly competent drivers of very fast cars, so Hutchinson operated on a level incomprehensible to the finest of amateur yachtsmen. Search your ocean racing clubs and Olympic yachting teams the world over and you will not find men like this. They are to be found, and even then so very seldom, only in the ranks of the professional deep sea fishermen.

Those huge hands on throttle and wheel had the delicacy of a moth. He had the night sight of a barn owl and an ear which could infallibly distinguish between waves breaking in the open sea, on reefs or on shores: he could invariably tell the size and direction of seas coming at him out of the darkness and mist and touch wheel to throttle as need be: he had an inbuilt computer which provided instant correlation of wind, tide, current and our own speed and always let him know exactly where he was. And I'll swear he could smell land, even on a lee shore and with the rest of us suffering olfactory paralysis from the fumes of the big black cigars which seemed to be an inseparable part of the man. It required only ten minutes beside him to realise that one's ignorance of the sea and ships was almost total. A chastening discovery.

He took the *Charmaine* out through the Scylla and Charybidis of that evil alleged harbor entrance under full throttle. Foaming white-fanged reefs reached out at us, bare feet away, on either side. He didn't seem to notice them. He certainly didn't look at them. The two "boys" he'd brought with him, a couple of stunted lads of about six foot two or thereabouts, yawned prodigiously. Hutchinson located the *Firecrest* a hundred yards before I could even begin to imagine I could see any shape at all and brought the *Charmaine* alongside as neatly as I could park my car by the kerb in broad daylight—on one of my better days, that was. I went aboard the *Firecrest* to the vast alarm of Uncle Arthur and Charlotte who'd heard no whisper of our arrival, explained the situation, introduced Hutchinson and went back aboard the *Charmaine*. Fifteen minutes later, the radio call over, I was back aboard the *Firecrest*.

Uncle Arthur and Tim Hutchinson were already thick as thieves. The bearded Australian giant was extremely courteous and respectful, calling Uncle Arthur "Admiral" every other sentence while Uncle Arthur was plainly delighted and vastly relieved to have him on board. If I felt this was a slight on my own seamanlike qualities, I was undoubtedly correct.

"Where are we off to now?" Charlotte Skouras asked. I was disappointed to see that she was just as relieved as Uncle Arthur.

"Dubh Sgeir," I said. "To pay a call on Lord Kirkside and his charming daughter."

"Dubh Sgeir!" She seemed taken aback. "I thought you said the answer lay in Eilean Oran and Craigmore?"

"So I did. The answers to some essential preliminary questions. But the end of the road lies in Dubh Sgeir. And the foot of the rainbow."

"You talk in riddles," she said impatiently.

"Not to me, he doesn't," Hutchinson said jovially. "The

foot of the rainbow, ma'am. That's where the pot of gold lies."

"Here and now I'd settle for a pot of coffee," I said. "Coffee for four and I'll make it with my own fair hands."

"I think I would rather go to bed," Charlotte said. "I am very tired."

"You made me drink your coffee," I said threateningly. "Now you drink mine. Fair's fair."

"If you are quick, then."

I was quick. I'd four cups on a little tin tray in nothing flat, a powerful mixture of instant coffee, milk and sugar in all of them and a little something extra in one of them. There were no complaints about the coffee. Hutchinson drained his cup and said: "Can't see why you three shouldn't get your heads down for a little. Unless you think I need help?"

No one thought he needed help. Charlotte Skouras was the first to go, saying she felt very sleepy, which I didn't doubt. She sounded it. Uncle Arthur and I left a moment later, Tim Hutchinson promising to call me when we neared the landing stage of the west side of Dubh Sgeir. Uncle Arthur wrapped himself in a rug on the saloon settee. I went to my own cabin and lay down.

I lay for three minutes, then rose, picked up a three-cornered file, softly opened my cabin door and as softly knocked on Charlotte's door. There was no reply, so I opened the door, passed in, silently closed it and switched on the lights.

She was asleep all right, she was a million miles away. She hadn't even managed to make it to bed, she was lying on the carpet, still fully clothed. I put her on the bunk and pulled a couple of blankets over her. I pushed up a sleeve and examined the mark left by the rope burn.

It wasn't a very big cabin and it took me only a minute to find what I was looking for.

It made a pleasant change and a very refreshing one to transfer myself from the *Firecrest* to land without that damned clammy scuba suit impeding every stroke or step of the way.

How Tim Hutchinson located that old stone pier in the rain, the fog and the darkness was something that would have been forever beyond me—if he hadn't told me later that night. He sent me to the bows with a torch in my hand and damned if the thing didn't loom out of the darkness as if he'd gone in on a radio bearing. He went into reverse, brought the bows, plunging heavily in the deep troughs, to within two feet of the pier, waited till I picked my moment to jump off, then went full astern and disappeared into the fog and darkness. I tried to imagine Uncle Arthur executing that lot, but my imagination wasn't up to it. It boggled. Uncle Arthur, thank heaven, slept the sleep of the just. Drake was in his hammock and a thousand miles away, dreaming all the time of W.C.1.

The path from the landing stage to the plateau above was steep and crumbling and someone had carelessly forgotten to equip it with a handrail on the seaward side. I was in no way heavily burdened. All I was carrying apart from the weight of my own years was a torch, gun and coil of rope—I'd neither the intention nor the expectation of doing a Douglas Fairbanks on the outer battlements of the Dubh Sgeir castle, but experience had taught me that a rope was the most essential piece of equipment to carry along on a jaunt on a precipitously walled island—but even so I was breathing pretty heavily by the time I reached the top.

I turned not towards the castle but north along the grass strip that led to the cliff at the northern end of the island. The strip that Lord Kirkside's elder son had taken off from in his Beechcraft on the day when he and his brother-in-law to be had died, the strip that Williams and I had flown along less than twelve hours previously after our talk with Lord Kirkside and his daughter, the strip at the abrupt northern end of which I'd imagined I'd seen what I'd wanted to see, but couldn't be sure. Now I was going to make sure.

The strip was smooth and flat and I made good time without having to use the big rubber torch I had with me. I didn't dare use it anyway, not so close to the castle. There was no light to be seen from there but that was no guarantee that the ungodly weren't maintaining a sleepless watch on the battlements. If I were the ungodly, I'd have been maintaining a sleepless watch on the battlements. I stumbled over something warm and soft and alive and hit the ground hard.

My nerves weren't what they had been forty-eight hours ago and my reactions were comparatively fast. I had the knife in my hand and was on him before he could get to his feet. To his four feet. He had about him the pungent aroma of a refugee from Tim Hutchinson's flensing shed. Well might they say why stinks the goat on yonder hill who seems to dote on chlorophyll. I said a few conciliatory words to our four-footed friend and it seemed to work for he kept his horns to himself. I went on my way.

This humiliating sort of encounter, I'd noticed, never happened to the Errol Flynns of this world. Moreover, if Errol Flynn had been carrying a torch a little fall like that would not have smashed it. Had he been carrying only a candle it would still have kept burning brightly in the darkness. But not my torch. Not my rubber encased, rubber mounted bulb, plexiglass guaranteed unbreakable torch. It was kaput. I fished out the little pencil torch and tried it inside my jacket. I could have spared myself the caution, a glowworm would have sneered at it. I stuck it back in my pocket and kept going.

I didn't know how far I was from the precipitous end of the cliff and I'd no intention of finding out the hard way. I dropped to my hands and knees and crawled forward, the glowworm leading the way. I reached the cliff edge in five minutes and found what I was looking for almost at once. The deep score on the cliff edge was almost eighteen inches in width and four in depth in the center. The mark was fresh but not too fresh. The grass had grown in again in most places. The time factor would be just about right. It was the mark that had been left by the tail fuselage of the Beechcraft plane when, with no one aboard, it had been started up, throttle opened and then the chocks removed. It hadn't had enough speed to become airborne and had fallen over the cliff edge, ripping this score in the earth as it had gone. That was all I needed, that and the holed hull of the Oxford expedition boat and the dark circles under the blue eyes of Susan Kirkside. Here was certainty.

I heard a slight noise behind me. A moderately fit five-year-old grabbing me by the ankles could have had me over the edge with nothing I could do to prevent it. Or maybe it was Billy the Kid back to wreak vengeance for the rude interruption of his night's sleep. I swung round with torch and gun at the ready. It *was* Billy the Kid, his yellow eyes staring balefully out of the night. But his eyes belied him, he was just curious or friendly or both. I moved back slowly till I was out of butting range, patted him weakly on the head and left. At this rate I'd die of heart failure before the night was out.

The rain had eased by this time and the wind fallen away quite a bit, but to compensate for this the mist was worse than ever. It swirled clammily around me and I couldn't see

166

four feet in front of my face. I wondered grimly how Hutchinson was getting on in this lot, but put him quickly out of my mind. I'd no doubt he was a damned sight better at his job than I was at mine. I kept the wind on my right cheek and continued towards the castle. Under my rubber-canvas raincoat my last suit was sodden. The civil service was going to be faced with a cleaner's bill of some note.

I near as a toucher walked into the castle wall but saw its loom just in time. I didn't know whether I was to the right or the left of the entrance gate on the landward side, so I felt my way cautiously to the left to find out. After about ten feet the wall fell away at right angles to another wall. That meant I'd arrived at the left or eastern side of the gate. I began to feel my way to the right.

It was as well I had come upon the castle wall where I had done: had I arrived at the right-hand side I'd have been up-wind of the central gate and would never have smelled the tobacco smoke. It wasn't much as tobacco went, nothing like as robust as Uncle Arthur's cheroots and positively anaemic as compared to Tim Hutchinson's portable poison gas factories, but tobacco smoke for all that. Someone at the entrance gate was smoking a cigarette. It was axiomatic that sentries should never smoke cigarettes. This I could deal with. They'd never trained me on how to handle billy goats on the edge of the precipice but on this subject they had become boringly repetitive.

I held the gun by the barrel and moved quietly forwards. He was leaning against the corner of the entrance, a hardly seen shape, but his position outlined clearly enough by the movement of his cigarette end. I waited till he brought it to his mouth for the third time, and when it was glowing at its brightest and his night vision consequently most affected I took one step forward and brought the butt down where by extension of the curve and subsequent glow of the cigarette end the back of the head of a normal man ought to have been. Fortunately, he was a normal man.

He fell back against me. I caught him and something jabbed painfully into my ribs. I let him finish the trip down on his own and removed this item that had become stuck in my coat. A bayonet, and, what was more, a bayonet with a very nasty point to it. Attached to the bayonet was a Lee Enfield 303. Very military. It seemed unlikely that this was just a routine precaution. Our friends were becoming worried and I had no means of knowing how much they knew or guessed.

Time was running very short for them. Almost as short as it was for me. In a few hours it would be dawn.

I took the rifle and moved cautiously toward the edge of the cliff, the bayonet prodding the earth ahead of me as I went. By this time I was becoming quite adept at not falling over the edges of precipices and, besides, with a rifle and bayonet stretched out in advance you have five feet notification of where eternity begins. I found the edge, stepped back, reversed the rifle, made two parallel scores in the sodden turf about a foot apart and eighteen inches in length, terminating on the very edge. I wiped the butt clean and placed the rifle on the ground. When the dawn came, the sentry changed and a search made, I trusted the proper conclusions would be drawn.

I hadn't hit him as hard as I'd thought, he was beginning to stir and moan feebly by the time I got back to him. This was all to the good, the alternative would have been to carry him and I was in no fit state to carry anyone. I stuffed a handkerchief into his mouth and the moaning stopped. Bad practice, I knew, for a gagged man with a head cold or nasal obstruction can die of suffocation in four minutes, but I hadn't the facilities to carry out a sinus examination, and, more importantly, it was his health or mine.

He was up on his feet in two minutes. He didn't try to run away or offer resistance, for by this time he had his ankles on a short hobble, his hands tied securely behind his back and the barrel of an automatic pressing into the side of his neck. I told him to walk, and he walked. Two hundred yards away, at the head of the path leading down to the landing stage, I led him off to one side, tied his wrists and ankles together and left him there. He seemed to be breathing without too much difficulty.

There were no other sentries, at least not on the main gate. I crossed the hollow square of a courtyard and came to the main door. It was closed but not locked. I passed inside and said a few hard things to myself about myself for not having searched that sentry for the torch he would almost certainly have been carrying. The window curtains must have been drawn and the darkness inside that hall was total. I didn't much fancy moving around a Scottish baronial hall in total darkness, the risk of bringing down a suit of armor with a resoundingly metallic crash or impaling oneself on targes, claymores or a royal set of antlers must be high. I took out my pencil flash but the glowworm inside was breathing its last, even when hard-pressed against the face of my wrist-watch it was impossible to tell the time. It was impossible to see the wristwatch.

From the air, yesterday, I'd seen that the castle had been built in perfect symmetry round three sides of a hollow square. It was a reasonable assumption then that if the main door was in the middle of the central or seaward-facing section then the main staircase would be directly opposite. It seemed likely that the middle of the hall would offer a passage unimpeded by either claymores or antlers.

It did. The stairs were where they should have been. Ten wide shallow steps and then the stairs branched both right and left. I chose the right-hand side because above me, on that side, I could see a faint loom of light. Six steps on the second flight of stairs, another right turn, eight more steps and then I was on the landing. Twenty-four steps and never a creak. I blessed the architect who had specified marble.

The light was much stronger now. I advanced towards its source, a door no more than an inch ajar, and applied a wary eye to the crack. All I could see was the corner of a wardrobe, a strip of carpet, the corner of the foot of a bed and, on the last, a muddy boot. A low-register cacophony of sound emerged, reminiscent of a boiler factory in the middle distance. I pushed the door and walked inside.

I'd come to see Lord Kirkside, and whoever this was it wasn't Lord Kirkside, for whatever Lord Kirkside was in the habit of doing I was fairly certain that he didn't go to bed in boots, braces and cloth cap, with a bayoneted rifle lying on the blankets beside him which was what this character had done. I couldn't see his face, because the cloth cap reached as far as his nose. On the bedside table beside him lay a torch and a half-empty whisky bottle. No glass, but from what little I could see of him I would have judged that he was, anyhow, one of those characters whose direct and simple enjoyment of life had not been impaired by the effete conventions of modern civilisation. The faithful watchman prudently preparing himself for the rigors of the West Highland night before taking his turn at sentry-go. But he wouldn't be making it at the appointed hour for there was no one now to call him. From the look of it, he'd be lucky to make it for lunch.

It was just possible that he might wake himself up, those stentorian snores wouldn't have gone unremarked in a mortuary. He had about him the look of a man who, on regaining consciousness, would find himself in need of thirst-quenching nourishment, so I unscrewed the bottle top, dropped in half-a-dozen of the tablets supplied by my pharmaceutical friend in Torbay, replaced the top, took the torch and left.

Behind the next door to the left lay a bathroom. A filthy basin with, above it, a water-stained mirror, two shaving brushes covered with lather, a jar of shaving cream with the top off, two unwashed razors and, on the floor, two towels that might just possibly have been white at some distant aeon in the past. The interior of the bath was immaculate. Here was where the watchman performed his rudimentary ablutions.

The next room was a bedroom as dirty and disorderly as the watchman's. It was a fair guess that this was the home of the man I'd left lying out among the gorse and stones on the hillside.

I moved across to the left-hand side of the central block—Lord Kirkside would have his room somewhere in that block. He did, but he wasn't at home. The first room beyond the sleeping warrior's was his all right, a glance at the contents of the nearest wardrobe confirmed this. But his bed hadn't been slept in.

Predictably in this symmetrically designed house, the next room was a bathroom. The watchman wouldn't have felt at all at home in here, this antiseptic cleanliness was the hallmark of an effete aristocracy. A medicine cabinet was fixed to the wall. I took out a tin of Elastoplast and covered the face of the torch till I was left with a hole no more than the size of a sixpence. I put the tin in my pocket.

The next door was locked but locks, in the days when the Dubh Sgeir castle had been built, were pretty rudimentary affairs. I took from my pocket the best skeleton key in the world—an oblong of stiff celluloid. I shived it between door and jam at bolt level, pulled the door handle back in the direction of the hinges, eased in the celluloid, released the handle, repeated the process and stood stock-still. That click might have wakened my watchman friend, it should certainly have wakened the person inside. But I heard no sound of movement.

I opened the door a fraction of an inch and went through the stock-still standing process once more. There was a light on inside the room. I changed the torch for the gun, went on my knees, crouched low and abruptly opened the door wide. I stood up, closed and locked the door and crossed over to the bed.

Susan Kirkside wasn't snoring but she was just as deep in sleep as the man I'd just left. She had a blue silk band round her hair, and all of her face was visible, a sight that must have been rare indeed during her waking hours. Twenty-one, her father had said she was, but lying there asleep, smudged eyes and all, she looked no older than seventeen. A magazine had slipped from her hands to the floor. On the bedside table was a half-empty glass of water and beside that a bottle containing a commercial brand of Nembutal tablets. Oblivion appeared to be a pretty hard thing to come by in Dubh Sgeir and I'd no doubt Susan Kirkside found it more difficult than most.

I picked up a towel from a basin in the corner of the room, removed the worst of the moisture and dirt from head and face, combed my hair into some semblance of order and gave my kindly reassuring smile a try-out in the mirror. I looked like someone from the pages of the *Police Gazette*.

It took almost two minutes to shake her awake or, at least, to pull her up from the dark depths of oblivion to a state of semiawareness. Full consciousness took another minute, and it was probably this that saved me from a screaming match, she had time to adjust herself to the slow realisation of the presence of a stranger in the middle of the night. Mind you, I had my kindly smile going full blast till my face ached, but I don't think it helped much.

"Who are you? Who *are* you?" Her voice was shaking, the blue eyes still misted with sleep, wide open and scared. "Don't you touch me! Don't you—I'll scream for help—I'll—"

I took her hand just to show her that there was touching and touching. "I won't touch you, Sue Kirkside. And a fat lot of good screaming for help would do around these parts. Don't scream, there's a good girl. In fact, don't even talk above a whisper. I don't think it would be very wise or safe, do you?"

She stared at me for a few seconds, her lips moving as if she were about to speak, but the fear slowly leaving her eyes. Suddenly she sat bolt upright. "You're Mr. Johnson. The man from the helicopter."

"You should be more careful," I said reproachfully. "They'd have you arrested for that in the *Folies Bergère*." Her free hand hauled the blankets up to her chin and I went on: "My name is Calvert. I work for the Government. I'm a friend. I think you need a friend, don't you, Susan? You and your old man—Lord Kirkside, that is."

"What do you want?" she whispered. "What are you doing here?"

"I'm here to end your troubles," I said. "I'm here to cadge an invitation to your wedding to the Honorable John Rollinson. Make it about the end of next month, will you? I'm due some leave, then."

"Go away from here." Her voice was low and desperate. "Go away from here or you'll ruin everything. Please, please, *please* go away. I'm begging you, I'm begging you. Go away. If you're a friend, go away. Please, oh please go away!"

It seemed that she wanted me to leave. I said: "It appears that they have you pretty well brainwashed. If you believe their promise, you'll believe anything in the world. They won't let you go, they daren't let you go, they'll destroy every shred and trace of evidence that might ever point a finger at them. That includes anyone who has ever had anything to do with them."

"They won't, they *won't*. I was with Mr. Lavorski when he promised Daddy that no one would come to any harm. He said they were businessmen, and killing was no part of business. He meant it."

"Lavorski, is it? It had to be." I looked at the earnest scared face. "He may have meant it when he said it. He couldn't have mentioned that they've murdered four people in the last three days, or that they have tried to murder me four times in the last three days."

"You're lying! You're making this up. Things like that— things like that don't happen any more. For pity's sake leave us alone!"

"There speaks the true daughter of the old Scottish clan chieftain," I said roughly. "You're no good to me. Where's your father?"

"I don't know. Mr. Lavorski and Captain Imrie—he's another of them—came for him at eleven tonight. Daddy didn't say where he was going. He tells me nothing." She paused and snatched her hand away. Faint red patches stained her cheeks. "What do you mean I'm no good to you?"

"Did he say when he would be back?"

"What do you mean I'm no good to you?"

"Because you're young and not very clever and you don't know too much about this world and you'll believe anything a hardened criminal will tell you. But most especially because you won't believe me. You won't believe the one person who can save you all. You're a stupid and pig-headed young fool, Miss Kirkside. If it wasn't that he was jumping from the frying-pan into the fire, I'd say the Honorable Rollinson has had a lucky escape."

"What do you mean?" It is hard for a mobile young face to be expressionless, but hers was then.

"He can't marry you when he is dead," I said brutally. "And he is going to die. He's going to die because Sue Kirkside let him die. Because she was too blind to know truth when she saw it." I had what was, for me, an inspiration. I turned down my collar and pulled my scarf away. "Like it?" I asked.

She didn't like it at all. The red faded from her cheeks. I could see myself in her dressing-table mirror and I didn't like it either. Quinn's handiwork was in full bloom. The kaleidoscope of color now made a complete ring round my neck.

"Quinn?" she whispered.

"You know his name. You know him?"

"I know them all. Most of them, anyway. Cook said that one night, after he'd too much to drink, he'd been boasting in the kitchen about how he'd once been the strong man in a stage act. He'd an argument one night with his partner. About a woman. He killed his partner. That way." She had to make a physical effort to turn her eyes away from my neck. "I thought—I thought it was just talk."

"And do you still think our pals are unpaid missionaries for the Society for the Propagation of Christian Knowledge?" I sneered. "Do you know Jacques and Kramer?"

She nodded.

"I killed them both tonight. After they had killed a friend of mine. They broke his neck. Then they tried to kill my boss and myself. And I killed another. He came out of the dark to murder us. I think his name was Henry. Do you believe me now? Or do you still think we're all dancing round the old Maypole on the village green, singing ring-a-ring-o'-roses as we go?"

The shock treatment worked almost too well. Her face wasn't pale now, it was ashen. She said: "I think I'm going to be sick."

"Later," I said coldly. What little self-regard I had was down among my shoelaces, what I would have liked to do was to take her in my arms and say: "There, there, now, don't you worry your pretty head, just you leave everything

173

to your old Uncle Philip and all will be well at the end of the day." In fact, it was damned hard not to do it. Instead, what I said, still in the same nasty voice, was: "We've no time for those little fol-de-rols. You want to get married, don't you? Did your father say when he would be back?"

She looked at the washbasin in the corner of the room as if she were still making up her mind whether to be sick or not, then pulled her eyes back to me and whispered: "You're just as bad as they are. You're a terrible man. You're a killer."

I caught her shoulders and shook them. I said savagely: "Did he say when he would be back?"

"No." Her eyes were sick with revulsion. It was a long time since any woman had looked at me like that. I dropped my hands.

"Do you know what those men are doing here?"

"No."

I believed her. Her old man would know, but he wouldn't have told her. Lord Kirkside was too astute to believe that their uninvited guests would just up and leave them unharmed. Maybe he was just desperately gambling that if he told his daughter nothing and if he could swear she knew nothing then they would leave her be. If that was what he thought, he was in urgent need of an alienist. But that was being unjust, if I stood in his shoes—or, more accurately, was swimming in the murky waters he was in—I'd have grabbed at any straw.

"It's obvious that you know that your fiancé is still alive," I went on. "And your elder brother. And others. They're being held here, aren't they?"

She nodded silently. I wished she wouldn't look at me like that.

"Do you know how many?"

"A dozen. More than that. And I know there are children there. Three boys and a girl."

That would be right. Sergeant MacDonald's two sons and the boy and the girl that had been aboard the converted lifeboat that had disappeared after setting off on the night cruise from Torbay. I didn't believe a word that Lavorski had said to Susan about their reverence for human life. But I wasn't surprised that the people in the boats who had accidentally stumbled across his illegal operations were still alive. There were very good reasons for this.

174

"Do you know where they are kept? There should be any amount of handy dungeons in Dubh Sgeir castle."

"There are cellars deep underground. I've never been allowed to go near them in the past four months."

"This is your big chance come at last. Get your clothes on and take me there."

"Go down to the cellars?" Aghast was the word for her expression. "Are you mad? Daddy tells me there are at least three men on guard duty all night long." There were only two men now, but her opinion of me was low enough already, so I kept quiet. "They're armed. You *must* be mad. I'm not going!"

"I didn't think you would. You'll let your boy friend die just because you're a contemptible little coward." I could almost taste the self-loathing in my mouth. "Lord Kirkside and the Honorable Rollinson. What a lucky father. What a fortunate fiancé."

She hit me, and I knew I had won. I said without touching my face: "Don't do that. You'll waken up the guard. Get your clothes on."

I rose, sat on the footboard of the bed and contemplated the door and higher things while she changed. I was becoming tired of women telling me what a horrible character I was.

"I'm ready," she said.

She was back in her uniform of pirate's jersey and the denims she'd outgrown when she was about fifteen. Thirty seconds flat and nary a sound of a portable sewing machine. Baffling, that's what it was.

We went down the stairs hand in hand. I may have been the last man in the world she would have elected to be alone with on a desert island, but she clung on pretty tightly all the same.

At the foot of the steps we turned right. I flicked on the torch every few yards but it wasn't really necessary, Susan knew every yard of the way. At the end of the hall we turned left along the eastern wing. Eight yards and we stopped at a door on the right hand side.

"The pantry," she whispered. "The kitchen is beyond that."

I stooped and looked through the keyhole. Beyond was darkness. We passed through the doorway, then into an archway giving on to the kitchen. I flashed the tiny beam around the room. Empty.

There were three guards, Susan had said. The outside man, for whom I had accounted. The lad who patrolled the battlements. No, she didn't know what he did, but it was a good guess that he wasn't studying astronomy or guarding against parachutists. He'd have night glasses to his eyes and he'd be watching for fishing vessels, naval craft or fishery cruisers that might happen by and interrupt honest men at their work. He wouldn't see much on a night like this. And the third man, she said, guarded the back kitchen premises, the only entrance to the castle apart from the main gate—and the unfortunates in their cellars down below.

He wasn't in the kitchen premises, so he would be in the cellars down below.

A flight of steps led from the scullery beyond the kitchen down to a stone-flagged floor. To the right of this floor I could see the loom of light. Susan raised a finger to her lips and we made our way soundlessly down to the foot of the steps. I slid a cautious eye round the corner of this passageway.

It wasn't a passageway, it was the damnedest flight of steps

I'd ever come across. They were lit by two or three far-spaced and very weak electric bulbs, the walls coming together towards the foot like a pair of railway lines disappearing into the distance. Maybe fifty feet—or seventy steps—down, where the first light was, another passageway branched off to the right. There was a stool at the corner of the small stone landing there, and sitting on the stool a man. Across his knees lay a rifle. They certainly went in for the heavy artillery.

I drew back. I murmured to Susan: "Where in hell's name do those steps lead to?"

"The boathouse, of course." A surprised whisper. "Where else?"

Where else, indeed. Brilliant work, Calvert, brilliant work. You'd skirted the south side of the Dubh Sgeir in the helicopter, you'd seen the castle, you'd seen the boathouse, you'd seen nary a handhold on the sheer cliff separating them, and you'd never raised an eyebrow at the glaring obviousness of the fact that ne'er the twain did meet.

"Those are the cellars in that passage going off to the right?" She nodded. "Why so far down? It's a long walk to collect the bubbly."

"They're not really wine cellars. They used to be used as water reservoirs."

"No other way of getting down there?"

"No. Only this way."

"And if we take five steps down this way he shoots us full of holes with his Lee Enfield. Know who it is?"

"Harry. I don't know his other name. He's an Armenian, Daddy says. People can't pronounce his real name. He's young and smooth and greasy—and detestable."

"He had the effrontery to make a pass at the chieftain's daughter?"

"Yes. It was horrible." She touched her lips with the back of her hand. "He stank of garlic."

"I don't blame him. I'd do it myself if I didn't feel my pension creeping up on me. Call him up and make amends."

"What!"

"Tell him you're sorry. Tell him you misjudged his noble character. Tell him your father is away and this is the first chance you've had of speaking to him. Tell him anything."

"No!"

"Sue!"

"He'll never believe me," she said wildly.

"When he gets within two feet of you, he'll forget all about the reasoning why. He's a man, isn't he?"

"You're a man. And you're only six inches away." The eternal female illogic.

"I've told you how it is, it's my pension coming between us. Quickly!"

She nodded reluctantly and I disappeared into the shadows of the nearest cellar, reversed gun in hand. She called and he came a-running, his rifle at the ready. When he saw who it was, he forgot all about his rifle. Susan started to speak her lines but she might have saved her breath. Harry, if nothing else, was an impetuous young man. That wild Armenian blood. I stepped forward, arm swinging, and lowered him to the ground. I tied him up and, as I'd run out of handkerchiefs, ripped away part of his shirt-front and used it as a gag. Susan giggled, a giggle with a note of hysteria.

"What's up?" I asked.

"Harry. He's what they call a snappy dresser. That's a silk shirt. You're no respecter of persons, Mr. Calvert."

"Not persons like Harry. Congratulations. Wasn't so bad, was it?"

"It was still horrible." Again the hand to the mouth. "He's reeking of whisky."

"Youngsters have odd tastes," I said kindly. "You'll grow out of it. At least, it must have been an improvement on the garlic."

The boathouse wasn't really a boathouse at all, it was a large vaulting cave formed in a cleft in a natural fault in the cliff strata. At the inner end of the cave longitudinal tunnels stretched away on either side paralleling the coastline, until they vanished beyond the reach of my torch. From the air, the boathouse in the small artificial harbor, a structure of about twenty feet by twenty, had seemed incapable of housing more than two or three fair-sized rowing boats. Inside it was big enough to berth a boat the size of the *Firecrest*, and then leave room to spare. Mooring bollards, four in number, lined the eastern side of the boathouse. There were signs of recent work where the inner end of the cave had been lengthened in the direction of the longitudinal tunnels to increase the berthing space and provide a bigger working platform, but otherwise it was as it must have been for hundreds of years. I picked up a boathook and tried to test the depth, but couldn't find bottom. Any vessel small enough to be accommodated inside could enter and leave at any state of the tide. The two big doors looked solid, but not too solid. There was a small dry-land doorway on the eastern side.

The berth was empty, as I had expected to find it. Our friends were apprehensive and on piece-work rates. It wasn't difficult to guess what they were working at, the working platform was liberally stacked with the tools of their trade: an oil engine-driven air compressor with a steel reservoir with outlet valves, a manually-operated, two-cylinder double-acting air pump with two outlets, two helmets with attached corselets, flexible, non-collapsible air tubes with metal couplings, weighted boots, diving dresses, life-cum-telephone lines, lead weights and scuba equipment such as I had myself, with a stack of compressed air cylinders at the ready.

I felt neither surprise nor elation, I'd known this must exist for the past forty-eight hours although I'd become certain of the location only that night. I was faintly surprised, perhaps, to see all this equipment here, for this would surely be only the spares. But I shouldn't have been even vaguely surprised. Whatever this bunch lacked, it wasn't a genius for organisation.

I didn't see that night, nor did I ever see, the cellars where the prisoners were housed. After I'd huffed and pulled three quarters of the way up that interminable flight of steps, I turned left along the passageway where we'd first seen Harry taking his ease. After a few yards the passageway broadened out into a low damp chamber containing a table made of beer cases, some seats of the same and, in one corner, some whisky that hadn't yet been drunk. A bottle of whisky, nearly full, stood on the table: Harry's remedy for garlic halitosis.

Beyond this chamber was a massive wooden door secured by an equally massive looking lock with the key missing. All the celluloid in the world wouldn't open this lock but a bee-hive plastic explosive would do a very efficient job indeed. I made another of the many mental notes I'd made that night and went up the stairs to rejoin Susan.

Harry had come to. He was saying something in his throat which fortunately couldn't get past his silk-shirted gag to the delicate ears of the chieftain's young daughter, his eyes, to mint a phrase, spoke volumes and he was trying as best he could to do a Houdini with the ropes round his legs and arms. Susan Kirkside was pointing a rifle in his general direction and looking very apprehensive. She needn't have bothered, Harry was trussed like a turkey.

"Those people down in the cellars," I said. "They've been there for weeks, some for months. They'll be blind as bats and weak as kittens by the time they get out."

She shook her head. "I think they'll be all right. They're taken out on the landing strip there for an hour and a half every morning under guard. They can't be seen from the sea. We're not allowed to watch. Or not supposed to. I've seen them often. Daddy insisted on it. And Sir Anthony."

"Well, good old Daddy." I stared at her. "Old Man Skouras. He comes here?"

"Of course." She seemed surprised at my surprise. "He's one of them. Lavorski and this man Dollmann, the men that do all the arranging, they work for Sir Anthony. Didn't you know? Daddy and Sir Anthony are friends—were friends—before this. I've been in Sir Anthony's London home often."

"But they're not friends now?" I probed keenly.

"Sir Anthony has gone off his head since his first wife died," Susan said confidently. I looked at her in wonder and tried to remember when I'd last been so authoritatively dogmatic on subjects I knew nothing about. I couldn't remember. "He married again, you know. Some French actress or other. That wouldn't have helped. She's no good. She caught him on the rebound."

"Susan," I said reverently, "you're really wonderful. I don't believe you'll ever understand what I mean by my pension coming between us. You know her well?"

"I've never met her."

"You didn't have to tell me. And poor old Sir Anthony—he doesn't know what he's doing, is that it?"

"He's all mixed up," she said defensively. "He's sweet, really he is. Or was."

"All mixed up with the deaths of four men, not to mention three of his own," I said. Sergeant MacDonald thought him a good man. Susan thought him sweet. I wondered what she would say if she saw Charlotte Skouras' back. "How do the prisoners do for food?"

"We have two cooks. They do it all. The food is brought down to them."

"What other staff?"

"No other staff. Daddy was made to sack them all four months ago."

That accounted for the state of the watchman's bathroom.

I said: "My arrival in the helicopter here yesterday afternoon was duly reported by radio to the *Shangri-la*. A man with a badly scarred face. Where's the radio transmitter?"

"You know everything, don't you?"

"Know-all Calvert. Where is it?"

"Off the hall. In the room behind the stairs. It's locked."

"I have keys that'll open the Bank of England. Wait a minute." I went down to the guard's room outside the prisoners' cellar, brought the whisky bottle back up to where Susan was standing and handed it to her. "Hang on to this."

She looked at me steadily. "Do you really need this?"

"Oh my God, sweet youth," I said nastily. "Sure I need it. I'm an alcoholic."

I untied the rope round Harry's ankles and helped him to his feet. He repaid this Samaritan gesture by swinging at me with his right foot but fifteen minutes on the floor hadn't helped his circulation or reactions any and I forestalled him with the same maneuver. When I helped him up the second time there was no fight left in him.

"Did you—did you really have to do that?" The revulsion was back in her eyes.

"Did I—did you see what he tried to do to me?" I demanded.

"You men are all the same," she said.

"Oh, shut up!" I snarled. I was old and sick and tired and I'd run right out of the last of my witty ripostes.

The transceiver was a beauty, a big gleaming metallic RCA, the latest model as used in the naval vessels of a dozen nationalities. I didn't waste any time wondering where they had obtained it, that lot were fit for anything. I sat down and started tuning the set, then looked up at Susan. "Go and fetch me one of your father's razor blades."

"You don't want me to hear, is that it?"

"Think what you like. Just get it."

If she'd been wearing a skirt she'd have flounced out of the room. With what she was wearing flouncing was out of the question. The set covered every transmission frequency from the bottom of the long wave to the top of the VHF. It took only two minutes to raise SPFX. It was manned night and day the year round. It really was most considerate of the ungodly to provide me with such a magnificent instrument.

Sue Kirkside was back before I started speaking. I was ten minutes on the microphone altogether. Apart from code names and map references I used plain English throughout. I had to, I'd no book, and time was too short anyway. I spoke slowly and clearly, giving precise instructions about the movements of men, the alignment of radio frequencies, the minutest details of the layout of Dubh Sgeir castle and asking all-important questions about recent happenings on the Riviera. I didn't repeat myself once, and I asked for nothing to be repeated to me because every word was being recorded. Before I was halfway through Susan's eyebrows had disappeared up under the blonde fringe and Harry was looking as if he had been sandbagged. I signed off, reset the tuning band to its original position and stood up.

"That's it," I said. "I'm off."

"You're *what?*" The grey-blue eyes were wide, the eyebrows still up under the fringe, but with alarm, this time, not astonishment. "You're leaving. You're leaving me here?"

"I'm leaving. If you think I'd stay a minute longer in this damned castle than I have to, you must be nuts. I've played my hand far enough already. Do you think I want to be around here when the guards change over or when the toilers on the deep get back here?"

"Toilers on the deep? What do you mean?"

"Skip it." I'd forgotten she knew nothing about what our friends were doing. "It's Calvert for home."

"You've got a gun," she said wildly. "You could—you could capture them, couldn't you?"

"Capture who?" The hell with the grammar.

"The guards. They're on the second floor. They'll be asleep."

"How many?"

"Eight or nine. I'm not sure."

"Eight or nine, she's not sure! Who do you think I am, Superman. Stand aside, do you want me to get killed? And, Susan, tell nothing to anybody. Not even Daddy. Not if you want to see Johnny boy walk down that aisle. You understand?"

She put a hand on my arm and said quietly but with the fear still in her face, "You could take me with you."

"I could. I could take me with you and ruin everything. If I as much as fired a single shot at any of the sleeping warriors up top, I'd ruin everything. Everything depends on their never knowing that anybody was here tonight. If they suspected that, just had a hint of a suspicion of that, they'd pack their bags and take off into the night. Tonight. And I can't

182

possibly do anything until tomorrow night. You understand, of course, that they wouldn't leave until after they had killed everyone in the cellar. And your father, of course. And they'd stop off at Torbay and make sure that Sergeant Mac-Donald would never give evidence against them. Do you want that, Susan? God knows I'd love to take you out of here, I'm not made of portland cement, but if I take you the alarm bells will ring and then they'll pull the plug. Can't you see that? If they come back and find you gone, they'll have one thought and one thought only in their minds. Our little Susan has left the island. With, of course, one thought in mind. You must not be missing."

"All right." She was calm now. "But you've overlooked something."

"I'm a great old overlooker. What?"

"Harry. He'll be missing. He'll have to be. You can't leave him to talk."

"He'll be missing. So will the keeper of the gate. I clobbered him on the way in." She started to get all wide-eyed again but I held up my hand, stripped off coat and windbreaker, unwrapped the razor she'd brought me and nicked my forearm, not too deeply, the way I felt I needed all the blood I had, but enough to let me smear the bottom three inches of the bayonet on both sides. I handed her the tin of Elastoplast and without a word she stuck a strip across the incision. I dressed again and we left, Susan with the whisky bottle and torch, myself with the rifle, shepherding Harry in front of me. Once in the hall I relocked the door with the skeleton key I'd used to open it.

The rain had stopped and there was hardly any wind, but the mist was thicker than ever and the night had turned bitterly cold. The Highland Indian summer was in full swing. We made our way through the courtyard across to where I'd left the bayonet lying on the cliff edge using the torch, now with the Elastoplast removed from its face, quite freely, but keeping our voices low. The lad maintaining his ceaseless vigil on the battlements couldn't have seen us five yards away with the finest night glasses in the world, but sound in heavy mist has unpredictable qualities; it can be muffled, it can be distorted, or it can occasionally be heard with surprising clarity, and it was now too late in the day to take chances.

I located the bayonet and told Harry to lie face down in the grass, if I'd left him standing he just might have been tempted to kick me over the edge. I gouged the grass in assorted places with heel and toe, made a few more scores with the butt of a bayonet, stuck the blade of the gatekeeper's bayonet in the ground at a slight angle so that the rifle was just clear of the ground, laid Harry's down so that the blood-stained bayonet tip was also just clear of the ground, so preventing the blood from running off among the wet grass, scattered most of the contents of the whisky bottle around and carefully placed the bottle, about a quarter full now, close to one of the bayonets. I said to Susan: "And what happened here do you think?"

"It's obvious. They had a drunken fight and both of them slipped on the wet grass over the edge of the cliff."

"And what did you hear?"

"Oh! I heard the sound of two men shouting in the hall. I went out on the landing and I heard them shouting at the tops of their voices. I heard the one tell Harry to get back to his post and Harry saying, no, by God, he was going to settle it now. I'll say both men were drunk, and I won't repeat the kind of language they were using. The last I heard they were crossing the courtyard together, still arguing."

"Good girl. That's exactly what you heard."

She came with us as far as the place where I'd left the gatekeeper. He was still breathing. I used most of what rope I'd left to tie them together at the waist, a few feet apart, and wrapped the end of it in my hand. With their arms lashed behind their backs they weren't going to have much balancing power and no holding power at all on the way down that steep and crumbling path to the landing stage. If either slipped or stumbled I might be able to pull them back to safety with a sharp tug. There was going to be none of this Alpine stuff with the rope around my waist also. If they were going to step out into the darkness they were going to do it without me.

I said: "Thank you, Susan. You have been a great help. Don't take any more of those Nembutal tablets tonight. They'd think it damn funny if you were still asleep at midday tomorrow."

"I wish it were midday the next day. I won't let you down, Mr. Calvert. Everything is going to be all right, isn't it?"

"Of course."

There was a pause, then she said: "You could have pushed those two over the edge if you wanted to, couldn't you. But you didn't. You could have cut Harry's arm, but you cut your own. I'm sorry for what I said, Mr. Calvert. About you being horrible and terrible. You do what you have to do." Another pause. "I think you're rather wonderful."

"They all come round in the end," I said, but I was talking to myself, she'd vanished into the mist. I wished drearily that I could have agreed with her sentiments, I didn't feel wonderful at all, I just felt dead tired and worried stiff for with all the best planning in the world there were too many imponderables and I couldn't have bet a brass farthing on the next twenty-four hours. I got some of the worry and frustration out of my system by kicking the two prisoners to their feet.

We went slowly down that crumbling treacherous path in single file, myself last, torch in my left hand, rope tightly—but not too tightly—in my right hand. I wondered vaguely as we went why I *hadn't* nicked Harry instead of myself. It would have been so much more fitting, Harry's blood on Harry's bayonet.

"You had a pleasant outing, I trust?" Hutchinson asked courteously.

"It wasn't dull. You would have enjoyed it." I watched Hutchinson as he pushed the *Firecrest* into the fog and the darkness. "Let me into a professional secret. How in the world did you find your way back into this pier tonight? The mist is twice as bad as when I left. You cruise up and down for hours, impossible to take any bearings, there's the waves, tide, fog, currents—and yet there you are, right on the nose, to the minute. It can't be done."

"It was an extraordinary feat of navigation," Hutchinson said solemnly. "There are such things as charts, Calvert, and if you look at that large scale one for this area you'll see an eight fathom bank, maybe a cable in length, lying a cable and a half out to the west of the old pier there. I just steamed out straight into the wind and tide, waited till the depth-sounder showed I was over the bank and dropped the old hook. At the appointed hour the great navigator lifts his hook and lets wind and tide drift him ashore again. Not many men could have done it."

"I'm bitterly disappointed," I said. "I'll never think the same of you again. I suppose you used the same technique on the way in?"

"More or less. Only I used a series of five banks and patches. My secrets are gone forever. Where now?"

"Didn't Uncle Arthur say?"

"You misjudge Uncle Arthur. He says he never interferes with you in—what was it?—the execution of a field operation. 'I plan,' he says. 'I coordinate. Calvert finishes the job'."

"He has his decent moments," I admitted.

"He told me a few stories about you in the past hour. I guess it's a privilege to be along."

"Apart from the four hundred thousand quid or whatever?"

"Apart, as you say, from the green men. Where to, Calvert?"

"Home. If you can find it in this lot."

"Craigmore? I can find it." He puffed at his cigar and held the end close to his eyes. "I think I should put this out. It's getting so I can't even see the length of the wheelhouse windows, far less beyond them. Uncle Arthur's taking his time, isn't he?"

"Uncle Arthur is interrogating the prisoners."

"I wouldn't say he'd get much out of that lot."

"Neither would I. They're not too happy."

"Well, it *was* a nasty jump from the pier to the foredeck. Especially with the bows plunging up and down as they were. And more especially with their arms tied behind their backs."

"One broken ankle and one broken forearm," I said. "It could have been worse. They could have missed the foredeck altogether."

"You have a point," Hutchinson agreed. He stuck his head out the wide window and withdrew it again. "It's not the cigar," he announced. "No need to quit smoking. Visibility is zero, and I mean zero. We're flying blind on instruments. You may as well switch on the wheelhouse lights. Makes it all that easier to read the charts, depth-sounder and compass and doesn't affect the radar worth a damn." He stared at me as the light came on. "What the hell are you doing in that flaming awful outfit?"

"This is a dressing gown," I explained. "I've three suits and all three are soaked and ruined. Any luck, sir?" Uncle Arthur had just come in to the wheelhouse.

"One of them passed out." Uncle Arthur wasn't looking very pleased with himself. "The other kept moaning so loudly that I couldn't make myself heard. Well, Calvert, the story."

"The story, sir? I was just going to bed. I've told you the story."

"Half-a-dozen quick sentences that I couldn't hear above

186

their damned caterwauling," he said coldly. "The whole story, Calvert."

"I'm feeling weak, sir."

"I've rarely known a time when you weren't feeling weak, Calvert. You know where the whisky is."

Hutchinson coughed respectfully. "I wonder if the Admiral would permit—"

"Certainly, certainly," Uncle Arthur said in a quite different tone. "Of course, my boy." The boy was a clear foot taller than Uncle Arthur. "And while you're at it, Calvert, you might bring one for me, too, a normal-sized one." He had his hasty side to him, had Uncle Arthur.

I said "goodnight" five minutes later. Uncle Arthur wasn't too pleased, I'd the feeling he thought I'd missed out on the suspense and fancy descriptions, but I was as tired as the old man with the scythe after Hiroshima. I looked in on Charlotte Skouras, she was sleeping like the dead. I wondered about that chemist back in Torbay, he'd been three parts asleep, myopic as a barn owl and crowding eighty. He could have made a mistake. He could have had only a minimal experience in the prescribing of sleep-inducing drugs for those who lived in the land of the Hebridean prayer: "Would that the peats might cut themselves and the fish jump on the shore, that I upon my bed might lie, and sleep for ever more."

But I'd done the old boy an injustice. After what was, to me, our miraculous arrival in Craigmore's apology for a harbor it had taken me no more than a minute to shake Charlotte into something resembling wakefulness. I told her to get dressed—a cunning move this to make her think I didn't know she was still dressed—and come ashore. Fifteen minutes after that we were all inside Hutchinson's house and fifteen minutes still later, when Uncle Arthur and I had roughly splinted the prisoners' fractures and locked them in a room illuminated only by a skylight that would have taken Houdini all his time to wriggle through, I was in bed in another tiny box-room that was obviously the sleeping-quarters of the chairman of the Craigmore's art gallery selection committee, for he'd kept all the best exhibits to himself. I was just dropping off to sleep, thinking that if the universities ever got around to awarding Ph.Ds to house agents, the first degree would surely go to the first man who sold a Hebridean hut within sniffing distance of a flensing shed, when the door opened and the light came on. I blinked open exhausted eyes

187

and saw Charlotte Skouras softly closing the door behind her.

"Go away," I said. "I'm sleeping."

"May I come in?" she asked. She gazed around the art gallery and her lips moved in what could have been the beginnings of a smile. "I would have thought you would have gone to sleep with the lights on tonight."

"You should see the ones behind the wardrobe doors," I boasted. I slowly opened my eyes as far as I could without mechanical aid. "Sorry, I'm tired. What can I do? I'm not at my best receiving lady callers in the middle of the night."

"Uncle Arthur's next door. You can always scream for help if you want to." She looked at a moth-eaten armchair. "May I sit down?"

She sat down. She still wore that uncrushable white dress and her hair was neatly combed, but that was about all you could say for her. Attempts at humor there might have been in her voice, but there was none in her face and none in her eyes. Those brown, wise, knowing eyes, eyes that knew all about living and loving and laughter, the eyes that had once made her the most sought-after actress of her time now held only sadness and despair. And fear. Now that she had escaped from her husband and his accomplices, there should have been no need for fear. But it was there, half-buried in the tired brown eyes, but there. Fear was an expression I knew. The lines round the eyes and mouth that looked so right, so inevitable, when she smiled or laughed—in the days when she had smiled and laughed—looked as if they had been etched by time and suffering and sorrow and despair into a face that had never known laughter and love. Charlotte Skouras' face, without the Charlotte Meiner of old behind it, no longer looked as if it belonged to her. A worn, a weary and an alien face. She must have been about thirty-five, I guessed, but she looked a deal older. And yet when she sat in that chair, almost huddled in that chair, the Craigmore art gallery no longer existed.

"You don't trust me, Philip," she said flatly.

"What on earth makes you say that? Why shouldn't I?"

"You tell me. You are evasive, you will not answer questions, but I know enough of men to know that the answers you give me are the ones you want to give me and not the ones I should hear. Why should this be, Philip? What have I done that you should not trust me?"

"So the truth is not in me? Well, I suppose I do stretch it a bit at times, I may even occasionally tell a lie. Strictly in the line of business, of course. I wouldn't lie to a person like you." I meant it and intended not to—unless I had to do it for her sake, which was different.

"Why should you not lie to a person like me?"

"I don't know how to say it. I could say I don't usually lie to lovely and attractive women for whom I have a high regard, and then you'd cynically say I was stretching the truth till it snapped, and you'd be wrong because it is the truth, if truth lies in the eye of the beholder. I don't know if that sounds like an insult, it's never meant to be. I could say it's because I hate to see you sitting there all washed up and with no place to go and no one to turn to at the one time in your life when you need someplace to go and someone to turn to, but I suppose again that might sound like an insult. I could say I don't lie to my friends, but that again would be an insult, the Charlotte Skourases of this world don't make friends with government hirelings who kill for their wages. It's no good, I don't know what to say, Charlotte, except that it doesn't matter whether you believe me or not as long as you believe that no harm will come to you from me and, as long as I'm near you, no harm will come to you from anyone else either. Maybe you don't believe that either, maybe your feminine intuition has stopped working."

"It is working—what you say?—overtime. Very hard indeed." The brown eyes were still and the face without expression. "I do think I could place my life in your hands."

"You might not get it back again."

"It's not worth all that much. I might not want it back."

She looked at me for a long moment when there was no fear in her eyes, then stared down at her folded hands. She gazed at them so long that I finally looked in the same direction myself, but there was nothing wrong with her hands that I could see. Finally she looked up with an almost timid half-smile that didn't belong to her at all.

"You are wondering why I came," she asked.

"No. You've told me. You want me to tell you a story. Especially the beginning and end of the story."

She nodded. "When I began as a stage actress, I played very small parts, but I knew what the play was all about. In this real-life play, I'm still playing a very small part. Only, I no longer know what the play is all about. I come on for three minutes in Act 2, but I have no idea what has gone before. I'm back for another minute in Act 4, but I've no idea in the world what's happened between Acts 2 and 4. And I cannot begin to imagine how it will all end." She half-lifted her arms, turning the palms upwards. "You cannot imagine how frustrating this can be for a woman."

"You really know nothing of what has gone before this?"

"I ask you to believe me."

I believed her. I believed her because I knew it to be true.

"Go to the front room and bring me, as they say in these parts, a refreshment," I said. "I grow weaker by the hour."

So she rose obediently and went to the front room and brought me the refreshment which gave me just enough strength to tell her what she wanted to know.

"They were a triumvirate," I said, which if not strictly accurate, was close enough to the truth for my explanation. "Sir Anthony, Lavorski, who I gather, was not only his public and private accountant, but his over-all financial director as well, and John Dollmann, the managing director of the shipping companies—they were split up for tax reasons—associated with your husband's oil companies. I thought that MacCallum, the Scots lawyer, and Henry Biscarte, the lad with the beard who owns one of the biggest merchant banks in Paris, was in with them too. But they weren't. At least not Biscarte. I think he was invited aboard ostensibly to discuss business but actually to provide our triumvirate with information that would have given them the basis for their next coup, but he didn't like the way the wind was blowing and shied off. I know nothing about MacCallum."

"I know nothing about Biscarte," Charlotte said. "Neither he nor Mr. MacCallum stayed aboard the *Shangri-la*, they were at the Columba Hotel for a few days and were invited out twice for dinner. They haven't been aboard since the night you were there."

"Among other things they didn't care for your husband's treatment of you."

"I didn't care for it myself. I know what Mr. MacCallum was doing aboard. My husband was planning to build a refinery in the Clyde estuary this coming winter and MacCallum was negotiating the lease for him. My husband said that, by the end of the year, he expected to have a large amount of uncommitted capital for investment."

"I'll bet he did, that's as neat a phrase for the proceeds of grand larceny as ever I've come across. Lavorski, I think we'll find, was the instigator and guiding brain behind all this. Lavorski it would have been who discovered that the Skouras empire was badly in need of some new lifeblood in the way of hard cash and saw the way of putting matters right by using means they already had close to hand."

"But—but my husband was never short of money," Charlotte objected. "He had the best of everything, yachts, cars, houses—"

"He was never short in that sense. Neither were half the millionaires who jumped off the New York skyscrapers at the time of the stock market crash. Do be quiet, there's a good girl, you know nothing about high finance." Coming from a character who eked out a bare living from an inadequate salary, I reflected, that was very good indeed. "Lavorski struck upon the happy idea of piracy on a grand scale—vessels carrying not less than a million pounds' worth of specie at a time."

She stared at me, her lips parted. I wished I had teeth like that, instead of having had half of them knocked out by Uncle Arthur's enemies over the years. Uncle Arthur, I mused bitterly, was twenty-five years older than I was and was frequently heard to boast that he'd still to lose his first tooth. She whispered: "You're making all this up."

"Lavorski made it all up. I'm just telling you, I wouldn't have the brains to think of something like that. Having thought up this splendid scheme for making money, they found themselves with three problems to solve: how to discover when and where large quantities of specie were being shipped, how to seize those ships and how to hide them while they opened the strong room—a process which in ships fitted with the most modern strong rooms can take anything up to a day—and remove said specie.

"Problem number one was easy. I have no doubt they may have suborned high-ranking banking officials—the fact that they tried it on with Biscarte is proof of that—but I don't think it will ever be possible to bring those men to justice. But it will be possible to arrest and very successfully indict their ace informant, their trump card, our good friend the belted broker, Lord Charnley. To make a real good-going success of piracy you require the cooperation of Lloyd's. Well, that's an actionable statement, the cooperation of someone in Lloyd's. Someone like Lord Charnley. He is, by profession, a marine underwriter at Lloyd's. Stop staring at me like that, you're putting me off.

"A large proportion of valuable marine cargoes are insured at Lloyd's. Charnley would know of at least a number of those. He would know the amount, the firm or bank of dispatch, and possibly the date of dispatch and vessel."

"But Lord Charnley is a wealthy man," she said.

"Lord Charnley gives the appearance of being a wealthy man," I corrected. "Granted, he had to prove that he was a man of substance to gain admission to the old club, but he may have backed the wrong insurance horses or played the stock market. He either needed money or wanted money. He *may* have plenty but money is like alcohol, some people can take it and some can't, and with those who can't the more money they have the more they require.

"Dollmann solved problem two—the hi-jacking of the specie. I shouldn't imagine this strained his resources too far. Your husband ships his oil into some very odd and very tough places indeed and it goes without saying that he employs some very odd and very tough people to do it. Dollmann wouldn't have recruited the hi-jacking crew himself, he probably singled out our good friend Captain Imrie, who will prove to have a very interesting history, and gave him the authority to go through the Skouras fleets and hand-pick suitable men for the job. Once the hi-jacking crew was assembled and ready, Messrs. Skouras, Lavorski, and Dollmann waited till the victim was on the high seas, dumped you and the stewardess in a hotel, embarked the lads on the *Shangri-la*, intercepted the specie-carrying vessel and by one of a series of ruses I'll tell you about later, succeeded in boarding it and taking over. Then the *Shangri-la* landed the captured crew under guard while the prize crew sailed the hi-jacked vessel to the appointed hiding place."

"It can't be true, it can't be true," she murmured. It was a long time since I'd seen any woman wringing her hands but Charlotte Skouras was doing it then. Her face was quite drained of color. She knew that what I was saying was true and she'd never heard of any of it before. "Hiding place, Philip? What hiding place?"

"Where would you hide a ship, Charlotte?"

"How should I know?" She shrugged tiredly. "My mind is not very clear tonight. Up in the Arctic perhaps, or in a lonely Norwegian fjord or some desert island far away. I can't think any more, Philip. There cannot be many places. A ship is a big thing."

"There are millions of places. You can hide a ship practically anywhere in the world. All you have to do is to open the sea cocks."

"You mean—you mean that—"

"I mean just that. You send it to the bottom. The west side of the sound to the east of Dubh Sgeir island, a cheery stretch of water rejoicing in the name of Beul nan Uamh—the mouth of the grave—must be the most densely packed marine graveyard in Europe today. At dead slack water the sea cocks were opened at a very carefully selected spot in the Beul nan Uamh and down they went, all five of them, gurgle, gurgle, gurgle. Tide tables show that, coincidentally, most of them were sunk at or near midnight. Cease upon the midnight, as the poet says, only in this case with a very great deal of pain, at least for the underwriters involved. Beul nan Uamh. Odd, I never thought of it before. A very apt name indeed. The mouth of the grave. Damn place is printed far too large in the chart, it doesn't have to be very obvious to be too obvious for Calvert."

She hadn't been listening to my meanderings. She said: "Dubh Sgeir? But—but that's the home of Lord Kirkside."

"It's not but, it's because. The hiding place was picked either by your husband, or, if someone else, then the arrangement was made through your husband. I never knew until recently that your husband was an old drinking pal of Lord Kirkside. I saw him yesterday, but he wouldn't talk. Nor would his charming daughter."

"You do move around. I've never met the daughter."

"You should. She thinks you're an old gold-digging hag. A nice kid really. But terrified, terrified for her life and those of others."

"Why on earth should she be?"

"How do you think our triumvirate got Lord Kirkside to agree to their goings-on?"

"Money. Bribery."

I shook my head. "Lord Kirkside is a Highlander and a gentleman. It's a pretty fierce combination. Old Skouras could never lay hands on enough money to bribe Lord Kirkside to pass the uncollected fares box on a bus, if he hadn't paid. A poor illustration. Lord Kirkside wouldn't recognise a bus even if it ran over him, but what I mean is, the old boy is incorruptible. So your charming friends kidnapped old Kirkside's older son—the younger lives in Australia—and just to make sure that Susan Kirkside wouldn't be tempted to do anything silly, they kidnapped her fiancé. A guess, but a damned good one. They're supposed to be dead."

"No, no," she whispered. Her hand was to her mouth and her voice was shaking. "My God, no!"

"My God, yes. It's logical and tremendously effective. They also kidnapped Sergeant MacDonald's sons and Donald MacEachern's wife for the same reason. To buy silence and cooperation."

"But—but people just can't disappear like that."

"We're not dealing with street corner boys, we're dealing with criminal masterminds. Disappearances are rigged to look like accidental death. A few other people have disappeared also, people who had the misfortune to be hanging around in small private boats while our friends were waiting for the tide to be exactly right before opening the sea cocks on the hijacked ships."

"Didn't it arouse police suspicion? Having so many small boats disappear in the same place."

"They sailed or towed two of those boats fifty or more miles away and ran them on the rocks. Another could have disappeared anywhere. The fourth did set sail from Torbay and disappeared, but the disappearance of one boat is not enough to arouse suspicion."

"It must be true, I know it must be true." She shook her head as if she didn't believe it was true at all. "It all fits so well, it explains so many things and explains them perfectly. But—but what's the good of knowing all this now? They're on to you, they *know* you know that something is far wrong and that that something is in Loch Houron. They'll leave—"

"How do they know we suspect Loch Houron?"

"Uncle Arthur told me in the wheelhouse last night." Surprise in her voice. "Don't you remember?"

I hadn't remembered. I did now. I was half-dead from lack of sleep. A stupid remark. Perhaps even a give-away remark. I was glad Uncle Arthur hadn't heard that one.

"Calvert nears the sunset of his days," I said. "My mind's going. Sure they'll leave. But not for forty-eight hours yet. They will think they have plenty of time, it's less than eight hours since we instructed Sergeant MacDonald to tell them that we were going to the mainland for help."

"I see," she said dully. "And what did you do on Dubh Sgeir tonight, Philip?"

"Not much. But enough." Another little white lie. "Enough to confirm my every last suspicion. I swam ashore to the little harbor and picked the side door of the boathouse. It's quite a

194

boathouse. Not only is it three times as big on the inside as it is from the outside, but it's stacked with diving equipment."

"Diving equipment?"

"Heaven help us all, you're almost as stupid as I am. How on earth do you think they recover the stuff from the sunken vessels? They use a diving boat and the Dubh Sgeir boathouse is its home."

"Was—was that all you found out?"

"There was nothing more to find out. I had intended taking a look round the castle—there's a long flight of steps leading up to it from the boatyard inside the cliff itself—but there was some character sitting about three parts of the way up with a rifle in his hand. A guard of some sorts. He was drinking out of some sort of bottle, but he was doing his job for all that. I wouldn't have got within a hundred steps of him without being riddled. I left."

"Dear God," she murmured. "What a mess, what a terrible mess. And you've no radio, we're cut off from all help. What are we going to do? What *are* you going to do, Philip?"

"I'm going there in the *Firecrest* this coming night, that's what I'm going to do. I have a machine gun under the settee of the saloon in the *Firecrest* and Uncle Arthur and Tim Hutchinson will have a gun apiece. We'll reconnoitre. Their time is running short and they'll want to be gone tomorrow at the latest. The boathouse doors are ill-fitting and if there's no light showing that will mean they still haven't finished their diving. So we wait till they have finished and come in. We'll see the light two miles away when they open the door to let the diving boat in to load up all the stuff they've cached from the four other sunken ships. The front doors of the boathouse will be closed, of course, while they load up. So we go in through the front doors. On the deck of the *Firecrest*. The doors don't look all that strong to me. Surprise is everything. We'll catch them napping. A submachine in a small enclosed space is a deadly weapon."

"You'll be killed, you'll be killed!" She crossed to and sat on the bed-side, her eyes wide and scared. "Please, Philip! Please, *please* don't. You'll be killed, I tell you. I beg of you, don't do it!" She seemed very sure that I would be killed.

"I have to, Charlotte. Time has run out. There's no other way."

"Please." The brown eyes were full of unshed tears. This I couldn't believe. "Please, Philip. For my sake."

"No." A teardrop fell at the corner of my mouth, it tasted

as salt as the sea. "Anything else in the world. But not this."

She rose slowly to her feet and stood there, arms hanging limply by her side, tears trickling down her cheeks. She said dully: "It's the maddest plan I've ever heard in my life," turned and left the room, switching off the light as she went.

I lay there staring into the darkness. There was sense in what the lady said. It *was*, I thought, the maddest plan *I'd* ever heard in my life. I was damned glad I didn't have to use it.

10 • THURSDAY NOON—FRIDAY DAWN

"Let me sleep," I said. I kept my eyes shut. "I'm a dead man."

"Come on, come on." Another violent shake, a hand like a power shovel. "Up!"

"Oh, God!" I opened the corner of one eye. "What's the time?"

"Just after noon. I couldn't let you sleep any more."

"Noon! I asked to be shaken at five. Do you know——"

"Come here." He moved to the window, and I swung my legs stiffly out of bed and followed him. I'd been operated on during my sleep, no anaesthetic required in the condition I was in, and someone had removed the bones from my legs. I felt awful. Hutchinson nodded towards the window. "What do you think of that?"

I peered out into the grey opaque world. I said irritably: "What do you expect me to see in that damn fog?"

"The fog."

"I see," I said stupidly. "The fog."

"The 2 A.M. shipping forecast," Hutchinson said. He gave the impression of exercising a very great deal of patience. "It said the fog would clear away in the early morning. Well, the goddamned fog hasn't cleared away in the early morning."

The fog cleared away from my befuddled brain. I swore and jumped for my least sodden suit of clothing. It was damp and clammy and cold but I hardly noticed these things, except subconsciously; my conscious mind was frantically busy with something else. On Monday night they'd sunk the *Nantesville* at slack water but there wasn't a chance in a thousand that they would have been able to get something done that night or the Tuesday night, the weather had been bad enough in sheltered Torbay harbor, God alone knew what it would have been like in Beul nan Uamh. But they could have started last night, they *had* started last night for there had been no diving boat in the Dubh Sgeir boathouse,

197

and reports from the *Nantesville*'s owners had indicated that the strong room was a fairly antiquated one, not of hardened steel, that could be cut open in a couple of hours with the proper equipment. Lavorski and company would have the proper equipment. The rest of last night, even had they three divers and reliefs working all the time, they could have brought up a fair proportion of the bullion but I'd been damn sure they couldn't possibly bring up all eighteen tons of it. Marine salvage had been my business before Uncle Arthur had taken me away. They would have required another night or at least a good part of the night, because they only dared work when the sun was down. When no one could see them. But no one could see them in dense fog like this. This was as good as another night thrown in for free.

"Give Uncle Arthur a shake. Tell him we're on our way. In the *Firecrest*."

"He'll want to come."

"He'll have to stay. He'll know damn well he'll have to stay. Beul nan Uamh, tell him."

"Not Dubh Sgeir? Not the boathouse?"

"*You* know damn well we can't move in against that until midnight."

"I'd forgotten," Hutchinson said slowly. "We can't move in against it until midnight."

The Beul nan Uamh wasn't living up to its fearsome reputation. At that time in the afternoon it was dead slack water and there was only the gentlest of swells running up from the south-west. We crossed over from Ballara to the extreme north of the eastern shore of Dubh Sgeir and inched our way southward with bare steerage way on. We'd cut the bypass valve into the underwater exhaust and, even in the wheelhouse, we could barely hear the throb of the diesel. Even with both wheelhouse doors wide open, we could just hear it and no more. But we hadn't the wheelhouse doors open for the purpose of not hearing our own engine.

By this time we were almost half-way down the eastern patch of miraculously calm water that bordered the normal mill-race of Beul nan Uamh, the one that Williams and I had observed from the helicopter the previous afternoon. For the first time, Hutchinson was showing something approaching worry. He never spared a glance through the wheelhouse windows, and only a very occasional one for the compass: he was navigating almost entirely by chart and depth-sounder.

"Are you sure it'll be this fourteen-fathom ledge, Calvert?"

"It has to be. It damn well has to be. Out to the seven fathom mark there the sea bottom is pretty flat, but there's not enough depth to hide superstructure and masts at low tide. From there to fourteen it's practically a cliff. And beyond the fourteen-fathom ledge it goes down to thirty-five fathom, steep enough to roll a ship down there. You can't operate at those depths without very special equipment indeed."

"It's a damn narrow ledge," he grumbled. "Less than a cable. How could they be sure the scuttled ship would fetch up where they wanted it to?"

"They could be sure. In dead slack water, you can always be sure."

Hutchinson put the engine in neutral and went outside. We drifted on quietly through the greyly opaque world. Visibility didn't extend beyond our bows. The muffled beat of the diesel served only to enhance the quality of ghostly silence. Hutchinson came back into the wheelhouse, his vast bulk moving as unhurriedly as always.

"I'm afraid you're right. I hear an engine."

I listened, then I could hear it too, the unmistakable *thud-thud* of an air compressor. I said: "What do you mean afraid?"

"You know damn well." He touched the throttle, gave the wheel a quarter turn to port and we began to move out gently into deeper water. "You're going to go down."

"Do you think I'm a nut case? Do you think I *want* to go down? I bloody well don't want to go down—and you bloody well know that I *have* to go down. And you know why. You want them to finish up here, load up in Dubh Sgeir and the whole lot to be hell and gone before midnight?"

"Half, Calvert. Take half of our share. God, man, we do nothing."

"I'll settle for a pint in the Columba Hotel in Torbay. You just concentrate on putting this tub exactly where she ought to be. I don't want to spend the rest of my life swimming about the Atlantic when I come back up from the *Nantesville*."

He looked at me, the expression in his eyes saying "if," not "when," but kept quiet. He circled round to the south of the diving boat—we could faintly hear the compressor all the way—then slightly to the west. He turned the *Firecrest* towards the source of the sound, maneuvering with delicacy and precision. He said: "About a cable length."

"About that. Hard to judge in fog."

"North 22 east true. Let go the anchor."

I let go the anchor, not the normal heavy Admiralty type on the chain but a smaller CQR on the end of forty fathoms of rope. It disappeared silently over the side and the Terylene as silently slid down after it. I let out all forty fathoms and made fast. I went back to the wheelhouse and strapped the cylinders on my back.

"You won't forget, now," Hutchinson said. "When you come up, just let yourself drift. The ebb's just setting in from the nor'-nor'-east and will carry you back here. I'll keep the diesel ticking, you'll be able to hear the underwater exhaust twenty yards away. I hope to hell the mist doesn't clear. You'll just have to swim for Dubh Sgeir."

"That *will* be ducky. What happens to you if it clears?"

"I'll cut the anchor rope and take off."

"And if they come after you?"

"Come after me? Just like that? And leave two or three dead divers down inside the *Nantesville?*"

"I wish to God," I said irritably, "that you wouldn't talk about dead divers inside the *Nantesville.*"

There were three divers aboard the *Nantesville,* not dead but all working furiously, or as furiously as one can work in the pressurized slow-motion world of the undersea.

Getting down there had been no trouble. I'd swum on the surface towards the diving boat, the compressor giving me a clear bearing all the time, and dived when only three yards away. My hands touched cables, lifelines and finally an unmistakable wire hawser. The wire hawser was the one for me.

I stopped my descent on the wire when I saw the dim glow of light beneath me. I swam some distance to one side then down until my feet touched something solid. The deck of the *Nantesville.* I moved cautiously towards the source of the light.

There were two of them, standing in their weighted boots at the edge of an open hatchway. As I'd expected, they were wearing not my self-contained apparatus but regular helmet and corselet diving gear, with air lines and lifelines, the life-lines almost certainly with telephone wires imbedded inside them. Self-contained diving equipment wouldn't have been much use down here, it was too deep for oxygen and compressed air stores too limited. With those suits they could stay down an hour and a half, at least, although they'd have to spend thirty to forty minutes on decompression stops on the way up. I wanted to be gone in less than that, I wanted to be gone that very moment, my heart was banging away against my chest wall like a demented pop drummer with the ague but it was only the pressure of the water, I told myself, it couldn't be fear, I was far too brave for that.

The wire rope I'd used to guide me down to the *Nantesville* terminated in a metal ring from which splayed out four chains to the corners of a rectangular steel mesh basket. The two divers were loading this basket with wire- and wood-handled steel boxes that they were hauling up from the hold at the rate of, I guessed, about one every two minutes. The steel boxes were small but obviously heavy: each held four 28-lb. ingots of gold. Each box held a fortune. There were a hundred and sixty such fortunes aboard the *Nantesville*.

I tried to calculate the over-all rate of unloading. The steel basket held eight boxes. Sixteen minutes to load. Another ten minutes to winch up to the diving boat, unload and lower again. Say twenty an hour. In a ninety-minute stretch, about thirty. But after ninety minutes they would have to change divers. Forty minutes, including two decompression stops of, say, twelve and twenty-four minutes, to get to the surface, then twenty minutes to change over and get their divers down. An hour at least. So, in effect, they were clearing thirty boxes every two and a half hours, or twelve an hour. The only remaining question was, how many boxes were left in the *Nantesville*'s strong room.

I had to find out and I had to find out at once. I'd had only the two compressed air cylinders aboard the *Firecrest* and already their two hundred atmospheres were seriously depleted. The wire hawser jerked and the full basket started to rise, the divers guiding it clear of the superstructure with a trailing guide rope. I moved forward from the corner of the partially opened hatch remote from where they were standing and cautiously wriggled over and down. With excessive caution, I supposed: their lamp cast only a small pool of light and they couldn't possibly have seen me from where I was standing.

I felt my hands—already puffed and numbed by the icy water—touch a lifeline and airline and quickly withdrew them. Below and to my right I could see another faint pool of light. A few cautious strokes and I could see the source of the light.

The light was moving. It was moving because it was attached to the helmet of a diver, angled so as to point down at an angle of forty-five degrees. The diver was inside the strong room.

They hadn't opened that strong room with any Yale key. They'd opened it with underwater torches, cutting out a roughly rectangular section in the strong room's side, maybe six feet by four.

I moved up to this opening and pushed my head round the side. Beyond the now stooping diver was another light suspended from the deckhead. The bullion boxes were neatly stacked in racks round the side and it was a five-second job to estimate their number. Of the hundred and sixty bullion boxes, there were about sixty left.

Something brushed my arm, pulled past my arm. I glanced down and saw that it was a rope, a nylon line, that the diver was pulling in to attach to the handle of one of the boxes. I moved my arm quickly out of the way.

His back was towards me. He was having difficulty in fastening the rope but finally secured it with two half hitches, straightened and pulled a knife from his waist sheath. I wondered what the knife was for.

I found out what the knife was for. The knife was for me. Stooped over as he had been, he could just possibly have caught a glimpse of me from the corner of his eye: or he might have felt the sudden pressure, then release of pressure, on the nylon rope: or his sixth sense was in better working condition than mine. I won't say he whirled round, for in a heavy diving suit at that depth the tempo of movement becomes slowed down to that of a slow-motion film.

But he moved too quickly for me, it wasn't my body that was slowing down as much as my mind. He was completely round and facing me, not four feet away, and I was still where I'd been when he'd first moved, still displaying all the lightning reactions and coordinated activity of a bag of cement. The six-inch bladed knife was held in his lowered hand with thumb and forefinger towards me, which is the way that only nasty people with lethal matters on their minds hold knives, and I could see his face clearly. God knows what he wanted the knife for, it must have been a reflex action, he didn't require a knife to deal with me, he wouldn't have required a knife to deal with two of me.

It was Quinn.

I watched his face with a strangely paralyzed intentness. I watched his face to see if the head would jerk down to press the telephone call-up buzzer with his chin. But his head didn't move, Quinn had never required any help in his life and he didn't require any now. Instead his lips parted in a smile of almost beatific joy. My mask made it almost impossible for my face to be recognised but he knew whom he had, he knew whom he had without any doubt in the world. He had the face of a man in the moment of supreme religious ecstasy. He fell slowly forwards, his knees bending, till he was at an angle of almost forty-five degrees and launched himself forward, his right arm already swinging far behind his back.

The moment of thrall ended. I thrust off backwards from the strong room's outer wall with my left foot, saw the air-hose come looping down towards me as Quinn came through the jagged hole, caught it and jerked down with all my strength to pull him off-balance. A sharp stinging pain burned its way upwards from my lower ribs to my right shoulder. I felt a sudden jerk in my right hand. I fell backwards on to the floor of the hold and then I couldn't see Quinn any more, not because the fall had dazed me nor because Quinn had moved, but because he had vanished in the heart of an opaque, boiling, mushrooming cloud of dense air bubbles. A noncollapsible airhose can, and often has to, stand up to some pretty savage treatment, but it can't stand up to the wickedly slicing power of a razor-sharp knife in the hands of the strongest man I'd ever know. Quinn had cut his own air-hose, had slashed it cleanly in two.

No power on earth could save Quinn now. With a pressure of forty pounds to the square inch on that severed air line, he would be drowning already, his suit filling up with water and weighting him down so that he could never rise again. Almost without realising what I was doing I advanced with the nylon rope still in my hands and coiled it any old way round the madly threshing legs, taking great care indeed to keep clear of those flailing arms for Quinn could still have taken me with him, could have snapped my neck like a rotten stick. At the back of my mind I had the vague hope that when his comrades investigated, as they were bound to do immediately—those great clouds of bubbles must have already passed out through the hold on their way to the surface—they would think he'd become entangled and tried to cut himself free. I did not think it a callous action then nor do I now. I had no qualms about doing this to a dying man, and no compunction: he was doomed anyway, he was a psychopathic monster who killed for the love of it and, most of all, I had to think of the living who might die, the prisoners in the cellars of the Dubh Sgeir castle. I left him threshing there, dying there, and swam up and hid under the deckhead of the hold.

The two men who had been on deck were already on their way down, being slowly lowered on their lifelines. As soon as their air helmets sank below my level I came up through the hatchway, located the wire hawser and made my way up. I'd been down for just under ten minutes so when my wrist depth-gauge showed a depth of two fathoms I stopped for a three-minute decompression period. By now, Quinn would be dead.

I did as Hutchinson had told me, drifted my way back to the *Firecrest*—there was no hurry now—and located it without difficulty. Hutchinson was there to help me out of the water and I was glad of his help.

"Am I glad to see you, brother," he said. "Never thought the day would come when Tim Hutchinson would die a thousand deaths, but die a thousand deaths he did. How did it go?"

"All right. We've time. Five or six hours yet."

"I'll get the hook up." Three minutes later we were on our way and three minutes after that we were out near enough in the mid channel of the Beul nan Uamh, heading north-north-east against the gathering ebb. I could hear the helm going on auto-pilot and then Hutchinson came through the door into the lit saloon, curtains tightly if, in that fog, unnecessarily drawn, where I was rendering some first aid to myself, just beginning to tape up a patch of gauze over the ugly gash that stretched all the way from lowest rib to shoulder. I couldn't see the expression behind the darkly luxuriant foliage of that beard, but his sudden immobility was expression enough. He said, quietly: "What happened, Calvert?"

"Quinn. I met him in the strong room of the *Nantesville*."

He moved forward and in silence helped me to tape up the gauze. When it was finished, and not until then, he said: "Quinn is dead." It wasn't a question.

"Quinn is dead. He cut his own airhose." I told him what had happened and he said nothing. He didn't exchange a dozen words all the way back to Craigmore. I knew he didn't believe me. I knew he never would.

Neither did Uncle Arthur. He'd never believe me till the day he died. But his reaction was quite different, it was one of profound satisfaction. Uncle Arthur was, in his own avuncular fashion, possessed of an absolute ruthlessness. Indeed, he seemed to take half the credit for the alleged execution. "It's not twenty-four hours," he'd announced at the tea table, "that I told Calvert to seek out and destroy this man by whatever means that came to hand. I must confess that I never thought that the means would consist of the blade of a sharp knife against an airhose. A neat touch, my boy, a very neat touch indeed."

Charlotte Skouras believed me. I don't know why, but she believed me. While she was stripping off my makeshift bandage, cleaning the wound and rebandaging it very efficiently, a process I suffered with unflinching fortitude because I didn't want to destroy her image of a secret service agent by bellowing out loud at the top of my voice, I told her what had happened and there was no doubt that she believed me without question. I thanked her, for bandage and belief, and she smiled.

Six hours later, twenty minutes before our eleven P.M. deadline for taking off in the *Firecrest*, she was no longer smiling. She was looking at me the way women usually look at you when they have their minds set on something and can see that they are not going to get their own way: a rather less than affectionate look.

"I'm sorry, Charlotte," I said. "I'm genuinely sorry, but it's not on. You are not coming with us, and that's that." She was dressed in dark slacks and sweater, like one who had—or had had—every intention of coming with us on a midnight jaunt. "We're not going picnicking on the Thames. Remember what you said yourself this morning. There will be shooting. Do you think I want to see you killed?"

"I'll stay below," she pleaded. "I'll stay out of harm's way. Please, Philip, let me come."

"No."

"You said you'd do anything in the world for me. Remember?"

"That's unfair, and you know it. Anything to help you, I meant. Not anything to get you killed. Not you, of all people."

"Of all people? You think so much of me?"
I nodded.

"I mean so much to you?"

I nodded again. She looked at me for a long time, her eyes wide and questioning, her lips moving as if about to speak and yet not speaking, then took a step forward, latched her arms around my neck and tried to break it. At least, that was the way it felt, the dead Quinn's handiwork was still with me, but it wasn't that at all, she was clinging to me as she might cling to a person who she knew she would never see again. Maybe she was fey, maybe she had second sight, maybe she could see old Calvert floating, face down, in the murky waters of the Dubh Sgeir boathouse. When I thought about it I could see it myself, and it wasn't an attractive sight at all. I was beginning to have some difficulty with my breathing when she suddenly let me go, half-led, half-pushed me from the room and closed the door behind me. I heard the key turn in the lock.

"Our friends are at home," Tim Hutchinson said. We'd circled far to the south of Dubh Sgeir, close in to the southern shore of Loch Houron and were now drifting quickly on the flood tide, engines stopped, in an east by northerly direction past the little man-made harbor on Dubh Sgeir. "You were right, Calvert. They're getting all ready for their moonlit flitting."

"Calvert is usually right," Uncle Arthur said in his best trained-him-myself voice. "And now, my boy?"

The mist had thinned now, giving maybe a hundred yards visibility. I looked at the T-shaped crack of light where the boathouse doors didn't quite meet each other in the middle and where the tops of the doors sagged away from the main structure.

"Now it is," I said. I turned to Hutchinson. "We've all of a fifteen-foot beam. That entrance is not more than twenty wide. There's not a beacon or a mark on it. There's a four-knot tide running. You really think it can be done—taking her through that entrance at four or five knots, fast enough to smash open those doors without piling ourselves up on the rocks on the way in?"

"There's only one way to find out." He pressed the starter button and the warm diesel caught fire at once, its underpass exhaust barely audible. He swung her round to the south on minimum revs, continued on this course for two cables, westwards for the same distance, curved round to the north, pushed the throttle wide open and lit a cigar. Tim Hutchinson preparing for action. In the flare of the match the dark face was quiet and thoughtful, no more.

For just over a minute there was nothing to be seen, just the darkness and patches of grey mist swirling past our bows. Hutchinson was heading a few degrees west of north, making allowance for the set of the tide. All at once we could see it, slightly off the starboard bow as it had to be to correct for the tide, that big T-shaped light in the darkness, fairly jumping at us. I picked up the submachine gun, opened and latched back the port wheelhouse door and stood there, gun in left hand, doorjamb in right, with one foot on the outside deck and the other still in the wheelhouse. Uncle Arthur, I knew, was similarly positioned on the starboard side. We were as firmly braced as it was possible to be. When the *Firecrest* stopped, it would stop very suddenly indeed.

Forty yards away Hutchinson eased the throttle and gave the wheel a touch to port. That bright T was even further round on our starboard side now, but directly in line with us and the patch of dark water to the west of the almost phosphorescently foaming whiteness that marked the point where the flood tide ripped past the outer end of the eastern breakwater. Twenty yards away he pushed the throttle open again, we were heading straight for where the unseen west breakwater must be, we were far too far over to port, it was impossible now that we could avoid smashing bow first into it, then suddenly Hutchinson had the wheel spinning to starboard, the tide pushing him the same way, and we were through and not an inch of Uncle Arthur's precious paintwork had been removed. Hutchinson had the engine in neutral. I wondered briefly whether, if I practiced for the rest of my life, I could effect a maneuver like that: I knew damned well that I couldn't.

I'd told Hutchinson that the bollards were on the starboard side of the boathouse, so that the diving boat would be tied up on that side. He angled the boat across the tiny harbor towards the right-hand crack of light, spun the wheel to port till we were angling in towards the central crack of light and put the engine full astern. It was no part of the plan to telescope the *Firecrest*'s bows against the wall of the boathouse and send it—and us—to the bottom.

As an entrance it erred, if anything, on the spectacular side. The doors, instead of bursting open at their central hasps, broke off at the hinges and we carried the whole lot before us with a thunderous crash. This took a good knot off our speed. The aluminium foremast, with Uncle Arthur's fancy telescopic aerial inside, almost tore the tabernacle clear of the deck before it sheared off, just above wheelhouse level, with a most unpleasant metallic shrieking. That took another knot off. The screw, biting deep in maximum revs astern, took off yet another knot, but we still had a fair way on when, amid a crackling splintering of wood, partly of our planking but mainly of the doors, and the screeching of the rubber tyres on our well-fendered bows, we stopped short with a jarring shock, firmly wedged between the port quarter of the diving boat and the port wall of the boathouse. Uncle Arthur's feeling must have been almost as bruised and lacerated as the planking of his beloved *Firecrest*. Hutchinson moved the throttle to slow ahead to keep us wedged in position and switched on the five-inch searchlight, less to illuminate the already sufficiently well-lit shed than to dazzle bystanders ashore. I stepped out on the deck with the machine pistol in my hands.

We were confronted, as the travel books put it, with a scene of bustling activity, or, more precisely, what had been a scene of bustling activity before our entrance had apparently paralyzed them all in whatever positions they had been at the time. On the extreme right three faces stared at us over the edge of the hold of the diving-boat, a typical forty-five foot MFV about the same size as the *Charmaine*. Two men on deck were frozen in the act of lifting a box across to the hold. Another two were standing upright, one with his hands stretched above his head, waiting for another box swinging gently from a rope suspended from a loading boom. That box was the only moving thing in the boathouse. The winchman himself, who bore an uncommon resemblance to Thomas, the bogus Customs officer, one lever against his chest and another held in his outstretched right hand, looked as if the lavas of Vesuvius had washed over him twenty centuries ago and left him frozen there for ever. Two others, backs bent, were standing on the wall at the head of the boathouse, holding a rope attached to a very large box which two frogmen were helping to lift clear of the water. When it came to hiding specie, they had one-track minds. On the extreme left stood Captain Imrie, presumably there to supervise operations and, beside him, his patrons, Lavorski and Dollmann. This was the big day, this was the culmination of all their dreams, and they weren't going to miss a moment of it.

Imrie, Lavorski and Dollmann were the ones for me. I moved forward until I could see the barrel of the machine gun and until they could also see that it was pointing at them.

"Come close," I said. "Yes, you three. Captain Imrie, speak to your men. Tell them that if they move, if they try anything at all, I'll kill all three of you. I've killed four of you already. If I double the number, what then? Under the new laws you get only fifteen years. For murderous vermin, that is not enough. I'd rather you died here. Do you believe me, Captain Imrie?"

"I believe you." The guttural voice was deep and sombre. "You killed Quinn this afternoon."

"He deserved to die."

"He should have killed you that night on the *Nantesville*," Imrie said. "Then none of this would have happened."

"You will come aboard our boat one at a time," I said. "In this situation, Captain Imrie, you are without question the most dangerous man. After you, Lavorski, then—"

"Please keep very still. Terribly still." The voice behind me was totally lacking in inflection, but the gun pressed hard against my spine carried its own message, one not easily misunderstood. "Good. Take a pace forward and take your right hand away from the gun."

I took a pace forward and removed my right hand. This left me holding the machine pistol by the barrel.

"Lay the gun on the deck."

It obviously wasn't going to be much use to me as a club, so I laid it on the deck. I'd been caught like this before, once or twice, and just to show that I was a true professional I raised my hands high and turned slowly round.

"Why, Charlotte Skouras!" I said. Again I knew what to do, how to act, the correct tone for the circumvented agent, bantering but bitter. "Fancy meeting you here. Thank you very much my dear." She was still dressed in the dark sweater and slacks, only they weren't quite as spruce as the last time I'd seen them. They were soaking wet. Her face was dead white and without expression. The brown eyes were very still. "And how in God's name did you get here?"

"I escaped through the bedroom window and swam out. I hid in the after cabin."

"Did you indeed? Why don't you change out of those wet clothes?"

She ignored me. She said to Hutchinson: "Turn off that searchlight."

"Do as the lady says," I advised.

He did as the lady said. The light went out and we were all now in full view of the men ashore. Imrie said: "Throw that gun over the side, Admiral."

"Do as the gentleman says," I advised.

Uncle Arthur threw the gun over the side. Captain Imrie and Lavorski came walking confidently towards us. They could afford to walk confidently, the three men in the hold, the two men who had suddenly appeared far behind the diving boat's wheelhouse and the winchdriver—a nice round total of six—had suddenly sprouted guns. I looked over this show of armed strength and said slowly: "You were waiting for us."

"Certainly we were waiting for you," Lavorski said jovially. "Our dear Charlotte announced the exact time of your arrival. Haven't you guessed that yet, Calvert?"

"How do you know my name?"

"Charlotte, you fool. By heavens, I believe we have been grievously guilty of overestimating you."

"Mrs. Skouras was a plant," I said.

"A bait," Lavorski said cheerfully. I wasn't fooled by his cheerfulness, he'd have gone into hysterics of laughter when I came apart on the rack. "Swallowed hook, line and sinker. A bait with a highly effective if tiny transmitter and a gun in a polythene bag. We found the transmitter in your starboard engine." He laughed again until he seemed in danger of going into convulsions. "We've known of every move you've made since you left Torbay. And how do you like that, Mr. Secret Agent Calvert?"

"I don't like it at all. What are you going to do with us?"

"Don't be childish. What are you going to do with us, asks he naïvely. I'm afraid you know all too well. How did you locate this place?"

"I don't talk to executioners."

"I think we'll shoot the admiral through the foot, to begin with," Lavorski beamed. "A minute afterwards through the arm, then the thigh——"

"All right. We had a radio transmitter aboard the *Nantesville.*"

"We know that. How did you pinpoint Dubh Sgeir?"

"The boat belonging to the Oxford geological expedition. It is moored fore and aft in a little natural harbor south of here. It's well clear of any rock yet it's badly holed. It's impossible that it would be holed naturally where it lay. It was holed unnaturally, shall we say. Any other boat you could have seen coming from a long way off, but that boat had only to move out to be in full sight of the boathouse—and the anchored diving-boat. It was very clumsy."

Lavorski looked at Imrie, who nodded. "He would notice that. I advised against it at the time. Was there more, Calvert?"

"Donald MacEachern on Eilean Oran. You should have taken him, not his wife. Susan Kirkside—you shouldn't have allowed her out and about, when did you last see a fit young twenty-one-year-old with blue shadows that size under her eyes. A fit young twenty-one-year-old with nothing in the world to worry about, that is? And you should have disguised that mark made by the tail fuselage of the Beechcraft belonging to Lord Kirkside's elder son when you ran it over the edge of the north cliff. I saw it from the helicopter."

"That's all?" Lavorski asked. I nodded, and he looked again at Imrie.

"I believe him," Imrie said. "No one talked. That's all we need to know. Calvert first, Mr. Lavorski?" They were certainly a brisk and businesslike outfit.

I said quickly: "Two questions. The courtesy of two answers. I'm a professional. I'd like to know. I don't know if you understand."

"And two minutes," Lavorski smiled. "Make it quick. We have business on hand."

"Where is Sir Anthony Skouras? He should be here."

"He is. He's up in the castle with Lord Kirkside and Lord Charnley. The *Shangri-la*'s tied up at the west landing stage."

"Is it true that you and Dollmann engineered the whole plan, that you bribed Charnley to betray insurance secrets, that you—or Dollmann, rather—selected Captain Imrie to pick his crew of cutthroats, and that you were responsible for the capture and sinking of the ships and the subsequent salvaging of the cargoes. And, incidentally, the deaths, directly or indirectly, of our men?"

"It's late in the day to deny the obvious." Again Lavorski's booming laugh. "We think we did rather well, eh, John?"

"Very well, indeed," Dollmann said coldly. "We're wasting time."

I turned to Charlotte Skouras. The gun was still pointing at me. I said: "I have to be killed, it seems. As you will be responsible for my death, you might as well finish the job." I reached down, caught the hand with the gun in it and placed it against my chest, letting my own hand fall away. "Please do it quickly."

There was no sound to be heard other than the soft throb of the *Firecrest*'s diesel. Every pair of eyes in that boat-shed were on us, my back was to them all, but I knew it beyond any question. I wanted every pair of eyes in that boat-shed to be on us. Uncle Arthur took a step inside the starboard door and said urgently: "Are you mad, Calvert? She'll kill you! She's one of them."

The brown eyes were stricken, there was no other expression for it, the eyes of one who knows her world is coming to an end. The finger came off the trigger, the hand opened slowly and the gun fell to the deck with a clatter that seemed to echo through the boat-shed and the tunnels leading off on either side. I took her left arm and said: "It seems Mrs. Skouras doesn't feel quite up to it. I'm afraid you'll have to find someone else to—"

Charlotte cried out in sharp pain as her legs caught the wheelhouse sill and maybe I did shove her through that doorway with unnecessary force, but it was too late in the day to take chances now. Hutchinson had been waiting and caught her as she fell, dropping to his knees at the same time. I went through that door after her like an international rugby three-quarter diving for the line with a dozen hands reaching out for him, but even so Uncle Arthur beat me to it. Uncle Arthur had a lively sense of self-preservation. Even as I fell, my hand reached out for the loud-hailer that had been placed in position on the wheelhouse deck.

"Don't fire!" The amplified voice boomed cavernously against the rock faces and the wooden walls of the boat-shed. "If you shoot, you'll die! One shot, and you may all die. There's a machine gun lined up on the back of every man in this boathouse. Just turn round, very very slowly, and see for yourselves."

I half rose to my feet, hoisted a wary eye over the lower edge of a wheelhouse window, got the rest of the way to my feet, went outside and picked up the machine gun on the deck.

Picking up that machine gun was the most superfluous and unnecessary action I had performed for many a long day. If there was one thing that boathouse was suffering from at the moment it was a plethora of machine guns. There were twelve of them in all, shoulder-slung machine pistols, in twelve of the most remarkably steady pairs of hands I'd ever

212

seen. The twelve men were ranged in a rough semicircle round the inner end of the boathouse, big, quiet, purposeful-looking men dressed in woolen caps, grey and black camouflaged smocks and trousers and rubber boots. Their hands and faces were the color of coal. Their eyes gleamed whitely, like performers in the Black and White Minstrel show but with that every hint of light entertainment ended.

"Lower your hands to your sides and let your guns fall." The order came from a figure in the middle of the group, a man indistinguishable from the others. "Do please be very careful. Slowly down, drop the guns, utter stillness. My men are very highly trained commandos. They have been trained to shoot on suspicion. They know only how to kill. They have not been trained to wound or cripple."

They believed him. I believed him. They dropped their guns and stood very still indeed.

"Now clasp your hands behind your necks."

They did. All but one. Lavorski. He wasn't smiling any more and his language had little to recommend it.

That they were highly trained I could believe. No word or signal passed. The commando nearest Lavorski walked towards him on soundless soles, machine pistol held across his chest. The butt seemed to move no more than three inches. When Lavorski picked himself up the lower part of his face was covered in blood and I could see the hole where some teeth had been. He clasped his hands behind his neck.

"Mr. Calvert?" the officer asked.

"Me," I said.

"Captain Rawley, sir. Royal Marine Commandos."

"The castle, captain?"

"In our hands."

"The *Shangri-la*?"

"In our hands."

"The prisoners?"

"Two men are on their way up, sir."

I said to Imrie: "How many guards?"

He spat and said nothing. The commando who had dealt with Lavorski moved forward, machine pistol high. Imrie said: "Two."

I said to Rawley: "Two men enough?"

"I hope, sir, that the guards will not be so foolish as to offer resistance."

Even as he finished speaking the flat rapid-fire chatter of a

213

submachine gun came echoing down the long flight of stone steps. Rawley shrugged.

"They'll never learn to be wise now. Robinson?" This to a man with a waterproof bag over his shoulder. "Go up and open the cellar door. Sergeant Evans, line them up in two rows against the wall there, one standing, one sitting."

Sergeant Evans did. Now that there was no danger of being caught in cross fire we landed and I introduced Uncle Arthur, full military honors and all, to Captain Rawley. Captain Rawley's salute was something to see. Uncle Arthur beamed. Uncle Arthur took over.

"Capitally done, my boy!" he said to Rawley. "Capitally. There'll be a little something for you in this New Year's List. Ah! Here come some friends."

They weren't all exactly friends, this group that appeared at the bottom of the steps. There were four tough but dispirited-looking characters whom I'd never seen before, but unquestionably Imrie's men, closely followed by Sir Anthony Skouras and Lord Charnley. They, in their turn, were closely followed by four commandos with the very steady hands that were a hallmark of Rawley's men. Behind them came Lord Kirkside and his daughter. It was impossible to tell what the black-faced commandos were thinking, but the other eight had the same expression on their faces, dazed and utter bewilderment.

"My dear Kirkside! My dear fellow!" Uncle Arthur hurried forward and shook him by the hand, I'd quite forgotten that they knew one another. "Delighted to see you safe and sound, my dear chap. Absolutely delighted. It's all over now."

"What in God's name is happening?" Lord Kirkside asked. "You—you've got them? You have them all? Where is my boy? Where is Rollinson. What—"

An explosive crack, curiously muffled, came down the flight of steps. Uncle Arthur looked at Rawley, who nodded. "Plastic explosive, sir."

"Excellent, excellent," Uncle Arthur beamed. "You'll see them any minute, Kirkside." He crossed over to where old Skouras was lined up against the wall, hands clasped behind his neck reached up both his own, pulled Skouras' down and shook his right hand as if he were attempting to tear it off.

"You're lined up with the wrong team, Tony, my boy." This was one of the great moments of Uncle Arthur's life. He led him across to where Lord Kirkside was standing. "It's been a frightful nightmare, my boy, a frightful nightmare. But it's all over now."

"Why did you do it," Skouras said dully. "Why did you do it? God, oh God, you don't know what you've done."

"Mrs. Skouras? The *real* Mrs. Skouras?" There is the ham actor in all of us, but more than most in Uncle Arthur. He pushed back his sleeve and studied his watch carefully. "She arrived in London by air from Nice just over three hours ago. She's in the Clinic now as well as can be expected."

"What in God's name do you mean. You don't know what you are saying. My wife——"

"Your wife is in London. Charlotte here is Charlotte Meiner and always was." I looked at Charlotte. A total incomprehension and the tentative beginnings of a dazed hope. "Earlier this year, blazing the trail for many kidnappings that were to follow, your friends Lavorski and Dollmann had your wife seized and hidden away to force you to act with them, to put your resources at their disposal. I think they felt aggrieved, Tony, that you should be a millionaire while they were executives: they had it all worked out, even to having the effrontery of intending to invest the proceeds in your empire. However, your wife managed to escape, so they seized her cousin and best friend, Charlotte—a friend upon whom, shall we say, your wife was emotionally very dependent—and threatened to kill her unless they got Mrs. Skouras back again. Mrs. Skouras surrendered immediately. This gave them the bright idea of having two swords of Damocles hanging over your head, so, being men of honor, they decided to keep Charlotte as well as your imprisoned wife. Then, they knew, you would do exactly as they wanted, when and as they wanted. To have a good excuse to keep both you and Charlotte under their surveillance at the same time, and to reinforce the idea that your wife was well and truly dead, they gave out that you had been secretly married." Uncle Arthur was a kind man: no mention of the fact that it was common knowledge that, at the time of her alleged death, brain injuries sustained by Mrs. Skouras in a car crash two years previously had become steadily worse and it was known that she would never leave hospital again.

"How on earth did you guess that?" Lord Kirkside asked.

"No guess. Must give my lieutenants their due," Uncle Arthur said in his best magnanimous taught-'em-all-I-know voice. "Hunslett radioed me at midnight on Tuesday. He gave me a list of names of people about whom Calvert wanted immediate and exhaustive inquiries made. That call was tapped by the *Shangri-la* but they didn't know what Hunslett was talking about because in our radio transmissions all proper names are invariably coded. Calvert told me later that when he'd seen Sir Anthony on Tuesday night he thought Sir Anthony was putting on a bit of an act. He said it wasn't all act. He said Sir Anthony was completely broken and desolated by the thought of his dead wife. He said he believed the original Mrs. Skouras was still alive, that it was totally inconceivable that a man who so patently cherished the memory of his wife should have married again two or three months later, that he could only have pretended to marry again for the sake of the one person whom he ever and so obviously loved.

"I radioed France. Riviera police dug up the grave in Beaulieu where she had been buried near the nursing home where she'd died. They found a coffin full of logs. You knew this, Tony."

Old Skouras nodded. He was a man in a dream.

"It took them half an hour to find out who had signed the death certificate and most of the rest of the day to find the doctor himself. They charged him with murder. This can be done in France on the basis of a missing body. The doctor wasted no time at all in taking them to his own private nursing home, where Mrs. Skouras was in a locked room. The doctor, matron and a few others are in custody now. Why in God's name didn't you come to us before?"

"They had Charlotte and they said they would kill my wife out of hand. What—what would you have done?"

"God knows," Uncle Arthur said frankly. "She's in fair health, Tony. Calvert got radio confirmation at 5 A.M." Uncle Arthur jerked a thumb upwards. "On Lavorski's big transceiver in the castle."

Both Skouras and Lord Kirkside had their mouths open. Lavorski, blood still flowing from his mouth, and Dollmann looked as if they had been sandbagged. Charlotte's eyes were the widest wide I'd ever seen. She was looking at me in a very peculiar way.

"It's true," Susan Kirkside said. "I was with him. He told me to tell nobody." She crossed to take my arm and smiled up at me. "I'm sorry again for what I said last night. I think you're the most wonderful man I've ever known. Except Rolly, of course." She turned round at the sound of footsteps coming down the stairs and promptly forgot all about the second most wonderful man she'd ever known. "Rolly!" she cried. "Rolly!" I could see Rolly bracing himself.

They were all there, I counted them, Kirkside's son, the Hon. Rollinson, the policeman's sons, the missing members of the small boats and, behind them all, a small brown-faced old woman in a long dark dress with a black shawl over her head. I went forward and took her arm.

"Mrs. MacEachern," I said. "I'll take you home soon. Your husband is waiting."

"Thank you, young man," she said calmly. "That will be very nice." She shifted her arm and held mine in a proprietorial fashion.

Charlotte Skouras came and held my other arm, not in quite so proprietorial a fashion, but there for everyone to see. I didn't mind. She said: "You were on to me? You were on to me all the time?"

"He was," Uncle Arthur said thoughtfully. "He just said he knew. You never quite got round to explaining that bit, Calvert."

"It wasn't difficult, sir—if you knew all the facts, that is," I added hastily. "Sir Anthony put me on to you. That visit he paid me on the *Firecrest* to allay any suspicion we might have had about our smashed radio set only served, I'm afraid, to make me suspicious. You wouldn't have normally come to me, you'd have gone ashore immediately to the police or to a phone, sir. Then, in order to get me talking about the cut telephone wires, you wondered if the radio-wrecker, to complete our isolation from the mainland, had smashed the two public call boxes. From a man of your intelligence, such a suggestion was fatuous, there must be scores of houses in Torbay with their private phone. But you thought it might sound suspicious if you suggested cut lines so you didn't. Then Sergeant MacDonald gave me a glowing report about you, said you were the most respected man in Torbay and your public reputation contrasted so sharply with your private behavior in the *Shangri-la* on Tuesday night—well, I just couldn't buy it.

"That nineteenth-century late Victorian melodrama act that you and Charlotte put on in the saloon that night had me fooled for all of five seconds. It was inconceivable that any man so devoted to his wife could be vicious towards another obviously nice woman—"

"Thank you kindly, sir," Charlotte murmured.

"It was inconceivable that he send her for his wife's photograph, unless he had been ordered to do so. And you had been ordered to do so, by Lavorski and Dollmann. And it was inconceivable that she would have gone—the Charlotte Meiner I knew would have clobbered you over the head with a marlin spike. Ergo, if you weren't what you appeared to be, neither were you, Charlotte.

"The villains, they thought, were laying a foundation for an excellent reason for your flight from the wicked baron to the *Firecrest,* where you could become their eyes and ears and keep them informed of all our plans and moves, because they'd no idea how long their secret little transmitter in the engine room would remain undetected. After they knew we'd found Hunslett—they'd removed the transmitter by that time—it was inevitable that they would try to get you aboard the *Firecrest.* So they laid a little more groundwork by giving you a bruised eye—the dye is nearly off already—and some wicked weals across your back and dumped you into the water with your little polythene kitbag with the microtransmitter and gun inside it. Do this, they said, or Mrs. Skouras will get it."

She nodded. "They said that."

"I have twenty-twenty eyesight. Sir Arthur hasn't—his eyes were badly damaged in the war. I had a close look at those weals on your back. Genuine weals. Also genuine pinpricks where the hypodermic with the anaesthetic had been inserted before the lashes were inflicted. To that degree, at least, someone was humane."

"I could stand most things," Skouras said heavily. "I couldn't stand the thought of—the thought of—"

"I guessed you had insisted on the anaesthetic, sir. No, I knew. The same way that I knew that you had insisted that the crews of all those small yachts be kept alive or the hell with the consequences. Charlotte, I ran a fingernail down one of those weals. You should have jumped through the saloon roof. You never batted an eyelid. After submersion in salt water. After that, I knew.

"I have devious reasons for the things I do. You told us that you had come to warn us of our deadly danger—as if we didn't know. I told you we were leaving Torbay within the hour, so off you trotted to your little cabin and told them we were going to leave within the hour. So Quinn, Jacques, and Kramer came paddling across well in advance of the time you'd told us they would be coming, trusting we would have

218

been lulled into a sense of false security. You must love Mrs. Skouras very much, Charlotte. A clearcut choice, she or us, and you made your choice. But I was waiting for them, so Jacques and Kramer died. I told you we were going to Eilean Oran and Craigmore, so off you trotted down to your little cabin and told them we were going to Eilean Oran and Craigmore, which wouldn't have worried them at all. Later on I told you we were going to Dubh Sgeir. So off you trotted down to your little cabin again, but before you could tell them anything you passed out on your cabin deck, possibly as a result of a little nightcap I'd put in your coffee. I couldn't have you telling your friends here that I was going to Dubh Sgeir, could I now? They would have had a reception committee all nicely organised."

"You—you were in my cabin? You said I was on the floor?"

"Don Juan has nothing on me. I flit in and out of ladies' bedrooms like anything. Ask Susan Kirkside. You were on the floor. I put you to bed. I looked at your arms, incidentally, and the rope marks were gone. They'd used rubber bands, twisted pretty tightly, just before Hunslett and I had arrived."

She nodded. She looked dazed.

"I also, of course, found the transmitter and gun. Then, back in Craigmore, you came and pumped me for some more information. And you did try to warn me, you were about torn in half by that time. I gave you that information. It wasn't the whole truth, I regret, but it was what I wanted you to tell Lavorski and company, which," I said approvingly, "like a good little girl you did. Off you trotted to your little whitewashed bedroom—"

"Philip Calvert," she said slowly, "you are the nastiest, sneakingest, most low-down double-crossing—"

"There are some of Lavorski's men aboard the *Shangri-la*," old Skouras interrupted excitedly. He had rejoined the human race. "They'll get away—"

"They'll get life," I said. "They're in irons, or whatever Captain Rawley's men here are in the habit of using."

"But how did you—how did you know where the *Shangri-la* was? In the darkness, in the mist, it's impossible—"

"How's the *Shangri-la*'s tender working?" I asked.

"The what? The *Shangri-la*'s—what the devil?—" He calmed down. "It's not working. Engines out of order."

"Demerara sugar has that effect upon them," I explained.

219

"Any sugar has, in fact, when dumped in the petrol tanks, but Demerara was all I could lay hands on that Wednesday night after Sir Arthur and I had left you but before we took the *Firecrest* into the pier. I went aboard the tender with a couple of pounds of the stuff. I'm afraid you'll find the valves are ruined. I also took with me a homing signal transmitter, a transistorized battery-powered job, which I attached to the inner after bulkhead of the anchor locker, a place that's not looked at once a year. So, when you hauled the incapacitated tender aboard the *Shangri-la*—well, we knew where the *Shangri-la* was."

"I'm afraid I don't follow, Calvert."

"Look at Messrs Dollmann, Lavorski, and Imrie. They follow all right. I know the exact frequency that transmitter sends on—after all, it *was* my transmitter. One of Mr. Hutchinson's skippers was given this frequency and tuned in to it. Like all MFVs it has a loop aerial for direction finding, he just had to keep turning the loop till the signal was at full strength. He couldn't miss. He didn't miss."

"Mr. Hutchinson's skippers?" Skouras said carefully. "MFVs, you said?"

It was as well, I reflected, that I wasn't overly troubled with self-consciousness, what with Mrs. MacEachern on one hand, Charlotte on the other, and every eye, a large proportion of them hostile to a degree, bent upon me, it could have been embarrassing to a degree. "Mr. Hutchinson has two shark-fishing boats. Before I came to Dubh Sgeir last night I radioed from one of his boats asking for help—the gentlemen you see here. They said they couldn't send boats or helicopters in this weather, in almost zero visibility. I told them the last thing I wanted was their damned noisy helicopters, secrecy was everything, and not to worry about the sea transport, I knew some men for whom the phrase 'zero visibility' was only a joke. Mr. Hutchinson's skippers. They went to the mainland and brought Captain Rawley and his men back here. I didn't think they'd arrive until late at night, that's why Sir Arthur and I were afraid to move before midnight. What time did you get here, Captain Rawley?"

"Nine-thirty."

"So early? I must admit it was a bit awkward without a radio. Then ashore in your little rubber boats, through the side door, waited until the diving boat came back—and waited and waited."

"We were getting pretty stiff, sir."

Lord Kirkside cleared his throat. Maybe he was thinking of my nocturnal assignation with his daughter.

"Tell me this, Mr. Calvert. If you radioed from Mr. Hutchinson's boat in Craigmore, why did you have to radio again from here later that night?"

"If I didn't, you'd be down among the dead men by this time. I spent the best part of fifteen minutes giving highly detailed descriptions, of Dubh Sgeir externally and of the castle and boathouse layout internally. Everything that Captain Rawley and his men have done had to be done in total darkness. You'll keep an eye on our friends, Captain Rawley? A fishery cruiser will be off Dubh Sgeir shortly after dawn."

The Marines herded them off into the left hand cave, set three powerful lights shining into the prisoners' faces and mounted a four man guard with machine pistols at the ready. Our friends would undoubtedly keep until the fishery cruiser came in the morning.

Charlotte said slowly: "That was why Sir Arthur remained behind this afternoon when you and Mr. Hutchinson went to the *Nantesville?* To see that I didn't talk to the guards and find out the truth?"

"Why else?"

She took her arm away and looked at me without affection. "So you put me through the hoop," she said quietly. "You let me suffer like this for thirty hours while you knew all the time."

"Fair's fair. You were doing me down, I was doing you down."

"I'm very grateful to you," she said bitterly.

"If you aren't, you damn well ought to be," Uncle Arthur said coldly. This was one for the books, Uncle Arthur talking to the aristocracy, even if only the aristocracy by marriage, in this waspish tone. "If Calvert won't speak for himself, I will.

"Point one: if you hadn't kept on sending your little radio messages, Lavorski would have thought that there was something damned fishy going on and might well have left the last ton or two of gold in the *Nantesville* and taken off before we got there. People like Lavorski have a highly attuned sixth sense of danger. Point two: they wouldn't have confessed to their crimes unless they thought we were finished. Point three: Calvert wanted to engineer a situation where all attention was on the *Firecrest* so that Captain Rawley and his men could move into position and so eliminate all fear of unnecessary bloodshed—maybe *your* blood, my dear Charlotte. Point four, and more important: if you hadn't been in constant radio contact with them, advising them of our impending arrival right up to the moment we came through those doors—we'd even left the saloon door open so that you could clearly overhear us and know all we were doing—there would have been a pitched battle, guns firing as soon as those doors were breached, and who knows how many lives would have been lost. But they *knew* they were in control, they *knew* the trap was set, they *knew* you were aboard with that gun to spring the trap. Point five, and most important of all: Captain Rawley here was hidden almost a hundred yards away along the cross tunnel and the detachment up above were concealed in a store room in the castle. How do you think *they* knew when to move in and move in simultaneously? Because, like all commandos, they had portable radio sets and were listening in to every word of your running commentary. Don't forget your transmitter was stolen from the *Firecrest*. It was *Calvert's* transmitter, my dear. He knew the transmitting frequency you were using and radioed that frequency to the mainland last night. That was after he had—um—given you a little something to drink and checked your transmitter before using the one up in the castle last night."

Charlotte said to me: "I think you are the most devious and detestable and untrustworthy man I've ever met." Her eyes were shining, whether from tears or whatever I didn't know. I felt acutely embarrassed and uncomfortable. She put her hand on my arm and said in a low voice: "You fool, oh, you fool! That gun might have gone off. I—I might have killed you, Philip!"

I patted her hand and said: "You don't even begin to believe that yourself." In the circumstances, I thought it better not to say that if that gun had gone off I'd never have trusted a three-cornered file again.

The grey mist was slowly clearing away and the dawn coming up on the quiet dark sea when Tim Hutchinson eased the *Firecrest* in towards Eilean Oran.

There were only four of us on the boat, Hutchinson, myself, Mrs. MacEachern and Charlotte. I'd told Charlotte to find a bed in Dubh Sgeir castle for the night, but she'd simply ignored me, helped Mrs. MacEachern on to the *Firecrest* and had made no move to go ashore again. Very self-willed, she

222

was, and I could see that this was going to cause a lot of trouble in the years to come.

Uncle Arthur wasn't with us. A team of wild horses couldn't have dragged Uncle Arthur aboard the *Firecrest* that night. Uncle Arthur was having his foretaste of Paradise, sitting in front of a log fire in the Dubh Sgeir castle drawing room, knocking back old Kirkside's superlative whisky and retailing his exploits to a breathless and spellbound aristocracy. If I were lucky, maybe he'd mention my name a couple of times in the course of his recounting of the epic. On the other hand, maybe he wouldn't.

Mrs. MacEachern wasn't having her foretaste of Paradise, she was there already, a calm dark old lady with a wrinkled brown face who smiled and smiled and smiled all the way to her home on Eilean Oran. I hoped to God old Donald MacEachern had remembered to change his shirt.